The next rush of conversation surged with static and was full of overlay so that it was difficult for Shirer to know exactly who was speaking. Battling with the yoke in heavy turbulence at ten thousand feet, he first heard his copilot yelling, "There they go!" then the exhaust of the 524-pound American missiles lighting the clouds nearby in a momentary and astonishingly beautiful peach glow, and then six seconds later, a fast, broken chorus of "Good kill! Good kill! . . . Shoot him! . . ."

Shirer was fighting to keep the Boeing in the steep dive, slipping farther away from the point of intercept. The babble of the Tomcats was now interspersed with Russian: *"Unichtozhit' . . . Unichtozhit' "—"Finish him off! . . . Finish him off!"*

The Russian missile, a quarter mile away, curled hard left and exploded. Seconds later the shock wave and debris hit the Boeing, and Shirer saw the warning light for the starboard two engine flashing, its intake fouled, temperature soaring. He shut it down but still kept diving, hard to port, down toward the sea. . . .

Also by Ian Slater:

FIRESPILL
SEA GOLD
AIR GLOW RED
ORWELL: THE ROAD TO AIRSTRIP ONE
STORM
DEEP CHILL
FORBIDDEN ZONE*
WW III*
WW III: RAGE OF BATTLE*

**Published by Fawcett Books*

WW III:
WORLD IN FLAMES

Ian Slater

FAWCETT GOLD MEDAL • NEW YORK

A Fawcett Gold Medal Book
Published by Ballantine Books
 Published in the United States by Ballantine Books, a division of Random House, Inc., New York, and simultaneously in Canada by Random House of Canada Limited, Toronto.

Library of Congress Catalog Card Number: 91-91899

ISBN 0-449-14564-6

Manufactured in the United States of America

First Edition: August 1991

For Marian, Serena, and Blair

ACKNOWLEDGMENTS

I would like to thank Professors Peter Petro and Charles Slonecker, two colleagues and friends of mine at the University of British Columbia. Once again I am indebted to my wife, Marian, whose patience, typing, and editorial skills continue to give me invaluable support in my work.

In the assessment of every member—not only of the United States, but of all NATO allies—of all the intelligence agencies, the strategic capability of the Soviet Union today is much, much greater than it was before Mr. Gorbachev came on the scene.

—Senator Daniel Inouye,
United States Congress

July 1990

PROLOGUE

THE COMMANDANT FOR Kremlin or "Citadel" security is always a general, and he uses falconers to send their goshawks to attack and frighten away the hundreds of crows. If the crows were left alone, they would defecate on and otherwise disturb the peace and dignity of the seat of Soviet government.

The falcons in the Kremlin date back at least fifty years, the use of gunfire to rid pests from the Kremlin's sixty-three acres strictly forbidden, for in times of political unrest, as in the Gorbachev days when the Yeltsin-ites and other "anti-Soviet elements" were allowed to mass in Red Square, it was feared that even a single shot from within the Citadel might be interpreted by the masses outside as the signal of a *new* revolution. In wartime it becomes imperative that no shots be heard coming from within the seat of government and that therefore only falcons be used to kill pests.

CHAPTER ONE

AS EASILY AS he had shed his naval uniform for his civilian clothes, Robert Brentwood slipped a pillow beneath his new bride and immediately felt the difference—their bodies closer now, her fragrance rising, engulfing him as in a dream. But he knew anything could break the spell.

Outside, the winter darkness howled along Scotland's rugged west coast, and from the upstairs bedroom of the bed-and-breakfast, they could hear the proprietor's dog challenging late arrivals, the spaniel's barking rising above the crashing of the waves. Moments later they heard the slam of a car door, saw the glow of the front porch light immediately beneath their upstairs room, heard voices, then felt the tremor as the door banged shut, the old stairs groaning as the owner—his hushed voice as off-putting to Rosemary as the dog's barking—led his guests, two of them, as far as Robert could tell, up to the other oceanfront room across the hall from Robert and Rosemary's. It was well past midnight, unusually late for checking into a B and B, but Rosemary thought nothing of it at the time. Instead she was wondering how it was that her husband of only a few days knew to do that with the pillows. For her there had been no one else before their marriage, and when they were first engaged in Surrey, while he was on leave from his command of his sub, the USS *Roosevelt,* and they'd first made love, he had told her that it had been the same for him—that despite the myths about sailors, especially American ones, there'd been no one else but her.

But now her mounting pleasure was stemmed. By itself her moment of doubt mightn't have bothered her, but she was carrying his child, and any passing suspicion was in danger of becoming an idée fixe. "Where did you learn to do that?" she asked, trying not to sound concerned. "With the pillows. In one of your submarine manuals?"

Everything slowed and Robert sensed there'd be "time out" before she could relax enough for them to start again, but he knew better than to show any annoyance. "Matter of fact," he replied, "I *did* get it from a manual. 'Missile Launch.' "

"Don't be vulgar," she said, smiling, but he could tell the tone was conditional. He loved her very much, but the war and his part in it as captain of the most powerful ship in history, a Sea Wolf II—dual-purpose Hunter/Killer and ballistic missile nuclear submarine—had already taken its toll on Rosemary since they had become engaged. He couldn't deny that her worry was justified—the Sea Wolf IIs with their six 8-warhead Trident "C" missiles were the most sought-after targets of the Russian navy. But in just the few days since they had been married, on their way up to the honeymoon in Scotland, he had noticed how her worry had become tinged with obsession. She was like a student before formal exams or a job applicant before an all-important interview—a case of free-floating anxiety—in her case, about the war she could do nothing about, the anxiety searching, albeit unconsciously, for something tangible, like a dog with a bone, over which it might worry and have some measure of control.

The only problem was that her anxiety was nondiscriminating, as likely to alight on a minor inconvenience of food rationing as it was to shift abruptly to the difficulties of teaching Shakespeare to her St. Anselm's sixth form in Surrey, or the terror of the increasing Russian rocket attacks across the Channel. At other times she would be seized by the kind of debilitating depression that still assailed her mother following the loss of young William Spence, Rosemary's brother, killed on one of the Atlantic convoys which Robert Brentwood and other sub skippers had been assigned to protect. Tonight her anxiety about the future manifested itself in the suspicion that she had not been Robert's only love.

When they'd first met, Robert had found her more confident, even fatalistic, about the war, but now it was as if their marriage, the very thing that should fill them with hope and optimism in hard times, had suddenly inundated her with concerns she'd never had before. Would the child be all right, or would the severe wartime rationing deform him or her? And what kind of a world would it be after the war—if there would be any world at all if it should suddenly go nuclear?

She pulled the bedclothes up protectively about her against

the mournful moaning of the wind. Perhaps, like the change in the weather, everything had happened too fast, she mused. Perhaps they should have waited longer—got to know one another better.

"You told me," Robert said quietly, "that knowing someone isn't a matter of time—and you were right. Besides, there's nothing—"

"And you told me," she said, lowering her voice, suddenly aware of how sound carried in the old house, "that I was your first and only—"

"You *were* the first," he said, his finger cupping her chin, turning her head toward his on the pillow, his right arm cradling her so close, he could feel her heart thumping. "There wasn't anyone before you."

She sighed. "I wouldn't really care if there had—"

"Yes you would," he told her softly.

"I'm glad." She snuggled into him. "Oh—I know it's terribly old-fashioned—that it's not *supposed* to matter anymore how many people you've slept with—or whom. But it does to me."

He said nothing, watching her breasts rising and falling. "I did read about the pillows in a magazine," he said, kissing her cheek.

"Hmm—" she teased. He pulled her closer, her breasts warm and full, her nipples hardening against him.

"You must think me an awful old prude," she said.

"In the first place, thirty isn't exactly old—*I'm* the one that's old. When I hit forty-four next year, they'll retire me from *Roosevelt*. That's old. In the second place, you're not a prude."

"What magazine did you get it from?" she asked. "*Playboy*, I expect?"

"Actually, I think it was *Cosmopolitan*. Article on 'Navy Wives'—how to home in your torpedo!"

"*Robert!*" she said, her expression halfway between laughter and feigned shock. "You certainly wouldn't have said *that* before we were married."

"No," he admitted, his hands slipping beneath the covers. The faint glow from the porch light disappeared, the room plunged again into total darkness, and they heard the proprietor walking creakily along the corridor on the ground floor.

Rosemary pulled the covers over them. "Father warned me the Scots didn't believe in central heating. It's freezing in here."

"Never mind," said Robert, "I'll keep you warm."

Rosemary, her jasmine perfume filling their cave, moved closer to him, kissing him, gently at first, then her tongue hungrily seeking his.

When he came up for air, he asked, "Where did you learn *that?*"

"Oh, I've had at least a dozen lovers. You wouldn't believe—"

His hand slipped down between her thighs and soon he entered her and slowly they began moving in harmony, then bone-hard against each other, she clutching at him tightly, wantonly, exciting him so much, he knew that unless he diverted his attention, he would climax first. Easing himself up slightly on his elbows, not breaking the rhythm but decreasing pressure, he tried to think of something completely nonsexual, something to do with his work. He seized upon the deliberately repetitious, almost mechanical, routine of *Roosevelt's* missile control verification procedure for the Hunter/Killer's six Trident C missiles, in two rows of three situated immediately aft of the sail, each of the forty-eight warheads containing more then forty times the power of the Hiroshima bomb. Should the war go nuclear, they'd be fired in "ripple" or alternate sequence, the first, number one, missile sliding out of its sheath being the first one on the port side behind the sail, the next missile to be fired not one adjacent to it but rather number six—diagonally opposite to it and farthest away on the starboard side. This would maintain the most stable buoyancy mode for the 360-foot-long sub, preventing excessive "lean," which, if not corrected for, would cause "wobble," which in turn would upset the launch trajectory of the remaining missiles. It was a sequence that Robert Brentwood nightly prayed he'd never have to set in motion but was prepared to do so if it came to that. Meanwhile, the thought of a missile breaking through its protective sheath, he discovered, was no help in calming him down.

"Robert—" Rosemary murmured, arching her back, her breathing faster, shallower. He lowered himself closer to her and could feel her nipples pressing into him. "Robert—Robert—" Then he could hear the latecomers again, in the room across the hallway, talking. Rosemary was moving faster and faster beneath him, clutching his buttocks so tightly, he could feel her nails digging in. His left hand beneath her neck lifting her, he kissed her, his other hand grasping the edge of the mattress so hard, its inner spring gave like foam rubber, his fist squeezing it to nothing.

"Darling—darling," she murmured, almost beyond control, and he could hear one of the latecomers padding out into the hall, heading toward the bathroom. If they flushed the toilet and put her off—

In Moscow, General Kiril Marchenko, once special adviser to President Suzlov and now minister for war, was strolling in the Kremlin's snow-manteled Taynitsky Garden. It was the coldest December night in fifteen years, but Marchenko had ignored the plummeting temperatures, eagerly seeking the fresh, albeit frigid, air during the recess from the STAVKA—Supreme Headquarters—meeting, where the atmosphere had been thick with bluish-gray smoke, giving him a throbbing headache. And if Marchenko had ever needed a clear head, it was now. The NATO armor, led by the eccentric but brilliant American general Douglas Freeman, reinforced by the NATO convoys from America, had broken out from near certain defeat in the Soviet-ringed Dortmund/Bielefeld Pocket on the North German Plain.

The American general, whose reputation had been made early in the war by a daring nighttime air cavalry raid behind enemy lines in Korea on the North Korean capital of Pyongyang, hadn't merely breached the Russian encirclement around the hundred-mile-long Dortmund/Bielefeld pocket but was turning it into a rout of Soviet armor. And as the Soviet troops withdrew, Marchenko knew his career was also in danger. As architect of the stunning SPETS—special forces—paratroop attack against Adak, the American submarine base in the Aleutians, Marchenko was now being held responsible for having committed Russian forces to a two-front war. His comrades in the STAVKA were charging, correctly, that had Marchenko not advised President Suzlov to attack the U.S. submarine base east of Kamchatka Peninsula and west of Alaska, the thousands of supply and support, as well as combat, troops that had been funneled to the Aleutian front could have been used to plug the gap punched out by the American armor on the European front. Marchenko knew that unless he could stop, or at least slow down, the NATO breakout, led by the Americans under Freeman, he could look forward to a demotion as rapid as his previous promotion had been.

To make matters worse, his son Sergei, a pilot attached to Far Eastern Command HQ at Khabarovsk in eastern Siberia but presently serving in the Aleutian Islands, had written home that the ''millimaws''—the storm winds born in the confluence of the westward-flowing Japanese Current and the eastward-flowing Alaska Current—had been unusually severe in the past few weeks. His comments about the weather were a shorthand Sergei used in order to get his letter past the squadron censor, the millimaws an Aleut word used by Sergei and his father to mean Americans. It wasn't the speed of the American fighting Falcons and carrier-borne Tomcats that had Sergei and the other MiG-25 Foxbat pilots worried—after all, the Russian MiG-25s and Sukhoi-15s at Mach 2.8 and 2.5 were faster than the American planes. Nor had it been the daring of the American pilots that had caused Sergei and his friends concern, for they knew about this from the North Korean pilots who had done battle with the American carrier-borne fighters providing cover for Freeman's raid on Pyongyang at the beginning of the war. What *did* astonish the Soviet pilots was that even in the worst weather—in the massive fog banks that covered most of the far-flung islands in the crescent-shaped arc between the Soviet Union and America—the American pilots had an edge because of their improved radar technology. Though the MiG Foxbats' state-of-the-art ''Fox Fire'' look-down 54-mile-range radar had been thought equal to anything the Americans had at the beginning of the war, the upgraded U.S. pulse-Doppler look-up, look-down radar in the American F-16 Falcons had caught up. And the F-14 Tomcats' AN/AWG-9 weapon-control system with its 195-mile-range radar, the latter capable of simultaneously tracking twenty-four targets and attacking eight of them at different altitudes, had brought the temporary Soviet air superiority over the western Aleutians to a screaming halt. Now, instead of being able to keep sending supplies to Adak, building it up as Russia's advance springboard for the Soviet attacks against NORAD's Alaskan flank, taking pressure off the Soviet forces in Europe, it looked as if the Americans might try to retake Adak Island and Shemya. The capture of the huge U.S. early-warning radar station at Shemya by the Second Soviet Airborne only weeks after Adak had fallen had been Marchenko's proudest boast.

As for Europe, Marchenko had sought help from the Soviet Northern Fleet to increase ''convoy interdiction'' all along the NATO sea lanes between North America and Europe—to cut off NATO's vital supply line from America. But following the sinking of the *Yumashev*, the pride of the Russian Kresta II–class guided missile cruiser, by the American submarine USS

Roosevelt in the Celtic Sea off southwestern England, the battle for the Atlantic had also momentarily swung in the Americans' favor. For the first time since the war began, more merchantmen were reaching the French and English Channel ports than were being sunk.

On the far eastern front, the Soviet navy had assured Marchenko and the other members of the Politburo that it was working as fast as possible, including using forced-labor battalions from the hitherto upstart Baltic republics and the troublesome minority groups on the Sino-Soviet border regions near Vladivostok, readying to launch a hitherto undreamt-of and highly secret submarine offensive against the U.S. West Coast. But until the two new subs were ready—another two months—the NATO convoys to the Aleutians, the Soviet admirals conceded, while sustaining heavy losses, would not be stopped. Momentarily oblivious to his surroundings, Marchenko had stopped walking in the garden, the blizzard swirling about him stinging his face as he realized he was going to have to make the most humiliating decision of his life. With the Soviet army withdrawing on the European front, the air battle over Europe, like the air war over the Aleutians, in uncertain flux, and the navy's promises not realizable for at least two, possibly four, months, the minister of war knew that only one man, Vladimir Chernko, head of the Committee for State Security, and whom Marchenko detested, could help remedy the crisis in Western Europe.

The feud between the short, stocky Marchenko and the tall, steely-eyed Chernko, whose ambition was to become president, had begun in what the Committee for State Security, the KGB, had called its *vershina,* or "high summer," of the West's honeymoon with Gorbachev. The British, as usual, had been standoffish, the Germans willing to accept Gorbachev's line in return for Moscow's support of reunification, and the Americans, Chernko said, gullible and deluded, wanting everyone to be happy, believing you could fix everything that was wrong in the world with goodwill and Yankee know-how. Chernko had served under Vladimir Kryuchkov, whom Gorbachev in 1988 had ordered to launch a massive industrial and military espionage offensive against the West in order to save millions of rubles for *perestroika,* rubles that would otherwise have to be spent for weapons and technological catch-up with the West. It was much easier to steal or buy Western technological secrets.

Under Chernko's direction, the KGB had outdone Madison

Avenue in its new image making, even going so far as to invite American counterparts from the CIA to "tour" the old Dzherzinsky Square headquarters and the new offices in the outer ring. In an effort to convince the world of just how reformed the KGB was, Chernko made highly publicized arrests in the Gorbachev years of certain "outlaw elements" among the Soviet elite who had "illegally profited" at the expense of the Soviet people. Chernko promised they would be severely "disciplined." One of those so punished was Kiril Marchenko's brother, Fyodor, accused of "profiteering" in one of the now-not-so-secret party specialty stores. As far as Kiril could find out, Fyodor had been chosen at random by Chernko. Publicly accused by Chernko, he was tried and sentenced to fifteen years, reduced to five as a humanitarian "gesture" by Gorbachev's administration. Chernko had meanwhile been featured on the cover of *Time* magazine as being typical of the "new breed in the KGB"—technocrats "more interested in rooting out inefficiency at home than in spying abroad." Fyodor Marchenko hung himself after one month in Lefortevo Prison. Kiril Marchenko remembered that Chernko had sent flowers.

"Comrade Marchenko!"

Marchenko turned to see one of the Kremlin's guards, ruddy-faced, his breath coming out like a hot tap in the icy air, the red piping on his bluish-gray greatcoat ruby-colored like thin lines of blood, the pea-sized snow bouncing off his fur-lined cap.

"Yes?" answered Marchenko irritably. "What is it?"

"The STAVKA meeting, Comrade. It is about to reconvene."

Marchenko looked nonplussed at the guard. "But it is—" he glanced at his watch "—not yet one A.M. The adjournment was for another—" Marchenko saw that the second hand on his watch had stopped. His father, who had died in one of the gulags that were supposed to have disappeared under Gorbachev, had once told him that when a man's watch stops, it is a warning his life is in imminent danger. Of course, Marchenko knew it was a ridiculous peasant superstition of his father's. Nevertheless, in his present mood, it jolted him, and he resolved that, unpalatable as it was, he would have to ask—beg, if necessary, Chernko to help him deal a death blow to the NATO advance which had become embodied by one man: the American, Freeman. After all, it had been Chernko who had successfully purged the Politburo of Siberian separatists who hated Moscow as much as they hated America and who had been plotting to overthrow Suzlov. It was also Chernko who had come up with the idea of sending SPETS commandos, dressed in captured American uniforms, to infiltrate the NATO lines and sow confusion among the Allied troops in the Dortmund-Bielefeld pocket. What Marchenko needed now was someone with the training to again pose as an American or some other NATO officer but who could penetrate right through to Freeman's headquarters and kill the American general. Perhaps, thought Marchenko, it could be done in the same way as some of Chernko's men already "in place" overseas had been ordered, as well as carrying out sabotage, to track down and "eliminate" the commanders of America's weapons of last resort, the Sea Wolf nuclear subs. If Chernko would support such an audacious plan, then Marchenko would support Chernko in his bid for the presidency, if and when President Suzlov was replaced or died—whichever came first. "If you mean to get ahead in this world," Marchenko could still hear his father say, "you must swallow your pride now and then." Kiril Marchenko told himself it was time he did so, to ask Chernko's help, not only for himself but for Mother Russia—for his family.

As he headed back for the STAVKA meeting in the Council of Ministers, Marchenko saw that the guard, about his son Sergei's age, could very well be his guard in some godforsaken prison in the Transbaikal if he, Kiril Marchenko, didn't quickly restore his own reputation in the Politburo and STAVKA.

"You ever been to the Far Eastern Theater?" he asked the guard. "To Khabarovsk?"

"No, Comrade General."

"You're lucky then," replied Marchenko morosely, a sudden flurry of snow swirling about him. "It's much colder than here. My son tells me that in Khabarovsk, the winds come all the way down from the Kara Sea—the prisoners have to dig through the ice of the Amur River so they can fish. The trouble is, the ice is jagged, you see—not at all smooth and flat as some people imagine. Chaotic—going this way and that at impossible angles."

The guard was feeling nervous—it was highly unusual for a general to be conversing in such a way with a mere private, especially the celebrated general who was minister of war and who had engineered the penetration of NATO's Fulda Gap, where the masses of Russian armor had burst through before heading north to the German Plain and south to the Danube Valley, sending the NATO defenses reeling.

"I—I don't know anything about the Far Eastern Theater, Comrade General. I didn't know we had taken prisoners east of—"

"No, no, boy," said Marchenko irritably. "Our *own* people—in the gulags."

The guard was doubly perplexed—as far as he knew, gulags had been banned ever since the time of the revisionist Gorbachev.

Marchenko had only a few minutes before the STAVKA meeting would be called to order, and presented his deal to Chernko quickly, succinctly.

Chernko rejected it out of hand. "This is not possible," Chernko said icily. "The American, Freeman, moves too fast. We never know where he is." Chernko signaled an aide.

"I need help, Comrade," repeated Marchenko. "If you assist—I will support you wholeheartedly."

"For what?" asked Chernko, feigning ignorance.

"For whatever you wish, Comrade."

Chernko replied that perhaps something could be worked out. He did have a plan to stop the Americans, but it was nothing like Marchenko's "amateur" proposal of assassination behind enemy lines. Nevertheless, he conceded he would welcome Marchenko's support when he presented his plan to the Politburo at tomorrow's meeting.

"Can you tell me what it is now?" asked Marchenko.

"Tomorrow," answered Chernko. "Meanwhile I will welcome your support in *this* meeting." Chernko was looking directly at him.

"Support of what?" asked Marchenko.

"Of anything I say."

Marchenko felt his blood rising at Chernko's contemptuous tone but held himself in check. President Suzlov was calling the meeting to order. As the members took their positions either side of the long, baize-covered table, with the portrait of Marx gazing down behind them, Chernko's aide slid in beside his boss, pencil and paper in hand. "Yes, Comrade?"

"Draw up the plan at once," Chernko informed him. "Two teams—twenty in each—neither must have any knowledge of the other. Purpose—penetrate NATO front lines. Target—the American general, Freeman."

"Code name?" asked the aide.

"Trojan," said Chernko. "And Colonel!"

"Sir?"

"Book an appointment for General Marchenko—tomorrow morning. Early."

"Yes, Comrade Director."

The room was soon full of blue-gray smoke, and Chernko could see Marchenko sitting glumly, pinching the bridge of his nose.

Lingering for a moment before he got out of bed, Robert Brentwood watched Rosemary, her face childlike, her breasts pressing against the turquoise negligee in her contented sleep, and he had the urge to make love again. But dawn was creeping over the western sea, and though this time of day had long ceased to have any meaning for him aboard the *Roosevelt* on patrol in the perennial darkness four hundred meters beneath the sea, once ashore, he found that he quickly reverted to the dawn-to-dusk habits of Annapolis: up early, ready to go.

One foot on the windowsill, looking out at the wind-lashed ocean, he began stretching his legs, preparatory to his fifteen-minute workout. He hated it, but—a believer, albeit reluctantly, in the "no gain without pain" school—he forced himself through it twice every twenty-four hours whether he was at sea or not. Out on the storm-cut swells, he could see the bobbing of a trawler, probably from Ballantrae several miles to the north, its mast momentarily spearing the cold blue sky, then disappearing in deep troughs. The constant vigilance bred at sea never left him, and he reminded himself that just over forty miles to the west, beyond the tempestuous North channel, lay Northern Ireland in the grip of continuing internecine strife between IRA terrorists and Orangemen.

The IRA had become increasingly active against the British military, who had been stretched thin in Northern Ireland because of the heavy losses suffered over the Channel by the British Army of the Rhine in the battle for the Dortmund/Bielefeld pocket. And Robert recalled the talk between his executive officer, Peter Zeldman, and the other officers aboard the *Roosevelt* about reports from CINCLANT—Commander in Chief Atlantic—to head of security for Holy Loch to be alert for IRA provisionals. Britain's military intelligence, MI5, warned that IRA "provos" might try coming across in trawlers. If they landed farther north near the Firth of Lorn, they could fairly quickly head inland through the wilderness of the sparsely populated Argyll to Loch Lomond, then down the fifteen miles to Holy Loch. Despite the base's reinforced concrete pens, a well-aimed shoulder-borne antitank missile could take out the *Roosevelt* or any other sub.

Not surprisingly, Robert hadn't mentioned any of this to Rosemary, knowing how the very mention of a submarine got her worrying. Indeed, he'd gone so far as to promise her that they wouldn't go near the base during the honeymoon but rather head inland a little, go north along Loch Lomond's western shore, then north again along the Firth of Lorn on their way to the ancient and picturesque fishing village of Mallaig near the fabled Isle of Skye.

Rosemary murmured in her sleep and rolled over to his side of the old-fashioned four-poster bed, her right hand moving to where he had lain, her lips in a smile that at once touched Robert with its simplicity and aroused him in its sensuousness. Below, he could hear someone stirring—the proprietor's wife in the kitchen, he guessed—and he caught a whiff of kippers cooking, the one thing Rosemary couldn't bring herself to eat on the honeymoon. Scottish blood ran in her veins, but the thought of smoked fish for breakfast appalled her—and no, she'd told him, it didn't have anything to do with morning sickness, which so far she'd escaped.

Halfway through a head-to-knee stretch, while still watching her, Robert wondered whether there'd be enough time before breakfast for what his horny crewmen ashore habitually referred to as a "dawn breaker." He could hear the floorboards creaking outside in the upstairs hallway as early risers made their way to the bathroom and down to the dining room. He began the last stretch, right heel on the windowsill, his hands fully extended in unison to touch his toes. For a moment he glimpsed the trawler again on the pewter sea. The wind had died, but it seemed only temporary, a scud of cloud invading from the north.

"Robert—"

When he turned, he saw she had pulled the bedding tightly about her with one hand, the other patting the sheet on his side. "Coming back to bed?"

"Funny you mentioned that," Brentwood said in midstretch. "I was just thinking about it. Hadn't decided—"

"Yes you have," she said, a cheeky glint in her eyes, her gaze wandering below his navel, "unless it's an optical illusion?"

"Rosemary!" He was genuinely and pleasantly shocked at her impishness after her fretting the night before. It was as if the worries of the night about his old girlfriends, et cetera, et

cetera, had vanished with the howling of the wind. "We might be late for breakfast," he cautioned, sliding eagerly in beside her.

"No we won't," she assured him happily.

"I'll take the Fifth on that," he told her.

"What do you mean?"

As she spoke, he detected the scent of fresh mint about her doing battle with the smell of kippers wafting up from below. "I mean," he explained, "that I refuse to answer on the grounds that it might incriminate me."

The phrase sounded familiar to her—from the American films she'd seen. She popped a mint candy in his mouth. "I thought only gangsters talked like that—"

"Well, you don't know much about me. Maybe I run a still aboard *Roosevelt.*" The sub's name was out before he could stop himself, but it didn't matter—it was lovers' talk, easy, without strain, and he was glad to see he could mention the sub without her getting upset again about him, the war, about what might happen. The Rosemary of the morning had put her worried self to flight—as if sometime during the sweet darkness after he'd settled her down following the latecomers' arrival, she had decided once and for all to live in the present, that the world and all its troubles were too big for them to control, that their time together was too precious to permit armies of "what ifs" to sabotage what happiness they might find before he went back to war. He pulled her toward him. "No," she said teasingly, giggling.

"Yes."

"No."

"My God," he said, "if you don't let me, I'll explode."

"The answer's still no. I won't let you."

His left arm curved beneath her and he raised her, kissing her nipples through the negligee. "I love you," he said breathlessly.

"Are you always . . . like this?" she asked, her hand sliding beneath the warm sheets, squeezing him.

"When I'm with you—" he said, kissing her again, "all the time."

"Robert—" her tone was soft, urgent "—don't leave me."

"I won't, sweetheart. I won't."

CHAPTER TWO

THOUGH FASHIONABLY SMART in a tweed jacket, tie, and flannels that Rosemary had chosen for him, Robert still wasn't used to being out of uniform and felt more self-conscious than his bride as they entered the B and B's dining room. They were relieved to receive a jolly greeting, without any honeymoon jokes, from Mrs. McRae, a small, dumpy, and irrepressible Scot who had been running the B and B sixty-five miles southwest of Glasgow for the past forty years, and her husband, Alfred, a partially incapacitated veteran of the Falklands War. The battle that left McRae with a gammy leg and intense pain, especially now in the depth of the Scottish winter, had been the single most important event of his life. It had also left him with a growing conviction that next to Napoleon, Montgomery of Alamein, and Robert the Bruce, he was one of the great unsung strategists of warfare. His greeting to the honeymooners and the other five guests, two couples and a single commercial traveler, consisted of a throat clearing and a stiff nod as he read the latest war news in the *Edinburgh Herald*.

"What'll it be, lass?" asked the ebullient Mrs. McRae. "Porridge to start?"

"No, thank you," Rosemary declined, opting instead for corn flakes—a choice that she had the distinct impression Mr. McRae didn't approve of. Robert asked for kippers, his request receiving an appreciative nod from Mrs. McRae and one of the other two couples.

Meanwhile Alfred McRae, head buried in the paper, let out his breath in short, audible bursts of disgust, his head shaking at something he'd just read. One of the other two couples, in their late twenties, were finishing their ersatz chicory coffee, excusing themselves from the table. Robert handed a dozen or so one-cup instant coffee packets he had brought with him from *Roosevelt* to Mrs. McRae.

"Och, mon, will ye look at this, Alfred? Real coffee from America."

McRae grunted behind the paper while the other of the two couples, a pair in their early forties, Robert guessed, their accents distinctly upper middle class, beamed, as did the lone commercial traveler. "I say," began the husband, sitting forward, the pale, cloud-sieved sunlight shining on his tan Dutch corduroy jacket. "Haven't seen anything like that for months."

"And ye're no likely to again," put in Mr. McRae suddenly. "And tha's a fact. The convoys are doomed."

"Oh?" said the Englishman in the corduroy jacket, who by now had introduced himself and his wife as James and Joan Price of London, a rather pinched yet tight good-humored look about him, his wife clearly deferring to him, though at the moment she was picking a pill of fluff from his jacket. Wearing a tartan shirt with nonmatching maroon necktie, he was the type of Englishman, Robert thought, who'd wear a necktie to the beach. His wife, a thin woman with mousy brown hair, wearing a beige tweed skirt, white blouse, socks, and what Rosemary's father would have called "sensible" walking shoes, smiled pleasantly at Rosemary as she flicked the fluff away from her husband's sleeve. Her husband looked up at the proprietor of the B and B. "Why do you say that, Mr. McRae?"

"What's tha'?"

The commercial traveler, a tired, overweight, stocky man in his late fifties, was torn between listening closely to what appeared to be a developing argument and watching to see whether Mrs. McRae was going to offer him one of the packets of American coffee. "You say the convoys are doomed?" said Price.

"Aye—we're all doomed."

"Och—noo," interjected Mrs. McRae, sliding the steaming kippers in front of Robert Brentwood. "It's not as bad as that, surely!"

"Then ye've no read the paper."

"I've noo had time," she said, eyebrows raised good-naturedly.

"They've attacked Sullom Voe," McRae announced gloomily, yet somehow sounding strangely triumphant. "Just as I said they would."

Robert Brentwood, though he had difficulty understanding

the Scotsman's brogue, knew that Sullom Voe, one of the Shetland Islands, three hundred miles off Scotland's northeast corner, was the site of a big oil refinery servicing the major part of the North Sea oil fields. He was interested but said nothing, finding McRae's melodramatic air irritating.

"Aye," went on McRae, "biggest terminal in Europe 'tis, Sullom Voe. Tankers line up there like buses." With that he suddenly swung the front page of the *Herald*—"RUSSIANS HIT SULLOM VOE!"—for all to see, the color photograph having captured great curling plumes of dense black smoke rising over a glint of gold sea, two tankers barely discernible in the bottom right of the photograph. "*Sooper*tankers at that," continued McRae, to add to the horror he was clearly enjoying. "God knows how many casualties. Och—" He put the paper down disgustedly on the linen tablecloth and pushed a large, thick china mug marked "British Rail" over his place mat of Burns's poetry toward his wife for more tea. "It was daft of 'em not to have more air cover. What did they expect? I told them, Maggie—didn't I? But noo—the *experts* in London knew best. Air-to-air missile batteries would be 'sufficient,' they said—with some fighter cover." He shot a glance across at Brentwood. "Drained Scotland, they did, and sent everything across the water to save the Frogs. What do they care aboot Scotland?"

"A great deal, I should imagine," put in Price. "It's always a problem, I suspect—how many to put where." He, too, looked across at the Brentwoods. "Wouldn't you agree?"

"Yes," said Brentwood. "There's never enough to go around."

"Precisely," enjoined Price.

"Ye no think the oil's important, laddie?" said McRae, wincing in pain as he abruptly turned around in his chair, left hand vigorously massaging his left kneecap, his right hand ladling heaping teaspoons of sugar into his milky tea.

"Not at all," answered Price, while his wife, Rosemary noticed, tugged as surreptitiously as she could on her husband's sleeve, her eyes rolling heavenward as she caught Rosemary's glance. Rosemary smiled sympathetically.

But Price wouldn't be restrained. "Oil's vital, of course," he said, "but I suppose there was enough in storage in the first few months until the convoys—"

"Och—" said McRae, his tone one of sneering contempt, his left hand continuing to massage his knee. "There might have been reserves for a wee while, but it was obvious right from the very first shot that we'd be in a right pickle. Started rationing straight off, they did. London wasn't prepared, laddie—and that's all there is to it. Only thing that surprises me is that the Russians haven't hit it sooner."

"I daresay they could use your prescience in London," said Price. "You should be in the Admiralty."

There was a flash of anger in McRae's eyes, his face clouding. "I've done my bit, laddie. Aye—and got this for it." He smacked his leg, glancing at the Brentwoods for moral support. Rosemary reached for more corn flakes while Robert, diplomatically, gave all his attention to separating the second kipper from its spine.

Mrs. McRae suddenly emerged from the kitchen. "Now, who'd like some of Mr. Brentwood's coffee?"

"I'd love a cup," said the commercial traveler, rising eagerly, toast crumbs tumbling from his napkin.

"And," said McRae, staring at Price, who was now looking rather sullen himself, "how old are you, laddie?"

"I'm a lecturer," Price replied defiantly, quick to the intimation of McRae's question. "LSE."

Rosemary looked up. McRae's chin jutted forward combatively. "Och, never heard of it." He returned noisily to his mug of tea.

"London School of Economics," said Price crisply.

"Perhaps," put in Rosemary, half out of genuine interest, half in an effort to calm things down, "you know my sister—Georgina Spence?"

Price looked at her blankly. "I—can't say I do. Sorry. I'm—I'm in political studies actually. Theory."

"Oh, aye," said McRae, "we certainly need that. A good dose of political theory. Essential war work, is it?"

"She's in her final year," Rosemary continued, Price trying to be polite to her while clearly furious at the Scot.

"Georgina . . . Spence—you said? Spence—yes—I do remember the name, I think. But can't put a face to it, I'm afraid. It's a big place. To tell you the truth—"

"Of course," said Rosemary. "I know what it's like. I'm a teacher myself and—"

"A lot of people studying politics then, are there?" cut in McRae, ignoring Rosemary and shoveling several more spoonfuls of sugar into his tea. "Special rations—along with exemptions from active duty, is it? For the important work at the university, I mean?" McRae's gray eyes sparkled even in the dim light of the dining room.

"No," said Price, hands clasped before him, "no, same ration as everyone else actually. Though we don't have everything, of course. Sometimes we've *no* sugar *at all.*"

The door from the hallway opened and the young couple who had excused themselves earlier, as Rosemary and Robert had arrived, came into the dining room—a spot or two of confetti still on the woman's lambswool coat. The husband, despite the civilian garb, was a young serviceman, Robert guessed as he watched the way the man pulled out and carefully counted the five-pound notes. The man, a little younger than his bride, Robert thought, had the look of a junior officer—anxious to take the lead in front of her but not quite sure of what he was doing. Turning to his wife, he whispered something, Robert detecting a distinctly New York accent as the man finally gave up trying to understand the British currency, handing his bride a clutch of ten-p notes.

By the time the couple had left, their interruption of the table conversation long enough to have cooled tempers, the Prices were completing their meal in silence and, seeing that Mrs. McRae wasn't going to bring out any more "real" coffee packets, politely fended off further offers of tea. As he rose to leave, Price asked Robert, "You on holiday?"

"Yes."

"Thought so. I suspect we'll see you again. Joan and I are doing a spot of sight-seeing ourselves. Few weeks off till the new term."

"Well," said Robert, rising and offering his hand, "next time I hope you'll have time for more coffee."

"So do *I*," said Joan, an edge to her voice, smiling at Rosemary. "And not so much talk!"

There was a long silence after the couple left, Robert finishing his kipper, the commercial traveler sitting quietly, hands about the cup of coffee in a warm embrace, but looking as pained as McRae, who was now avidly reading the obituaries. Finally the traveler spoke. "Excuse me. Ah—" He had the look of a petty criminal. "Does anyone mind if I smoke?" He glanced awkwardly at Rosemary.

"Not at all," she lied. Next, the salesman sought Mr. McRae's permission, the Scot shifting in his chair again, pushing his tea mug to a new position. "I'll not mind." Mrs. McRae was busy in the kitchen. The commercial traveler sat back, eyes closed to luxuriate in the twin pleasures of smoke and coffee. Through the dining room window they could see the young newlyweds getting into a yellow Honda Civic, the faint remnant of "Just Married" visible across the passenger door.

"That's a silly thing to do," observed McRae. "Cost him a packet to get that painted over."

Mrs. McRae put a new pot of tea before him, smoothing its cozy. "Perhaps they don't want to paint it over, McRae."

"Aye," conceded McRae, knowing he'd gone too far for her liking with the Prices but still grumpily eager to get in a last salvo at the world. "Well, they certainly didn't mind who heard 'em during the night."

Robert saw Rosemary blush. The commercial traveler had his eyes closed in a grin of contentment as he exhaled, the long stream of smoke swirling in the air, as gray and turbulent as the storm clouds scudding in from the Irish Sea.

"You'll be heading north, then?" said McRae.

"Yes," answered Robert, his hand beneath the table on Rosemary's thigh. "Yes, we're off to Mallaig."

"What?" said McRae, as if they'd taken leave of their senses. "That'd be nigh on two hundred miles!"

It always amazed Brentwood how the British sense of what distance it was proper or possible to travel in a day was so different from how the Americans viewed it, even accounting for the fact that the long, lonely roads over the moors and through the highlands were often one-way and certainly a far cry from any freeway—or motorway, as the British called it. "We should be there by dark," said Robert confidently.

"You'll be seeing Robbie's cottage first?" It sounded more like an order from Commander in Chief Atlantic than a question.

"Yes," said Robert.

"And Glencoe?"

It didn't ring a bell with Robert. Rosemary came to her husband's rescue even as she was trying to fend off his groping beneath the table. "You remember, Robert. I told you—it was the site of a great battle between the Scots and the English."

"Who won?" asked Robert, smiling. "The Scots, I guess."

McRae's face was swept by squall, eyes brooding and sullen as the clouds congealing over the sea. "It wasn't a *battle*," said McRae. "It was a *massacre*. MacIain Macdonald, his wife, and thirty-six of the clan. Slain by the English. And by men who had supped with them." McRae paused. "You'll not be calling into your Holy Loch then?"

Robert reacted quickly, trying to hide his surprise, turning the question back to McRae. "Holy Loch?"

"Aye. You're a submariner, aren't you?"

Robert didn't answer.

"You're American, aren't you?" pressed McRae.

"Yes, but—"

"Your face, laddie," said McRae. "Clean as a bairn's bottom. You've no seen the sun or any kind of weather for a wee while, have you?"

"You're very observant, Mr. McRae," Robert complimented him. McRae came around the table, face grimacing, his limp favoring the stiff left leg. Then, quite unexpectedly, he offered his hand to Brentwood. "Mind how ye go." Next, his steel-grey eyes shifted from Robert to Rosemary. "And take good care of the lassie."

Robert nodded his head. "Thank you, sir. I will."

After they'd packed their bags into the trunk or, as Rosemary insisted on calling it, the "boot" of the Morris and driven off, Rosemary waving back to the lone Mrs. McRae on the porch, Robert wondered aloud why, if McRae was such a determined Scot, he had bothered fighting for the British in the Falklands War.

"The Scots love to fight," she said simply, winding up her window against the splatter of rain and taking out the map of Scotland's west coast, looking down at the thin, solitary roads winding up past Ayre to the Highlands and beyond—to Cape Wrath.

CHAPTER THREE

FROM THE HIGH-RESOLUTION satellite pictures, the Politburo had clearly seen the vast North German Plain streaked with a white mange of snow, crisscrossed with Allied pontoon bridges over the tributaries to the Elbe and strewn with all the detritus of war: eviscerated, still-smoking armored columns, gutted empty gasoline dumps, and bloated bodies, all indicating how rapidly the Americans were advancing and the Russians retreating. The American general, Freeman, was obviously moving so fast that Soviet divisions hadn't time to bury their dead.

Sergei Marchenko, one of the Soviet fighter pilots temporarily seconded from the Far Eastern TVD Aleutian section to plug the gaps opened up by the American breakout from the Dortmund-Bielefeld pocket to the North German Plain, was coming in low over the white ribbon of the E-8, the 120-mile autobahn between Berlin and what, before Gorbachev, used to be the frontier of Western Germany. His Foxbat-A MiG-25, one of a combat pair, crossed the Elbe seven miles northeast of Magdeburg. He pressed the "ARM" switch for four Acrid 6 air-to-air missiles, two of them infrared-homing, the other two radar-homing. The two fighter interceptors, with no internal armament, were equipped with external pod-mounted twenty-three-millimeter cannons to be used strafing either NATO supply lines or NATO fighters covering the American advance.

Sergei Marchenko was no coward, but he, like the other pilots rushed to the western front, hoped that the SPETS units, long in place in Western Europe, would help slow the American advance by sabotaging their forward airfields, which the Americans were so good at laying down despite the slushy conditions of a temporary thaw in the freezing weather.

Besides, as much as Sergei Marchenko enjoyed being a fighter pilot after his military slog through the armored corps, to which he had originally been assigned because of his height, he would have preferred to be flying the somewhat slower but more maneuverable Sukhoi-15 Flagon. It had served him so well at his home base in the Aleutians during the attacks on the American outposts of Adak submarine base and Shemya Island. In supporting the SPETS operation against Shemya, the United States' largest western radar warning post, the Sukhois, flying out of the Komandorskiye Islands less than two hundred miles from the Americans' westernmost island, had performed exceptionally well. It was true that Marchenko, despite his impressive record of five *unichtozhennykh*—"kills"—had been shot down by an American F-14 Tomcat from the U.S. carrier *Salt Lake City*, reputedly flown by the American ace Shirer. Marchenko had ejected, been picked up within ten minutes, and was back at Komandorskiye base within three hours. But pilots who survived a plane shot up in a dogfight tended to grow more, not less, attached to the make, and so it was with Marchenko.

Still, he knew it was silly to become sentimental about such things, and one had to learn to adapt quickly amid the vicissitudes of a rapidly changing war. In any event, Marchenko and his wingman had been buoyed by the information given them during engine-start that intelligence reports showed Allied pilots in Europe were being forced to fly in excess of six sorties a day in order to try to deal with the swarms of Russian fighters now being funneled in from the eastern sectors of the USSR.

It was predicted that at this unheard-of—except for the Battle of Britain—sortie rate, sooner or later the unrelenting fatigue would take its toll, not only on pilots and the radar-intercept officers who flew with them, but also on the ground crews. But the Russian estimates were wide of the mark, for while there had been even more casualties than they thought, British and American pilots were not about to ease off or pause to catch their breath—not after the American army, spearheaded by Freeman's corps, had finally breached the Soviet ring of steel. The Allied pilots were like marathon runners, worn down but suddenly invigorated by a second wind—in this case provided by Freeman's breakout from the DB pocket and by the possibility of quickly gaining ground. To make up for air crew losses, many of the British and American aircraft normally crewed by pilot and RIOs were being flown with pilot only—doing what he could with the electronic countermeasures but going up anyway, disdaining second-by-second control over all the avionics in favor of pressing home the attack, going air-to-air, giving maximum attention to dogfight maneuvers.

Coming in from the southwest over Göttingen and the recaptured airfields of lower Saxony, a flight of two F-16A Fighting Falcons, though not yet visible against the bright whiteness of blue-patched nimbostratus, could be seen quite clearly on Marchenko's fifty-two-mile look-down Fox Fire radar.

Unaware he was already on the Soviets' radar, Kurt Schulz, an American from Los Angeles, now picked up one of the Russians on his Dalmo Victor AN/ALR radar-warning receiver, the computer telling him the Russian fighters were now in excess of Mach 2.3—his Falcon's top speed, Mach 2. Lying back in full recline, sidestick mode of the F-16 to reduce the G force, Schulz pressed the zoom toggle, bringing up the DAA—designated area of attack—the blipping rectangle showing cattle grazing against sodden, snow-slushed fields either side of the highway where once the tall barbed wire had stood. The black streaks Schulz could see in the zoom shot were slicks of oil visible against the unthawed shoulder of the road where snow had remained. Then there were other streaks against the snow—these rising from the ground toward him, as SAM sites opened up from the Harz foothills to the south. Schulz immediately noted on his kneepad that the SAM sites had shifted from the day before and so were presumed to be mobile launchers. In the distance he could now see the two Russians, specks of silver, closing fast, and he was alert for an ELOK—enemy lock-on tone. Radio silence was pointless now that visual ID had been made, and he asked his wingman, "That barn down there—eleven o'clock—was it there yesterday?"

There was such a deafening noise, it made Shulz grimace. He lost the video image momentarily as the plane shifted violently left. He went to "jammer" to play havoc with the SAM radars. Coming up at him at over five hundred miles an hour from less than three hundred feet, the terrain below him now a racing white-green blur, Schulz dropped two iron bombs and let the afterburner have its head. The barn was gone; so was his wingman, a young pilot he'd met only that morning as they'd raced from the ready room in response to the scramble horn. At five thousand, Schulz banked hard, the sun glinting behind him as he turned to take another run at the broken span across the Elbe, where he'd spotted the black marks against the snow. Possibly they were tire ruts, leading down from the highway to the water's edge, more tracks coming up from the other side of the river through snow. "A "sunken" pontoon bridge?

The flak was thick, and he saw a burst of red tracer catching the sun, fading, climbing leisurely up toward him through the smoke of the barn, more tracer now coming from the direction of Magdeburg. He was into the smoke, turning tightly, coming in low again, the HUD lines flicking rapidly, the four green diamonds closing spastically. The smoke was gone. He saw the wreckage of the SAM site in the barn he'd destroyed littering the icy green fields, some of its debris caught in a high mesh fence either side of the autobahn. Schulz knew it was only a matter of minutes before the MiGs, rising like silver gnats in his rear vision from Stendal, would be on him. He set the "clicker"—automatic release—when the river section he'd chosen on his TV zoom was mirrored in the radar image. The Falcon rose as the bombs released. The plane yawed slightly and he headed south, climbing to clear the Harz, hoping to lose himself in cloud, black puffs of flak from the AA batteries around Stassfurt and Aschersleben smudging the air about him.

CHAPTER FOUR

THREE MILES SOUTH of Burns's cottage outside Ayre, occasional spots of rain turned to sleet and Robert turned on the wipers. In the drowsy hum he and Rosemary were lost in their own thoughts—she wondering how her younger sister, Georgina, and Robert's executive officer, Peter Zeldman, were getting along—or if they were getting along at all after having graciously performed their official roles as best man and maid of honor at Robert and Rosemary's wedding.

Georgina's beauty was matched by her pride and a strong streak of leftist feminism that Rosemary surmised might not "go down" or, as Robert would say, "sit well" with the plainspoken, somewhat taciturn Zeldman. On the other hand, Rosemary, after the years of teaching all types of students in her Shakespeare class, was aware that sometimes opposites attract in the most unpredictable way. She hoped so, suspecting that, deep down, Georgina, though too proud to admit it, wanted a relationship that would give her a measure of certainty and stability in the world of "avant-garde" politics at the LSE and in a world made daily more uncertain by war.

She thought of her brother William's death in the convoy and of how terrified he must have been, his ship torpedoed in the middle of the Atlantic. She thought, too, of Robert's sister, Lana, who, as William's nurse, had written them about William, and without whom Rosemary would never have met Robert, who'd so kindly brought the letter down to Surrey on his first leave. Lana Brentwood, it seemed, had been with William in the final days of his life on the Halifax-bound hospital ship where he died. Rosemary thought, too, of Robert's youngest brother, David, twenty-four, who, though now safe in Liège in Belgium, had been listed as an MIA for several weeks after he and others, in the big drop by the American airborne over the Dortmund-Bielefeld pocket, had been swept off course by crosswinds into enemy territory. She wondered what he was like. There was still so much she didn't know about Robert's family. "Does your brother David have a girlfriend?" she asked.

Robert shrugged. "Sort of, I guess."

"What does that mean?"

"I'm not sure. Had a girl he liked back in the States—" He paused. "High school sweetheart—far as I can recall. But that was before the war. Don't know if it's still on between them."

"Do you know her name?"

"Mmm—" Robert pondered the question while using another tissue to clear the semicircle of mist above the dash. "Now there," he said, "you've got me."

"Oh, Robert—you *must* know!"

"Mel . . . Mel . . . Melanie, I think." It bugged him that he couldn't remember, a nuclear sub skipper who, like Zeldman and others in the service, was expected to have a photographic memory of enemy maneuvers and myriad descriptions of ships and armaments. But he was having trouble even trying to visualize the girl's face.

"Melanie who?" pressed Rosemary. "He must have spoken about her?"

"Not David," said Robert. "Very closemouthed about dating. We all were. All I remember is that he and a guy called Rick Stacy were in competition for her."

"Sounds serious."

"I guess. She was a nice kid—well, a kid *then*."

"So you've met her?"

"Once. On leave. She was a coed."

"A first-year student?"

"What—oh, yes," replied Robert. "First year at Oregon State. She was a bright—hold on!"

Rosemary was thrown forward, the car's rear end skewing hard right, skidding to a stop on the rain-slicked road. "You okay, honey?" he asked her quickly.

Off to her left, Rosemary caught the auburn blur of a deer slipping through the mist. "I'm all right," she said. "For a second—" she sat back against the headrest and turned to him, hand over her heart "—I thought it was another car."

"Figured the honeymoon was over, eh?" he said, swinging the Morris back onto the left-hand side of the road.

"Yes," she said. "I did."

He put a hand on her knee. "Sorry, sweetie."

"It's all right—not your fault." The fog was so thick, it made day seem like night, and for a moment Robert realized again how close the line was between survival and death—if it *had* been another car—a head-on collision on the lonely, narrow road across the moor. The irony of him and Rosemary dying on their honeymoon while David, having weathered the vicissitudes of the Dortmund-Bielefeld pocket, was now safe in Liège, awaiting transport back to England, struck with full force. Even hitting the deer could have been disastrous for them, and in a second he found himself envisaging Rosemary's face slashed bloody with broken glass and saw his other brother, Ray, the thirty-seven-year-old ex-captain of a missile frigate, the USS *Blaine*.

Ray, once nicknamed "Cruise" because of his resemblance to the onetime Hollywood idol, had been wounded in the flash fire following the attack of a swarm of fast, small North Korean attack boats, one of whose missiles had exploded on the *Blaine*'s bridge. Ray's face was now a horror mask of tight, polished skin, and he was still convalescing after a long, painful, and still unfinished series of plastic surgery operations. Robert had been revolted when he'd first seen the pictures of Ray and then felt guilty. He had never been close to either Ray or David. Perhaps, he thought, it wasn't so much a matter of different personalities as the gap in ages between him and his two younger brothers. It was like the age of "Bing" Crosby, as Robert was called by his crew, meeting Springsteen. After a certain age, your tastes just didn't change much, "nor your tactics," as one of the submarine instructors had told them, which is why anyone heading into his "deep" forties was considered too old for submarines. The temptation to let old habits ride, never to change them, from music to tactics, he knew could be fatal aboard the most complex fighting machine in history.

"Burns's cottage," said Rosemary, looking down at the map, "should be about five miles further on." Robert was feeling unusually drowsy, a temporary reaction, he knew from his war patrols on the sub, to the rush of adrenaline caused by a near miss—in this case a deer standing in for a Russian depth charge.

"Robert—I don't want to be a backseat driver, but you're going awfully fast." He glanced at the speedometer—seventy kilometers per hour.

"Just a tad over forty," he said, and almost added that *Roosevelt* went faster than this when she was submerged—but he stopped himself.

"You're angry?" she said, turning to him.

"Nope."

"Yes you are."

"No, seriously. I was—*Melissa!* That's it."

"What—?"

"David's girlfriend. Melissa Lange."

"Have you been thinking of her all this time?" Rosemary pressed mischievously. "I supposed that's why we almost hit that poor deer."

"No," he said, smiling across at her. "That had nothing to do with it. You were right. I was going too fast for fog like this."

" *'Och, och—'* as Mr. McRae would say, 'ye're noo tellin' me the truth, Robert Brentwood. You were going fast because you were thinking of her. This Melissa creature. 'Turns you on,' I suppose, as you Americans say."

"Aye," he joked, in an atrocious imitation of a Scottish accent. The car slowed to twenty kilometers, the fog so thick, visibility was near zero. Now the car was at a crawl, Robert sitting well forward in the seat. He flicked on the left turn signal.

"What are you doing?" asked Rosemary, alarmed. "We're not there—"

"I know that, but this is unsafe at any speed. There should be one of those staggered pull-offs the Scots are so fond—ah, there we are!"

Ahead, no more than fifteen feet away, Rosemary glimpsed a black rectangle of macadam or, as Robert would call it, blacktop, barely big enough for a car, bracken blurring its edge. She couldn't imagine a more forlorn spot to stop, but Robert was right—it was riskier to go on. Besides, at most it would mean a late arrival at the bed-and-breakfast-house at Mallaig.

Pulling off, leaving the parking lights on, Robert let the motor run for a little until it was cozily warm, Rosemary lying back against the headrest, closing her eyes. "It's ridiculous," she said, excusing a yawn. "I feel tired and we've just started."

"Make the most of it, sailor," he said, reaching over, taking the map from her lap, and adjusting the seat into the semirecline. "You're beautiful. I ever tell you that?"

She smiled dreamily. "All the time, kind sir." As he began folding the map, he glimpsed a filigree of black lace against the stockinged tan of her thigh. She began to say something, but gently he placed his finger on her lips and felt the moistness of her tongue, his hand slipping beneath her skirt.

"We can't," she said, hushed. "What if—"

"We'd hear anyone coming a mile away."

"Don't be vulgar—"

"What? Oh, I wasn't." He laughed. "I didn't mean to be, honest."

"Yes you did."

"No I didn't—" She made sweet murmuring sounds, her thighs trapping his hand. "I want—" he began, "I want to—"

"What's that?" she said suddenly, stiffening, pushing him away.

He stopped, listening. There was only the sound of the sleet pelting against the car. "Nothing," he assured her, adding, "Submariners can tell, honey. If I can't hear it, it isn't there. We can pick out a noise short for miles and—" He didn't finish, her embrace smothering all talk, his eyes closing with hers as his hands slid further beneath the lace to her secret warmth. She whimpered ever so slightly in a mounting joy. The very moment she touched him, gripped him, he felt his whole body stiffening with a throbbing urgency the likes of which he'd never known.

Schulz heard a high, bipping tone—a radar-homing missile locked onto him, left quarter, from Dessau thirty miles away. He hit the jammer, went to full thrust, and felt the G force "dumping" on him as the Falcon's Pratt and Whitney F-100 afterburner screamed in the full vertical climb as he jettisoned sea urchin flares and three high-frequency "burp" box decoys, just in case—to sucker off the enemy missile.

Already, ten miles nearer American lines than the Dessau batteries, Sergei Marchenko fired his first Acrid AA missile.

Schulz saw one of the Acrids streak below in front of him, the second one passing above left, hitting a flare, disintegrating, a white cloud speckled black with debris coming down at him from the explosion. He flicked the sidestick for afterburner, but the engine was out and his tail radar warning receiver wasn't working, so he had no idea if the Russian fighter was in the Falcon's cone of vulnerability. Down below, he saw the snow-streaked blur of green plain start to spin, foothills moving to its periphery, mountains looming fast ahead. He pulled the Douglas eject.

Next moment he was soaking wet, the cloud he was in supersaturated, Schulz knowing only that he was alive, the ruby spot of the Falcon's dying jet vanishing in gray stratus.

"Christ!" He was above the Harz. His greatest fear of bailing out had always been that he would be hung up in a tree on one of the steep mountain sides, unable to free himself—with a hundred-foot drop or worse beneath him and no other way out. Search and Rescue had found a colleague of his on the American side of the Harz, on the run for weeks and, of course, dead when they found him, eyes pecked out, stomach bloated enormously, and every orifice oozing with maggots.

For Marchenko, the downed American plane not only added to his score of five NATO kills—three earned over the Aleutians, including his *otplata*—"payback"—downing of the American, Shirer—but it added enormously to his reputation as the up-and-coming Soviet ace who might take the title from the Belorussian, Gorich, who had eleven kills. This was Marchenko's second F-16, the first shot down over Adak in the Aleutians. And the F-16 was regarded by the Soviet pilots as one of the best all-around combination interceptor/ground attack aircraft ever built, bristling with American know-how. But if Marchenko was pleased with the kill, he showed no such emotion to his wingman. The truth was that though he was satisfied enough with the kill, he wasn't happy that the American flier might have gotten away by having ejected. You beat the Americans not by killing their machines—their industrial capacity was enormous. You had to kill their *pilots*. This was the Allies' critical vulnerability. And it irked him that the American ace, Shirer, had also survived and bailed out when Marchenko had shot him down over the Aleutians. The fact was, Sergei Marchenko was the only Soviet ace who had not killed an American ace. It rankled him, particularly when his critics charged that since the fierce dogfights over the Aleutians, he had only been up against second-stringers. Shirer became his obsession. Marchenko had a photograph of the American ace, taken from the German magazine *Der Spiegel*, pinned up in his home base at Khabarovsk; Shirer's face the center of his squadron's dart board.

Low on fuel, Marchenko and his wingman turned back toward Berlin.

* * *

In the shuddering moment of their ecstasy followed by the warm, flooding peace that enveloped them, neither Robert nor Rosemary was aware of any sound on the lonely Scottish road. It was only when he returned to the driver's seat that Robert saw the twin yellow spots of light in the rearview mirror. Still, there was no sound, and it was another several minutes before the car, feeling its way through the fog, could be heard. In the frantic race to button her blouse and make herself "respectable," Rosemary dropped her lipstick between the hand brake and the seat. As she and Robert reached for it, they crashed heads. "Och, we're doomed!" said Robert, mimicking McRae of the bed-and-breakfast. Rosemary began to laugh, and the more she laughed, the more uncontrollable it became so that soon she was weeping, Robert pulling her toward him, she fending him off, slumped down out of sight beneath the window level. The lights from the car, now no more than fifty yards behind them, disappeared momentarily, and at first Robert thought the car had stopped, before he saw more thick sheets of fog sweeping in from the coast, obliterating the approaching car and roiling over the road. "Rosemary—get up."

"I don't want anyone to see me!"

The car was almost on them. Its horn sounded as it drew level with them, the driver a dim outline waving, Robert acknowledging it from one driver on a lonely road to another. Rosemary sighed with relief, watching the red taillights of the car and a lorry that was obviously using it as a trailblazer on the fogbound highway disappearing like two sore eyes into the mist.

"Funny," commented Robert.

"What—me being ravaged out on the moor?"

"The car that passed us," Robert said. "Looked like the pair we saw at McRae's."

"There, I found it," Rosemary proclaimed victoriously, grimacing as she reached down behind the hand brake to retrieve her salmon-red lipstick. "Well, they did say they'd probably see us. They're sightseeing, too, remember?"

"No—" Robert replied, "not the Prices—that other couple. The soldier and the girl. Confetti still on them. Remember?"

"Soldier?"

"Well, he was wearing civvies, but he looked to me like a junior officer—NCO maybe."

"I don't understand," Rosemary said, winding her passenger window down a tad in an effort to thwart any more misting up on the inside of the windshield. "What's so funny about them being on the same road? There's no other highway to speak of. I should think it's likely we'll see them again."

Robert shrugged. He tried to remember whether the yellow Honda Civic that had passed them had had "Just Married" sprayed on the side, but he hadn't noticed. It was sprinkling rain again, and he turned on the wipers. "It's just that they started out long before we did."

"Maybe they stopped somewhere for the fog to clear, too."

He nodded in acquiescence. For several seconds they drove on in silence. Soon they saw the taillights again, at first thinking they were the lorry's but then realizing the two red lights weren't far enough apart for a truck, the lorry having apparently overtaken the car on one of the pass-bys. "Any other points of interest along this road—before Ayre?" he asked Rosemary casually. "Before we get to Burns's cottage?"

"I don't—" she began, stifling a yawn, "—know. Why?"

"Just wondered. Wouldn't want to miss anything. McRae'd send a lynch party."

"You want me to look up the map?" she offered unenthusiastically.

"Nope," he said. "Doesn't matter."

"I do hope this fog clears," said Rosemary, peering ahead at the dim gray strip of bitumen a few feet in front of them. "If not, we *will* be doomed up at Glencoe. Daddy told me the Highland mists are always much worse. Won't see a thing. Perhaps we should stop at Glasgow for a bite. Give the weather a chance to improve?"

"Aye, lass," he said.

"You have a terrible Scottish accent. Did you know that?"

"I'm working on it. You want to eat in Glasgow then?"

"Do you?" For a moment Robert Brentwood was back in his family's home in New York. It was his mother's habit to ask his father five or six times whether he was sure he wanted to do something after he'd said that's what he wanted to do. Drove him nuts. Her repetition, his father had written Robert, had been particularly bad after Ray had been wounded, her nerves shot to pieces—the trying repetition of every "goddamn question" clearly a symptom of her anxiety. Robert knew in Rosemary's case the repetition was thoughtfulness on her part, not wanting him to feel obligated to do anything he didn't really care to do, particularly given the short time he had ashore. But Rosemary, too, had changed between the engagement and the wedding, her nerves and her sense of self trembling like so many in Britain who'd experienced the sudden dangers of modern war. For the submariner, it might be the fear of ASROCs coming down at you out of nowhere—for civilians, like Rosemary and her family, it was the terrifying cacophony of massed Soviet rocket attacks.

"Fine," he said. "We'll eat in Glasgow."

"You sure? It might clear up. You never know in the Highlands apparently. Daddy told me you can have rain, sun, and sleet all in one morning."

"You're as cheerful as old McRae."

"I'm trying not to plan things too far in advance, that's all. On your honeymoon you're supposed to be carefree. Anyway, as your best man would say, I guess it's 'no use frettin'.' "

They were getting closer to the car.

"You know your southern accent is terrible?" he said.

"Yes, I know. So?"

"We'll stop for chow in Glasgow, and what happens, happens."

"Yes."

"They have any places to pull off up in the Highlands?"

"Oh, lots of them," Rosemary said encouragingly. "Or so Father says. Road's so narrow in places, you have to go off just to let another car pass."

"So who has right of way?"

"No one," she said. "First in, first served."

"Sounds like a Texas whorehouse."

"*Robert*—really! And what, pray, do *you* know about Texas whorehouses?"

"Nothing," he said. "Absolutely nothing. Shipboard talk, that's all. Tell me more about these Highlands."

"They're supposed to be wildly beautiful," she said. "Forlorn but beautiful."

"And there are *lots* of places to pull off?" he said, leering.

"My Lord, is that all you can think about? I would have thought you'd had enough for one day." She adopted her stern, schoolmarmish pose. "Anyway, you'll just have to wait till we get to Mallaig."

"How far's that?"

"About a hundred and sixty miles."

"Don't know if I'll make it," he said, reaching out for her.

She pushed his hand away. "You stay alert, Captain, otherwise neither of us'll make it. You'll have us in the bracken, and tha's a fact."

For a moment he glimpsed red taillights again, but then the rain came down in sheets and they had to slow to a crawl.

"Damn," he said, above the whine of the wipers, "this is tougher than driving a sub."

In the heavy rain, they missed Burns's cottage. Rosemary was disappointed but didn't press to go back. They'd only a week left of his leave before he'd once again set out on war patrol.

"Sorry, sweetie," he apologized. "I was so busy looking at the damn road—"

"Oh, never mind," she said gaily. "We'll see it another time."

"Yes," he said, "that's a promise." Both of them fell silent, the rain coming down so hard on the roof, it made a steady drumming sound and was splashing up from the narrow road, but they didn't mind. It gave them a cozy feeling together inside the car, like being in a cave, safe from the raging forces outside their control.

"We'll stop at Glasgow," he said, "if we find it."

When Kurt Schulz entered the swirling grayness of the stratus above the Harz and could no longer glimpse the reassuring green khaki parachute above him, he had the distinct sensation of going down a lot more slowly than he really was. His worst fear was not realized as he saw the tall pines glide past, his landing on open ground in the mist-shrouded outskirts of Stolberg in the Harz Mountains near a copse of poplar, and spotted by an old villager out walking his dog. As the German shepherd ran toward Schulz, the pilot, a dog lover, intuitively went down on his left knee, left hand resting on it, his right hand hanging loosely, fingers cupped, his body loose in as nonthreatening a pose as he could make, fingers snapping. "Here, boy! Good boy!" The villager stood and watched, his pipe hanging loosely from aged, stained teeth above a stomach that, despite the economic hardships of living in the GDR, had consumed its fair share of German beer. His dog's tail began wagging. The villager whistled quietly over to the flier, looking about them anxiously, almost tripping on a patch of moss. *"Hier kommen!"*

It looked all right, but Shulz knew that if the *Grenztruppen*—"border troops"—had seen him coming down, the villager would have no alternative. Then he saw the man's short-barreled shotgun slung across his back.

"Haben Sie amerikanisch Zigaretten?"—"Have you any American cigarettes?"—asked the villager.

"No," Schulz told him, astonished by the question. He wished he had a bagful. A truckload.

The old man shrugged philosophically. Schulz decided to act quickly, to take no chances. He could easily overpower the old man if he was quick enough and shot the dog first. But then the dog began pawing at him, tail wagging. Intuitively, or perhaps because of his long boyhood association with pets of his own, Schulz began scratching behind the dog's ear, the shepherd nuzzling into him the harder he scratched.

"The border," said the old man, "is sixteen kilometers. We will have to leave now—the patrols are much heavier at night."

Schulz trusted the dog but not the old man. He'd heard a number of tales of would-be rescuers leading fliers into a *Grenztruppen* trap.

They heard one patrol, but it was a long way off—the German shepherd the best early-warning radar Schulz had ever seen.

Four hours later, Schulz was across into West Germany.

Afterward, Schulz tried to dress it up a bit. With each retelling, it sounded more and more like a harrowing escape with the entire East German army pursuing him. In fact, it had been little more than a hike through one of the most beautiful wooded parts of Germany. Schulz knew that whether or not he survived the war, to his last day he would think of the old villager whenever he smelled wood smoke.

When they had parted, Schulz asked for the old man's name so that if ever he had the chance to repay, he could. But the old man wouldn't give it. If ever such a thing should slip out, he explained, he would be a dead man.

CHAPTER FIVE

NORTHEAST OF THE Bronx, on the placid waters of Croton Reservoir, the water police helicopter was carrying out its normal patrol to ensure that no power boats were churning up the surface. If left undisturbed, the water would be aerated through the action of the sun's ultraviolet light, and once rid of impurities, would pass through the aqueducts and tunnels, built a hundred years before, and become part of the one and a half billion gallons of water that New Yorkers consumed every day. The chopper came down as it spotted the quality-control men on the only power boat allowed in the lake lowering the seki disc—which they could see was visible down to about three and a quarter meters, much deeper than the "two-meter clarity" required by law. When the chopper had gone, a man in his late fifties, taking his usual walk by the dam, sat down by the edge of the spillway, fascinated as always at how quickly the placid surface of the lake became a cascade of white water over the elegant beveled curves of the dam. He emptied the thermos into the water.

CHAPTER SIX

IN THE STORM-WHIPPED night of the northern Pacific, the USS *Salt Lake City* turned her bow into the wind, the jet engines on her flight deck screaming from ruby red to an urgent white, the catapult officer, his head barely visible in the slightly raised Perspex-covered hatch, peeking above the flight deck, knowing he had only fifty seconds to launch each fighter, cursing the condensation building up inside his bubble despite the heating duct, his eyes having to strain to get a visual verification of takeoff weight for the F-14 Tomcat on the waist catapult so that he could set the appropriate steam pressure for the cat and crosswind. The catapult officer thought he heard "six eight zero," indicating steam pressure on the cat for around sixty-eight thousand pounds—about right for a Tomcat, with ordnance on its four underfuselage points and the two hard points closer in under the wings. But still he couldn't make out whether the rain-smeared digit on the "board," a tray-sized counter held up by the yellow-jacketed member of the flight deck, was a six or a five. He had to get it right, but if he took much longer, he knew the air boss, a hundred feet up in the carrier's island, would be onto him. The catapult officer pushed his earphones in hard, trying to hear the yellow jacket's voice above the screaming of the twin twenty-one-thousand-pound Pratt and Whitney turbofans, but still couldn't make out what the other man was saying. He looked again through his deck bubble at the board, saw a "six" for only a fraction of a second, but it was enough. The cat was set for sixty-two thousand pounds. He saw the last yellow jacket running from the plane, his right thumb up, indicating "all set"—the launch bar between the fighter's nose and catapult rail connected. He pushed the button, the jet shot forward in a blur of battle gray and swirling steam that momentarily obliterated the blast deflector.

The launch had taken forty-nine seconds. There wasn't even time to grimace at his assistant that he'd made it under fifty seconds before the next plane, an A-10 Intruder, was on the waist cat, screaming just as insistently for release. The catapult officer prayed he got every one of them right this night. "Damn!" The bubble was fogging up again.

High above the flight deck, the captain of the USS carrier *Salt Lake City* battle group received an urgent request from COMPAC—Commander Pacific—Pearl Harbor, that one of the carrier's pilots, Lt. Comdr. F. Shirer, be reassigned to Washington, D.C. Knowing there were over five thousand men and women aboard and that there could easily be two with the same name, even the same rank, the director of personnel, a new man on the *Salt Lake City,* waited for the computer to come back on line to double-check the flier's service number. He was pretty sure it was the Shirer of the Pyongyang raid fame who, in the midst of the North Korean army's invasion, or rather rout, of the South Korean and American forces, had led the second wave of Tomcats through a raging monsoon over the North Korean capital. The raid of American airborne troops, led by Gen. Douglas Freeman against "Kim Il Suck," as the general called him, deep behind the North Korean lines, had electrified the world, and in a way reminiscent of Doolittle's raid on Tokyo in World War Two, it had given American morale at home, and particularly in the shrinking Pusan-Yosu perimeter, a much-needed boost. It had also bought precious time for the U.S. troops en route from Japan to "restock" the perimeter in time to start the counterattacks that were now driving Kim Il Sung's forces across the wide, frozen wastes of the Yalu into the mountain fastness of Manchuria.

For the men like Shirer, who'd been in on Freeman's raid, it had given them an élan not normally found in battle-hardened men until they are much older. Even now, Shirer's exploit in downing four Sukhois over the Aleutian Islands was overshadowed by his reputation as the cool warrior who had gone in over Pyongyang, his flight through flak- and missile-thick air giving crucial support to Freeman and his troops engaged in a fierce firefight outside Mansudae Hall. Here a young American marine, David Brentwood, had been busy winning the Silver Star, flushing out the enemy in a vicious room-to-room battle, seeking the NKA's General Kim. Kim either escaped shortly after the defenses of the Koreans' supposed impenetrable fortress of Pyongyang had been penetrated or, as intelligence suggested, might have been shot on the orders of Kim Il Sung. The failure to get Kim had bitterly disappointed General Freeman; the TV pictures of the successful sweep of Mansudae Hall, its windows now roaring with flame, and the felled statue of Kim Il Sung, once sixty feet of solid bronze, seconds later shattered by the American demolition teams, reasserted, however, the American determination to go on the attack even though they had been retreating in the South. The American public made heroes of young David Brentwood and the others who deserved it, and some who didn't but who had been in the right place at the right time.

For most of the men, the reputation of having been in on the Pyongyang raid proved as much a burden as a blessing. Later, in Europe, during a night drop when Brentwood's battalion had bailed out over the Dortmund-Bielefeld pocket as part of the American airborne's drop to relieve pressure from the trapped British Army of the Rhine, four American brigades, and a German division, David, like most in Charlie company, had been blown into enemy territory by crosswinds.

He had lain against a fetid, disemboweled corpse in a shell-pocked field under enemy artillery barrage, too paralyzed to move. At dawn, when he did go forward and found himself looking through the foresight of a Russian AK-47, he was secretly relieved. That was, until he saw the Russian SPETS commandos herding American and British prisoners, making them take off their uniforms and dog tags and issuing the shivering NATO POWs only one coarse blanket apiece.

The Russians were preparing to infiltrate the NATO lines and blow up the Allied "prepo" supply depots. Subsequently, Brentwood, after seeing a British officer and Americans murdered in cold blood on a forced march through deep snow, had been jolted out of his funk. Escaping from the column, using two of the enemy's stick, male-female connector grenades, he'd single-handedly set a huge Soviet oil dump near Stadthagen afire, robbing Marshal Kirov's armored columns of their critical fuel supply during the assault by over five thousand Russian T-90 and T-84 tanks against the Dortmund-Bielefeld pocket.

For that, David Brentwood had been awarded the Congressional Medal of Honor to add to the Silver Star earned at Pyongyang.

Now, recuperating in a Belgian NATO hospital outside Brussels, the exhilaration of having found his courage at Stadthagen was quelled by the burden of his memory—of those hours alone before dawn in the shell-cratered field outside the DB pocket when only he and God knew he'd been immobilized with fear. The wounds caused by flying shrapnel from the stick grenades he'd used at Stadthagen to blow up the dump were superficial but extremely painful. Yet he bore the pain without any ill will, his stoicism born of the gnawing guilt that festered out of those two hours—for him, two hours of cowardice.

To make matters worse, everyone he spoke to, from the pretty, young admitting receptionist at Lille to reporters from the *Stars and Stripes*, kept admiring his courage, and the more reticent he became to give yet another interview, the more he was celebrated as the modest hero, and the more the guilt of those two hours mounted.

Finally David felt literally weighed down, longing for the Dutch harbors to be cleared of the Soviet air-drop mines and Allied wrecks so that he could be shipped back to a convalescent hospital in England. There, hopefully, he could bury himself among the anonymity of the half million Allied soldiers in the vast encampments of southern England and East Anglia who, fed and resupplied by the convoys now getting through from the States, would be far too busy to worry about any one individual.

As the personnel officer aboard the USS *Salt Lake City* waited to get confirmation that it was *Frank* Shirer whom Washington was requesting, David Brentwood on the other side of the world sought solitude along the banks of one of the narrow, olive-drab canals. But the denuded winter poplars and the flat, lush green of Flanders Fields beyond only nurtured his gloomy mood. He wondered how much of his attack on the Soviet fuel dump had been due to having seen other prisoners shot at the whim of a Soviet guard and how much of his desperate run through the blizzard that night with the grenades had been motivated by nothing else than fear of meeting the other prisoners' fate—instead of by any conscious plan to strike back at the Russians. One-half of him told him that the reason he did it wasn't important. Who cares? as his marine buddy, Thelman, would say. "What matters, babe, is you did it." Yet the other half of David Brentwood, his father the admiral's side, was unmoved. For Adm. John Brentwood, the reason for doing something was almost as important as the deed itself.

A phantom breeze ruffled the canal water, its leaden surface shivering like a living thing apprehensive of the gunmetal skies gathering ominously overhead. David turned around to head back to the hospital, smelling rain in the air, wondering whether this tug-of-war within him afflicted others who, like him, had been singled out for public celebration—"Best of Show" propaganda!—at a time when Allied commanders well knew the war could easily go either way despite Freeman's breakout from the DB pocket.

Or was his condition peculiar to himself? Was he in some way abnormal? He had tried to visualize confiding in his brothers to find the answer, but he felt too far away in years from Robert. And his older brother wasn't given to opening up about himself. Like all submariners, cocooned in a world of secrecy, he had a natural reticence to discuss personal matters or, for that matter, anything else, outside the sub. He'd only told David of his impending marriage to Rosemary Spence a month before it took place. In any case, like their father, Robert probably wouldn't want to discuss personal matters, perceiving such self-absorption as a sign of weakness, an inability on David's part to handle his own problems. Perhaps it was?

David heard the high thunder of bombers, probably B-1s—the so-called Stealth B-2 a disaster, easily picked up by the enemy's low, long-wave radar despite the Pentagon's claims and assurances otherwise. Looking up, seeing nothing but thick overcast, David felt more depressed than ever. Someone said that coming off the painkillers helped induce depression. Or was he just feeling downright sorry for himself?—a thing neither of his two brothers or father would abide, especially not after Ray's burn trauma.

He had thought of writing Lana—sure she'd understand his doubts and fears about having so much expected of him. Once you'd been a winner, you were supposed to go on winning, distinguishing yourself. What had old George Patton said? "Americans love to win and will not tolerate a loser." But the problem with trying to talk about any problem in a letter, to Lana or anyone else, was the damned censor. Oh, the censor would keep it to himself, all right—wouldn't go about blabbing a Medal of Honor winner's doubts about himself—but the thought of anyone, especially another marine, seeing his innermost doubts revealed was too humiliating to contemplate. No—he'd just have to "bear up," as his DI had bellowed at him and "Thelma" at Parris Island. "Flush all the shit out!" and "Go forward." Or, as Adm. John Brentwood had said ad nauseum, "When the going gets tough . . ."

"Yes, I know," David could hear his mother saying. "But we're not all as tough as you, John."

David smiled at the memory despite his dark mood. He longed to see his mom, remembering how, as a small child, he could go to her in the mornings and cuddle up, the warm, soft smell of her enfolding him. Safe from the world. And he thought of Melissa Lange, his last day with her, a rushed lovemaking torn by anxiety about his posting to Korea and by the memory of Rick Stacy, a political science major. Stacy, the weasel—bow tie and forced preppy charm, except he was from Oregon, having no doubt waited for David to move out so he could try a move on Melissa. The thought of her with Stacy, even though she'd said her relationship with the weasel was "strictly platonic," was damn near unbearable.

In her most recent letter, Melissa had said Stacy was applying for an M.B.A. program scholarship, his tuition to graduate school being paid by an air force scholarship, providing he would serve four years as a crewman in one of the air force's two-man, or was it "two-person," missile silos. "It's a very popular program," Melissa had written David. Sure it was—sixty feet underground, wanking yourself off while everyone else was overseas with the crap coming from every direction. David could see Stacy now, waltzing about in his missile crewman's blue jumpsuit, cravat and missile shoulder patch for everyone to see. The thought of Stacy with his finger on the button—

David could imagine him strutting across campus, writing A-plus papers on the "nuclear threat"—and how taking out a whole city wouldn't worry him one little bit. Trouble was, after seeing the way the Russians had shot Americans out of hand, David knew he wouldn't have much trouble pushing the button either if it came to that.

"Brentwood!" It was like being woken up from a sleep, the

British sergeant's bullish voice rolling down the embankment of the canal. "Brentwood?"

"Yo," answered David.

"You're to report to Brussels, lad."

"There are no hospital ships in Brussels," he told the sergeant, who was one of the military policy detachments assigned to Liège.

"Nothing about hospital ships, lad—HQ wants you. Something about prisoners. They suspect there might be a few of those bloody fancy-dress artistes." Sometimes David didn't know what the British were talking about. Churchill was right: the English and Americans were two races divided by a common language.

"*You* know!" said the sergeant, taking off his beret, bowing and slapping it hard against his thigh before putting it on again. "*Artistes*. Actors! Those bastards who took our blokes' uniforms and—"

"Oh, SPETS," said David. "What about them?"

"Brussels thinks they might have captured some of the swine. But they need positive ID, see. We're rounding up all you blokes from the DB pocket who might have seen 'em—least, all of you who are still around. London's dead set on making an example of 'em. Shoot a few of the pricks. Send a big message to Moscow, right?"

David was surprised to find himself out of breath after walking up from the canal. His old DI would've been disgusted, and he made a mental note right then and there that he'd better get back into shape. "I doubt it'll make any difference," he told the sergeant, pausing for breath. "SPETS are very professional. Won't stop them sending more."

"Like you marines, eh?" said the sergeant. He was a much taller man than David, an angry glint in his eye. "Well, I'm inclined to agree, mate," continued the Brit. "Won't stop 'em, I reckon. But London wants to let 'em know that it's the high jump if they're caught. Bump off a couple anyway. Hell—you shouldn't worry. Free trip to Brussels, lad. See the sights. Wine, women, and song, eh? Train leaves in two hours."

"Don't think I could identify any of the SPETS," said David, glancing worriedly up at the sergeant. Ahead were long, white, loamy cart tracks beside the canal. Some parts of Europe hadn't changed in three hundred years. "Except for the guy who shot your lieutenant," said David.

"Couple of birds among them, I hear," said the sergeant, bending down, cracking a fallen branch from one of the poplars, stripping the bark in no time and slapping it under his left arm as if he were the regimental sergeant major on parade.

David looked up at him, puzzled. "Birds?"

"Women, lad! You know. Tits and—"

"Yeah, yeah, I know," said David. He'd been thinking about Melissa, and, whenever he did, crude descriptions of the female anatomy bothered him.

"Not interested?" charged the sergeant as they walked along the path, David finding it hard to keep up. The cart track stopped and became a bicycle path by the canal. "Maybe," said the sergeant lecherously, "you're dipping your wick into that Admitting filly, eh? Young Lili." He laughed so loudly, anyone could easily have heard him on the far side of the bank.

"No such luck," answered David. The truth was, he hadn't really tried—he guessed she mustn't be more than seventeen.

"Well," boomed the sergeant, "she's got the hots for you, boy. Medal of Honor winner and all that—"

"Yeah, sure," said David.

"I'm serious, lad. I've seen her giving you the once-over when you pick up your hero mail. Cat, if ever I saw it, mark my words."

"Cat?"

The sergeant thought for a moment, slowed, then stopped. "Ah—" he said, swiping the top off a long stem of reed grass, "pussy, I mean. Isn't that what you call it?"

"Cat!" said David, starting to laugh.

The sergeant was exploding in laughter again. When he finally got control, he told David that several of the female POWs were supposedly "smashing!"

"You've seen them?" David asked, surprised.

"No—but word has it."

"They'll be ugly as sin," said David. "Beards most likely."

"Now, don't be particular, laddie. It's wartime."

"No kiddin'," David replied.

"I'm not kidding," said the sergeant. "It's in all the newspapers."

"You're nuts," said David. He was starting to like the Limey.

"Here," said the sergeant, thrusting his right hand out, a packet in his hand.

"What's this?" It was a strip panel of condoms.

"If you don't know what to do with 'em," ordered the sergeant, "read the instructions after you get through your fan mail." He tapped them with his poplar stick. "See?" The condom instructions were in Dutch. "Course," the sergeant said, "it's all Greek to me!" and began another belly roll of laughter. But he kept laughing and wouldn't stop, wildly swiping at more reed grass, tears rolling down his face, until the fixed glint in the Britisher's eye told David the man was quite mad.

Despite the stinking kerosene fumes from the Avgas sucked in by the air-conditioning, there was a half-hearted cheer in Personnel two levels below the *Salt Lake City's* flight deck when the computers came back on line. But they told the personnel director that Lt. Comdr. Frank Shirer was presently assigned to the Tomcat squadron at Dutch Harbor on Unalaska in the easternmost sector of the Aleutian arc. Shot down over the western Aleutians eight weeks before, following an air strike from the carrier, and picked up by a helo from one of the nine escorts in the battle group, Shirer had been taken to Unalaska. Because of the "big show" in Europe, pilots were in short supply on the Aleutian front, and Shirer had quickly found himself seconded to the air force's Sixty-Fifth Wing stationed at Dutch Harbor.

What the computer didn't reveal was that between sorties over the Russian-captured outposts of Adak and Shemya at the westernmost reaches of the Aleutian arc, Shirer had renewed a fleeting romance in Dutch Harbor with a Wave nurse, Lana Brentwood, whom he'd met years before in Washington. But the screen did show that Shirer was "AFR-CD—available for recall" to the carrier at the captain's discretion.

"Very well," the captain informed the personnel director, "check with Dutch Harbor. My hunch is they'll be about as unhappy as I am to have one of our top guns reassigned to Washington. But if the Pentagon wants him, I'm not going to stand in their way. Any advisory on why they want him back east?"

The personnel officer's reply was drowned by the roar of a Grumman EA-Prowler, or "Wild Weasel," one of the ship's electronic countermeasures aircraft, landing on the "roof."

"Say again?" asked the captain, his eyes on a yellow jacket far below whose thumb was held high in the air as he sprinted away from the nose of the Prowler, the wash of jet engines flapping the man's vest, the plane's proboscislike midair refueling spout giving it the look of some giant insect anxious to be on its way.

"COMPAC gives no reason for requesting Shirer, sir." The Prowler was off, swallowed by the darkness.

"Very well," said the captain, slapping the personnel director on the shoulder. "Ours not to reason why, Phil. Draw up the papers. I'll sign them end of the watch. Where's Shirer now?"

"Dutch Harbor, sir."

The captain nodded "okay," but the personnel director knew the old man was still trying to figure out why the hell Washington, awash in top brass, would bother to recall one of the fleet's top aces at a time when the damn Russians were at the back door in the Aleutians, clearly using Shemya and Adak as advance carriers to island-hop along the island chain, readying to hit America's western and most vulnerable flank. For his part, the PD was concerned it might be a bureaucratic screw-up. It had happened before—a liaison officer in San Diego ordered verbally by Washington to grab the first available flight to what was supposed to be Oakland, the guy ending up twenty-four hours later in *Auck*land, New Zealand.

"We have any other Shirers aboard?" asked the captain. As he waited for the answer from the PD, he never shifted his gaze from the flight deck, watching the crews working feverishly, the carrier launching a plane every forty-seven seconds. Meanwhile, other aircraft from the battle group's constant combat patrols were coming in to land at over 150 miles an hour. One slip could take out two pilots, flight deck crew, and billion-dollar aircraft in milliseconds.

"Captain," came the PD's reply. "We've got four Shirers. One also a Frank. A purple jacket. But his number's—"

"Never mind the number. Get a repeat from Washington, Phil. Son of a bitch, what'd I tell you? Another Pentagon snafu."

The PD requested verification of Shirer's service number. One wrong digit was all it would take.

The confirmation came back within the hour. It *was* Frank Shirer, the fighter ace at Dutch Harbor, whom Washington wanted. When he received the information, the captain sighed resignedly, telling his executive officer that neither *Salt Lake City* nor the Aleutian command could afford the loss of even one pilot, with more air-supported land battles shaping up in the Aleutians. "Very well," he instructed the personnel director. "Send message to Dutch Harbor—immediate for Shirer."

"Yes, sir."

"But, Phil—"

"Sir?"

"I want that F-14 back *here*. He can be ferried back to Pearl from here and then to Washington via San Diego. He might be their fair-haired boy, but the plane's *ours!* Got it?"

"Yes, sir."

"Washington," put in the executive officer, "is probably going to give him another medal."

The skipper shrugged. "Even Washington's not that stupid. He could receive it in the field. It's got me beat, I'm tellin' ya. It's ridiculous." The executive officer agreed.

So did Shirer.

CHAPTER SEVEN

WHETHER IT HAD been McRae's morbid description of how MacIain Macdonald and his clan had been cut down or whether it was the strange effect of the subdued light in the western Highlands that was responsible for his sense of unease, Robert Brentwood wasn't sure, but the sight of the Glencoe Massacre was unexpectedly grim and unsettling. Looking over the jagged outcrops of the gloomy glen, he understood how it was the stuff not only of the inevitable ghost stories but of many a Highlander's sense of separation from other men. More than one Scot, sober as the bitter cold, had sworn by everything holy that he'd seen the blood-streaked face of Alasdair MacIain Macdonald.

"By God, this is a barren place," he said to Rosemary as he stopped the car in one of the pull-outs, the sight of a red English phone booth standing by the road a hundred yards away distinctly anachronistic to the mournful, wind-riven nature of the place, the booth's solitary presence only adding to Robert's sense of anomie and to what Rosemary called the "spirit-filled" strangeness of the place.

Soon, out of the bruised sky above Ben Nevis ten miles to the north, more mist descended and at times completely obscured the long ribbon of narrow road behind them that had wound through the lonely valley to the desolate glen. Despite the mist, Robert was able to see a lone car.

"Second time," said Robert.

"Second time for what?" asked Rosemary as they paused on their way back from the monument, walking toward what Rosemary called their car of "ill repute."

"What? Oh—" Brentwood caught himself. "Nothing. Just noticed that car down there's a yellow Honda Civic. Didn't realize there were so many in Scotland."

"Lord," said Rosemary easily. "They're common as colds in England. That other couple at the B and B had one as well—the Prices."

"Did they?" Robert asked surprised.

"Yes. Rental companies love them."

"Why?"

"Easy, silly. Less accidents in the fog. Best color, yellow—though I think it's ghastly." Then she surprised him again. "Besides, Robert, if they were following us, I should think they'd be a little more subtle than that. I mean, the only other car on the road."

"Huh—" grunted Robert. Perhaps he was being a little paranoid. But as one of the elite skippers whose sub was one of the most powerful in the world as well as being his country's last line of defense in the event the war went nuclear, he and everyone else on the Sea Wolf II knew their vigilance didn't start and end with the sub. Even so, Rosie had a point. Why would the Prices, if it was them—or the other people, or anyone—be so obvious as to be seen? "Unless . . ." he began, but trailed off as more thick clouds born about the summit of Ben Nevis gathered and came rolling down, obliterating Glencoe's stark beauty.

It wasn't until they were halfway to the ferry that Rosemary, struck by Robert's unusual bout of suspicion, felt her chest tightening in a rush of fear as she realized Russian agents would have no compunction in murdering a nuclear submarine's captain. She turned to him wide-eyed in terror.

"It's an occupational hazard," he explained quietly. "Everybody knows about it when they join up."

"Is that supposed to comfort me?"

"Guess not. Sorry—I shouldn't have . . ." He paused, smiling. "Hell, we could get hit by a bus. You can't live in a box."

"You can die in one," she said. "My God, you mean you accept this as a normal part of your—"

"Right. Besides, honey, I do have my executive officer here."

For a second, Rosemary was nonplussed.

"No," Robert explained, shifting down, using the gears as a brake on the narrow, wet road. "I don't mean Pete Zeldman," he said.

"Well then, who do you . . ."

Robert pressed the glove box button. Nothing happened. He punched it and the compartment lid dropped, spilling out road maps as well as a Smith & Wesson .45.

Rosemary, gasping for breath, recoiled from it as if it were a snake.

"Don't worry," he said casually. "Safety's on."

Steering with his right hand, he slipped the .45 between them and stuffed the maps back into the glove box. "Don't look so shocked, honey. It's only a gun.

There *is* a war going on."

Rosemary started to say something but was still too astonished by the sight of the gun.

"Hey," he said, slipping his arm around her shoulder, "it was supposed to reassure you. That's what it's for."

"Well, it doesn't," she answered emphatically, looking up at him as if in some way she were seeing him for the first time. "Why didn't you tell me this before?"

"They issue them for protection while we're ashore—not to frighten brides."

"It doesn't frighten me," she said, staring at the gun, its khaki-green camouflage pattern making it appear more ominous to her. "It *terrifies* me."

"Hon," he assured her, "I wasn't going to show you, but you seemed so wound up about these—"

"You were wound up," she answered.

"Yeah—well—" He was using his left sleeve to wipe condensation off the windshield, the diaphanous fog now pierced by rays of sunlight streaming down on the moss-covered crags.

"They're gone!" she said, watching the rearview mirror. Robert adjusted it from where she'd twisted it to one side, combing her hair before they'd got out to see the Glencoe memorial. Now he could see the road farther back, but she was right—the long stretch of blacktop along the valley floor was bereft of movement. Ahead lay Loch Ballachulish, where, Rosemary informed him, they would have to catch a ferry across the loch on their way to Mallaig, the fishing village six miles farther up on the rugged west coast. In the prewar days, Mallaig had been a "repairs" port for Russian trawlers out of the Kola Peninsula, some suspected of being SIGLINT—signal intelligence—listening for NATO sub traffic around the Holy Loch sub pens eighty miles south from which, all being well, *Roosevelt* would set out on another war patrol as soon as Robert Brentwood returned from his honeymoon a week from now.

"I hope the ferry's on time," said Rosemary anxiously as they rounded the U-bend leading down to the loch.

"Doesn't matter," said Robert. "We can fill in the time."

She looked quickly at him. "Oh no you don't! Not again. I'm not—"

"No," he said, "I didn't mean that."

"You didn't?" she asked, feigning astonishment. "You're ill!" She took in a deep breath, leaning back on the headrest, telling herself not to be a ninny—feeling better now that the car hadn't been seen following them after all. "You're getting tired of me," she charged playfully.

"I'll never get tired of you," he said, doing a W. C. Fields: "My little cooing turtle dove." He took her hand in his. "Never."

"Hmm—a likely story."

Robert could see a long, calm, cobalt-colored tongue of water coming into view, their first sight of the loch and a welcome one after the unrelieved wildness and isolation of Glencoe. Driving through the mist-shrouded valley had been cozy enough, part of the coziness coming from the safety of the warm car and its comforting dash lights, which, like those aboard a sub, created a sense of security, when in fact the line between civilization and the wild, safety and danger, was very thin.

"Where did you put the—gun?" she asked suddenly. It was no longer between them.

"In my jacket," he said.

It was blustery outside as they pulled up to wait for the ferry, and cold, despite the sun's attempt to break free of the low stratus.

"Think I'll hop out and stretch my legs," he said.

"You'll freeze."

"Nah—put on my old tweed coat here. No problem."

She watched him draw up the collar of the tweed jacket as he walked away and waved back at her. She loved watching the way he walked—a purposeful yet relaxed stride that was somehow distinctly American, part and parcel of their optimism, which, no matter what the odds, refused to be dimmed. She'd noticed it the first time Robert had met her great-uncle Geoffrey. Robert, and some Australians she'd known, had no sense of class difference and so weren't even aware they were crashing right through it with a friendly handshake and first-name familiarity. They didn't give a fig about social status; simply rode over it, judging what a man said more than the way he said it.

She wound down the window. "Don't go too far!" she called out over the howl of wind that was ruffling parts of the loch while other stretches of water remained surprisingly, almost alarmingly, calm. He strode back down the hill.

"What's wrong?"

"Nothing—oh dear, I'm sorry, pet. Just didn't want you to go too far. The ferry'll be here in ten minutes or so. Besides, I don't want you to catch a cold. You must be freezing."

"Have to spend a shilling," he said.

"Oh—" she began, perplexed. *"Oh!"* She felt herself blushing and laughing at the same time. He was walking away again.

"It's 'spend a penny,' " she said.

"Well," he said, without turning around, "I was close."

"You were not."

Rosemary kept watching him and suddenly her smile and laughter vanished. Surely he could have waited until they'd reached the ferry. And wasn't that one of those portable lavatories she'd seen parked down by the ferry ramp? "All right, Rosemary Brentwood," she addressed herself sternly, as if bringing one of her sixth-form boys to order. "That will be quite enough of your morbidity."

It had been the sight of the loch that had upset her—the unforgiving aspect of its gunmetal surface now that the sun was momentarily shut out again. It called up the memory of her brother William's death on the Atlantic convoy—how one day he had sailed out, never to be seen again. So young. She took a tissue from her purse and, adjusting the rearview mirror, began making herself look presentable. "Good grief," she told her reflection. "Will you stop worrying? Robert'll probably outlive you." Yes, he would undoubtedly die an old man and in bed—with her. She used just a dab of blusher, recalling Georgina's rather high-minded counsel about how makeup was a "bourgeois conceit." It always astonished Rosemary that here the whole world was at war, the Communist ideology so utterly discredited despite Gorbachev's attempted reforms, and yet there were still young intellectuals like Georgina, fresh from the "thesis" and "antithesis" of university and who, filled with the outrage of people who know they will never actually have the responsibility of power, could still be drawn to the left's unholy mysteries. She closed the lipstick holder, adjusted the mirror, and froze. Coming over the last dip before the long hill leading to the ferry was a yellow car.

CHAPTER EIGHT

SHIRER SAW THERE were fourteen minutes to go, the sea hidden from him beneath the flat gray expanse that seemed to go on forever. The edge of the front had come down from the Bering Sea over the Aleutians even before Shirer had taken off in his F-14 Tomcat, number 203, the second fighter assigned him, the first lost when he was shot down by Sergei Marchenko's Sukhoi and had to bail out over Adak Island before being picked up and taken to Dutch Harbor.

There he and Lana Brentwood had taken up where they had left off before the war. But just when he was getting used to the idea that he'd probably be with Lana and flying out of Dutch Harbor for the foreseeable future, he was jolted back to the bleak reality of just how unforeseeable any future was when he received the terse instruction from *Salt Lake City* that he was to deliver his jet back to the carrier.

Shirer glanced at his vector control on "radio silence" approach toward the carrier, his plane on a passive, not active, radar to warn him of any approaching Bandits. Unless the Russians had launched midair refuelers without Aleutian radar picking them up, there shouldn't be any danger.

By nature, he was an optimist. Lana wasn't. She had been through the trauma of a failed marriage with Jay La Roche, the boss, or some said "don," of La Roche Pharmaceuticals, a multinational spread over twenty-three countries, including China. Shirer remembered that China was one of the countries because Lana had told him it had been in Shanghai that the three-year marriage had ended in a violent attack on her by La Roche, who had beaten her so badly that only his money and influence with corrupt Chinese officials had prevented charges being laid. She had long ago learned to suffer the carefully chosen and medically screened stable of call girls and boys La Roche had used on his business trips abroad. But when his anal and oral fixations went beyond all bounds with her to the point at which excreta became inextricably linked in La Roche's mind with sex, she had drawn the line and La Roche had stepped over it. He couldn't prevent her from leaving him, from joining the navy's "whores," as he jeeringly referred to the Waves. But no way, he told her, would he ever allow her to divorce him, to cause him to lose face. If she tried it, La Roche warned, he'd unleash his chain of tabloids and "throw so much muck around" about her parents that the family would be ruined.

"There's no muck to throw around," she'd challenged him bravely. She remembered his sneering, cold reply. "You're so fucking naive, Lana, I don't believe it. Doesn't matter whether it's true or not. Once it hits the street on page one, it's game over for the Brentwoods, sweetheart."

It was little wonder, Shirer realized as they had parted in Dutch Harbor, that she'd learned to roll with life's punches—their Washington-enforced separation not upsetting her as much as he had expected, or secretly hoped, it might. And yet he knew she loved him. Still, her greatest fear wasn't of separation but of him simply vanishing somewhere over the vastness of the Pacific, more terrifying to her than anything Jay La Roche might have done.

"I won't get shot down, honey," he'd tried to assure her, recognizing the hollowness of it as soon as he spoke.

"You have been already."

"Then it's over. Finished. One time is all you're allowed. If you get out of that—you're home and—"

A luminescent green dot, the size of a pinhead, was blipping on his radar screen. The carrier.

He had done it hundreds of times before, but during the approach, his stomach still knotted, his G suit warmer as the perspiration increased, his heartbeat, like most pilots', faster now than when in a dogfight. He still couldn't see the ship through the gray candy floss cloud flitting below him like a black river. With air brakes full on, he was coming in at over 150 miles an hour. He remembered that during Freeman's raid on Pyongyang, *Salt Lake City* had lost more planes on landing than in combat—the slightest thing going wrong could mean curtains. But it hadn't happened to him yet and—hell, he told himself cavalierly, it wasn't going to happen now, even if *Salt Lake City*'s air boss was always claiming a fighter pilot's worst enemy wasn't the Russians but a woman who took your mind off "one joystick onto another."

No way, Shirer told himself, feeling the slight vibration of his oxygen mask, convinced that the thought of making sweet, unhurried love with Lana was the best guarantee in the world that he wouldn't foul up. His vector was dead on—five minutes to the carrier, the possibility of enemy fighters suddenly appearing and pouncing remoter than ever.

In *Salt Lake City*'s air traffic control with the CIC—combat information center—and in PRIFLY—primary flight control, above flight deck control—computers and status boards showed Tomcat 203 approaching the carrier with fifty-seven thousand pounds gross weight—information conveyed instantaneously to the LSO—landing signal officer—in the flight deck's trench. The LSO, his Day-Glo orange vest only dimly visible above the deck's skirting, kept one eye on the video recording 203's approach, and the SPIN, or speed indicator, that showed the Tomcat's approach speed. This speed, together with that of the crosswind and carrier, aided the LSO in deciding the correct tension for the four arrestor wires. Too little would fail to stop the fighter within the three hundred feet—too much could snap the cable, with the same result.

"Tomcat two zero three, five seven zero," came the confirmation from the arresting gear room, whose crew of four set the dials for fifty-seven-thousand pounds. Shirer was looking for the orange ball of light in the big convex mirror mounted on the carrier's starboard side. If centered, the orange blob of light would be a second visual confirmation of the glide path projected by his computer. There were so many variables: state of sea, humidity, cloud cover, wind sheer . . .

He saw the orange ball between two horizontal green lights, but it was above the mirror's midline. He was too high. Quickly he realigned degrees of flap, saw the orange orb go dead center, and called, "Meatball," which told the LSO he was "on the ball''—locked into the correct glide path, the relief in his voice palpable despite his long experience.

The LSO's voice blasted Shirer's earpiece and suddenly, either side of the meatball, he saw two vertical red lines appear. A wave off. ''Damn!''

''Try again,'' instructed the LSO, Shirer hitting the button for full afterburner, the Tomcat veering hard left, engines screaming in a banshee howl as it climbed, leaving the carrier's island leaning hard right and slipping downhill. Then the carrier was gone, below cloud.

''Try again two oh three,'' repeated the LSO. ''Nose wheel not lowered.''

In flight deck control, a man on the ''Ouija'' board moved the plastic model of 203 to the side while another crewman took up his grease pencil, a backup in case of power failure, and marked 203's position on the transparent plastic screen, asking, ''He a nugget?''

''No,'' replied Comdr. Phil Harris, the officer in charge of FDC—flight deck control—''nothing green about him. Been on this tub longer than you have.''

''Two oh three?'' said the crewman disbelievingly. ''I haven't heard of a Tomcat of ours with that number.''

''It's been in Dutch Harbor. Watch him—he's turning.''

''Got him,'' replied the seaman cockily, skidding the plastic model around. Two oh three was already on infrared video, its ghostly outline like an underdeveloped negative, a heat blur around the twin twenty-one-thousand pound Pratt and Whitney exhausts, heat streamers trailing from the fuselage's shimmering edge.

Shirer pressed the nose wheel release button again, unable to hear whether or not it was coming out of its well because of the noise of the fighter's engines, the indicator nevertheless showing the wheel was down, his G suit feeling like a sauna as he took another run over the carrier, alert for other incoming aircraft. He was on a vector that would take him fifty feet above the flight deck, giving the LSO and other deck crew plus everyone in PRIFLY a chance to see whether the wheel was in fact down.

''There it is!'' said one of the red-jacketed ordnance crew.

''No,'' responded a green jacket from electronics maintenance, his arm following the line of the plane, ''it's only half-extended.''

''You sure?''

"Sure I'm sure."

The LSO saw it swooping directly overhead through the mist. "LSO to two oh three. Your nose wheel is only half-extended. Do you read me?"

"Affirmative. Nose wheel half-extended," came Shirer's voice, crackling through static.

"LSO to two oh three. Go to five thousand. Repeat, five thousand. Minimum radius ten miles. Repeat ten miles and hold pattern. I say again, hold pattern."

"Going to five thousand," confirmed Shirer, silently cursing the nose wheel. "Will hold pattern." The carrier couldn't waste any more time on him at the moment. He would have to hold pattern until *Salt Lake City* got all its other planes, which included combat patrols approaching "Bingo"—fuel exhausted—status, and only then, when his Tomcat's fuel was all but gone, reducing the risk of fire, could they try to bring him in.

His eyes refocused on his helmet display, which remained steady, despite the motion of the fighter. Shirer could see he had fifty-seven minutes of fuel remaining. Meantime he'd try the wheel again. He thought he felt it give a little—hoped that it might only be a bird jamming the lower gear. A bird's body, most likely a gull, would compress on retraction—unless it was one of the big wandering albatross with a wingspan up to seven feet, but he'd felt no impact.

He tried the release again and it seemed to give, but only a fraction. Trouble was, it was so damn hard to be certain, given all the noise. Simultaneously the indicator panel's constant flickering demanded close attention if he was to avoid midair collision.

With the ferry almost at the dock and the yellow Honda rolling slowly up behind theirs, Rosemary looked about anxiously for Robert. She saw him walk out from the bracken behind the Prices, coming up to them on the driver's side, rapping on the window. Rosemary saw Price start, winding down the window, looking flustered.

"Going to Mallaig?" Robert asked Price, his tone convivial.

"Ah, yes—" Price turned to his wife. "Joan said we'd probably meet up with you."

"Small world," said Robert, still smiling. "Rosemary'll be glad to see you." He indicated the ferry at the dock. "Better be getting back to the car. See you on board."

"Ah, yes."

By the time Robert reached the car, the ferry attendant was waiting for him to drive on down the ramp. There obviously wasn't any hurry about it—not until the Christmas rush in a few days time would the lonely road see a line of cars and trucks backed impatiently waiting to cross the loch.

"Well?" asked Rosemary. "What did they say?"

"Not much," answered Robert. "Seemed surprised." He pulled his seat belt strap across, looking at Rosemary. "Better buckle up. More accidents happen leaving port."

"Except we're not on your submarine," she replied affably, "and we're not leaving port exactly."

"Buckle up. Accidents happen when you least expect them."

As they approached the ferry and he was watching the Prices in the rearview, Rosemary saw that on the other side of the loch, mist had crept right down to the bank, and she pointed out patches of old snow discolored by pink algae visible among the heather. In a few more seconds the mist was replaced by heavy fog, tongues of it tumbling like dry ice over the embankment, spreading quickly, turning what had been the cobalt blue of the loch into a monotonous gray sheet. "I don't fancy being ahead of them in that," she said, indicating the fog on the far side of the loch.

"Neither do I."

"How can we avoid it?" said Rosemary, almost as if she were asking him to turn back, her suspicion of the Prices now complete. "Not like the big ferry, is it? I mean, we'll be first on and first off." They went over the bump of the ramp, the metal drop plate reverberating under them, followed by a quieter sound as the tires "burred" on the grooved steel decking.

"It'll be all right," Robert told her.

"What are you going to do?"

"I'll think of something."

"What did *she* say—Mrs. Price?"

"Nothing. All smiles. Didn't seem surprised at all. Very cool."

"Perhaps she doesn't know?"

Robert looked across at Rosemary. It was the kind of glance she used to give a student when he didn't know what came after Hamlet's "To be or . . ."

"All right then," she conceded. "So she would have to know—if she's with him all the time. I mean *if* she *is* his wife? Was she wearing a ring?"

"What—oh, I don't know. Never noticed."

"Men never do."

"Ring wouldn't prove anything. Not these days—" He saw the hood of the Prices' Honda dip toward the deck as it pulled up behind them. "Keep the doors locked," he told Rosemary. "I won't be—"

"Stay here? Locked in?" she said, adopting a cockney accent to convey the apprehension an upper-middle-class upbringing wanted to subdue. "Not ruddy likely. I'm coming with you." As Robert walked around to the left side of the car and opened her door, the wind buffeting his tweed jacket, he felt the bulk of the gun against his chest. If there was any comfort in it, it was also a reminder that he hadn't practiced with the service-issued sidearm for at least three years—at Norfolk, Virginia, when he'd first taken command of *Roosevelt*. Opening her door, he gave her his hand and flashed a honeymoon smile. "Get Mrs. Price—if that's who she is—off to one side. Get her talking. I want to jaw with her old man."

"Yes," Rosemary said hesitantly. "All right. You know—"

"He was very defensive about not having joined up. When old McRae, remember, challenged him about being a lecturer at LSE."

"Hello!" Mrs. Price called out jovially. "A bit nippy, isn't it?"

"Yes," said Rosemary. "Still, expect it won't do us any harm."

"Do us the world of good, I should think," said Mrs. Price. "Fresh air. James smokes a pipe."

They were drawing level with a yellow school bus from some girls' school, a few giggling as Robert walked by, one of them calling out, "I say there, tall, dark, and—" There was more laughing.

Robert nodded at Mrs. Price, but kept walking toward her husband at the stern, addressing him with a questioning air. "I've never seen snow like that before. Have you?"

"Oh—" said Price, looking up, "the pink stuff? Yes—it's quite common up here." Both men were close to the rail, spray catching their face, Robert, despite his preoccupation about the Prices, automatically wondering what the fresh-to-salt-water ratio was in the loch. For a sub diving, it would be critical information, altering the density and therefore the sub's buoyancy. If you didn't react fast enough to a sudden change, you'd be dead.

"You're familiar with these parts then?" he said to Price while leaning eagerly into the wind against the rail without looking at Price but remembering that at the bed-and-breakfast place, Price had said it was his first trip to Scotland.

"Ah—yes," Price conceded, adding hastily, "well, you know—I've read a lot about Scotland. Before I came."

Robert said nothing for a second or two, his gaze fixed on the fog cascading down the bank they had just left, encircling them. "I heard an interesting story the other day."

"Oh—yes?" said Price politely.

Brentwood was still watching the shore. "Yeah. It was about this guy—kept following a sergeant and his wife. They were taking a trip through the Sierras—back in California. Wherever they went, he went. Well, after a couple of days, this sergeant pulled the guy over and told him that if he didn't bug off, he'd get his head blown off."

There was a long silence, and all Brentwood could hear was the ferry's wake boiling furiously into the calm loch.

"Rather silly of the sergeant," said Price. "I mean, to threaten people like that. I would have thought all he needed to do was call up the local constabulary. You know, the police. Register a complaint."

Robert turned to look at Price, noticing the man's hairline was receding—something he hadn't been aware of at the McRaes'. There Price had looked well groomed, hair combed down over the front in a stylishly casual forelock. He wondered how much else he hadn't noticed about Price.

"Funny you mentioned that," said Brentwood, "about calling the police. The sergeant did look for a phone. It was high in the mountains, you see. Not many people around. When he did find one, it had been trashed. Line cut."

Price shook his head, tut-tutting. "Vandals everywhere."

The change in Price's tone from his off-balance surprise in the car to his present air of confidence told Brentwood his bluff wasn't working. He should have asked the Englishman point-blank. Instead he'd given the man time to think, regain his balance.

"Anyway," continued Price, "what do you think the police could have done—to help the sergeant? The sergeant could have been delusional."

"I don't think he was," said Brentwood, his eyes fixing Price.

"Look, old chap," said Price. "You're making me a bit nervous with that bulge in your jacket. I've made a bit of a cock-up with all this, but—well, I suppose this won't assuage you very much, but I'm not who you think I am. Nor is Joan."

Robert Brentwood said nothing, waiting.

"Point is," continued Price, pushing the disobedient lock of hair back, "Special Branch didn't see much point in unduly alarming you—certainly not on your honeymoon. And especially given what you sub chaps've done for us re the convoys. We're all terribly grateful."

Brentwood let the flattery go by him like the spray. "What Special Branch?"

"Scotland Yard. Joan and I have been tailing you ever since you left Surrey. Your wedding."

"What the hell—"

"Peter Zeldman," Price cut in, "your executive officer, was best man. Georgina Spence—your wife's sister—was bridesmaid. Young William Spence was killed in the Atlantic—looked after by Lana Brentwood—your sister. It's through her looking after him that you met Rosemary, correct? I mean, you took young Spence's personal effects to his parents during one of your shore leaves from the *Roosevelt*. How am I doing?"

"Anyone could have learned all that stuff," said Brentwood, "reading a paper down in Surrey."

"Do be reasonable, old sport!" said Price, flashing a Special Branch card.

"You've got American Express, too, and you're a blood donor. Right?" Robert challenged him. "Anyone can get cards printed up, sport! Many as they like."

Price slipped the card away, glanced behind them, squinting in the sun-infused fog, seeing Rosemary and Joan Price ambling from the ferry's bow back toward the cars. Another few minutes and the ferry'd be across the loch. "Look," said Price, "I don't want to be indelicate, old boy, but d'you know your sister Lana was transferred to the Aleutians?"

"Sure I know," responded Robert Brentwood. "She wrote me. Her ex is a string-puller. Congressmen in his pocket. What's indelicate about that?"

"I mean the *real* reason she was transferred?"

Robert Brentwood shrugged. "I told you La Roche is the original sleaze-ball. Besides, Aleutians is a combat zone." He paused, looking hard at Price. "The *Russians* are trying to get through the back door. There's a navy hospital at Dutch Harbor. So?"

"Well, I'm not saying La Roche had nothing to do with it,

but he 'lucked out,' as you Americans put it. The navy already had a good reason to banish her up there.'' He paused, still looking at the far shore. ''Your sister was transferred to the Aleutian theater, old boy, because her care of young William Spence, shall we say, *exceeded* the requirements of duty.'' He paused to let it sink in. ''Not to put too fine a point on it, Captain, she performed certain—shall we say—'favors.' ''

''What the hell d'you mean?''

''I think you Americans call it a blow job.''

Rosemary heard a crack—Price's watch smashing against the ferry's bulkhead as Robert Brentwood felled him with one blow. ''You son of a bitch!'' Price stayed down, only daring to raise himself slightly on one arm, the other held up in submission.

Rosemary made to run toward them, but Joan Price grabbed her arm. ''No. Stay here!''

''Get up, you son of a bitch!'' yelled Robert Brentwood, his voice all but inaudible to the women, his face red, tweed jacket ballooning in the wind. ''Get up or I'll—''

''I'm not making—'' began Price, fearing the blow to his chin had fractured his jaw, his voice breathless. ''I'm not making a moral judgment. The Spence boy was dying. Perhaps it was an act of—look, I'm sorry, but if you don't believe I'm from Special Branch, I had to convince—'' Price paused, his face grimacing in pain. ''We haven't been following you—well, we have, but it's the other two newlyweds that we were really shadowing. You're in-between as it were.''

Brentwood looked blank.

''Your innocent young GI,'' Price continued, easing himself back so he could rest against the bulkhead. ''You know, the young couple at the B and B—confetti still in their hair. And his lovely wife. Real charmer, she is—been to bed with two of your sub captains already. Found them—should say what was left of 'em—down by Loch Lomond. We had to change everything—including their sub's ETD from Holy Loch—just in case our bonny pair got anything out of them. He paused, feeling his jaw, wishing he hadn't. ''We're your minders,'' he told Brentwood. ''We caught up with them just before you reached the B and B. They were your late arrivals. You were bloody lucky you didn't make it to Burns's cottage. The sweet young thing was carrying a Beretta and two shrapnel grenades. Very nice.''

By now, Price felt safe enough to get up. ''I'm afraid we're on duty till we see you safely back at Holy Loch. Sorry to dampen your nuptial bliss, but we can't afford to lose a Sea Wolf skipper. Especially now."

Robert Brentwood gave a grunt. "Sorry—I—such a fool . . . didn't realize . . ."

"Not to worry," Price assured him, dusting himself down, the wind from the loch playing havoc with his hairpiece. "National Health'll take care of the teeth. I hope." He tried a grin, but his jaw hurt too much.

"I feel like a goddamned idiot," said Robert, his face still red from wind chill and embarrassment. "Here they are protecting us and we think—"

"Well," responded Rosemary, chagrined by her own embarrassment but her tone more defensive. "They should have told us."

"No," said Brentwood. He glanced in the rearview and gave a friendly wave. Price honked in reply. "If we'd known they were following us, it wouldn't have been much of a honeymoon. Would've seemed like someone was watching us through the keyhole all the time." Rosemary didn't like it, but she had to agree. The thought of her and Robert trying to make love with two people staking the place out from across the hallway of the B and B would certainly have put her right off. "Oh no!" she said. "They must have heard everything." Her face was between her fingers, looking at Robert. "Tell me, was I—"

"Screaming with joy!" he said. "All the time!"

She slid down into her seat as they drove off.

Five miles on, both cars disappearing into fog, Rosemary gasped in fright, turning to Robert. "My God—he mightn't be from Special Branch at all. I mean, he could be just saying that to—"

"No," Robert interjected. "He told me some stuff that only someone in the know could have a handle on. They couldn't have found it out in Surrey."

"Found out what? What kind of things?"

"About my family," Robert answered, gearing down on a hill, the fog so thick, he could barely see the front of the hood. "I don't want to talk about it. Damn it! I wish this goddamned demister would work."

The car slowed, Robert unconsciously taking his foot off the gas pedal, not because of the fog or his preoccupation with the windshield misting, but because he realized a Russian agent could as easily have had contacts in North America and the

Aleutians as in Surrey—that the information about Lana—if it was true—

"What's *assuage* mean?" he asked Rosemary, a little embarrassed.

"To allay," she explained eagerly, without a trace of surprise. "Why?" she pressed. "Did Price use it?"

"Yes, he said he hoped he'd assuaged my suspicions."

"Has he?"

Robert pushed himself backward from the steering wheel, his back hard against the seat, arms still, as if bracing himself for a crash. It was one of the isometric exercises he often used during the long watches aboard the sub and which he would be doing in several days time when, *if*, he returned safely to Holy Loch. "I don't know, hon," he told Rosemary. "He could have got all the stuff about my family from some—I don't know—some intelligence network in the States."

Price's jaw was throbbing and badly swollen on the left side. "Could you hand me one of those towelettes from the glove compartment?" he mumbled. "Or are they in the boot?"

Joan opened her purse, took out the Beretta nine-millimeter, and rummaged through the contents. "Here's one!" she pronounced triumphantly, tearing it open and passing the towelette to him. Dabbing it gently on his chin, he relished the temporary cold that took the edge off the pain. "By God, he can pack a wallop. Hope he isn't like that on his submarine. A man like that in charge of—how many is it—forty-eight nuclear warheads? Gives me the willies, I can tell you. Thought they were supposed to be the silent type. Not bloody rowdies."

"You *were* talking about his sister. How did you know all that about her anyway?"

"Because," he replied, "I do my homework. That's why."

The thing Robert Brentwood found unforgivable in himself was that, try as he might to push the image of Lana performing oral sex on young Spence from his mind, the more he fantasized about whether Rosemary would do it for him. The moment he thought he had evicted the scene from his mind as unworthy of him, the more pervasive it became until he had such an erection, he thought Rosemary would be sure to notice. At least he hoped she would. The image of her moist, red lips encasing him, her tongue darting with abandon, sucking him dry, made him doubt whether they could make Mallaig without him having to pull over. Returning again and again to what

Price had said about Lana, he remembered Price also saying something about how grateful the Admiralty was for the protection afforded by the Sea Wolfs, "especially now." But surely the subs had always been important to Admiralty. Why *"especially now"?* He mentioned it to Rosemary.

"Perhaps something's happened," she proffered, "that we haven't heard yet on the news?"

Robert switched on the radio, but Highlands static crackled like a log fire. Anyway, it was a violation of their pledge not to listen to any newscasts while on their honeymoon, not to let anything intrude on their all-too-brief time together. But now he wondered whether their pact had been a good idea after all. He hated not knowing what was going on. He looked in the rearview again but couldn't see Price's car, not even the yellow eyes of fog lights. He was unsure as to whether he should pull over and wait or keep going.

CHAPTER NINE

The White House

WHEN THE ARMY chief of staff, General Grey, arrived from the Pentagon and was ushered into the Oval Office by press aide Trainor, he wasn't sure whether the president had heard him and so coughed politely to announce his presence.

The chief executive of the United States was reclining in the black leather chair behind the dark oak desk from HMS *Resolute*—given to the much earlier President Hayes by Queen Victoria in 1878, the great seal of the United States carved on its front adding to the quiet dignity of the office that General Grey found distinctly gloomy in the fading evening light. Outside, the darkening magnolia bushes and stark brambles of the rose garden added to the heavy, oppressive atmosphere that had descended about the White House since the news had come in from the big aerial arrays at Fort Meade in Maryland.

The ELINT—electronic intelligence—experts had picked up FORCOMPS—forward command post signals—between the U.S. and South Korean armies under the command of Gen. B. W. Anderson, supreme commander of all Allied forces in Southeast Asia. On top of this, Mayne was in the throes of a migraine attack—it being no consolation to him, as Trainor well knew, that other presidents, too, had been victims of disease while in office, that Ulysses S. Grant had suffered one of his worst migraine attacks the night before Lee's surrender.

"Take a seat, General," said Mayne, waving him in the gloom to the red-and-yellow-striped cushioned chair to the left of the president's desk and directly in front of the presidential flag. As the general's eyes adjusted to the dim light, he could see the president wasn't looking directly at him but was deep in thought in the island of soft, peach-colored light casting its glow on the portrait of George Washington, in full uniform, above the mantel.

"I was told . . ." began the president, his voice quiet, measured. "Your intelligence boys told me Beijing couldn't do—what they've now done?" Mayne's right arm came into view indicating the map of the "big prick," as the Pentagon called the Korean Peninsula, set up to the right of him. Already, in the first twenty-four hours of heavy fighting between the enemy and U.S.-ROK forces, there were over eleven thousand American casualties. The Chinese–North Korean breakthrough was threatening to be an even bigger rout of the U.S.-ROK forces than that suffered by them at the beginning of the war around the Pusan-Masan perimeter in the far south.

The president turned to the general. "How many Chinese have crossed already?"

Grey rose and reluctantly took up the retractable pointer, its tip sliding from southwest along the line of the Yalu to the northeastern end of the eight-hundred-mile-long river that had been the border between the Korean Peninsula and Manchuria for a thousand years. "They moved down from up here, Mr. President, in Shenyang—China's most northeasterly province. The Thirty-ninth Army out of Anshan, the Fortieth from Shenyang City itself, and the Sixty-fourth from Fushun. Possibly they've moved the Twenty-fourth up from Yangshan—but that would have to be seconded from Beijing command."

"How many troops altogether?" asked Mayne.

"Ah—a hundred and twenty thousand, thereabouts, Mr. President."

Grey paused for a second or two to collect his spittle. "Give or take a division."

"How in Jesus' name," began Mayne, turning on the general, "can a one-hundred-and-twenty-thousand-man army and their equipment move—" looking back at the map, he eyeballed the distance south from Shenyang to the Yalu "—a hundred and fifty miles over mountainous terrain—in the dead of winter—cross a goddamn river, and take us by surprise?"

"The river's frozen over, sir."

"All right then—a hundred and twenty thousand of them crossing a *frozen* river and taking us by surprise. And our intelligence units didn't see *any* of them until I get this ELINT report—until it's too late? Come on, General." Mayne's voice was rising. "Where are all those super-duper movement sensors and infrared nighttime scopes we used in Vietnam? And for which I had to fight Congress?"

The general didn't think it appropriate to remind the president of the United States that sensors hadn't stopped General Giap in Vietnam either. Though Grey had to concede the president had a point, he nevertheless felt obliged on behalf of the U.S. Army to explain. "The difference here, Mr. President, is that under the terms of your—our—agreement with Beijing, any overflights by us to drop those sensors on the Yalu's northern bank would have violated Chinese air space."

"All right, Jimmy. But what's wrong with your men's *eyes?*" He gave the Yalu the back of his hand, the map stand shaking from the impact. "How the hell do a hundred and twenty thousand Chinese regulars, give or take a *division,* General—that'd be another thirteen thousand, right?"

"Yes, sir."

"How do a hundred and thirty-three thousand men move up and down mountains and get across the Yalu without us seeing a goddamned one of them?"

"Sir—it's an old Chinese maneuver. They used it on Doug MacArthur. They travel only at night. Hide by day. Anyone moves—they execute them—by bayonet—on the spot. Saves a bullet and there's not even the noise of a shot we can pick up."

Mayne returned to the desk, his face contorted as much by pain, despite his effort not to show it, as by the sudden catastrophe of China, with its standing army, not counting reserves, of over three million men, having entered and suddenly exploded what the Pentagon in their report to the president were pleased to call "the *parameters* of the war."

"*Parameters!*" said Mayne. "They've blown the gate wide

open, Jimmy! They've—" He sat down in the chair and was silent for a moment. "Jimmy, I don't want to sound like a hard-ass or anything, but if this is an 'old Chinese trick,' like firecrackers, why the hell weren't you ready for it? Didn't we have reconnaissance patrols? Aircraft?"

"Yes, sir, but we could only go as far as the Yalu."

"Christ, Jimmy, I'm no—" Mayne hesitated, his mind searching for the name of an ace pilot. "Frank Shirer. I don't even have a pilot's license. But even I know if you fly high enough, you can see over a damn river. See anything move. Our satellite's supposed to read *Pravda* in Red Square from space—right?"

"I don't know who made up that old crock, Mr. President, but it's far from accurate. More a PR—"

"Don't nitpick, Jimmy. You know what I mean. How come the first I hear of it is in a national intelligence digest out of Fort Meade who picked up a radio intercept from some poor kid in one of our forward observation posts screaming that he was being overrun by Chinese?"

"The weather, sir. It's been snowing like crazy the last few days. Not even the satellites could get through that."

"Before *that?*" pressed Mayne relentlessly. He wasn't interested in assigning guilt, but he damn well didn't want it to happen anywhere else—in Europe, for instance. Or, God forbid, at the Aleutian back door. Or the Middle East. General Grey retracted the pointer. "Sir. We just plain didn't see them. I mean, that's pretty tough discipline they have, sir." The general could see Mayne behind the desk, sitting well back in his chair but far from relaxed, hand massaging his temple.

"Well, I wish we had that kind of discipline. Our boys and the South Koreans are on the defensive again just when I thought we could wrap it up in Korea and divert some of our divisions up to the Aleutians and Europe, now that Doug Freeman's got us moving again over there." He sat forward, hands clasped on the green blotter, speaking more slowly now, more reflectively. "Course, if we were like them—had the kind of army where you could shoot a man for moving—I suppose we wouldn't be fighting them. But—hell, Jimmy, we've got to do something. Fast. By pulling back—retreating like this—"

"Some units just plain broke, Mr. President, and ran."

Mayne's arms were cradling his head, the thumbs pressing hard into tense neck muscle. "Got to get some stiffener over there or else—" His voice was more agitated than the general had ever heard it. "Or we'll have a goddamn A-grade, number one, full-blown political and military disaster on our hands." He was out of the chair again, fingers running about his belt, glancing up at the map for several seconds, then turning toward Grey. "If we lost Korea, Jimmy, as a base—the only one we have on mainland Asia from which to harass Russia's southern flank, then—" He broke off, his tone suddenly infused with new energy. "Jimmy—we're still pressing ahead in Europe, am I right? No surprises in the last twenty-four hours or anything?"

"No, sir. Everything's going as well as can be expected. Doug Freeman's got the Russkis retreating so fast, he's in danger of outrunning his own supply line. The British and Norwegians are worried Moscow could panic—throw in the conventional towel and go nuclear while they've still got time."

"They'll talk peace before that," said Mayne.

"I'm not so sure, sir. I mean, it might be Politburo policy to talk before anyone pushes the button, but policy gets the bum's rush when panic sets in. It only takes some nut, some kid on an SS-18 battery, to start it. And remember, the Russians and Chinese have huge shelters. Haven't a hope of saving most of their population and industry, of course, and they know it, but the Chinese figure on, say, saving twenty percent of their population in the worst possible case. For us that'd be totally unacceptable, but in China, that's two hundred million people left. Russian estimate used to be they'd lose twenty-four million and still they'd have more than twice our population. We haven't got anything like their civil defense. Our public was so pummeled with that 'nuclear winter' shit—excuse me, sir—that we didn't think there was any point to civil defense. So if the Russians do panic in the face of Freeman's advance, we're in one hell of a lot of—"

"Then we'd better slow down the advance. Tell Freeman to consolidate, give him time to build up supplies. Good point, Jimmy, about the supply lines. Will the joint chiefs go for a halt?"

"They will, sir."

From the general's quick response, Mayne guessed the C in Cs had instructed him to make that very argument. "Then I suggest we transfer Doug Freeman immediately—to C in C Korea. Get Anderson out of there. Put Freeman back on his old turf for a while."

This the general wasn't ready for. "But—Mr. President. We

want to slow down in Europe, yes. But if we take General Freeman out and there's a Russian counterattack, then—"

"Don't tell me we haven't got any other generals over there, Jimmy? Defensive backs?"

"Of course not, sir. I simply mean that Freeman has a high profile. If the Russkis see him withdrawing—"

"It'll be a demonstration of enormous confidence in all our other field commanders," countered Mayne. "Most of them trained by you, Jimmy, I might add."

"Maybe, sir, but still—"

"Jimmy, Freeman *knows* Korea. He attacked the North Korean capital at night, got in, got out, and gave us time to reinforce the Pusan-Masan perimeter. We *need* a man like that."

"You mean someone a little bit crazy?"

"We have to get those Chinese back across the Yalu."

"I don't know if even Doug Freeman can do that, Mr. President."

"Let's try."

The general nodded his assent. "Very well, sir."

"Jimmy?"

"Sir?"

"If you aren't happy with bringing him out of Europe, how about we play a shell game?"

General Grey frowned.

"General, we live in a country that produces more actors than any other. We breed them by the bushel. Hell, if I remember correctly, one of them occupied this office."

There was subdued laughter from Trainor. General Grey was warming to the idea. "A double?"

"You won't have much time," conceded Mayne.

But Grey, pursing his lips, was considering the logistics. "It might just work. They did it with Montgomery. But how about Freeman's getting to Korea? If that gets out, the Russians—"

"It won't," said Mayne, turning to Trainor. "Under wraps. No press. Shut everything down like Reagan did in Grenada and Bush in Panama. Keep the press right out of it—and only allow two or three of Doug's top aides to go with him. Leave the rest in Europe. Hell—he'll need to leave most of them in Europe to execute his strategy over there—until he gets back."

"Mr. President," General Grey told his commander in chief, "Doug Freeman'll die without the press—without an audience."

"Then he'll die in a good cause," said Mayne, reaching for the water decanter, a signal to Trainor it was time for the pain pills.

"Think positive, Frank," Shirer told himself, as one by one he saw the green blips of *Salt Lake City*'s brood of aircraft disappearing from his radar screen as they landed safely on the carrier. Finally only one blip remained, approximately three miles starboard aft of the carrier: the "Sea King" helo on its plane guard station. Shirer had been making pattern for thirty minutes, and the nose wheel hadn't budged, so that now he knew that he had only twenty-seven minutes remaining before he'd have to take her in. "Like a bird, like a bird," he repeated to himself, recalling the words of his old instructor during his first carrier landing. "Coming in on a carrier's way different from having a mile of runway to screw around on. Go in like the birds—feet first, get your rear rubber down, hook the wire, and the nose'll take care of itself." The only trouble was, this time Shirer knew the nose wouldn't take care of itself, not with the wheel only halfway down. He tried to remember whether there had ever been a barricade engagement on *Salt Lake City*—a crash landing racing at 150 miles an hour into the nylon net.

In another three minutes, Commander Harris in flight deck control was watching the last of the *Salt Lake City*'s air umbrella, an E-C Hawkeye long-range warning aircraft, its rotodome stem retracting, the dome sitting on the plane's fuselage like a huge white pancake, wings already folding up and back as the plane was being hauled by a mule, a flat yellow tractor, to the port elevator as fast as the crosswind would allow so that it could be moved out of harm's way in the hangar deck below.

"Soon as that baby's in the dungeon," instructed Harris, "let me know."

"Yes, sir," replied a tired assistant one deck below in air traffic control, which was part of the combat information center. "Sir—LSO says we may have a foul deck."

"Chri—" Harris began, checked himself, and asked, "How long's two oh three got fuel for?"

"Twenty-four minutes, sir."

The flight deck commander called the LSO. What he needed to know was whether the LSO had any idea of what the debris on the deck might be. And where?

"Can't tell you, Phil," came the LSO's reply. "Might be

nothing, but thought I saw something drop off when the last Hawkeye came in.''

''It was a clean trap, wasn't it?'' the FDC asked the LSO.

''Yeah—clean trap. But I thought I saw something after she hit. Could have been thrown up in her wash.''

''Okay. We'd better check it out.''

''Looked like it was near three cat.'' He meant the white line that marked the waist catapult run.

''Thanks, Pete,'' answered the worried FDC. If it was an obstacle near the waist catapult line, it could be a dislodged nut, fuel tank flap—or anything from the scores of deck vehicles used to push and pull the planes into position. A nut sucked into either one of the Tomcat's intakes could mean a multimillion-dollar engine gone, or a seabird that had been hit and knocked to the steel-grooved deck could become an instant lubricant the moment the twenty-five-ton aircraft, its nose wheel not fully extended, landed, sending the Tomcat sliding an inch or two out of alignment—which, at over a hundred miles an hour, could wipe out the aircraft and anyone nearby. The FDC lifted the phone for the air boss six decks above him, depressed the other phone atop his right shoulder, and requested a search party for the area around the four arrestor wires. They simply didn't have time for a full-fledged ''walk-down'' to make sure the deck was sterile.

Within a minute, the chief petty officer and the sixteen-man search party team were scouring the deck, and it was Seaman First Class S1c. Elmer Ventral, who'd been on the *Salt Lake* less than a year, who spotted the oil rag caught in the corner of one of the four-feet-diameter circular steel mountings that houses the one-and-a-half-inch-thick cable to which the number one arrestor wire was attached. Whenever the wire hooked an aircraft, the big cable took the strain.

''All right,'' said the chief petty officer, whose job it would be to report to flight deck control. ''Let's get inside before we all freeze our butts off.''

Young Ventral, two days away from his twenty-first birthday, married little more than fourteen months and already a father, felt good about having found the oil rag. It couldn't really have caused that much damage—unless it got sucked in by an air intake—but the air boss was a fanatic about a sterile deck, and Ventral knew it would stand him in good stead.

The CPO who had to tell the FDC wasn't so lucky.

''Jesus Christ!'' Harris bellowed. ''What was that doing there?''

"Somebody must have dropped it, sir."

"I know somebody dropped it, Chief. And I want his ass. You read me?"

"Yes, sir," said the CPO, but he knew the task would be hopeless. So did the FDC. They were both feeling bad about it, both having worked with the air boss long enough to know that when any single player screwed up, the team screwed up. FDC called PRIFLY and told the air boss what had fouled his deck.

"A rag!" said the air boss, his voice rising like a tenor going for the high C as he walked, or rather stalked, behind the grease pencil status board and stared down into the bluish light that washed the flight deck. "We've got a man to come down and some joker's dropped a fuckin' rag?"

"Yes, sir."

"Listen, Phil, I want his ass."

"Yes, sir."

The moment he put the phone down, the air boss turned to PRIFLY's mini boss. "Get Lieutenant Ronson up here pronto."

"Yes, sir."

Ronson was the chief of the *Salt Lake City*'s TV station. The air boss knew there was no chance of finding out who exactly dropped the rag, but he was going to make it item one—cut right into the movie and play it on every shift for the next forty-eight hours. They'd be so goddamned sick of that oil rag—

Meantime he had a plane to get down and, glancing at the real-time PRIFLY clock, saw he had seventeen minutes.

"We going to get this barricade up in time?"

It was more an order than a question, but the mini boss complied. "They're working on it, sir. They think they'll make it."

The air boss picked up his binoculars, looking down at the barricade, a series of tough, hydraulically anchored nylon ribbons forming a vertical netting that stood twenty-four feet high, strung across the flight deck and which he hoped would catch the Tomcat if, due to the necessarily high "up" angle the pilot would have to have on the nose, the Tomcat missed the three wire.

"You done one of these before, Henry?" the air boss asked his assistant.

"No, sir."

"What time we got, Henry?"

"Sixteen minutes, sir," replied the mini boss, wondering

whether his superior had ever handled a barricade engagement himself.

"Weather report, sir," interjected a seaman, handing him the printout. "Wind's dying, but more fog."

"Great," said the air boss sardonically. "Just what we fucking need. Be lucky if he can see the meatball. We got rescue and fire all set, Henry?"

"All set, sir."

"Anyone loses a goddamned oil rag in future and the whole shift pays. Beer ration cut to one can—or zilch." He shifted his binoculars to look down at the port side of the barricade being laid out, its nylon ribbons flapping furiously in the crosswind. "How much time we got, Henry?"

"Fourteen minutes, sir," said the mini boss, the other spotter trying to keep visual contact with Shirer's blinking red light along with the radar blip. The mini boss looked teed off—couldn't the air boss read a goddamned clock? Everyone was getting too tense.

Five decks below, TV technicians were plugging into the flight deck camera feed. With the crew of over five thousand below decks run ragged by the day-in, day-out dangerous task of keeping planes constantly airborne, the Tomcat's final approach might as well entertain as instruct. In the dungeon, above the noise of the mules pushing and pulling planes about and scores of technicians swarming over parked planes, many of the aircraft looking as if they'd been roughly cannibalized for spare parts, some green jackets checking Tomcat avionic "slip-in, pull-out" circuit boards in the black boxes started making book on whether Shirer would make it or not. More navy pilots had been lost in accidents than had been shot down.

Up on the flight deck in the wait room, S1c. Elmer Ventral, whose job it was to race out to release the hook immediately after a plane caught the wire, was being ribbed by the rest of the work crew, who'd awarded him the "ROFOR"—royal order of the fucking oil rag.

Unbeknownst to Ventral, the CPO in charge of the shift Ventral was part of, following carrier tradition, had called down to one of the bakeries aboard to have them bake a cake for Ventral's birthday—and to decorate it with something that looked like an oil rag.

Up in PRIFLY, the air boss was going over everything that could possibly go wrong. He called down to flight deck control. "Harris!"

"Yes, sir?"

"Phil—you have the new weight for two oh three?" The loss of weight occasioned by the Tomcat burning up as much fuel as possible before landing would have to be vectored in so the arrestor wires wouldn't be too taut.

"We've got it covered, sir."

"Good man."

"Barricade's up, sir," reported the mini boss.

"Clear the deck!" ordered the air boss, his voice projected by the powerful PA system designed to cut through any noise on the carrier, including the cacophony of noise attending the launch of a full air operation, when the air boss dispatched the carrier's planes at a rate of one every thirty seconds.

"Decks clear," came the confirmation two minutes later.

"Very good," acknowledged the air boss.

"Fog bank closing," another voice informed him.

"Not good," said the air boss, turning around. There was a nervous chuckle. The air boss then ordered the Sea King helo off the starboard beam to move from its plane guard position three miles away from the carrier to one mile. If the pilot overshot and had to ditch, there was no way the ninety-thousand ton ship, at twenty-two knots, could stop or alter course to assist, risking the integrity of the entire battle group. Besides, even if all engines were shut down, it would still take the ship over a mile to stop.

After crossing the loch, Robert and Rosemary noticed how many more cars were coming south from Mallaig than those, like themselves, heading north toward the fishing port. And after a while, when the Prices' car hadn't shown up behind them, Robert Brentwood grew even more suspicious of the Englishman's story. If the Prices, or whatever their real name was, were really protecting him and Rosemary, then they'd be going on to Mallaig. For Robert, the choice was clear. Either he and Rose could go on ahead to Mallaig, looking over their shoulders all the time in the fog—"a hell of a way," he murmured, "to spend your honeymoon"—or he could do something about it. As he made the U-turn cautiously in the swirling fog, heading back in the direction of the ferry, Rosemary asked him to pass her another Gravol. Whether it was morning sickness or from their "run-in" with the Prices, she didn't know, but she felt "awful."

Brentwood saw the vague shape of a car coming at him from the direction of the ferry. It wasn't the Prices. It occurred to him they might have turned back to the ferry, recrossed the loch, and made a call perhaps—arranged a little surprise for the captain of the Sea Wolf in Mallaig—away from witnesses and the busload of kids on the ferry?

After another five minutes or so, he saw what at first seemed to be a cluster of lambs and a shepherd at the roadside, but on getting closer, he could see it was a group of teenage girls and, immediately behind them, the school bus. The girls, in buff-colored skirts and maroon blazers, stood near the bus, which had a miter with a scroll underneath painted on its side. It was pulled off on the opposite side of the road where it had been heading for Mallaig, and soon he could read "St. Mark's" written in black letters above the more colorful school emblem. The girls were all standing in a group, subdued. A moment later he saw two figures, a man and a woman, emerging from behind the bus, but saw it wasn't the Prices. The woman, in a gray pleated skirt and coat, was walking toward him briskly, and behind her was a man who appeared to be the bus driver, wearing an anorak. The woman, obviously in charge, nodded brusquely.

"Anything the matter?" he asked.

"There's been an accident," she replied matter-of-factly. "Can you help?"

"I know first aid," said Brentwood, getting out of the car. "What—"

"It's too late for that, I'm afraid," she said. "First aid." The bus driver looked shaken, turning, his arm pointing behind the bus to a car, lopsided in a ditch, almost completely hidden by bracken. Brentwood's first thought was that it was the Prices, but he couldn't tell from this distance.

"I think," began the bus driver, "what Miss Sawyers means, sir, is that you could help us if you'd take a message for us to Mallaig. We can't go over sixty kilometers an hour on the bus. Be a while 'afore we get in."

"If you're *going* in that direction," said the schoolmistress.

"No problem," said Robert. "Be glad to help. Just give me the message and I'll—"

"Noo, lass—" called out the bus driver. ". . . Miss Wilson! Where you think you're going?" Robert saw it was one of the schoolgirls across the road moving away from the group.

"Mother nature," the girl replied.

"Up t'other way," the driver instructed her. "And not too far from the bus, mind. We could lose you in this lot."

The schoolmistress was leading Brentwood back to the car obscured by the bracken. It *was* the Prices's.

"A terrible accident," she said. "Perhaps we shouldn't touch anything."

"Christ!" said Brentwood, the mistress wincing at his blasphemy. "Sorry—" he went on, not wanting to look any further but feeling compelled.

"I think we should keep it quiet," she said, her voice calm but nevertheless strained. "Until you reach Mallaig. No point in upsetting the girls any more than they have been. One or two of them saw the broken glass—otherwise we wouldn't have seen the car in the bracken. Thank goodness Wilkins—our bus driver—had the sense to keep them away from it."

"Yes," agreed Robert. "Well, leave it to me, miss. I'll tell the police in Mallaig. Maybe you should give me your name."

"And you?" she asked. Robert showed her the U.S. Navy card with his photo. She was visibly relieved.

"Oh, thank goodness. I saw you leaving the ferry, you see, and wondered—"

Brentwood suddenly remembered something, too—the car speeding past him in the rain, shortly after he'd made the U-turn to come back. What if he and Rosemary hadn't turned but, like the Prices, had kept on in the fog toward Mallaig?

"Listen, Miss Sawyers," he said urgently. "I think we should all go into Mallaig. On your bus. Can we hitch a ride with you?"

"Why, yes, but—"

"I haven't time to explain fully yet."

He saw her suspicion return. "Look, when we get to Mallaig, you can call this number—here on my card. It's the U.S. Navy attaché at the U.S. Embassy in London. But right now I think it'd be best if we all go in together to Mallaig."

"Perhaps one of us should stay here and—" she began.

"No," cut in Brentwood. "No one stays here. Everyone gets on the bus." The teacher and the driver looked uneasily at one another. "Trust me!" said Brentwood. "I know what I'm doing, believe me." The driver made noises about sweeping the glass off the road. "Leave it," said Brentwood. "Believe me, I know what I'm doing."

"Very well, I suppose —" began Miss Sawyers. "You'd best get the girls back on the bus, Wilkins."

"Yes, miss."

The drive to Mallaig was a mournful one, only a few of the girls talking, a few giggling, trying to act nonchalant despite their having come across what Miss Sawyers had somberly told them was a "fatal accident."

"But I didn't see any damage to the car," Rosemary insisted.

"It was on the driver's-side fender," Robert told her. "On the right side—you couldn't see it from where our car was parked. Slammed right into the ditch. Price probably dozed off at the wheel."

"How dreadful." The Gravol hadn't worked yet, and she felt so ill, she thought she was going to throw up.

When the bus reached the Mallaig police station, it was an anticlimax for the girls of St. Mark's, who had thought they were in sole possession of knowledge of the accident. But the police said someone had already called it in. That being the case, Robert told the desk sergeant he was surprised he hadn't seen any ambulance or rescue vehicle passing them on the way in.

"Ah," replied the desk sergeant good-naturedly, "we wouldn't be using flashing lights unless it's an extreme emergency, sir. Air raid regulations, you see."

The sergeant took down the statements from the three of them, spun the log book about, thanked Miss Sawyers and Wilkins for their help, and informed Robert that "the super'd like a word with you, Captain Brentwood, if you don't mind, sir. I'll have the corporal make Mrs. Brentwood a cuppa. Come inside the staff room if she likes, sir."

"Thanks."

The superintendent had Brentwood draw up a chair. "Well, Captain, I know you're not a police officer, but I'd appreciate your assessment of the situation. In your line of country, I expect you've seen a few injuries?"

"Yes," acknowledged Brentwood. "Well, from what I saw through the shattered window, I'd say the car was forced off the road, *then* they were shot. Both between the eyes—at short range. Bullet holes in the windshield. You couldn't do that at speed—I mean, from a moving vehicle."

"Were the doors locked, Captain?"

"I think so. If I remember correctly, on the way up here, the bus driver said he'd had to reach in through the shattered window glass to pull up the lock."

"Silly man," said the superintendent.

"He told me he used a handkerchief," said Robert.

"Oh, aye. But now any other fingerprints on the door lock are probably gone." The superintendent paused, running fingers through thinning white hair. "You've no idea of the weapon, I suppose?"

"Small-bore, I'd say. Neat hole in the forehead—the back of the skull was something else."

"Strewn about, was it?"

Robert sat back in the uncomfortable wooden chair, face grim with the recollection. "Never seen anything like it."

The superintendent was nodding. "A high-vel, most probably," he mused. "Not much noise, faster than most, with a mercury-filled head. They like twenty-two-caliber. That'd explain the back-of-the-head business." He looked across the desk at Brentwood. "Did none of the girls see tha'?"

"No. Wilkins, the bus driver, kept them away."

"And quite right, too. How's your wife taking this?"

"She'll be fine. I told her it was an accident. I doubt she believes me but, well, when she's feeling better, maybe . . ."

"Not much of a honeymoon you've had, lad?" the superintendent cut in.

Robert couldn't remember telling him they were on their honeymoon. The sergeant saw his surprise. "Oh, we've been given the gen on you, lad. Ever since our boys got on to them in Surrey."

"You've circulated their descriptions, I hope?" said Brentwood.

The corporal came in with two teas and the station's ration of Peek Frean biscuits on a tray.

The superintendent dunked a chocolate sandwich, tapping it on the large mug showing President Suzlov being kicked in the butt. "I'm sorry, Captain. I'm not with you. How do you mean—'circulated their descriptions'?"

"Well, I mean whoever's chasing us. Whoever's trying to kill nuclear sub captains. Of course, I know they're special Soviet agents—SPETS, I suppose—but I assume you know what they look like by now—or don't you?"

"Och, mon, you've got it all mixed up. " 'Twas those bloody Prices who were gunning for you. Hoping for a lonely place on the stretch after the ferry. If our boys hadn't caught up with 'em, you'd be dead, lad."

Brentwood slowly put his tea down on the superintendent's desk. "Then who in hell were—" He gave the superintendent the description of the young newlyweds they'd met in the B and B. The ones with the confetti still in their hair.

The superintendent fished a file from his top drawer and, opening the folder, passed over an ID kit sketch. It was them.

"The 'charmers,' we call 'em," said the super. "Real charmers, they are. Bastards change their name every other week." The super hesitated. "Captain Brentwood, I hate to say this, but—well, first of all, I'd better make sure I've got the right info from London. Your naval attaché informed us your leave's up in a few days. Correct?"

"Yes."

"Now, this is up to you, mind, but if I were you, I'd get back to Holy Loch. Out of danger—if you see what I mean?"

"How about my wife?"

"It's you they want, lad. Not her. 'Sides, we'll keep a close eye on her. We do it for a lot of you chaps. But they've not grabbed any of the womenfolk yet. They know we'd never give in to a kidnapping situation. No, as I say, it's you they're after."

There was a long silence, broken finally by the superintendent. "Would you like a wee dram of something stronger in that tea?"

"Yes," Robert Brentwood replied, "I would."

"Corporal?"

While they were waiting, the superintendent told the nuclear sub skipper, "She won't like it, of course—wives never do—but tell her you've got orders to sail a few days earlier. Won't be much of a Christmas, I'm afraid."

Brentwood nodded tiredly. He realized that then and there, police protection or not, he was going to give Spence Senior his .45, along with the police ID sketch of the two charmers from the B and B. And he was going to tell Richard Spence that if either of the charmers ever showed up around the Spence house, he was to call police emergency straightaway. And if he couldn't he was to shoot the charmers dead.

Robert Brentwood took the tea and double Scotch in one gulp. It wasn't safe anywhere.

Coming down toward the postage-stamp-size deck of the carrier, Shirer knew it would be his last chance. He had the carrier's meatball centered, the green dots either side of it confirming he was on the right glide path, despite the buffeting of the crosswind. The wind had blown the deck clear of fog, and while the salt spray on his cockpit obscured his view, it wasn't enough to trouble him.

While flying in pattern to use up his fuel, he'd had time to psyche himself up for a barricade engagement should he fail to make a clean-trap, hooking the three wire. Besides this, there was the four wire, and providing he could keep the Tomcat's ass low, nose high, most of the braking would be over before the nose could lunge and take out the fighter's Hughes radar and the long-range Northrop target-TV. If all went well, he'd halt the plane fast enough so that even if he slid, the Tomcat would stop before reaching the net. His major problem, which the LSO calmly reminded him of, was that unlike the normal landing when, after hitting the deck at 150 miles an hour, the pilot kept the engine at 75 percent power, ready for touch and go should there be anything wrong, Shirer's approach on Bingo fuel would be his only one. And with the barricade up, the Tomcat would be fully committed once it touched the deck, Shirer having to immediately cut power. If he hit the net at three-quarter power, he could "total" any or all of the other aircraft clustered cheek to jowl on the cramped parking area of the flight deck, the carrier able to house only half her aircraft belowdecks.

"Beautiful, two oh three," came the landing officer's voice. "Beautiful—on the glide path—on the glide path—"

The bluish-white blot of the deck suddenly became a blur of lights, the narrow deck widened, the orange ball centered, the twenty-five-ton fighter hitting the deck with a force of over forty tons. Below the flight deck, the cable housings crashed like two freight trains. Shirer felt the harness jerk, his body slammed back into the seat with a force of over seventy tons. He cut power and left it to God.

The Tomcat skewed, and halted abruptly, the wire's "pull-back" failing to release the hook so that Elmer Ventral and two other green shirts following a brown-shirted plane captain raced to unhook the plane, but the three wire snapped. The cable whipped through the air. Ventral disappeared, two men near him smacked clear off the deck. As the petty officer and two other men attended the plane's chocks, another sounded the "man overboard" alarm of his fiber mike, the Klaxon wailing throughout the enormous ship. Immediately the Sea King helo hovering a quarter mile astern moved in.

Ventral's top half continued writhing close to the island, slithering in its own entrails, the green jackets helping Shirer unstrap, leading him quickly off to flight deck control and debriefing.

The Sea King's searchlights crisscrossed the sea, the helo hovering above the wide, bubbling wake, whose luminescent plankton made it look like wild, undulating hills of cream.

Neither of the two men were found.

As both the captain's and the flight deck controller's investigation would reveal, the oil rag should have raised the alarm that the big one-and-a-half-inch "braking" cable, to which the arrester wires were anchored, had been strained—a loose strand hooking the oil-stained cloth, the worst section of frayed cable hidden from view in the cable's housing.

Shirer, sitting exhausted in his cabin, knew it wasn't the first time a wire had gone, and it wouldn't be the last. He felt bad about it but not guilty. If you went "into guilt," as the air boss often repeated, you'd soon be "out of" flying.

It was announced on all three of the carrier's TV channels that there would be a service for Leading Seaman Ventral and the other two flight deck crewmen at 1400 hours next day—"Air Ops permitting."

Most of the five thousand men aboard *Salt Lake City* had never heard of Ventral or the other two men, but this made it all the more important for those who could to attend.

"Shirer?"

It was the air boss's voice outside his cabin. Shirer found the effort of getting up off his bunk and going to the door as tiring as if he were dragging a bag of cement. "Yes, sir?"

"You okay?"

"Yes, sir."

"No you're not." The air boss slapped him on the shoulder. "You're off to Pearl in the morning. Then San Diego and Washington."

"What's the scuttlebutt?" Shirer asked.

"Don't know. Haven't got a clue."

"Guess I'll find out soon enough, sir."

The air boss smiled and turned to go. "Need anything tonight? We can lay on room service if you like."

"No, thanks, sir," replied Shirer. "D'we know what screwed up on that nose wheel?"

"Not as yet. By morning."

"Yes, sir. Ah—I'd like to attend the burial service for . . ."

The air boss was shaking his head. "Sorry, but Washington wants you ASAP. Don't worry—I'll explain it to the men."

"Appreciate that, sir."

"You get some shut-eye."

Shirer didn't need an order to sleep. He hadn't been as tired as this since the dogfights over Adak, when, after three or four sorties, you were ready to sleep on the tarmac. Lying on the bunk, he looked down at his boots. He'd have to undo them before he— His head lolled and he was fast asleep.

CHAPTER TEN

Belgium

DAVID BRENTWOOD HAD never dreamed that he would get fan mail as a soldier, and yet here it was: over two hundred letters from admirers waiting to touch, however indirectly, one of the few who had won what General Freeman, in the manner of congratulating an Olympian, had called the "gold and silver"—the Congressional Medal of Honor for David's single-handed destruction of the Russian fuel dump at Stadthagen, the silver for "conspicuous bravery above and beyond the call of duty" during the assault on Pyongyang.

The letters depressed him. Their writers trusted him so much. They didn't know, unless they'd been in combat themselves, how thin the line could be between cowardice and bravery, between "thumbs up" and "screw up." David had seen men, officers like Freeman, who, though they could understand fear, were able to disdain it. For them the adulation of the public was fuel for their fire. For David, adulation only did what high marks did for him in college—drove him on not because he wanted to but because it was expected—had been expected by generations of Brentwoods in the armed services. Personal achievements were nothing for a Brentwood if they weren't surpassed the next time around. The pressure was enormous. Dutifully he opened the next letter without having taken any notice of whom it was from. Only when he unfolded it did he recognize the handwriting—Melissa Lange's.

"Hey, Yank!"

David turned around and saw it was the mad British sergeant, perched high in the back of a lizard-camouflaged Humvee, using its swivel-mounted .50-millimeter machine gun as an armrest. "Got you a seat on the hospital train to Brussels. Ten minutes. Better get a move on."

"Right," answered David, quickly folding the letter, slipping it into his top breast pocket as he headed toward the Humvee.

" 'Ere, 'ere!" bellowed the sergeant, albeit good-naturedly. "Where's your gear?"

David stopped, feeling as foolish as he had in the first terrible hours at Parris Island. He'd forgotten his kit bag in the excitement of receiving Melissa's letter. As he climbed aboard the Humvee, he saw the sergeant pointing toward the administration building. "Hear about your little sweetie?" The sergeant was talking again about the young admitting clerk, Lili, who had flirted with David when he'd first arrived at the Belgian hospital on convalescent leave after Stadthagen. "She's coming along, too," the British sergeant informed him. "Which reminds me. You ever see that old cartoon—barrack room full of birds all stripped down to their waists. Tits sticking out all over the place. Sar' major comes in, beet red. 'Good God!' he says. 'I said *kit* inspection!' "

"That's terrible," said David.

"Never mind, lad. I'll 'ave another one for you when you get back."

David never liked people saying things like "when you get back." Always made him nervous.

Lili was helping some of the nurses load the last of the abdominal cases that were being transferred to Brussels on the train. She waved, smiling at him.

" 'Ello, 'ello," the sergeant teased David. "Bit of the old in-out for you, Jack. Eh?"

Before David could answer, the Humvee jerked to a stop at the gate, throwing them both against the driver's cabin. The guards were demanding ID. "This man's got a train to catch," the sergeant informed the corporal of the guard.

"We must check all passes," said the Belgian sentry in impeccably stilted English.

"We much check all passes," said the sergeant, mimicking him to David.

"What for?" the sergeant asked the corporal. "Think I'm a bloody spy?" He dug David in the ribs, sending shooting pains down to the scar tissue.

"No, I do not think so," replied the Belgian corporal, unfazed. "You are too fat, I think."

"What? You cheeky bastard!" said the sergeant, passing his and David's ID down. "Don't give me any of your lip.

I'm responsible for this hero, see. And if we don't catch that train—"

"You will catch the train."

"We'd better," the sergeant retorted, snatching back the ID, and, indicating the younger guard, asked David, "You fancy the young one?—bit of lance corporal on the side?" He roared laughing, David leaning against the machine gun, shaking his head as the truck moved out.

CHAPTER ELEVEN

AS THE RED Cross hospital train headed for Brussels from Liège, diverted south because of a rocket-torn section of track on the more direct westward line, David fell under the slow, hypnotic sway of the carriage, the train restricted for a time to no more than forty kilometers an hour because of the danger of air-sewn mines that might still be in the area, hidden by snow.

The clickety clack of the wheels passing over the ties took David back to his childhood of going up from New York to Albany, the River Meuse, effortlessly slipping by him now, a stand-in for the narrower reaches of the Hudson River. But he knew the analogy was a strained one, more a pining for home than an accurate remembrance of things past. America was not only a long way off in his mind, it was another time, so remote, so unlike the war-filled continent that he was part of, that it might as well be on another planet. It wasn't simply that the snow-dusted flat country around the Meuse didn't approximate the heavily wooded banks along the upper reaches of the Hudson, but the smells were so unfamiliar.

Europe always smelled different—an older, colder brick smell, and especially in winter, with all the fumes of coal-burning furnaces that had come back into use as North Sea gasoline supplies that came from England via the Channel's "subfloat" pipeline were jealously coveted by the armed forces. The brownish haze from the coal fires created at once the most polluted and beautiful sunsets Europe had seen in the last hundred years.

David saw a Red Cross nurse coming through from the carriage loaded with badly wounded abdominal cases into the walking-wounded carriage, where David and the British sergeant were sitting with a number of other American, British, and Belgian troops. The nurse's experienced eye was looking for repatriation cases, which, if they were up to it, would be sent on from Brussels to the Channel ports, when these were cleared of debris, and sent back to England. The sergeant dug David in the ribs. "Look at the knockers on that, Davey boy. Imagine those dangling—"

"All right," said David, thwarting more detailed description. The sergeant, he decided, was one of those who took a perverse pleasure in getting the sexually deprived soldiers worked up about "dipping your wick." David turned his attention to the scenery, the train picking up speed, as he heard an American in front of him, in a neck brace, telling his buddy the train's engineer had told him they would pass through Waterloo on their way up from Namur to Brussels. Right now David didn't care about Waterloo—last thing he needed was to see another battlefield, no matter how historic it was. What he wanted was privacy, longing to read Melissa's letter, to hear her voice. But he wasn't going to spoil it like a dessert you're so hungry for that it's gone before you've time to savor the taste. Letters from home, like everything else in this war, had to be rationed carefully. He glanced back at the toilet lineup, but there were too many.

Soon his eyes were tearing because of the cigarette smoke in the carriage. The war, he mused, had been a monumental setback for the antismoking lobby. His older brother, Robert, or so his mother had told him, had mentioned it in his letters home, too, opining that sometimes he felt that, along with looking to escape unhappy situations back home, half the sub crews had joined the silent service because on a sub, you could smoke all you wanted.

"You are enjoying the scenery, yes?"

David looked up and saw the pretty young admitting clerk, Lili, the British sergeant already unabashedly leering at her, his cockney tone taking on a decidedly vulgar edge. " 'Ello, luv!" he said, patting the inside of his thigh. "Want to sit on Daddy's knee then?"

"No, thank you, Daddy." She smiled.

David burst out laughing, sending a burning pain down his arm, but he didn't care. Momentarily he forgot everything unpleasant in his life—the heart-thumping run he'd made on the Stadthagen dump, the raid on Pyongyang, and the churning doubt inside him about whether or not he could withstand the strain of any more combat, wondering how close he was—his body was—to simply throwing in the towel, his will exhausted by the combination of physical and mental fatigue.

The sergeant wasn't amused by Lili's repartee, a burning resentment in his eyes against the young girl, a resentment that David felt partly responsible for because of having laughed at him. "Ah—" said David in an effort to change the subject. "Someone was saying we'll be going through Waterloo?"

"Yes," said Lili. "It is very famous. You know about this?"

"He doesn't know anything, luv," cut in the sergeant. " 'E's just a boy. What you need, luv—"

"My name is Lili." She said it without rancor but evenly.

"All right, Lili luv—listen. You know where we can get a snort?"

She looked blankly at him.

"You know," said the sergeant as he motioned, knocking back a drink. "Booze? Ah—*le vin,* eh?"

"No," she said, "I—" The train lurched, approaching the bend near Auvelais, and Lili bumped into the sergeant, quickly righting herself, blushing. "I am sorry, I—"

"Sorry!" said the sergeant. "Don't you apologize, Lili. Just what we need on this—"

"Lay off," said David.

"My, my," the sergeant snorted at David. "I think he's jealous, Lili. And 'im wiv all those lovely letters. 'Please, Davey, my hero—I want to marry you.' Eh?" The sergeant was digging his elbow further into David. "Eh—that's what they want, isn't it, Brentwood? A bit of the old stick?"

David turned on him, but the sergeant, his face having lost all trace of humor, wasn't to be interrupted, his grin the same expression he'd worn when whacking the heads off the brambles by the canal. "Can't you take a fucking joke, matey? Eh?" Lili moved off.

"She's gone now, Sarge," said David icily. "You don't have to—"

"*Sergeant* to you, Dick!"

"All right, sergeant," said David quietly. "She's gone."

The sergeant sneered. "You fucking heros are all the same. Get a bit of fucking tin on your chest and you think you've got it on tap, right?" David turned away, refusing to be drawn further into argument, fixing his gaze back on the white-snow-dusted blur of the hills to the southeast, where the low country of Wallonia gave way to the formidable barrier of the Ardennes. His great-grandfather had been there—when Hitler's panzers had broken through to make their last great counter-attack of the Second World War, bringing the U.S. Allied advance to a bloody halt, inflicting over fifty-five thousand casualties on First Army's Eighth Corps, and destroying more than seven hundred American tanks.

Soon David heard a noise like someone farting in a bathtub—it was the sergeant asleep, David marveling at yet another example of Murphy's Law run rampant. If the army, concerned that David's injuries might give him some trouble en route to Brussels, had wanted to choose a more unsuitable candidate for escorting him to identify the SPETS at the in-camera trials in Brussels, it couldn't have chosen anyone as unsuitable as the British sergeant.

The sergeant's mouth was agape, revealing a row of tobacco- and tea-stained teeth. The English, David had discovered, drank enormous quantities of tea. Now and then at the front he'd seen British Centurion tanks in revetment areas, the drivers jerry-rigging a small can of water by the exhaust, the water quickly coming to a roiling boil, and they'd let the tea stew until it was the color of Coca-Cola.

The sergeant mumbled something and closed his mouth, issuing a nasal whistle that immediately caused a stir farther down the aisle, a British naval rating, head bandaged, shouting, "Shut his cake hole!" The man across the aisle calmed the seaman down. Later the American sitting directly in front of David said the Limey sailor was probably freaking out because the whistle sounded just like the Russian RU-six thousands. "Depth charge rockets," the American explained. "Russkis fire 'em in horseshoe pattern—twelve at once. Only, they've put whistles on 'em. Like the Stukas in World War Two. Frightens the piss out of you, the sub boys say."

"You couldn't hear 'em under the water, though, could you?" proffered a sapper across the aisle who looked as if there was nothing wrong with him until David saw the man had no left hand.

"Like hell you can't," answered the man in front of David.

"One of my buddies is on one of those pigboats—says underwater, you can hear sound four times easier."

"Faster," commented David. "Four times faster."

"You been in subs? A *marine?*"

"No," answered David. "One of my brothers."

"No way, man," said the sapper across the aisle. "I want something I can get out of. In a hurry."

"Like what?" challenged someone else.

"Yankee Stadium," came the answer, the man who said it turning self-congratulatingly to David. But David was no longer there, having seen the line for the john was no more, easing his way out past the sergeant. Outside, canals flashed by under a leaden sky, the train picking up more speed, its sound louder now there wasn't so much snow to muffle it, the train heading away from Wallonia, where Lili came from, and toward Waterloo, where Wellington had stopped Bonaparte.

Sitting in the relative peace of the washroom, David took out Melissa's letter. A salvo of Russian rockets couldn't have stunned him more than the first sentence:

> Richard and I are engaged. I know this might be quite a shock, but I wanted to tell you straightaway. You always told me, Davey, that we should be honest with one another—that's what I'm trying to do now. I hope you understand. It just sort of happened between Rick and me. I thought we were "just good friends"—I know you'll think that sounds awfully corny, but honestly, we were—I mean we *are.* I mean we are friends, you know, but, well, Rick has really become quite a different person since you left. Oh, I know I'm not saying this right but—gee, I guess that makes it sound like your going overseas had something to do with it. Not really. It was actually sort of accidental and—

The train took a corner at speed, its rails squealing, throwing David hard against the hold bar. His stomach tightened. Christ! The thought of the wimp in bed with her made him want to throw up. While others were fighting and dying thousands of miles from home, the bow-tied weasel had got into her. Mr. Bland, cost-benefit analysis Stacy would no doubt have meticulously planned his moves. First, exemption from the draft in return for a four-year stint as an SAC missile silo jockey, sitting sixty feet under the ground in his protected, superhardened shelter, wearing his fucking cravat. It was true—women went for the uniform. Hell, what were a grunt's fatigues next to sharp air force blue?

"Rick feels bad about it," Melissa explained. "He hadn't planned it that way."

"No!" said David. "What other way did he plan it, the fucking—"

There was a thump on the door. "Hey, you all right in there?"

"What—?" shouted Brentwood. "Yeah. I'm having a crap. You mind?"

"Enjoy, man! Enjoy!"

"Damn!" said David, skimming over the rest of the letter, one phrase leaping out at him. "Richard—" Funny how women always used the guy's full name when they were going to shaft you. Made it sound more civilized, David guessed.

> . . . Richard has gotten me interested in the SAC program, too. I didn't want to write you until I'd qualified. It's a very intensive course, as you probably know. Didn't want to talk about it too much for fear it mightn't happen. Well—I *passed!* Not only that, but with "outstanding" commendation. So there, Davey! Who said women couldn't *man* the silos? Of course, they've been doing it for years, I know, so I'm hardly breaking new ground. But—and this is so ridiculous—SAC won't permit mixed teams—both operators have to be of the same sex. Can you imagine? TV cameras all over the place.

The next word was blocked out by the censor. Jesus, thought David, even the censor knew he, Brentwood, D., Medal of Honor and Silver Star, was being dumped. ". . . As if," the letter went on,

> anyone would try any hanky panky down there! Even if you wanted to, there are too many drills to keep you busy the whole shift. Anyway, I *really* like it, Davey. And it's kind of nice, I think, that you're over there doing your thing for the war and I'm here. Sort of keeps us closer. At least we can write, I hope. Some of the girls who have steadies on the subs say they don't get replies for months on end. Hope you can write me more often than *that!* I called your mom the other day. She seems fine but is worried, of course, about your brother Ray, well, all of you, of course. But at least she more or less knows how things are with you and Robert and

Lana. I mean you *do* write, but Ray, she says, has just stopped writing altogether. He's had more laser plastic surgery apparently and it's amazing what they can do nowadays. But apparently he's been *really* depressed lately. He's asked his wife (sorry—I can't remember her name) to stop bringing down their two kids because he doesn't want them to see him that way. Or so your mom says. Your dad's taking it hardest, I think, though of course he would never admit it!!! Your mom says he keeps telling Ray, you know, "When the going gets tough," etc., etc., etc.

"Oh Jesus," David sighed, "no, no—"

He also told Ray the doctors told him that despite the severity of the burns, Ray's physical condition isn't too bad really and that he could get another command in time. Of course, your dad means something like a minesweeper. Important, I guess, like trash collectors, but hardly a command—at least not for someone who used to run a guided missile frigate off Korea. Talking of Korea, I guess you've heard as much as we have. Aren't you glad you're not there *now!* It really is scary. Rick says that we should've nuked them soon as they came across the Yalu. He says that what we should do now is—

The rest of it was crossed out by the censor's pen.

Just like Stacy, thought David. They put him in a hole somewhere in the Midwest in some friggin' wheat field and he thinks he's an authority on how to run the war. "Very scary in Canada," Melissa went on.

Six big grain silos—huge things like round skyscrapers—no windows and full of wheat, waiting for rail transport to the Great Lakes. They were blown up. ABC Late Night showed shots of one of them—terrific explosion. Apparently they build up a lot of electricity from the dry grain dust and it makes for a very explosive atmosphere, but of course, sabotage is suspected. There's a big row about how come ABC got an exclusive—live coverage of one of the silos blowing its top. They said they got an anonymous tip, which is probably right—I mean whoever blew it up probably *wanted* us to see it. Just to show how vulnerable we are. Now everyone's saying our big mistake was to have let so many so-called "refugees' into the States during the Gorbachev years—turns out apparently that the head of the KGB was stuffing in as many agents as possible. Nobody figured what would happen after Gorbachev, I guess.

Must run now. I am sorry, Davey, but I wanted to tell you right away. Please write. I'd love to hear from you.

Love, Lissa.

There were hugs and kisses.

"Hey!" came a British voice from outside. "Don't make a meal of it, Yank."

"Hero's probably wanking himself off," said another voice. It sounded like the sergeant, so that when David came out, he was ready for him. But it wasn't. Instinctively the British soldiers stepped back, one pinned up against the water fountain, his sleeve getting wet. Brentwood's face was white with anger. As he passed them, the men waiting for the toilet fell silent, and for a moment it was as if the noise of the train drowned all else, even the sergeant's snoring, while David, mumbling, "Excuse me," made his way back to his seat by the window, the letter now a crumpled, tight ball in his fist.

One of the soldiers waiting outside the toilet, a corporal, lit a cigarette and noted quietly, "A Dear John letter. You think?"

"I'll put a fiver on it," said an Australian gunner, arm in a sling.

"Dear John in the john," a cockney quipped.

"Not funny, mate," said the corporal. "Knock the piss out of you, that will. Rotten bitch."

"He should chuck it. Throw it away," said the corporal's mate.

"Nah," said the cockney. "Our 'ero's a bloody brooder, I reckon. 'E'll covet that, '*e* will. Read it over an' over. Torture 'imself proper. Drop 'is bundle, 'e will. No more gongs for him, mate."

"Ah, I dunno," said the Australian reflectively, drawing thoughtfully on the cigarette. "Might take it out on the Russkis and win another friggin' gong."

"A Purple 'Eart's only medal 'e'll get," rejoined the cockney. "A loser."

"Dunno," opined the Australian, lighting a cigarette from the corporal. "Hears his bird's getting screwed by the milkman. First he's mad, full 'o piss and vinegar, know what I mean? Then he goes really crazy—runs at a fucking machine gun. He'll get his gong." The Australian blew out a cloud of smoke and looked down at the cockney. "But it'll be posthumous."

"Well," answered the cockney, " 'e won't get it in bloody Brussels. All 'e'll get there is the clap."

"No way," concluded the Australian definitively. "Right now he hates all women, I reckon."

"Who are you?" asked the cockney derisively. "Dr. Freud?"

"Listen, mate, I know about those blokes. Overachievers. Type A. Go, go, go, and then suddenly they look around and there's no one there. Then they can go either way. He's on a high wire, mate, make no mistake."

When Lili came through the carriage again, clutching a sheaf of papers in her hands, checking each patient had the right chart to avoid the kinds of bureaucratic foul-ups that so often bedeviled administrators trying to keep track of wounded as they moved from train to buses to ships, she saw David and could tell instantly something dreadful had happened to him. He was staring out the carriage window like an old man, the coloration in his face splotchy, teeth clenched like those patients she'd seen who ground their teeth at night and wondered why they woke up with a pounding headache—a look of such unrelieved bitterness in his eyes that it seemed to distort the very contours of his face.

Lili could only wonder what might have caused it. Her heart wanted to go out to him not only because she had found him attractive when she'd first seen him but because he was an American. In her father's house the word "American" had always been uttered in reverential tones. When she was a child, her father had taken her to the South, deep into French-speaking Wallonia, to Bastogne, where the Nazis had made their deep armored thrust through Belgium in December of 1944. Lili had stood in awe of the huge monument outside the town with the Latin inscription, which her father translated: "To the American liberators. The Belgian people remember." He had told her of how his great-grandfather and his wife and two children, like so many other Belgians, owed their lives to the Americans who, though surrounded by a ring of German steel in that bitter Christmas, wouldn't surrender. At school, Lili had heard the story of how the American general, given the surrender terms by the German commander, had replied, "Nuts," though her father—"in the interest of truth," as he gravely told her—felt compelled to explain to her in order to save her any "embarrassment" as she grew older that what the American general, McAuliffe, after whom the town square in Bastogne was named, had actually said was not "Nuts" but an English synonym to do with, as Lili's father put it, a part of the male anatomy.

Because of the fearlessness of her youth and because she had always assumed Americans were heroes, Lili felt that no matter how off-putting David's mood or appearance was now, she must try to help him. He was, after all, far away from his home, and to have fought with such courage must have exacted a terrible cost. She was so used to seeing soldiers whose wounds were external, she had to remind herself that some of the most terrible wounds, as her father had so often told her, were unseen, inside the heart. Perhaps, she thought, he was worried about the coming ordeal of identifying the captive SPETS. It was not a thing, she imagined, that a soldier liked doing, even to his most bitter enemy, even though she knew such people must be punished. Perhaps after he had been to the NATO HQ, she could help him forget the ordeal by showing him around Brussels. She must be brave, she resolved, brace herself and risk his anger. The Belgians' debt of honor to the Americans, her father had said, was eternal, and every generation must do its best to repay.

CHAPTER TWELVE

FIVE HUNDRED MILES to the east, on the snowy vastness of the alluvial Polish plain, the thunder of artillery was intense. Along the C-shaped front that took in Gdansk in the north to Poznan, 250 miles to the southwest, and Krakow, 250 miles to the southeast, the crashing of the artillery was so constant that it was said newborn babies were accepting the noise as normal. Since December 21, over a thousand Russian self-propelled 152-millimeter gun-howitzers, refueled by urgently rushed oil supplies from the Estonian shale fields, were mobile again and, together with the 2,037 lighter 122-millimeter guns still in action on the front, were laying down a wall of steel that had already destroyed advanced elements of the Dutch Forty-first and German Third Armored. And with blizzards moving in from the Baltic, advance Allied air cover was soon reduced to almost nil except for the all-weather ground-hugging Tornadoes whose British and German pilots were flying often no more than a hundred feet above ground level, denying Russian antiaircraft radar stations any telltale "bounce-back."

The situation was made even worse for the Allies when the American helicopters, which had performed so magnificently at Fulda Gap when the Russian armored surges had first breached the NATO defenses, now found themselves hampered by lack of refueling depots. The helos, including the redoubtable Black Hawk UH-60—three-man-crewed air cavalry choppers, capable of carrying up to eleven fully equipped troops, antitank and antihelo missiles, plus M-52 mine disposal baskets—were fuel-limited to a hundred minutes in the air. Drop tanks could be fitted, but then the fuel weight/weapons equation shifted dramatically, making the missions doubly dangerous for the pilot. In short, as General Freeman was first to recognize in his forward HQ bunker less than forty miles from Poznan, his armies were the victims of their own success.

"Like small businesses," he had told his aides. "All the business we want, fellas, and too little inventory." After he'd broken out of the Dortmund-Bielefeld pocket, the speed of his advance from NATO's central front had been such that urgently needed fuel, ammunition, and food supplies had either been slowed or stopped altogether in the truck convoys' attempt to keep up with the troops in the blizzards sweeping down from the Baltic and the North Sea. In such weather, artillery notwithstanding, the opinion of most Allied commanders was that neither side could mount major offensives, particularly fighter sorties—NATO air forces, as much as the Soviets, thankful for the respite of the snowstorms so they could attend to the high levels of maintenance demanded by state-of-the-art aircraft. In any case, the pilots of the "super" birds like the F-15 Eagles and MiG Foxbats were presently as worn out as their fighters' engines. Furthermore, apart from the Luftwaffe and RAF risking their Tornadoes in zero visibility, subjecting other billion-dollar airplanes and pilots to dogfights in blizzard conditions was a losing proposition. For the Allied chiefs, it was viewed as a good time to pause and consolidate. In this they were in concert with Washington.

Not so for Douglas Freeman. He wanted to press on.

"Give me a fuel dump, Lord," Freeman declared, studying the headquarters map of the curving Polish front beyond Poznan, "and I'll be in Warsaw in two weeks! In another week I'll be over the River Bug into Russia."

Without turning from the map, Freeman addressed his aide, Colonel Norton. "Jim, I've gotta have gas. By God, we'll fly fuel in here by the pallet if we have to. Like we did it inside the DB pocket. Meanwhile I don't want anybody digging in for Christmas. Get as much as we can as far forward as we can. We can't stop. Attack! Attack! Attack!—that's the strategy. That's the *only* strategy. You start letting troops dig in, they start thinking it's R and R. Start putting up pictures of the girl back home and their dog. Next thing you know, you have to stick a bayonet up their ass to get 'em moving again. No, sir, now we've got the bastards on the ropes—finish them off. That's the plan."

"I needn't tell you it's a risk, General," cautioned Norton anyway. "You could lose everything you've gained."

"I know—I know. It's against every military credo. But all we need is the gas, goddamn it! If we can get the gas up here, we can kick ass from here to Moscow." Freeman paused, arms akimbo, looking up at the huge operations map, shaking his head. "We made one hell of a mistake, Jim—and I'll be the first to admit it—" He paused. "Though I wouldn't want that to get around."

"What's that, General?"

"That we—meaning everybody from the president down—screwed up royally when we thought that once we hit the Russian regulars, all their frappin' republics would take advantage of it. Try like Siberia to break free of Moscow. Even help us. But—" the general sighed, his right-hand glove sweeping over the map beyond the Urals and the Caucasus. "—we should have known. *Mother Russia* isn't politics. It's an emotion. Republics'll hang together to beat us, no matter they hate one another's guts." Freeman lifted a mug of coffee, holding it thoughtfully between his hands, still studying the map. "But I do believe the Baltics will be different. They'll help us. Oh, not much—only a handful of troops compared to the Russians. But—look what Finland did in forty-one, Jim." He put his coffee down, making short, skirting movements about the Russian Baltic seaports. "If they can harass the

Russians, a week, ten days—long enough for us to drive a wedge here, into Lithuania, and out—we can do it, Jim. We can do it."

"I hope so, General."

"So do I." It was such a shocking, unpredictable thing for the general to say—to concede even the slightest doubt—that it had the effect of jolting Norton.

"General."

"No, no." Freeman shook his head. "I have no doubt about my troops. About the ground war. What I'm alluding to, Colonel, is a matter of time. What I'm concerned about is that if we don't hit hard, and fast enough . . ." He paused and took a sip of coffee.

"What, General?"

"That some bastard'll push the button."

Knowing the general as well as he did, what disturbed Norton most was that if the general had seemingly envisaged the possibility of the Russians going nuclear—then Freeman had probably thought of doing it himself.

CHAPTER THIRTEEN

IN ATLANTA CDC—Center for Disease Control—another skull-and-crossbones pin, this one for the state of New York, was stuck into the map of the United States. There were now twenty-three pins clustered along the eastern seaboard, near Chicago and the Midwest, the others sprinkled throughout California, the major clusters of "stings," meaning five or more acts of sabotage, in Silicone Valley, the site of some of the country's leading electronic defense system manufacturers.

What was first thought to be only a New York problem because of the sabotage of Croton, Hillsview, and the other main reservoirs for New York, affecting eleven million people, was now a national crisis, affecting seventy-two million. Over a thousand cases of "arson" had been reported—many of the fires impossible to extinguish by water from city reservoirs because the water, once evaporated, left lethal residues of airborne poison. All but two of the twenty-three cities, Salt Lake City and Portland, declared martial law and curfews in an effort to contain growing crowds clamoring for water supplies. In Norfolk, Virginia, and in Puget Sound, north of Seattle, at the Bangor Sub Base, several nuclear submarines in for maintenance were ordered to stay in port, their salt/freshwater converters providing emergency drinking water for households with a ration of two gallons of water per day for a family of four.

National Guard units throughout the country on "shoot-to-kill" orders surrounded distilleries and bottled water depots, and in Colorado, more Guard units were deployed to turn back ad hoc convoys of armed civilians heading for Aspen and other winter resorts where fresh snow had not yet melted down into the contaminated water tables. Atlanta CDC issued a national alert—so urgent that it could not wait for the chiefs of staff's normal clearance and so was disseminated under President Mayne's "Executive Order" signature. The CDC alert was a warning that because of the poisoning that by now had been conveyed via myriad underground aquifers into the major U.S. water tables, "no water other than rainwater directly trapped by uncontaminated vessels would be safe" for at least three months. When President Mayne realized the enormity of the problem, he knew he was confronted by a danger whose implications posed a greater threat to the public than that posed to Lincoln during the threat of disunion. Already looting and attendant crime were the worst they had ever been.

As the president moved from his White House work study around to the Oval Office to address the nation, the kleig lights seemed to stun him momentarily and he used his notes, with Xeroxes of the Atlanta CDC crisis map, to shield himself from the glare.

"How long have we got?" he asked Trainor, who was grumpily telling the CBS mobile crew to clear the hallway.

"Six minutes, Mr. President," Trainor replied.

As he raised his cup of coffee seconds before going on national TV to try to calm the nation, Mayne looked at the black liquid and put the cup down.

"It's been tested, Mr. President," an aide informed him. "Washington's supply hasn't been affected—so far."

"Why not?" he asked. "Surely the capital would be the prime target?"

"We think," suggested Trainor, "it's a message. U.S. leadership can survive if it comes to terms."

"With what? Chemical warfare?" snapped Mayne.

"With their terms," responded Trainor.

One of the TV crew stepped forward beneath the kleig lights and put a glass of water on the president's desk. There were ten seconds to go. "Take it away," said Mayne, indicating the glass. "Can't show that on television. Cause a goddamn revolution!"

"Get it away!" hissed the TV producer. The red light turned green.

Unbeknownst to President Mayne as he began his speech, red lights all across the frozen tundra of northern Canada and Alaska came on in every one of NORAD's—North American Air Defense—early-warning stations reporting "Bogeys, fifty plus."

It was the third time that week that NORAD jets, engines constantly warmed in the hardened snow-white hangars, scrambled to meet the Soviet bombers who, with all Canadian and American F-18s airborne, turned back before they reached the BI—Baffin Island—circle. Duty officers were watching the operators as much as the big screens. This game of cat and mouse, constantly testing each other's state of readiness, did much more than tell the other side whether you were ready or not, forcing the NORAD fighters to gulp thousands of gallons of precious fuel during each scramble. It also wore down the nerves of potential attackers and defenders alike, especially those of radar operators on the NORAD line, any one of whose "yea" or "nay" could inadvertently start the chain of events catapulting both sides into all-out nuclear war.

Trainor read the message handed him by the TV producer. Ahead of the Pentagon, the wire services were reporting ten massive forest fires, apparently deliberately set and now raging on the north-south spine of the Sierra Nevada, causing the evacuation of over thirty communities and producing a thick pall of smoke and ash over ten thousand square miles in the western United States. As Trainor walked quietly back to the White House press room, he glanced at the monitor, ever conscious of the president's appearance as well as what he was saying. But in this crisis, Trainor knew that it hardly mattered what the president looked like so long as he projected calm—and did not come across as being as stressed out as he was.

Hearing the president's speech en route to Washington, D.C., on Eastern Airlines flight 147 out of San Diego, Frank Shirer, who had been dreaming of Lana, now had a fairly good idea of why he, as one of the top five American aces, had been recalled. What bothered him, however, was that if SAC had recalled him to pilot one of the two "Looking Glass" twenty-four-hour command planes, each E-48 with fifty battle staff and communications experts, a week *before* the president's speech, then things must be much worse now. Or perhaps he hadn't been recalled to fly Looking Glass at all.

Perhaps, Shirer flattered himself, the president, like the country's chief executives before him, wanted a firsthand account of exactly what the precarious Aleutians campaign was like.

Within a few minutes of touching down at Dulles International in Washington, D.C., Shirer would learn he was wrong on both counts.

The sixteen SPETS who carried out the sabotage in New York were among the first citizens to support the president, and joined crowds in burning effigies of Premier Suzlov outside the now boarded-up though still guarded Soviet Embassy. In the next twenty-four hours, more than three thousand reports of sabotage poured in, the most hysterical callers screaming about the vulnerability of the country's nuclear power plants, which had already been placed under heavy protection by National Guard units.

In Detroit it was reported that large concentrations of deadly PCBs, once used in old electric power station generators, had been dumped into Detroit's, and on the Canadian side, Windsor's, water supply. A bottler of "mountain-fresh water" in Cleveland, Ohio, was arrested when tests showed he'd been bottling water that had been contaminated by highly toxic PCBs.

CHAPTER FOURTEEN

DAVID BRENTWOOD'S FIRST shock upon reaching the outskirts of Brussels was to see just how badly damaged the city was. Like so many other soldiers who'd seen action at the front and the terrible punishment meted out by the Russian rocket artillery attacks, he knew that civilian centers behind the front were being hit, but he hadn't imagined it would be as bad as this. Piles of red and yellow brick rubble were everywhere as the train slowly crept in from the southern outskirts, the rockets clearly having made no distinction between residential areas and military targets—not that David could blame Russians for that any more than he could the Allies' artillery for the havoc their short-range rockets were now wreaking on the ancient capitals of eastern Europe, church spires and stained glass mixed in with the rubble of thousands of homes as well as the officially designated targets. There was very little wood around, he noticed, most of it already scavenged for fuel, the Atlantic convoys having been hit again by Soviet sub packs.

His second shock in Brussels was that he had not been summoned to identify any of the SPETS he'd seen in U.S. and British uniform around Stadthagen and who had murdered British and American POWs.

Instead David found himself being escorted by the MP sergeant, then by an American captain, to a rather nondescript, musty-smelling basement room in the pockmarked Brussels HQ. A U.S. Marine major sat at a long plywood table supported by sawhorses in front of a crumbling plaster wall, the major flanked by another American, a captain, on his left, and a British captain to the major's right. It was a recruiting committee for the elite, and now joint, British and American SAS, or Special Air Service, of which little was known by regular units except that elements of the joint SAS regiment sometimes made tactical strikes deep behind enemy lines. They were the British and American equivalent of the SPETS Kommandos, some of whom were believed to be operating in civilian garb behind NATO lines.

David's orders that he was to ID captured SPETS were, as the American army captain from the three-man interviewing board had put it before taking him inside, merely a "cover." "Limeys are very careful about recruitment," the captain explained. "Special Air Service personnel are never identified—not even in their own regiments. It's always put down as a transfer. Anyway, there are no SPETS for you to identify, Brentwood. We haven't caught any." The captain had paused, looking David over carefully before entering the room. "You in the picture?"

"Yes, sir," David answered unenthusiastically. He didn't like it. He'd had enough.

Inside the windowless interview room, he could hear the faint hum of the furnace heat recirculating the cloying dust particles from the bomb rubble above.

"Quite an honor, Lieutenant," the marine major sitting in the center told him.

"Yes, sir." David wasn't sure whether the major was talking about the honor of him having been selected for interview or whether it was meant as a compliment to David's decorations.

There was an awkward silence, the U.S. Army captain glancing up at Brentwood's regulation somber straight-headed gaze, then at the marine major and British SAS liaison captain.

The marine major cleared his throat. "Course, it's purely voluntary, but a man with your experience, Brentwood, would—" He looked at the British officer, who was showing no sign of embarrassment over Brentwood's obvious hesitation. "I think," continued the major, "your experience in Pyongyang and—" he glanced down at a file "—Stadthagen would prove invaluable to SAS."

So that's it, thought David. The major was now pointing out that in keeping with NATO policy, Washington and Whitehall were "actively encouraging" joint Allied participation in both SAS in Europe and further afield in the Pacific, with U.S. Special Forces. It was either Korea, concluded David, or the Russian front.

Then the major threw him the curveball. "General Freeman recommended you—personally."

The British captain, a bent-stem pipe in his right hand, was scooping dark Erinmore Flake from its pouch and palming it into a stringy consistency before stuffing the bowl. "Please don't feel pressed, old man," he told Brentwood. The U.S. Marine major was looking down hard at the pencil he held captive between his burly hands.

"Purely voluntary," the Englishman continued, "as your chaps have already told you. And Heaven knows—Medal of Honor, Silver Star . . . I should say you've done your bit and more. Just thought you might like a crack at it, that's all. Heard so much about you." He smiled, and what made it worse for David, the Englishman's smile seemed genuine, without the trace of irony he'd come to expect of some of the other British officers he'd met. The Englishman was now tamping the tobacco into the pipe's bowl, blowing through it before waving a lighted match back and forth over it. "Just thought you might be a beggar for punishment," he told David congenially. "Getting a bit bored—" he paused to suck in hard on the pipe "—with all those Flemish girls and *couques*. Given your record, thought you might be craving a little action again." The very thought of action produced in David the chilled-bowel feeling he'd experienced before final exams at college, his throat dry, face feeling strangely hot yet cold at the same time, his heart racing, thumping so loudly, he was afraid they might hear it. "Thanks, sir," he said in a parched voice, "but—ah—I don't think I'm fit enough for your SAS or any other—"

"Quite understandable, old man," cut in the British captain. "No apologies needed. We're scouting for new chaps, that's all. We got rather a bloody nose up in Schleswig-Holstein when the balloon went up." He flashed another smile. "Just looking around." Proceeding to draw heavily on the pipe, the Brit winked at him understandingly, then glanced at the U.S. Marine major and Army captain at the same time. "Tell you the truth, if I had half the chance, shouldn't be surprised if I gave the bloody lot up myself. Off to sunnier climes, I should expect. Next to the Pole, Scotland must be the chilliest place on earth."

The mention of Scotland made David wonder if they weren't trying to use the fact of his brother operating out of Holy Loch as a possible lure. But he rejected the possibility as soon as he'd thought of it. They probably didn't even know his brother was there—if he still was. And the last thing the military cared about was trying to reunite family members. In fact, in time of war, it was the *last* thing they wanted to do. Besides, nothing

David could think of could overcome the gut-gnawing fear he seemed incapable of shucking ever since Stadthagen.

The British captain had risen, extending his hand. "Thank you for your time, Lieutenant."

David shook the Englishman's hand. The marine major tried to look understanding but came off as grim. The U.S. Army captain meanwhile had opened the door to take Brentwood down to pick up his travel voucher for the trip back to Liège, where he was to await further orders.

After David saluted and left, the marine major shook his head at his British colleague. "I'm sorry, Captain."

The Englishman held up the pipe in protest. "Not to worry, Major."

"I *do* worry. He's a marine. Hell—I know it was rough at Pyongyang—and at Stadthagen, too, from all accounts. Damn rough! But it wasn't a sustained action. Some of my boys on the Polish front—"

"No doubt, Major," responded the English captain gracefully. "But at Stadthagen the lad was completely on his own, and in that kind of situation, at least in my experience, how long a man's actually been at the front has little meaning. He was captured by SPETS—saw men all around him being murdered in cold blood before he managed to make his break and was hunted to ground again in raging blizzard. Dogs after him. With all that, he kept his head and blew up an ammo dump. After you've been through that lot, Medal of Honor notwithstanding, I should think the nerves are never quite the same. Damned sure mine wouldn't be."

The marine major conceded the point, but true or not, his pride in the corps had taken a blow because of Brentwood's refusal to join the joint SAS team.

"Some chaps do recuperate, of course," the English captain continued, another match scratching, circling the pipe's bowl as he blew voluminous curls of grayish-blue smoke into the high, windowless room. "In Malaya I remember—"

"I don't think so," cut in the major. "In my experience, Captain, once they go to pieces, they stay in pieces. Best thing we can do is ship him home."

The Englishman was expansive in his agreement. "By all means, old chap. He's earned it."

"He has," replied the major, his tone not so gruff now, but the Englishman knew the major, a row of ribbons attesting to his own valor under fire, still didn't approve.

"How about his comrade-in-arms?" asked the Englishman. "Black chappie. Thelman, I think the name was? Another one on Freeman's recommendation list."

"Yes," said the major. "We should try him. They went to Parris Island together."

"Parris Island," said the U.S. captain, turning to the marine major. "Well, at least we know Brentwood's a survivor then."

"I wonder?"

Peter Zeldman, the *Roosevelt*'s executive officer, was enjoying his leave down in Surrey with the Spences following the wedding, knowing nothing of Robert and Rosemary's near brush with what MI6 were convinced had been SPETS "sleepers." Neither did Rosemary's parents, Richard and Anne Spence, until a registered letter arrived one morning for Richard Spence marked "Personal and Confidential." It was Robert's letter of warning about the "charmers" and about a "package" Robert would be sending Richard via Rose when she returned to Surrey.

Till this letter from Robert, the previous postcards of wild, heather-covered Highlands—in reality, rather forlorn and snow-covered at this time of year—had borne no hint to Richard Spence of the danger his daughter and new son-in-law had been in during the final days of their aborted honeymoon. Up to now, the cards, full of a carefree optimism, had been gratefully received by Anne and Richard Spence, whose loss of their son on convoy escort duty still cast a pall over the house. Young William's death was something they knew they had to accept but which they also realized they would never become reconciled to in a world where so often the good seemed defeated by the bad.

Georgina Spence, Rosemary's younger and vivacious sister, was down from the London School of Economics and Political Science for Christmas, but careful not to let Peter Zeldman think for a moment her visit had anything to do with his presence in the house. It was this haughty indifference to him that attracted Zeldman to her. He was sure that behind the sophisticated leftist chitchat and learned allusions, there was a woman waiting to be let out. And he was sure that she couldn't be so naive as not to think how downright sexual she appeared in front of men. The fact that she disdained makeup as a "bourgeois affectation," as he'd overheard her telling her mother, only highlighted her natural beauty, the kind of woman, Zeldman believed, who would look as good first thing in the morning as she had the night before.

After six tension-filled months without a woman, the mere sight of her was a feast—and every time he saw her move, he was tantalized by wondering whether or not she wore a bra. Still, he refused to play a game. There was "no time for dancing," as his Uncle Saul would say. "You want—you ask—you get or you don't get. That's all." Some enjoyed the chase. He enjoyed the sex—all the maneuvering he wanted to do was in bed. He decided he'd give her the weekend to show some interest in him, or rather admit her interest in him, or he was off up to London to take in a few shows and wait for his orders there. Brentwood had told him what a sharp mind Rosemary's sister had. That was nice, but he didn't care. He wanted her body. He'd had enough of her mind. Students at LSE, she'd announced, were going to prepare a "pretty deadly broadside" in a petition to the government on the wartime limits on individual freedom. He said nothing. He'd seen good men die so that she could sign petitions, and the only broadside he had in mind was a chance to get her in bed and "fire all tubes." What bugged him was she knew they were mutually attracted—sexually anyhow. He'd admitted it every time their eyes had met. She couldn't—or wouldn't.

"Close the curtains, will you?" he heard Richard Spence asking her in the living room. "Been a bit overcast tonight, I'm afraid." Spence was referring to the fact that Russian rocket attacks launched from the Baltic usually came over on stormy, cloudy nights when the fighters scrambling from East Anglia had more difficulty seeing them. The problem was that in bad cloud conditions, if the IDD, or identification friend or foe, signals sometimes got jammed, pilots had to go to infrared for air-to-air missile launch, which had caused a number of them to shoot down missiles sent up by their own AA batteries. On occasion, in the split-second world of the dogfight, they'd even shot down friendly fighters in the darkness whose exhaust they'd mistaken for that of an enemy rocket.

Zeldman heard Georgina drawing the drapes shut, and saw her mother, the heavy lines in Mrs. Spence's face belying the determined charm with which she had tried to hide the pain of her son's death.

"We'll be late, dear," she called out to Richard, who still hadn't solved the *Telegraph*'s crossword. Mrs. Spence smiled at Zeldman. "Sure you don't want to come, Commander?

Being a submariner, you might have some very practical suggestions about recycling. I imagine you—''

''Leave him alone, Mother,'' said Richard, folding the paper and at last making a move to haul himself out of the lounge chair. ''I'm sure Commander Zeldman has far better things to do than turn his energies to the Oxshott Recycling Society. Tell you the truth, I'm not sure I want to.''

''Very well. The commander must do as he likes, of course.'' It made Zeldman feel uncomfortable and old, being referred to as ''commander,'' but despite his telling them to call him ''Pete,'' English reserve carried the day.

''Oh, do get a move on, Richard,'' said Anne impatiently.

''Yes, yes,'' he said irritably, reaching for his jacket. ''Suppose I must.''

''Don't come if you're going to be cross.'' She turned to Zeldman. ''Last time he came, he just sat there and harrumphed at the professor.'' As Richard slipped off his bifocals, popping them into his jacket pocket, he explained to Zeldman, ''Professor Knowlton. A bag of wind. Apparently he's got some mad scheme now for the local councils to recycle shoes. Can you imagine? Last thing I'd want to wear is another man's shoes.''

''Here,'' said Anne, holding his scarf out to him. ''Don't be so negative. You thought he was crazy about everyone handing in their hair dryers.'' Helping him on with his coat, she turned to Peter Zeldman. ''When they make those jump-up planes—''

''*Jump jets*, Anne. For Heaven's sake. Vertical takeoff and landing, to be precise.''

''Well, whatever. I'm sure the commander would like to know,'' she added, turning back to Zeldman. ''Did you know that the Harriers—those jets were made from layers and layers of material that had to be hand-dried? Presto! The hair dryers. It was very original. I think they'll give him an OBE.''

Zeldman looked perplexed.

''Order of the British Empire,'' Anne explained.

''*OPE*, more like it,'' said Richard, doubling his scarf about his neck. ''Order of Pompous Eccentrics. Honestly, the man's so inflated with his own importance, it's a wonder *he* doesn't take off.''

''Well,'' said his wife as they went out the door, glancing back at Peter Zeldman and Georgina, ''enjoy yourselves.''

Outside, Richard turned to Anne. ''I hardly thought that was necessary, Anne.''

''What?''

"Telling them to enjoy themselves. Sounds like you're—well—matchmaking."

"I wouldn't mind."

"Good grief, woman, we've just got over Rosemary's wedding. Have you seen our bank account?"

"Oh, stop fretting. It's like chalk and cheese with those two. He's interested, I think, but not Georgina. I'm afraid she considers him 'unsuitable.' "

"She's probably right. Don't mind putting the chap up. Nice enough, and it's our duty really, as the government says. If it wasn't for the American submariners, we'd be starving. Everyone knows that. No, I don't mind billeting the chap at all. Pleasant enough. But we're not obliged to open a marriage bureau. In any case, Georgina's far too young."

"She's twenty-five, Richard."

"Yes, and he's what?"

"Late twenties, that's all."

"I'm not talking number of years," Richard replied. "It's a matter of maturity. She's not ready—"

"Oh, stop fretting so. I told you, she has no interest in him whatsoever. Tell you the truth, she's been rather rude to him. Goes about the house as if he's not there."

"Well, she's studying. Her Michaelmas term paper—"

"Oh, you know what I mean. Or perhaps you don't. Every time I see you, you've got your head stuck in the paper."

"Leave off, old girl." It was said politely but firmly—the danger signal that they were close to reliving the terrible time when they'd heard young William had been killed, Richard retreating for days at a time, saying nothing, reading, burying his grief in his own silence, and the two of them quite apart at the very time they both knew they should have been closest.

They were approaching the parish hall. "A big crowd to hear Professor Knowlton. Now, don't worry, Richard. He's not Georgina's type. Nothing's going to happen."

"My God!" said Richard. "Look at Knowlton. Old fool. Looks like a recycled coat he's wearing."

"Richard! Behave yourself."

"Yes, yes." He glanced up at the brooding sky. Clouds were curdling ominously about one another but not yet a solid sheet of gray.

When the phone rang, Georgina jumped, her nerves on edge because of the expected Soviet missile raid, but as she rose to answer it, she pretended to Zeldman her fright was due to her having been absorbed in one of her textbooks.

"It's for you," she said, surprised.

As he took the phone from her, their fingers touched. He watched her walk away. The phone call was from Faslane, the village near Holy Loch, informing him the post office was holding a "familygram" for him—a fifteen-word message each submariner was allowed over a month. Did he want it forwarded to Surrey? The question about whether he wanted it "sent on" meant, however, that it wasn't from home. Instead, it was a message to him that he must report back to the Sea Wolf within seventy-two hours. He had counted on having several more days at the Spences'—at least till Christmas—if things worked out with Georgina, but now his time with her had suddenly been cut in half.

"Have to leave tomorrow," he said after putting the phone down.

Georgina said nothing.

At 9:17 P.M. the first Russian salvos could be heard several miles away, their distinctive shuffling noise sounding as if they were chopping the air instead of coming at supersonic speed toward their targets. Peter picked up the TV's remote control and turned the television off, for, as well as the increasing Russian salvos, an electrical storm was coming in from the Channel. "Better not use the phone either," he said. "Charge could throw you across the room."

She barely acknowledged his comment, continuing to read in the soft glow of an Edwardian lamp, its light trapped by heavy blackout drapes. Finally the din of missiles exploding came several miles closer. Suddenly the power was out.

"Okay if I open the drapes?" asked Zeldman. She didn't answer.

Looking outside at the garden pond, neglected through the winter, he could see, reflected in its icy surface, the stalks of searchlights starting to cluster and intertwine high in the sky to the east. Beyond the garden, yellow slits of headlights came to a standstill—everything stopping during the raid except for a blacked-out commuter train rumbling through the nearby culvert, making its run for the nearest tunnel.

"Right," said Peter. "I'm off for the shelter. Coming?"

"No, thank you." She said it as if the missile raid were a mere impertinence and that in any event, it was "too bourgeois" by half to go scuttling into the nearest shelter.

"Suit yourself," said Zeldman, walking out through the

wild shrubs of the English garden toward the shelter Richard Spence had dug not far from an old sun house.

In the momentary lighting of the Nike Hercules air defense batteries around Leatherhead, Georgina saw the ugly, leafless vines of morning glory which had strangled the best of the garden, its wild aspect the result of her mother's neglect following William's death. Suddenly, oppressively, the red and bluish flashes of the AA missile batteries nearby, the tang of ozone in the air, the decaying garden, seemed to leap at her in a series of strobe-lit pictures of primeval forces victorious not only in having run riot over the garden, the very semblance of civilization, but over civilization itself.

The Russian rockets were crashing closer and closer, and a rain of red-tailed missiles could be seen plummeting down over Leatherhead and nearby in Oxshott, devastating what had been heavily camouflaged army staging areas.

A salvo of Zhukov J rockets, their long crimson exhausts plainly, if only momentarily, visible, their harsh metallic retching sound rending the air, crashed into the nearby culvert, the explosion blowing out most of the Spences's windows, the living room's heavy blackout drapes sucked frighteningly inward, swirling about her but stopping most of the flying glass.

Zeldman, in the shelter, heard the implosion—glass shattering. Within seconds, drawing the Nansen slide bolt and wrenching the heavy door open, he was racing up the short flight of sunken brick steps as Georgina, her nerve breaking as more salvos rained about the culvert, fled the house toward the shelter.

In another flash of a Nike Hercules battery and the glow of fuel dump fires, the two of them all but crashed into one another in the garden. It would have been funny but for Georgina's frantic panic.

Leading her back to the shelter, Peter Zeldman said little apart from a few quietly given instructions, and sat holding her, stroking her hair, trying to calm her down. For a long time her body remained rigid, tense with fear, but then slowly she yielded—all her pretenses shattered by the closeness of death, their mutual longing unreined by the dull thumps of the rockets' explosions bringing danger ever closer, her fingers tearing into him as he lifted her high against the shelter's damp wall, penetrating her with equally wild abandon, the fullness of her release sweeping over her time and again, the air raid reaching its crescendo, their joy a reverie.

CHAPTER FIFTEEN

IN MONTANA, COYOTES howled in the foothills of Bear Paw Mountain while in the hardened shelters of Strategic Air Command on the snow-covered Great Plains, an air force instructor was telling Rick Stacy and the other eleven silo cadets not to hesitate. "If your partner goes berserk under pressure, you not only have the right but the *duty* to shoot him or her." He paused. None of them showed any surprise—which was good. "Now, the air force has taken great pains to select the best possible people for this job. But none of us knows for sure how we'll perform if things start coming apart—that is, if it comes to a nuclear exchange—if other silos in your sector were to be hit. You all passed A-okay on the simulators, but tomorrow you'll be in silo on solo ride."

Stacy smiled across at Melissa Lange. The instructor saw it, gave no sign of disapproval, but made a mental note that these two were to be kept apart in the two-member team drills. You couldn't stop fraternization. In fact, it could be a stabilizing factor off duty, but you kept them well apart in training and in the silo. Despite the advancement of women in the forces, the no-mixed-sex rule remained inviolate at "Ground Zero."

"There's something else I want to mention," the instructor continued, neat and tan in knife-edged ironed pale blue uniform and tie. "In any crew, you'll find there's a tendency for one partner to become leader by default. Know what I mean, Lieutenant Stacy?"

"Yes, sir. One team member relies too heavily on the other." Stacy looked pleased with himself.

"Not really," replied the instructor. "You're all taught to *rely* on one another, Lieutenant. The problem, however, is when one member *habitually* relies on the other so that in the event of a slipup by the one who's been leading, we are likely to risk either aborting launch or executing an inappropriate release at the critical moment. It is *not,*'' the instructor emphasized, ''a pilot-copilot situation down there. In the silo there are two of you with equal responsibility. You're a team. No one of you can launch. And forget all that BS you've read about a 'string and second key' game where one of you supposedly goes bonkers, shoots the other, and then catapults us into a nuclear exchange by using a connecting string to turn both keys at once. You can't. We fixed it. You need a two-key insert to initiate your launch procedure.'' The instructor paused. ''You got that, Corporal Lange?''

''Yes, sir.''

''Okay. Let's recap before you all head off to get drunk.'' There was a polite ripple of laughter. None of them were heavy drinkers. The air force had carefully checked that out in the psychiatric profile on each recruit. Besides, everyone knew that if they so much as took an aspirin, it had to be reported. If anyone climbed aboard the pickup van and had taken so much as an antihistamine, they'd have to immediately declare themselves DNIA—duty not involving alert. Not to do so carried the same penalty meted out to a fighter pilot who hadn't reported himself DNIF—a verbal reprimand, a fine, and confined to barracks. With launch crews of necessity required to live in and around the silos, being CB meant staying in the plusher SAC living quarters. But in the middle of the snow-covered prairie with all calls automatically monitored, the only recreation was to watch TV, get laid—difficult, given the long duty hours—eat, get overweight, and risk a WRC—weight reduction course.

For some reason Melissa couldn't understand, the U.S. Air Force did not want their missile shooters fat. Rick Stacy, a fitness fiend, postulated that ''excessive poundage,'' in his words, made people slower on the controls. Melissa said she knew a cab dispatcher who was fat, enormous, and the most competent dispatcher around.

''We're not dispatching cabs, Lissa,'' Stacy told her. ''We're into kilotons on the front line.''

Melissa didn't bother pursuing the fact that the front line was five thousand miles away in Europe, and nine thousand in Korea. In a way, she knew Rick was right, but his egocentric habit of automatically assuming the ''front line'' wherever he was annoyed her. Still, he was kind to her, considerate, and in this world where the casualties in Europe and Korea meant that there were about four women for every man back home,

Richard was a better catch than most. And he'd given her good advice. While some of her friends at college had put their professional goals on permanent hold to have a good time, "while the world lasts," as they'd put it, Melissa had signed up for the silo program, which would help pay for her degree. After the war, her degree and experience in such a highly skilled job would stand her in good stead.

In any case, she and Rick, by planning on getting married in the spring, were going to try both for the "good time" and, in Rick's words, improve their "marketable skills."

The only thing she regretted was that Rick was as organized and efficient in bed as he was in class. It was all very purposeful and unerringly "on target," as he so romantically put it. And it was all over in ten minutes. She was reminded of some vulgar engineering student in Portland talking about "slam, bam, thank you, ma'am." Part of the problem was that Rick detested sweat.

Now and then she found herself conscious of the stares of a local contractor, a man the air force used for base and silo support building repairs. He was a big man, very hairy, known to some of the unmarried women team members—and, it was said, some of the married women—as "KITS—Killerton in the SAC." Melissa hadn't been listening to the instructor, idly wondering whether "KITS" referred to his weight on top of you or to his actual performance in bed.

The instructor was rambling on about how "weather bias," such as differences in air density, could cause possible "skipping" of a reentry warhead vehicle and how one way around this was for the kiloton or megaton warhead to effect reentry at a steeper angle than usual, which would make it more accurate, but that this in turn would generate more heat.

"So be alert," said the instructor, "when we're going through PALFIR—which is?" He was pointing at Melissa. Rick Stacy was watching her.

"Prearming," she replied. "Arming, launching, firing, releasing," she added smartly.

"Very good! Okay, that wraps it up for today. Remember, tomorrow you're on solo, which may or may not include a problem with the blast valve. Three ways to clear?" He looked about the room, using a stick of chalk as a pointer. "Johnson?"

"Ah—"

The instructor laughed. "Unfair question. Tomorrow, right?"

"Yes, sir."

Zipping up his parka before going out in the thirty-below "icy hell," as Rick Stacy called it with what he thought was a fine piece of irony, he complimented Melissa on her PALFIR answer. "Right on the button, Lissa. Very impressive!"

"Don't call me that," she snapped.

"What?"

"Lissa."

"What's wrong with it?"

"What's right with it? My name's Melissa."

"Sorreeeee."

In the pickup van, there was a lot of loud talk as the class members unwound. No one spoke of estimating warhead yield, launch reliability factors, or reentry penetration. Only when it was suggested that the PX might have run out of Coors did one of the silo cadets, a tall youth from Louisiana, drawl that if the PX manager hadn't ordered in enough beer, the manager's TKP—terminal kill probability—would be 1.0—absolutely certain.

Melissa ignored the small talk, thinking instead about the bungalow she and another woman trainee shared. The bungalow had developed a leak in the roof. It would be all right for the time being, but once there was any melting, it'd be like a waterfall. "Be spring," Rick said sulkily, "before there's any melting around here."

"You might be right," she said, "but I thought you didn't like my place looking unkempt—the ceiling's stained."

"I don't."

"Well then?"

"Melissa, I have better things to do right now than to mend roofs. We go solo tomorrow, remember?"

"I remember," she said tartly.

"What's gotten into you?" he asked brusquely.

"Nothing."

"Well, if you want it fixed that badly, call Base Repairs. They'll send someone over."

"I thought you liked doing that kind of stuff."

"I would if I had the time. Okay?"

"*Okay*. I'll get Base Repairs."

"Right."

The van suddenly slid on black ice. There was a chorus of "*whoa*"s as it slithered further, then righted itself. It was all very funny, but for a second Melissa felt they were going to go right off the road and smash into the ice-hardened ditch. Life was too short—full of hazard.

CHAPTER SIXTEEN

AS DAVID BRENTWOOD left Brussels headquarters, stepping out onto the wet, black pavement, his mood was one of brooding self-condemnation—about Melissa's letter, the interview board—everything. His dejection wasn't helped any by the ceiling of overcast, drizzling gray clouds so low, they obscured the ornate spires of the Grand Place, or by the British military police sergeant waiting for him under a dark canvas awning. The last thing he needed was the Brit's nonstop patter, full of empty homilies and pubic jokes.

"What ho! Here comes our hero!" the sergeant said. Until then, David hadn't seen Lili with him. The rosy-faced girl smiled with such transparent pleasure at seeing David that momentarily his attention shifted from thoughts of Melissa, whose letter lay like a poison against his chest. So powerful was the effect of the letter that for a moment during the interview, he had petulantly thought of agreeing to join the joint British/American commandos out of pure pique. He'd show her—the bitch. But then the fear of sudden death had prevailed—and now he was glad. Lili's smile beneath the Flemish bonnet was so radiant and open that despite himself, he was smiling, too.

"You have forgotten," she said.

He looked blank.

"Well—are you ready?" she added, full of enthusiasm.

"Oh-oh—that's a leading question," guffawed the sergeant. David wished the MP would evaporate. Lili ignored the Englishman.

"You do not remember," she said, but it was uttered without rancor, almost alluringly. "I promised I would be your, ah—" She couldn't think of the English word, her hands gesticulating impatiently, but even this was done with an infectious eagerness, full of life, of the kind of spirit that David felt had deserted him, what the French call *joie de vivre*.

"My guide?" he proffered.

"*Oui*—yes. My guide."

"Lucky you!" said the sergeant. "Can I come along, too?"

"No." Lili said it with such unequivocal authority, given her age, that David found himself laughing. The sergeant, unamused, mumbled something ending with "bitch," adding officiously, "We're leaving Brussels at sixteen hundred hours. By rights I should accompany you—you being a big hero and all. You're my charge, you might say."

David wasn't listening. He was still watching Lili.

"Hey!" bellowed the sergeant.

"I'm a big boy, Sarge," said David. "You've done your duty directing me to HQ. I can find my way back to the station, thanks."

"Oh—all fit again, are we?"

"Fit enough," said David.

"Ah!" quipped the sergeant. "You signed up then?"

David stiffened. "What do you mean?"

"Come on, Yank," the sergeant said derisively. "The bloody commandos. Beret boys. They asked you to sign on the dotted line. Right?"

"You're in violation of secrecy," said David, looking anxiously around. "You're an MP. You should know—"

"Oh, pardon me, Sir Galahad," retorted the sergeant, buttoning up his greatcoat, one of the blackened brass buttons hanging by a thread. "I didn't realize you'd taken holy orders. And don't tell me my fucking job." He glared at Lili. "Anyway—common bloody knowledge, isn't it?"

"What?" said David, hard-eyed. He felt Lili's arm slip through his protectively, and for a second her perfume of roses washed over him and he was transported to a summer with Melissa, a warm breeze bending and teasing the young grass, Melissa's breasts warm and pliant beneath him. A surge of arousal outstripped his anger and he decided there wasn't any point in pursuing the question of security with the sergeant. The Brit was a little off the deep end anyway. Lili snuggled closer to David in the rain as the sergeant mockingly answered Brentwood's question by repeating it.

"What's common knowledge? For Christ's sake, Brentwood, anyone with half a brain knows HQ's recruiting. Fucking Arabs are threatening the Yids, right? Iraq's going to drop a few CBs on 'em. Right? So we're going to send in some of our heros to the rescue. Right? Or aren't you going?''

Brentwood saw the mad look in the sergeant's eyes again, remembering the first time he'd seen him bellowing down the canal bank. This time Lili's grip on David's arm was one of alarm.

''You're nuts,'' said David before he could stop himself.

''Hey, hey, Yank. Button your beak!'' the sergeant hissed. Lili moved in closer against David, holding him in tighter still.

''All right, old buddy,'' said David placatingly.

''All right then, *eh—eh?*'' The MP was getting out of control.

''David,'' said Lili quietly, ''please—''

As they walked off, Lili's free arm stretching high above her in an effort to bring her floral umbrella over him, the rain was drumming on the canvas canopy of the HQ building, rivulets pouring over the edge, the rain so heavy, it was pitting the snow that still lay in dirty mounds by the sidewalk. The sergeant was shouting after them. ''Better *come* by fifteen-thirty, mate. Or you'll be fucking AWOL. Understand?''

''He is the nuts!'' said Lili, wide-eyed, her bonnet shaking side to side.

David slipped his arm further about her. She told him first she would take him to the Grand Place to show him the four-hundred-year-old gilded Flemish gables surrounding the square; then they would go to the Museum of Art and she would present the ''immortal'' Rubens. ''Do you like the little people?'' she asked.

''Little people? Pygmies—in Brussels?''

''No, no, silly. The puppets.''

He didn't answer, preoccupied with crossing the rain-spattered street in what was now heavy military traffic and still thinking about the sergeant's blatant breach of security. David hated the idea of fingering anyone but knew he had no option. Too bad the sergeant had cracked, and the Englishman couldn't know how much David sympathized, but Brentwood knew if he didn't report what the sergeant had shouted about, a lot of American and British lives might be lost. What, for example, would have happened if Lili Malmédy had been a spy? ''What's that?'' David snapped at her. ''I mean pardon?''

''The puppets. Do you like them?''

''Yes,'' he said. ''Sure—I like puppets. I'll have to make a call, too, okay?''

"Okay." She said it with delight. "It is all right, we have time. After, we will go to the Toone."

"Toone?"

"A puppet theater for—how do you say?—adults?"

"I guess." It made him think of the British Special Air Service captain at the interview saying something about enjoying Flemish girls and what sounded like "Cokes." He pressed Lili for an explanation.

"The same as in your country," she answered. "Fizzy drinks."

"No," said David. "Way I heard it, I think it must be a Belgian word."

"Oh—you must mean a Walloonian, not Flemish."

"Okay," he said. "A Walloonian word."

"Then it must be C-O-U-Q-U-E-S. It is a—" she thought for a moment "—A vast cookie."

"A cookie?"

"Yes. Very large. As big as—" She withdrew her arm from his, holding her hands about two feet apart.

"A *cake!*" he said.

"No, no," she answered, "a cookie," her face suffused with such enthusiasm that momentarily David felt much older. "It is a cookie," she insisted. "You do not believe me?"

He took her hand and looked at her. "Yes," he said, "I do," and her smile told him unequivocally that she loved him.

CHAPTER SEVENTEEN

ROSEMARY STOOD ON the dockside at Holy Loch watching the USS *Roosevelt* slip her moorings from the sub pen inside the huge, floating dock and pass her tender, the USS *Topeka,* as she made her way through the oily calm of the loch past the crushed-stone houses that lined the shore and the magnificent snow-mantled hills of Scotland's western approaches, heading out toward the rougher water south in the Firth of Clyde.

She knew she might never see Robert again, and yet rather than the overwhelming sadness of saying good-bye numbing her as it had the first time, the clean, wintry smell of the loch, the snow-dusted blue of the hills, and the screech of gulls all came to her aid—their wild beauty enough to make the very idea of war seem momentarily unreal. Besides, the strain of these last few hours together before they'd reached the safety of Mallaig had worn her down so that she felt too tired to weep. In any case, with Robert on the *Roosevelt*'s bridge, the last thing she wanted him or any other of the crew aboard to see was a woman bawling her eyes out.

It was time to be strong, to return to Surrey, spend Christmas with her parents, and get on with her teaching again at St. Anselm's in the new term. And to keep herself and "Junior"—Robert still insisted it would be a boy—well nourished, no small feat with rationing becoming more severe, the Allied convoys under constant attack from the Russian subs.

Taking off a tartan scarf Robert had bought her in Mallaig, she waved once more, his captain's cap no more than a blip on the bridge atop the *Roosevelt*'s tall, tapered sail.

Robert had her framed in the circle of his binoculars. She was standing alone on the dock, dwarfed by the hills, and he was afraid for her. The "charmers" aside, who the police had told him had never bothered any of the wives, it was still possible in this war that a Soviet rocket attack from as far away as the Russians' Baltic bases could kill her as easily as a depth bomb could implode his sub, killing every man aboard in seconds.

Now fully provisional and reloaded with the latest D-5 Trident missiles, the Sea Wolf was passing through the aerial arrays of the degaussing station.

Beyond the few small surface craft of the Royal Navy that would run noise interference for him until he reached the more open water of the Firth of Clyde, the best way to avoid detection from either spy trawlers or satellites, which might pick up either the *Roosevelt*'s thermal patch, from even the minute heat exchange of the sub's exhaust systems, or its surface bulge, not visible to the naked eye, was to go deep. As well as the Sea Wolf's speed being greater beneath the water, because of the absence of roiling, depth was the best defense against aircraft with magnetic anomaly detectors looking for the sub and its lethal load of six missiles, each D-5 with a range of six-thousand-plus nautical miles and with fourteen MIRVs, independently targeted reentry vehicles, of 150 kilotons each.

Normally the crew's scuttlebutt would have been alive with rumor of where they were going based on a word here and there around the dry dock. But this trip, it was different. Britain's MI6—its secret services counterespionage branch—had discovered that a spy, a disc jockey on a Glasgow radio station, had, by using letter-for-letter code in his selection of record titles, been broadcasting departure times as well as the names of submarines egressing Holy Loch.

As a result, security at the base had been so tight that the base commander wouldn't even risk verbal instructions to his captains for fear of parabolic directional mikes being beamed in from the hills around the loch. The result was that it was only now that Robert Brentwood, his sub's food supplies the only factor limiting the normal war patrol of seventy-five days submerged, was going down below to Control, forward of the sail. As soon as he was clear of the firth, heading into the Irish Sea, he would dive, and only then would he open up the magnetic-tape-sealed heavy-gauge white plastic envelope to find out where he was going and what his mission was.

"Officer of the deck—last man down. Hatch secured."

Zeldman took up his position as officer of the deck. "Last man down. Hatch secured, aye. Captain, the ship is rigged for dive, current depth one three two fathoms. Checks with the chart. Request permission to submerge the ship."

"Very well, officer of the deck," said Brentwood. "Submerge the ship."

"Submerge the ship, aye, sir." Zeldman turned to the diving console. "Diving officer, submerge the ship."

"Submerge the ship, aye, sir. Dive—two blasts on the dive alarm. Dive, dive."

The wheezing sound of the alarm followed, loud enough for the crew in Control to hear but not powerful enough to resonate through the hull. A seaman shut all the main ballast tanks. "All vents are shut."

"Vents shut, aye."

A seaman was reading off the depth. "Fifty . . . fifty-two . . . fifty-four . . ."

One of the chiefs of the boat was watching the angle of the dive, trim, and speed. "Officer of the deck, conditions normal on the dive."

"Very well, diving officer," confirmed Zeldman, turning to

Brentwood. "Captain, at one-thirty feet, trim satisfactory."

"Very well," answered Brentwood. "Steer four hundred feet ahead standard."

Zeldman turned to the helmsman. "Helm all ahead standard. Diving officer, make the depth four hundred feet."

They were just flattening out at three ninety when Brentwood heard, "Sonar contact! Possible hostile surface warship, bearing two seven eight! Range, twenty-four miles."

Brentwood turned calmly to the attack island. "Very well. Man battle stations."

"Man battle stations, aye, sir," repeated a seaman, pressing the yellow button, a pulsing F sharp, slurring to G, sounding throughout the ship.

Brentwood turned to the diving officer. "Diving officer, periscope depth."

"Periscope depth, aye, sir."

Brentwood's hand reached up, taking the mike from its cradle without him even looking. "This is the captain. I have the con. Commander Zeldman retains the deck."

Beneath the purplish-blue light over the sonar consoles, the operator advised, "Range twenty-four point two miles. Possible surface hostile by nature of sound."

"Up scope," ordered Brentwood. "Ahead two-thirds."

"Scope's breaking," said one of the watchmen. "Scope's clear."

Brentwood's hands flicked down the scope's arms, and, his eyes to the cups, he moved around with the scope. On the COMPAC screen Zeldman could see the dot, moving so fast at forty knots, it had to be a hydrofoil.

Brentwood stopped moving the scope. "Bearing. Mark! Range. Mark! Down scope." Above the soft whine of the retracting periscope Brentwood reported, "I hold one visual contact. Range?"

"Twenty-two point three miles," came the reply.

"Range every thousand yards," ordered Brentwood.

"Range every thousand yards, aye, sir. Range forty-six thousand yards."

"Forty-six thousand yards," confirmed Brentwood. The possible hostile was almost within firing range. "Officer of the deck, confirm MOSS tube number."

"MOSS in for'ard tube four, sir."

"Very well. Angle on the bow," said Brentwood. "Starboard three point two."

"Check," came the confirmation.

"Range?" asked Brentwood.

"Forty-five thousand yards."

"Forty-five thousand yards," repeated Brentwood. "Firing point procedures. Master four five. Tube one."

"Firing point procedures, aye, sir. Master four five. Tube one, aye . . . solution ready . . . weapons ready . . . ship ready."

"Con," said Brentwood. "Not hostile. Repeat not hostile."

It was a British E-boat with a similar noise signature, probably due to repairs on its prop, to that of a 180-foot-long Russian Nanuchka attack boat. It was the fact that the British E-boat had suddenly increased speed to sixty-seven kilometers, at least nine kilometers an hour faster than a Russian Nanuchka missile boat, that had saved her from being sunk by *Roosevelt*.

As he gave the order to stand down from battle stations and began tearing open the "orders" envelope, Robert Brentwood recalled that it was an NKA Nanuchka that had crippled his brother Ray's fast-guided missile frigate off Korea.

With everyone still coming down from battle stations, Executive Officer Peter Zeldman kept a sharp eye on the planesmen and the other crew on watch, making sure the adrenaline didn't find its way into overcompensation in the controls.

Brentwood tore open the envelope then, having read his instructions, spoke calmly, purposefully, into the PA.

"This is the captain speaking. USS *Roosevelt* has been ordered north through the GI Gap to hold stations beneath the ice cap. Duration will be seventy-five days unless otherwise ordered by SACLANT during rendezvous with TACAMO aircraft. This will mean that we'll be in shallow waters part of the time, but we will have air cover from our bases in Greenland on our port flank as we head up, and some long-range ASW aircraft from Iceland on our starboard flank before we're in the safety of Molly Malone and environs." He paused, handing the envelope to Zeldman for countersignature. "Consequently, silent running is the order of the day. Soviets have been dropping buoy-attached hydrophone arrays all over the approaches whenever they can get through our air cover. Same as we do. I might as well tell you that there is no way we can completely avoid the arrays, which may send our signature to Soviet Hunter/Killers, but we can minimize the risk and could luck out. Once we're under the ice, our safety margin increases. If, however, we cannot avoid being heard, we'll be in a fight which we're ready for. That is all."

"Molly Malone?" asked a perplexed cook's helper, his first haul on the *Roosevelt.* A chief of the boat poured himself another coffee, offering the pot around. "Molloy Deep," he explained, "about seven hundred miles from the Pole. Over fifteen thousand feet straight down. Less chance of being detected."

"You mean we just sit there?"

"You hayseed," said a torpedoman's mate. "Christ, three thousand feet's our crush depth."

"What I mean," the chief told the newcomer, "is that there's lots of deep water room so we can keep moving to different launch spots." The chief quickly switching the subject to the chromium guard around the twin silex glass coffeepots. "Those are a bit loose," he told the cook's helper. "Better make sure they're secure. Don't want anything dropping. They'd hear it from here to Murmansk."

"No sweat," put in the cook. "Once we're north of sixty-five, we'll be under drift ice. North of seventy-five, we're under pack. Have a roof over our heads, eh, Chiefie?"

"Don't matter. Fix those guards."

"Will do."

As the chief walked out of the mess, the cook's helper noted, "He doesn't look too happy."

"Ah," retorted the cook, "probably put a packet on us going south—instead of north."

"What's wrong with north?"

"Friggin' dangerous," said a torpedoman's mate. "Ain't nothin' right with it. Fuckin' cold, too."

In Control, Robert Brentwood told the navigator to instruct the Cray NAVCOMP to plot a course for latitude sixty-two degrees north, longitude thirty-two degrees ten minutes west, which would bring *Roosevelt* to a point over the Reykaanes Ridge, south of Iceland. This position would put them 430 miles southwest of Iceland's North Cape before they headed for the narrow Denmark Strait of the GI—Greenland-Iceland—Gap, in parts no deeper than five hundred feet. From there Brentwood intended to execute a zigzag/weave pattern leading eleven hundred miles farther north to Koldewey Island at the southernmost extent of the pack ice that extended like a long, right-handed thumb pointing down from the Pole into the Greenland Sea.

In all, the war patrol would run west of Scotland to Reykaanes Ridge, then north beyond Koldewey Island to the fifteen-thousand foot deeps along the Fracture Zone around

Spitzbergen Island, putting the Sea Wolf between Greenland's northern reaches and northwestern Russia. In all, the journey of around three thousand miles would normally take her the best part of four days at her flank speed of thirty knots plus. But moving more slowly, at a third of her speed, so the cooling pumps would not have to work so hard, therefore limiting the sub's noise, the slower trip, while navigating through the ice fields and the southward-flowing East Greenland Current, would take around thirteen days.

While the Greenland-Iceland Gap was known to mariners at large as the GI Gap, to the NATO sub crews it was the "Gastro-Intestinal Tract"—the one where ships' quartermasters recorded a higher than usual consumption of Pepto-Bismol as drift ice, calved from the pack ice, ground together all around you like a giant grinding his teeth. It also added ominous and forbidding tones to the sound waves coming in via the Sea Wolf's towed passive sonar array, which was integrated with the conformal bow-mounted passive hydrophones. Which meant it could confuse sonar operators.

Brentwood bent over the chart, carefully circling the six stations he would have to maintain in the Arctic deep, ready on a moment's notice, should the occasion ever arise, to attack one or all of the more than forty-five Russian navy, army, and air force bases on Kola Peninsula—from the ice-free ports of Polyarnyy and Murmansk in the west as far east as Amderma on the Kara Sea and Uelen on Siberia's edge that looked out on the Bering Sea, less than a hundred miles from Alaska and only eleven hundred miles from Unalaska, where his sister, Lana, was stationed.

CHAPTER EIGHTEEN

AS COMMANDER OF all U.S. forces in Europe Gen. Douglas Freeman left Brussels with four F-18 fighters escorting him on the first leg of his circuitous ten-thousand-mile journey to Korea via a U.S. stopover where he would secretly consult with the president at Camp David, Freeman's look-alike, seconded from the Fifth Canadian Army's entertainment battalion, left the icy barrens of Newfoundland for the flight across the pole to Brussels' NATO headquarters.

David Brentwood and Lili were in the Brussels gallery, admiring the Rubens, which, along with other masterpieces, had been relegated to a rather poky basement of the museum because of the possibility of Soviet rocket salvos.

He admired Lili's knowledge of Rubens and other painters—Caravaggio, Bernini, Berckhuide, and Hals—he'd never heard of. Her mention of them made him feel "provincial," as his sister, Lana, and probably Melissa would have teasingly called him. He even felt prudish in front of Rubens's voluptuous women, whereas Lili talked about them at a deeper level with such affection and knowledge of detail that it was clear she had been nurtured by such paintings and felt a need for them, as much a part of her life as baseball was to him. His older brother, Robert, had written home in much the same vein about his fiancée, Rosemary, who taught Shakespeare.

It made David feel slightly inferior to Lili, despite the fact that he was older. But she had none of the pomposity of some of the self-proclaimed aficionados of art who flaunted their disdain for the neophyte.

He tried to understand the paintings, but at heart displayed more curiosity about how they were done than what they depicted. But Lili put him at ease, telling him he shouldn't even try to explain them. "It is better to feel them, David," she advised, happy with the joy of showing her handsome young American the best of her culture. "Do you feel them?" she asked.

He thought for a moment. "I suppose so. They look warm—"

"Yes!" she said triumphantly, squeezing his hand in delight. "Rubens always makes it come alive so." She glanced about the basement gallery. "Of course, they are not in a very nice setting, and the light is not good."

"It's fine," David assured her. "Makes them seem cozier."

She didn't understand the word. He explained by pulling her closer to him, to the stern disapproval of the security guard, and David felt the happiest he'd been since—he couldn't remember when. He told Lili. She said nothing, putting her head on his shoulder as they sat in silence on the bench in front of a Vermeer, each lost in one another until reluctantly David reminded her they must soon head for the train station.

"If only we could stay," she said, sighing. "Forever."

"We will," he said. Perhaps, he thought, remembering his mother's time-honored adage, God did work in mysterious ways. Perhaps Lili would take away the pain of losing Melissa.

"A penny for your thoughts?" said Lili, looking up at him.

"What—oh. I was thinking we'd better be going or the mad sergeant will have me down as AWOL." David stood up, searching for change in his pocket. "Which reminds me, I forgot to make that call. There a phone somewhere?"

"You can call from the station."

"All right."

As he waited for the British captain to answer, David realized that any line in NATO HQ might well be tapped by anyone from NATO's own intelligence to a SPETS undercover operative, and so he spoke to the British captain in deliberately vague terms about hearing news from a sergeant that perhaps HQ Brussels should know about.

"Oh?" said the captain, his tone clearly one of interest. "Then I think perhaps you'd better give us a verbal if you don't mind. Don't worry about your train. We'll lay on a driver to fetch you from the station and you can catch up with the train around Ezemaal. It has to stop at a few places to pick up more wounded anyway."

"I thought the line had been cut," replied David. "By SPETS or—"

"Yes, it was, but our erstwhile Belgian Railway chaps have put it right again. Don't worry, Lieutenant—I promise you

you'll catch up with your girl." David looked unhappily out of the phone booth at Lili. "Okay," he told the captain. "But can you send your driver right away?"

As he left the phone booth, David saw the sergeant, rheumy-eyed, looking as if he was drunk, giving Lili a flower, a single red rose. Where the hell had he got that? David walked up and, nodding curtly to the sergeant, turned to Lili and told her HQ wanted to see him again. "Oh no—" she said, the disappointment in her eyes making him wish his conscience had never prompted him to make the call about the sergeant's big mouth being a walking security risk.

"I won't be long," David assured her.

"Been a naughty boy?" said the sergeant, his breath reeking of beer. How the hell the man had become a military policeman, David couldn't fathom, and no longer cared much if he showed his disapproval of the sergeant's behavior. The Englishman's eyes narrowed. "What's up with you, Yank? Look like you've lost your virginity."

"I have to report back to HQ."

"Joining it, are you?"

"Joining what?" David parried.

"Bloody 'ush-'ush brigade?" spat out the sergeant.

David turned to Lili. "You okay?"

"Course she'll be okay, you bloody twit!" said the sergeant, lifting his head so fast as he spoke, he almost lost his balance. "She'll have a bloody trainful of wounded coming south from Hasselt. She'll have her hands full, mate." He winked lewdly at Brentwood. "If you get my meaning!"

"For two bits I'd punch you out," said David, taking a step forward.

"Bloody try!" snarled the sergeant. "C'mon, bloody try."

"You're drunk."

"Don't say—" the sergeant slurred contemptuously. " 'S'at a fact, Yank? And what're you?"

Ignoring him, David turned back to Lili. "Won't be long," he said, taking her hand for a moment, squeezing it reassuringly. She was holding the rose limply by her side in her left hand. Where in the hell, David wondered again, did the crazy sergeant manage to find a rose in the middle of winter—in a war? The sergeant no doubt knew the black market in the Belgian capital.

"See you at Ezemaal," he told Lili, and gave her a peck on the cheek.

As he walked down the platform toward the entrance, he

passed a long line of Belgian reserve medical corps moving collapsed tier hospital bunks into the first four carriages, French reinforcements and an American engineer company bound for the front being informed that they'd have to vacate the first four cars and move back to the rear of the train to leave enough room for the wounded who would be coming down from Hasselt.

When David turned at the entrance, he looked back in Lili's direction, but she'd disappeared among the troops.

The sergeant slouched into the phone booth, noisily inserting francs into the slot. The voice on the other end was friendly, almost desperately chipper: "Hello, Captain Smythe here."

The military sergeant identified himself.

"Yes, Sergeant?"

"He's passed with flying colors, sir. I've done everything to goad him. Insulted his piece of skirt. No go. Bit annoyed, mind—but held himself in check. Lots of self-discipline."

The sergeant could hear the captain exhale. "Pity he declined then, Sergeant. Just the kind of man we need."

"You going to have another crack at him, sir?" asked the sergeant.

"Yes. But I doubt he'll change his mind. Still—I appreciate what you've done, Sergeant. Let's know if you have any other chaps you think could do the job."

"Will do. Sorry he didn't turn out, sir. Thought he was made of sterner stuff. Maybe we could take another run at him in a month or so?"

"I doubt it, Sergeant. Especially given young Miss Malmédy. Good-bye."

"Good-bye, sir." It took the sergeant a second to remember "Malmédy" was Lili's last name. No flies on the SAS.

Captain Smythe's prognosis was borne out by David Brentwood. Upon arriving at HQ, Brentwood was clearly anxious to rejoin Lili after telling Smythe, albeit reluctantly, that in his opinion, the sergeant who had accompanied him to the SAS interview was a serious security risk, having blabbed something on the way out about an SAS attack against the Arabs.

Smythe thanked him and asked, "I don't suppose you've changed your mind—about joining the team?"

"No, sir. I haven't."

Typical Brits, thought David. Always making it sound like they were merely asking you to join a cricket club. One British officer he remembered insisted on referring to the whole war as the "unpleasantness."

"Very good, Brentwood," Smythe reacted heartily. "Don't mean to press you."

Like hell, thought David, who, before he left, turned to Smythe. "Sir—I've heard quite a few rumors about some kind of action in the Middle East—against the Arabs. No specific targets—until the sergeant, that is."

Smythe took his pipe out of his pocket, turning it upside-down, smacking it hard against the heel of his boot, then blowing through it, little pieces of charcoal flying out into the wastepaper basket. "Well, of course, it's hardly news—I mean, the possibility of us going into the Gulf, with Iraq threatening to go to war again with Iran. If that happened, it's possible, of course, we'd have to put pay to that chappie in Baghdad. We simply cannot tolerate disruption of oil supplies."

Smythe seemed to Brentwood far too unconcerned about the voluble sergeant mouthing off about an Allied attack against the Arabs. The British captain put his arm around David's shoulder as he escorted him toward the door. Momentarily it made David wince, but the Englishman's gesture was purely that of a comrade—or was it? he wondered. Or was he worrying about nothing? Again he realized how badly his whole sense of his own self—the confidence of his own masculinity and of the world around him—had been shattered by the nerve-pounding experiences of Pyongyang and Stadthagen. It was something he couldn't explain to anyone who hadn't been through it. War, he had once thought, was supposed to clarify conflicts—the enemy was there, you were here. But war had only made *his* life, at least his inner life, extraordinarily more complex. He felt at war with *himself*—his psyche a battlefront, never clearly defined and as changeable as any free-floating anxiety, constantly shifting in its attempt to escape a flak of uncertainty.

"Truth is," Smythe assured him, "we've been feeding the sergeant a lot of 'cockamamy' plans. He's known as 'Flapper Lips' around here, you know. Anyway, point is, everyone expects NATO to hit if the Iraqis and Iranians become difficult. So we might as well plant a few fake rumors about the actual targets to give us cover."

Cover for what? David wondered, but knew better than to ask. If he wasn't willing to volunteer for the "team," he had no right to know. Besides, he understood the general strategy well enough. The allies were simply going to have to punch out the Iraqis à la Desert Storm if they threatened to stop the oil. You'd have to go in and kill them to go on killing elsewhere. It was necessary and mad—like the sergeant.

"Thank you for coming, Lieutenant," said Smythe graciously.

"No problem, sir."

"Ta ta."

Outside the HQ, David waited impatiently for the Humvee from the transport pool to arrive.

The train had left fifteen minutes ago, and car traffic, he knew, would be slow due to the endless convoys heading east to Liège and on to the front. The driver was a British corporal, and David asked him if he thought they could get to Ezemaal in forty minutes.

"Dunno about that, Lieutenant," said the cockney, shaking his head morosely. "Bit of a squeeze."

"There's a ten in it for you if you can," David promised him.

"Marks or dollars, sir?"

"Fussy, aren't you?"

"Begging the lieutenant's pardon. Not fussy, sir. Practical. Dollar's worth more right now."

"Dollars," said David.

"Right you are, sir," said the driver, his mood suddenly upbeat as he rushed a yellow traffic light, an MP whistling and waving his baton to no effect. The driver was correct, thought David. You had to be practical. Look after yourself. No one else would.

"What does 'ta ta' mean?" David asked the corporal as the Humvee weaved its way through the Brussels traffic past the high gables of the Grand Place. "I guess it means good-bye, right?"

"Sort of," commented the corporal, turning sharply into one of the fashionable redbrick alleys leading from the Grand Place. "Not good-bye exactly—more like till we meet again."

"Hmm," mused David. "I don't think so."

Once on the highway heading eastward toward Liège, the corporal drove dangerously. "Get out of the bloody way!" he shouted, looking in the rearview, shaking his head at Brentwood. "Women drivers!"

David wondered if Lili drove. Melissa did.

CHAPTER NINETEEN

THE THING THAT puzzled Canadian Forces Base Esquimalt at the southern tip of Vancouver Island—the listening post for the U.S. and Canadian SOSUS network—was that the undersea hydrophone should have picked up a sub that had attacked a Canadian coastal steamer, the MV *Jervis*. The steamer, alerted by her shipboard lookout, had actually seen the wave of the torpedo that had struck her and failed to explode—a standard Soviet 530-millimeter-long fish of the type that had decimated the NATO convoys. What worried Esquimalt was that the SOSUS hydrophones should have heard the enemy sub much earlier. No matter how silent a nuclear sub was, its reactor wasn't noise-proof, and the reactor couldn't be shut down because it would take hours to "cook up"—suicidal for an operational sub as it would give ASW forces ample time to reach the area and pound it with ASROCs and depth charges. Besides, without the sub's prop going, it would not have been able to stalk the ships it attacked.

It continued to be a mystery until the CNO's office in Washington, on advice from COMSUBAT—Commander Submarines Atlantic—in Norfolk, Virginia, informed Esquimalt and Bangor, Washington State, Trident and Sea Wolf Base eighty miles to the south of Esquimalt that the reason a Russian sub had got so close to them was that the Russian navy yards at Leningrad and elsewhere must have improved even further on quietening their props after the gigantic advantage given them by the Walker spy ring and by Toshiba's sale in the 1980s of state-of-the-art prop technology to the Russians.

Either that, said Norfolk, or the SOSUS listening network of hydrophones on the sea floor had been cut or, more likely, "neutered" by synthesized noise "override," producing fake yet natural-sounding sea noise that would be interpreted by the

SOSUS's monitoring teams at Esquimalt and Bangor as phytoplankton scatter, or, as the sonar operators called it, "fish fry."

In any event, it was decided that deep-diving submersibles out of Vancouver should be used to inspect the network in the area of the attack. But if they were wrong about fish fry, Norfolk warned, it would mean that the United States had suddenly become vulnerable to close-in ICBM sub attack—America could be blindsided.

There was no malfunction in the SOSUS, however—the "sonograms" called up on the computer showed that like a seismograph picking up the slightest tremor, SOSUS had had no difficulty picking up the sound of the dud Soviet torpedo hitting the steamer, which had been well within the supposed impenetrable Anti–Submarine Warfare Zone. Something was wrong.

CHAPTER TWENTY

THE MOMENT FRANK Shirer was told he wouldn't be flying "Looking Glass" and instead was given the innocuous, flesh-colored eye patch from the outgoing pilot at Andrews, he understood his mission and was immeasurably depressed. He knew it meant his chances of seeing Lana for the next several months were zilch.

Oh, he realized full well that he was being accorded the highest honor—the "True Grit" or "Duke" eye patch the ultimate accolade a flyer could receive, its recipient being the man in whose hands the fate not only of America but of the West might reside.

"What's the matter with you?" asked the outgoing pilot. "Look like you've been poleaxed."

Shirer glanced down at the patch. "Yeah."

"Christ, man, this is it. As good as it gets. What d'you

want? You'll have to beat pussy off with a stick. Top Gun Shogun—that's what you are, buddy."

Shirer looked up at him. "What if the balloon goes up?"

The other man shrugged. "That's the downside. Comes with the territory. Hell, if I could stay on, I'd—" The man didn't finish.

Shirer thanked him, shook hands, and walked out on the tarmac toward the cavernous hangar containing the six-story-high "Taj Mahal," the most sophisticated command plane in history. He had mixed emotions. In a sense, coming back to the $400 million Boeing 747B was like coming home to the job of test pilot he had had before the war, as one of the elite, selected from among the top guns of the top guns—the few who were entrusted with the responsibility of flying Air Force One in the event of nuclear war. More important than Looking Glass.

The sight of the huge plane took him back before the war and to the day of the outbreak of hostilities, when, from the pool of peacetime Air Force One pilots, he'd requested active service with the F-14s. And now it had come full circle. They had recalled him. Which either meant that some member of the Taj Mahal's "pool" had cracked or was over forty, considered too old for the quick reflexes necessary should the president find himself aloft in a "nuclear exchange."

The conversation he'd had with the outgoing pilot had unsettled him, not only because piloting Air Force One would mean he and Lana would be separated longer than he'd thought, but because if nuclear war broke out, the Aleutians, where America herself had tested the A-bombs on Amchitka, would be a prime target for the Russians' ICBMs on Kamchatka Peninsula. Even those Americans, like Lana, at Dutch Harbor and the other easternmost islands of the chain close to Alaska which were not directly targeted would be in the path of the radioactive clouds, carried swiftly via the millimaws, engulfing the islands in the fallout. Lana and everyone else would die of radiation poisoning—a lingering, painful death which Shirer wouldn't wish on his worst enemy—not even La Roche.

The young communications lieutenant aboard Air Force One was eager to show him the latest wizardry, pointing proudly to a signal jammer. "Course, we'd still use basic flares against heat seekers as the first line of defense against incoming. Trouble is, Russians have reportedly got the French R-50 Air-to-Airs. They don't go for heat but home in on the radar beam."

"No kidding," said Shirer. The sarcasm was out before he could stop himself.

"Sorry, sir. Guess you're familiar with all this stuff."

"No," Shirer answered. He pointed to a console that he knew was another radar beam jammer. "What's that?"

"Echo delay mode, sir. Slows down the Bogey's radar pulse—so he gets the echo later than he normally would. Thinks his target is further off than it is."

"What happens if we're in the missile's path anyway?" Shirer asked.

"Console also has CDC—chaff-dispensing capability."

Shirer smiled despite himself. Give the military manufacturers a simple idea and they'd give it a fancy name to impress the congressmen on the defense budget committees. " 'CDC'—you mean it drops foil strips to scramble enemy radar?"

"Yes, sir. But we do have electronic jammer backups as well. This baby's got over two hundred and forty miles of sheathed wiring. Sixty-one antennas."

Shirer wasn't sure an electromagnetic pulse could be prevented by sheathed or "condom" wiring, as the technicians called the pulse-resistant fiber-optic cable. It was certainly better than the old microchip circuits, which an electromagnetic pulse would certainly knock out and which had been replaced to some extent by gallium arsenide chips. But he wondered aloud whether the cables could survive a close-in nuclear air burst.

"Ah—manual doesn't give minimum air burst radius, sir."

"Didn't think they would," said Shirer. "Don't think we'd like the answer."

The lieutenant was quickly getting teed off with the new pilot, as he told the ground crew later. "He's a moody son of a bitch," the lieutenant charged.

"Heard he was an okay guy," put in one of the electronic engineers. "One crackerjack of a pilot, by all accounts. An ace, my man!"

"Yeah—well, I'm not the fucking enemy."

"Probably lonesome for his missus," put in the engineer. "Though I thought they liked bachelors to drive the beast. No family to think about—might stop the trigger finger."

"Dunno whether he's married or not," said the lieutenant disinterestedly.

"Well," put in another technician. "Maybe something else is buggin' him. Maybe he's been drinking tap water."

"Then he wouldn't be sick," said the engineer. "He'd be dead."

"Could be he's lovesick," said another of the ground crew.

"I don't give a shit," said the communications lieutenant. "Whatever his problem is, I'd rather not be one of his crew if it hits the fan."

"Don't worry," said the engineer, tearing open a sugar packet, letting it stream into his coffee. "It won't go nuclear."

CHAPTER TWENTY-ONE

NORMALLY DAVID WOULDN'T have shown such irritability. Maybe it was the bad weather, the overcast still so low, you could almost touch it, and the rubble from the Soviet rocket attacks still not cleared, partially covered by snow turned dirty from the coal fire pollution—or "bad ions in the air," as his brother Ray would have said.

Whatever the reason for his mood, the Gallic shrug of the stationmaster at Ezemaal thirty miles east of Brussels bugged him. He suspected the man could speak English but was refusing to do so on principle, continuing to rattle away in either Flemish or French. As the unhelpful stationmaster walked on by them, a porter nearby told David slowly and clearly, *"Un train est déraillé! Près de Roosbeek."*

"Son of a bitch!" said David, turning and walking quickly back to the Humvee.

"Come on," he yelled to his driver, Corporal Parkin, who had just started to relax with a cigarette. "Let's go! They say a train's been derailed."

"Ours?"

"Don't know—at Roosbeek. You know it?"

"Not to worry, chief. Got a Michelin in the glove box. Has to be on the line 'tween here and Brussels, doesn't it?"

"Right," said David, with more optimism than he felt.

"Why don't we just go on to Liège, guv?" suggested Parkin. "It's not too far. Wait there. Nothing much we—"

"No!" said David. "Train's full of wounded. Need all the help they can get. Besides, I know some people on it."

"Oh. Yeah—well, that's different, in't?"

The stationmaster was coming back down the platform. Glancing quickly at them, his mood changed. "Be careful," he told David. "You must have your identification ready. There will be many people there by now."

"What you mean, guv?" put in the corporal, calling out over the rattle of the Humvee engine. "Lots of people?"

The stationmaster shrugged, as if the answer were surely obvious to all. "Police, the army—they might still be around, you see."

"Why?" asked Parkin.

"The SPETS, of course. It was they who attacked—"

Before the Belgian could finish, Parkin had unclipped his seat belt, reaching down into the backseat. He produced a red light, its magnetic base thudding on the roof over him as he plugged its adapter into the dashboard lug.

As they sped back from where they'd come, having to use several detours because of rocket damage to the main Brussels road, David told himself it probably wasn't Lili's train anyway. There were dozens—goods trains, troop trains, passenger—every day. Had to be one of the busiest lines in all Europe.

The red light swishing in the mist produced a surreal pink glow. David wasn't sure an illegal MP light was a good idea. It'd get them there faster, but if there were SPETS around, it could draw fire. Momentarily he was ashamed he was thinking about his safety rather than Lili's, but then again, his marine training had conditioned him against drawing undue attention to himself in any battle zone.

"Don't worry, sir," Parkin assured him. "SPETS would've been after them for the front—the troops. Wouldn't bother with anyone else on board. Anyway, this bird of yours—she's a noncombatant. Right?"

As if that made any difference, David thought. "More noncombatants are killed than soldiers, corporal. Besides, you obviously don't know about the SPETS." As he spoke, David instinctively felt for his .45 sidearm. "You carrying any weapons?" he asked Parkin.

The corporal was shocked by the suggestion. "Only my rifle—in the back. Haven't fired it since me national service. That was two years—" He paused. "Ah, not to worry, sir. The SPETS're hit-and-run types, right? Won't bother us. Hardly gonna go runnin' around in uniform, are they? Civilian garb, most likely."

"Allied uniforms," said David, not taking his eyes from the fields, dim outlines of farmhouses, and gaunt, stripped poplars racing by. "They've got nothing to lose. They'd be shot as spies either way, in civilian garb or military."

There was another flashing red light ahead and Parkin started pumping the brake. The Humvee slowed and though visibility was poor, they could soon make out six or seven men, all with submachine guns, possibly in Belgian military uniform, waving them down. Off to the right ahead, David spotted at least fifteen more—spread out—the same number to his left—all in all, a U-shaped formation running down either side of the road, the road blocked by two 3-ton trucks parked so they overlapped each other in a tight V—so you'd be forced to drop to five kilometers per hour in order to negotiate the S-turn.

"Bound to be our blokes, right?" proffered the corporal unconvincingly.

"Don't know," said David softly, watching the officer approaching him. "You any good at reversing this jalopy?"

"Not now," said the corporal. "No way." He was looking in the rearview mirror. The U-shape had closed to an O, with three men about twenty yards behind them advancing, submachine guns at the ready.

"Out!" shouted the officer ten yards in front of the Humvee. "With your hands up!"

"They're not Belgians," said the corporal. "English is too bloody good."

"Don't know," answered David quietly.

"I could try a run," said the corporal, his foot hovering above the accelerator. "We'd hit the ditch but take a few . . ."

"Out! Turn off the engine. This is an order! You!" The officer in a black beret was pointing the gun directly at Brentwood. "The holster. Take it off!"

Parkin switched off and David did as he was told, slowly, while trying to make out the insignia of the Belgian regiment. He became aware of a faint tinkling sound, like an old steam kettle all but boiled dry, its metal flexing, giving off the most mournful sound he'd ever heard.

It was only as the officer moved forward that he saw what it was. Beyond the roadblock, across the canal, the locomotive sat deserted, derailed, its boiler punctured, steam bleeding from it like vaporous ghosts floating this way and that until the white became absorbed by the gray of the mist.

There were small groups of men watching, further back behind the locomotive, their figures fading in and out of view in the mist, which, rising for a second, revealed a line of khaki trucks. Further beyond the train, on the canal's north side, off to his right, David saw a line of other figures, the sticklike projections of their rifles visible now and then as a breeze flustered the mist, which continued to roll across from the canal.

"Looks like a bloody firing squad!" said Parkin, joking uneasily. "Ah—bound to be our blokes."

"Taisez-vous!"—"Silence!"—said one of the soldiers on the road.

"Venez avec moi!"—"Come with me!"

"What's your business here?" demanded the senior Belgian officer, a colonel, his military police checking David Brentwood's ID as closely as the railway inspector had at Ezemaal. The other Belgian officer who'd escorted him and Parkin down the road had now turned back to the roadblock.

"I've got a friend on the train," David told the colonel.

The Belgian looked at David's face and back at the photograph. "All right, you may pass through," he said, returning the ID cards. "But don't get in the way of the ambulance teams. Wait until they tell you it's all right."

"The stationmaster at Ezemaal," said David, "told me SPETS had hit the train. Is that true?"

"Yes."

Neither in the fright-filled, bloody, and often confused fighting at Pyongyang nor the bone-chilling terror of Stadthagen—the bared teeth of the German shepherd at his throat near the ammunition dump—had David Brentwood felt as he did now, standing on the platform of the first carriage of the still mist-shrouded troop train. As David moved aside while the stretcher bearers negotiated the tight right-angle turn from the carriage down the steep steel-grate steps to the spongy turf, Parkin was standing by the nearest of the six ambulances, talking to one of the Belgian drivers. First aid attendants, who had at first swarmed over the train, were now poking carefully through the chaos on a second sweep. "How many survivors?" Parkin asked the driver.

"Don't know. We were among the last ambulances to arrive. But not many, I expect. When the SPETS hit, my friend, it is total." He offered Parkin a cigarette, which the Englishman eagerly accepted. "They leave no one," continued the Belgian, flicking open his lighter, "who might be able to identify them, you see."

"Course," said Parkin, cupping his hand around the flame. "Silly bloody question really."

"Ja," said the Belgian with a distinct Flemish accent. "They are marksmen, those ones, believe me. They are the best those bastards have got." The Belgian nodded toward the canals and poplar woods beyond. "Probably miles from here by now."

David overheard the conversation, but something, he couldn't explain what, told him Lili was alive. The next stretcher he saw coming out had the military police sergeant on it—a neat hole above the left ear—the small hole and dark color of the blood telling David the sergeant had been killed by an expert shot, quickly and some time ago. It fueled David's hope, for it meant the ambulance teams had probably left all the really hopeless cases till last, first having taken all the survivors, few though they may have been.

"Why aren't they using body bags?" asked Parkin tactlessly but with the directness of natural curiosity. "Poor buggers can hardly get 'round them corners with those friggin' stretchers." As if to underline his point, a swirl of thickening mist swept up against the carriage, momentarily hiding the ambulance team from view, the man carrying the front of the stretcher not having yet touched ground. The man stumbled for a moment, and had it not been for David helping the man at the rear of the stretcher to take the weight, the sharp angle of the stretcher would have caused the dead sergeant to slide forward beneath the restraining straps onto the sodden grass.

"Ran out of body bags," explained the Belgian driver. "Used over sixty already. We're running out of everything."

"How come?" asked Parkin, surprised. "Thought ruddy Antwerp and Ostend were fair flowin' over wiv supplies."

"Some more trouble with the convoys from America, they say."

"Blimey—I thought we'd fixed that lot."

"So did everyone else," shrugged the Belgian. "But apparently the Russians have something up their sleeve. New sonar, I guess."

Parkin was watching the ambulance men bringing off more of the dead.

"Jesus!" said Parkin. "They wipe out all the reinforcements?"

"*Ja.* Shot every one of them. Train staff as well and the hospital cases—the wounded."

Parkin could hear steam bubbling away, and he swung angrily toward the still locomotive. "Why the hell doesn't somebody turn that friggin' thing off?"

The engineer is dead, too," said the ambulance driver. "No one here, I think, knows how to shut it off."

"I'll have a go," said the corporal.

A whey-faced ambulance man emerged from the end of the third carriage and began to negotiate the steep stairway.

"Excuse me," began David.

"*Je ne parle pas anglais,*" said the stretcher bearer, using his head to indicate the driver who'd been talking with Parkin, who was now climbing aboard the engine whose mournful dying sound seemed to fill the forlorn field.

"Can I help you, sir?" the driver asked David.

"Is it all right if I go in now?" David told him. "Have a look around?" The driver spoke to one of the ambulance men, who managed to shrug despite the weight of the dead body—a marine, his arm in a cast, face jaundiced-looking and frozen in pain.

"They say you can have a look," the driver told David. "But do not move anything. More ambulances are on the way. The police may want photographs."

"What for?" put in Parkin, returning down the track. "Nothing to investigate, is there?"

The Belgian driver shrugged. "Regulations."

Parkin drew heavily on the cigarette. "Regulations ain't gonna help those poor bastards," he said, looking at the ambulances filling up on this, their second trip, eight shrouds in each, dead laid out on the wet grass for the additional ambulances on the way.

David hesitated before going in as Parkin, heading on down to the other end of the carriage, called out, "Beg pardon, Lieutenant, but what's she look like?"

"About five four," said David, entering the second to last carriage, looking at the slumped bodies which the ambulance men still had to clear. "Blue eyes—" he told Parkin.

"Very good, sir, but I mean, what was she—is she—wearing?"

Brentwood tried to think, recoiling from the stench. "Well, she had a sort of yellow raincoat on—the kind fishermen wear over here—"

"Slicker," said Parkin. "Right, but I mean, she wouldn't be wearing a coat in the train—probably bit stuffy in here before—I mean, not when she was busy looking after the wounded—"

"Yes," replied David, "I guess you're right. I don't know—a kind of floral patterned dress—skirt," he said. "Red and yellow flowers—I think—white sweater. A bonnet. Blue." David eased his way down the body-strewn aisle, each hand on the corner of one of the day-sitters, the upholstery torn here and there where the bullets had passed through, some of the beige-colored sponge rubber filler oozing from the seats speckled with blood. He remembered she was wearing a red poppy, too, for Remembrance Day, even though the actual day was weeks ago.

David paused, wiping the sweat from the cap's band before he could bring himself to move deeper into the carriage. He could still hear the heavy, muffled tinkling of the boiler, steam still rising, floating back past the carriages even though Parkin had shut down the main valve.

He moved farther into the carnage, having to step over the bodies gingerly, trying not to disturb anything, finding a footfall wherever he could and using the web of the overhead luggage racks to keep his balance, recoiling one moment from pinkish-gray ooze of brains sticking to one seat, the upholstery black with blood.

One of the American reinforcements was slumped in a corner, and from the pinkish-white pulp that David guessed must have been bone and flesh, David could tell the SPETS had probably used high-velocity mercury or depleted-uranium tips, which would penetrate the target like a white-hot rod, exploding through the other side with the force of a sledgehammer.

"Jesus!" said Parkin softly, now entering the carriage from the far end. "Get away, you bastard!" He was waving his hand ineffectually at a large blowfly crawling, bloated, through the mash of a GI's eye dangling by a thread. Suddenly Parkin put his hand to his mouth, and rushed back toward the toilet door. As it flung open, David heard Parkin utter another half-choked oath and saw him reappear, rushing out the doors at the end of the carriage.

As David reached the washroom, he saw the reason—another GI, crumpled against the outer wall, one leg bent impossibly between the toilet stem and sink pipe, hands protectively over his face—the impact of two SPETS bullets having blown him clean off the seat even as he'd tried to cower in the corner. Or had he simply been too terrified to move? Again it had been a head shot, and David saw the splattered slug that had ricocheted, ending up, after smashing the cistern, embedded in the copper float. There were empty nine-millimeter brass jackets all over the place—same ammunition as used by NATO forces.

David pushed open the carriage's end door and saw Parkin, head over the rail. Beyond him David could see through the doors of the fourth carriage, another carnage of khaki bodies strewn about, several of them clustered by the water fountain. "You okay?" he asked Parkin.

"No—Jesus, never seen anything like it. Bloody slaughter. The bastards."

David passed by him, heading for the doors of the fourth carriage, and heard ambulance men behind him starting to clean out the remaining bodies now that more stretchers had arrived. As he opened the door, he saw several bodies that had fallen from upper bunks where the wounded had been. David felt his nostrils assaulted by a stringent mixture of spilled antiseptic, saline drip bottles, medications, and excrement.

He stood still looking about for her, for any sign of movement, still having a gut feeling that as she was of slighter build than most, she could well be buried but alive under the crush of bodies. He heard something and motioned the ambulance men coming in behind him to be quiet, listening for the faintest sound of breathing—for anything. But all he could hear now was the sound of the boiler condensing, its melancholy sound still with them. Outside, more ambulances were arriving.

"Should check those who've been taken away," suggested Parkin, reappearing, smelling of sick. He meant those who the Belgian had told him had been stacked earlier in the Roosbeek morgue.

"Damn it—she isn't dead," David said. "I just know it." He turned, looking at Parkin. "Sorry. You don't have to come. Wait back at the Humvee if you like."

Parkin didn't answer but followed Brentwood as he entered the last carriage.

She was the first one he saw—spread across a wounded youth, both his arms in casts, one eye bandaged, the bandage bloodied now and rust-colored. At the base of her head there was a small, ugly hole, the edge of her white sweater stained. David knelt down and felt her wrist. No pulse. Cold. He couldn't breathe and tore at his collar. Parkin moved up behind him. "Oh Christ, Lieutenant! Oh, shit!"

David, biting his lip, bent over her, still clinging to hope, and saw a phantom breeze blow the soft baby hair on the nape of her neck. It was his own breath. He took her right hand in both of his, holding it gently, feeling for the faintest pulse. He doubled over, pulling her hands to his face, his head moving side to side, sobbing in desperate denial that it was Lili, that the bloody mush that had been her face was Lili. But the poppy of Flanders Field that she'd worn, like those poppies she had told him sprang forth from the artillery-plowed earth after the 1914 war, was still there, crushed against her by the body of the soldier she'd been trying to protect.

David didn't remember the walk back to the Humvee, nor much of the ride back to the convalescent military hospital in Liège where he was to await orders, possibly for light supply duties in France. Parkin had put the poppy, her ID bracelet, and a lock of her hair—he'd had to wash it first—in a white linen envelope marked "Lieutenant Brentwood—Personal" and left it at the front desk. He wanted to stay at Liège but couldn't. In the morning he'd have to report back to Brussels as what supplies were making it through the renewed Russian sub attacks on the convoys had to be shipped up quickly to the front if Freeman's army wasn't to be halted, and a counterattack risked all along the line. NATO needed every driver it could get its hands on.

"You take care of yourself, Lieutenant," Parkin enjoined.

David nodded. "Thanks for bringing me back, Corp."

"Anything I can do, sir? I mean, if you're not feeling up to it—someone should let your folks know." Parkin was holding out a packet of cigarettes, momentarily forgetting that the American didn't smoke.

"No," said David. "They know nothing about her." He looked up at the Englishman, his lip quivering. The corporal, embarrassed, offered him a light. Brentwood looked down, cleared his throat, and asked in a strained voice, "Can you fix me a ride to Bouillon? It's in the Ardennes. Her parents live there. I'd like to—I mean I should—"

"No problem!" said Parkin, relieved he could do something, anything, to help. "I'll go over to the motor pool right now."

"Thanks," said David.

Sitting on the edge of his bunk, eyes fixed on the drops of

rain slowly making their way down the window of the Quonset hut, he felt a hollowness—a vast emptiness and the beginning of rage—that they could waste someone so young, so beautiful—so good—the best thing, he now realized too late, that had happened to him in the whole rotten war.

Parkin's footsteps echoed on the highly polished linoleum. "Well, if you can put up with me, Lieutenant, they say I can drive you down. But I was thinking, maybe her folks wouldn't—I mean, maybe we should wait a few days."

"No," said David. "I'd like to go now."

"It's about ninety miles. Good three hours, Lieutenant. Maybe you should rest awhile. Go in the morning."

Parkin waited patiently for the lieutenant to reconsider, to at least put it off till the morning. Parkin knew he couldn't appeal to the American's convalescent status anymore either—the sister on the ward telling the Corporal that Brentwood was as fit as they could make him now and that he could certainly go to Bouillon if he wanted to. To cheer him up, the sister brought a pile of letters waiting for him from the United States. "And abroad," she said, showing him one with a Scottish postmark.

"Thank you," David said, looking at the bundle in his hand. He might as well have been looking at a relic from the ancient past. Right now nothing held any importance for him, not how Lana was faring in the Aleutians or Robert on the *Roosevelt*—if he was still on the *Roosevelt*—or even the state of Ray's progress in the burn unit of San Diego Vet's. The only thing that mattered was that Lili was gone. She had been a bright burst, a warmth in the winter of his recovery from Stadthagen. Only his anger at the Russians offered any salve for the emptiness that now engulfed him; he fed on it. On that anger and what he felt was his duty to go to Bouillon. He hoped they'd find each and every one of the SPETS and hang them. It hadn't been a military action—what was military about hitting a train and murdering wounded in cold blood? It was butchery. He only hoped he could keep the worst of it from Lili's father and mother.

" 'S all right with you, sir," said Parkin. "I wouldn't mind a kip before we go."

"All right," said Brentwood finally. "But I want to go down first thing in the morning." It was the most dispirited voice Parkin had ever heard.

CHAPTER TWENTY-TWO

THE DECEMBER SUN was weak in Khabarovsk, but its reflection off the snow dazzled the city, ice crystals sparkling in the pristine air. Apart from the massive underground supply depots and the munition factories on the city's outskirts, where the wind kept most of the industrial pollution blowing west, the city, though shabby up close, nevertheless looked stunningly clean and peaceful. Gen. Kiril Marchenko had sensed the difference in the air the moment he'd deplaned following the long, four-thousand-mile trip from Moscow.

After having received greetings from the Khabarovsk's KGB chief, Colonel Nefski, he went up the winding stone stairs of the jail. General Marchenko took off his greatcoat, cap, and gloves, and got right to it.

"Who put you up to this?" he asked the girl, Alexsandra Malof, the moment she was brought in.

She said nothing.

"It's a very grave matter."

It was worse than that, Nefski knew. Even suspected sabotage carried the death penalty. Several submarine captains from the Far Eastern Fleet out of Vladivostok had reported that some torpedoes were not detonating. A serial number check showed they all came from the munitions factory at Khabarovsk.

In a perverse way, Nefski admired the woman. Dark, in her late twenties, not much over five feet, she radiated defiance, her body stiffening the moment the two burly guards held her, one on each arm, when she looked as if she was about to spit at the general. The coarse woolen prison top could not hide her beauty, her breasts more alluring each time she resisted the pull of the guards, her eyes quick with rage, her whole body tense. Proud, too—wouldn't even acknowledge the presence of Nefski's subaltern near the window, overlooking the courtyard, whether from fear or contempt, he didn't know. Of course, she'd just been in the prison for a day—brought straight from the munitions factory. Anyone could act tough for the first couple of hours, and amateurs were always profligate with their resistance.

It never occurred to her interrogators that she might be innocent of any sabotage, either on the railway or in the munitions factories where the Jews were supplying what was euphemistically called "volunteer labor." She was also one of the young Jewish women *prorosili*—"requested"—to entertain the pilots at Khabarovsk air base. Refusal meant family harassment or most usually what the fliers called a "surprise party"—a pogrom—when things became too dull at the base.

"Is this how you Jews repay us?" pressed Marchenko. She glared at Colonel Nefski and his assistant looking on impassively.

"We give you your autonomous regions," said Marchenko. "Let you worship your God—and this is how you treat us?" He waited. Nefski and his assistant could see the general's patience was wearing thin.

"There are Jews in all our armed services, you know," continued Marchenko. "Loyal to the USSR. How do you think they must feel, knowing there are traitors among their own people?"

She smiled, but it was one of contempt, as if to say, "They are the ones who are the traitors."

Marchenko rose from behind the colonel's desk, put on his coat, and picked up his gloves from his cap. Holding his gloves in one hand, the general put the edge of his cap beneath her chin, forcing her to look up at him. "You think this Jewish stubbornness is a virtue?"

She remained silent, and Marchenko, sweeping the cap away, turned to Nefski. "I'm wasting my time. She's your charge." Putting on his cap, he gestured to Nefski with his gloves. "A moment, Comrade."

As the two men's footsteps echoed down the stone staircase toward the brilliant white rectangle of snow framed by the door of the KGB headquarters, Nefski's assistant asked the prisoner if she would like some tea. She made no sign.

Marchenko began putting on his fur-lined gloves. It might be sunny outside, but it was still twenty below. "She is banking on the *kosoglazy*—slant-eyes—being beaten by the Americans—*if* the Americans cross the Yalu."

"I think you may underestimate the Chinese, General," said

Nefski. "With all due respect. They may solve our problem for us. Look at the Americans in Vietnam. They failed miserably, and with overwhelming air superiority."

"They failed," said Marchenko, pulling the other glove on tightly and squinting against the brilliant reflection of the snow, "because they lacked national will, Colonel. They dropped more ordnance on the Vietnamese than in all of World War Two. But it does you no good if you don't have national will. This war, however, is very different, Comrade. The Americans see it as a Holy Grail. Vietnam veterans were spat on. In this war, Americans think God is back on their side. Like the Jews, which is why we must break that one upstairs. A dud torpedo that does not sink an American nuclear ship, a missile that fails to bring down an American nuclear bomber, could mean the difference between victory and defeat for us. Remember, Colonel, for the want of a nail, the shoe was lost, for the want of a shoe, the horse, for the want of the horse, the rider, for the want of the rider, the battle."

"I will get the information about the sabotage," said Nefski confidently.

"No doubt, Comrade. But *when?* It's all a matter of time. You remember the *Yumashev*—the best battle cruiser we had? Well, we found the Estonian bastards who sabotaged her depth charges—depth charges which might have saved her from the American Sea Wolf—the *Roosevelt*—that sank her."

"Luchshie umy mysliat odinakovo"—"Great minds think alike"—said Nefski. "I was telling my assistant only this morning, Comrade General, about the *Yumashev*." Nefski didn't go on to tell the general that his mention of the *Yumashev* to his assistant had been used to illustrate how Moscow's interference with local investigations could actually delay solving the problem.

"Good," said the general, "then we are in concert on this matter." The chauffeur opened the door of the hand-tooled Zil and Marchenko stepped into the warm, plush interior. "I will be here for another six hours before I return to Moscow with my report. I can be reached at Khabarovsk air base. It would go well for us both, Colonel, if I could tell the Politburo upon my return that the situation had been solved."

"Of course, General. I understand."

"I'm sure you do." The splash-green-and-white-camouflaged Zil moved slowly out of the compound, its tires crackling on the frozen sheet, the heavily coated KGB guards coming snappily to attention, rifles at the "present."

* * *

"You are as foolish as your grandfather, Alexsandra," Nefski told her. "You see, no matter what the official records show, we have always known your little secret. Oh yes, your grandfather paid his fifteen rubles like a good little boy to change the family name to Russian and thought he'd bought the family protection. I admit, for some, it worked. But you see, we—" he meant the KGB "—here at the local level have always known that you were Jews. And—" said Nefski, his tone magnanimous, "we told no one outside because we wanted to give you a chance. In return, this is how you repay—"

"You told no one outside," she said, sitting forward, Nefski's assistant grabbing her hair, pulling her back hard against the wooden chair, "because," she shouted, undaunted, "you were being bribed not to tell!"

Nefski pouted like a disappointed grandfather. "You see?" He turned to his assistant. "The old man's grandchildren are not grateful for his sacrifice. The poor old fool changes his name—he knows he can't change the noses—but the name will help. To make sure, he does not go to synagogue—for seventeen years—to show us he's sincere." Nefski walked over, lifting up her chin. "He does this for you. And you despise him." Nefski let her head drop. "He surrenders his faith and you spit on him."

"I didn't spit on him."

Nefski glanced at his assistant as if he could no longer be bothered with her. "She spits on him. She and her brothers." As Nefski stood by the window, the sunbeam caught his flat shoulder boards, and Alexsandra could see his red stars vibrant, like spots of blood, the sunbeam slicing the room in two, dust particles dancing madly in the beam, their randomness terrifying her. She didn't know how much longer she could be strong. She thought of her grandfather, a good man but a compromiser, deluded into thinking he could buy respectability and safety, believing that even if the secret of the family's origin got out, the very act of changing their name to Russian and not going to the synagogue would speak for itself. She despised Nefski and all those like him. In them, hatred of Jews ran as deep as it had in the Nazis. Gorbachev had not changed that. She remembered the resurgence of nationalism in the republics, all crying for more independence and, along with it, the wildfire of anti-Semitism. Even before that, she remembered the reports coming out of Hungary in the great days of the 1990 liberation, when at the beginning of the first big soccer game in free Hungary, the cry had gone up from the fans: "Kill the Jews! Kill the Jews!"

"You and your three brothers," said Nefski. "You worked in the Khabarovsk munition factory. Dispatch. Correct?"

"Yes," she said.

"The munitions are checked on the production line—so the logical place for sabotage is in dispatch. You agree?" She didn't answer.

"Your family worked the night shift. Correct?"

"Everyone worked night shift—sometimes."

"The midnight-to-dawn shift," said Nefski. "Before the transport trucks arrive."

"There are truck pickups all night," she retorted. "Can you loosen these handcuffs?"

He had gone to the window, where he had been distracted for a moment by watching a driver from one of the red-and-cream-colored trolley cars trying to realign its poles after they had been deflected by a glistening scab of ice. "He'll need his gloves on for that, Ilya," Nefski told his assistant, who was still watching Alexsandra. It was a ploy for the colonel to appear unconcerned, his confidence that he would break the prisoner transferring itself to the prisoner.

Nefski lit a cigarette, and soon Alexsandra could smell the strong, pungent Turkish tobacco, the interrogation room filling with swirling brownish smoke. She inhaled as much of it as she could.

"Don't think the fact that you've been fraternizing with our pilots will help you," Nefski told her, still ostensibly watching the trolley car. Before she could stop herself, Alexsandra had suddenly looked up, and Ilya knew the information was correct, and it all slid into place for him. She had been buying protection from officialdom through her pilots. Or so she had thought.

"Well, well," said Ilya. "And who would your pilot be, Alexsandra?"

She fell silent again.

"Maj. Sergei Marchenko," said Nefski, without turning around.

Nefski told Ilya to inform the guards it was time for her meal. Ilya lifted the phone and advised the guardhouse. As he put the phone back down, he had new respect for Nefski. Marchenko had obviously come all this way on a twofold mission: as Moscow's heavy—to "urge" the locals to get to the bottom of the sabotage—but also to show for the record that he himself had interrogated the girl. It had been so brief that in Ilya's eyes, it could hardly be called an interrogation at all, but it would allow the general to say he'd personally questioned her, showing no favoritism, even though his son had been seen in her company.

What his assistant admired most about Nefski was that while it would have been so easy for Nefski to do a deal, to protect the Marchenko name, he had stood firm. If the Jew had thought she'd compromised the KGB by making it with the son of one of the Supreme Soviet commanders, then she had made a serious mistake.

The phone jangled. Ilya answered it and, cupping the mouthpiece, told Nefski that the kitchen said her meal was ready. Should they bring it up to the office?

Alexsandra looked surprised. Since when did the KGB provide room service?

"It depends," answered Nefski. He beckoned to her, as a father to a child. "Come," he said. "Don't be afraid." And she walked slowly toward the window.

Down below in the high-wall quadrangle of the prison's exercise yard, she saw her three brothers: Ivan, Alexander, and Myshka—"little Michael"—who had just turned twelve. "*Little* Mike" because he so loved bears and, like the Yakuts, had always believed that if you shot one of the great beasts, save in self-defense, God would punish you. He looked so tiny, the drab khaki prison jacket and bulky trousers making him look even more diminutive. A guard stood near them, an officer, from his shoulder boards. A moment later she saw a squad of nine men in gray infantry caps, their earflaps down, which somehow made it even more ominous, Kalashnikovs slung over their shoulders, their boots crackling on the frozen snow, and the banana-shaped magazines of the rifles painted in winter-white camouflage pattern. Her attention to such details was an escape from what she knew was happening. Either the three brothers had not seen her or had been told not to look up, trudging out in the foot-deep snow, looking straight ahead, hands behind their backs, making them look strangely like holy men. It was only when they stopped and were told to face the wall that she saw they were handcuffed. Ivan, the oldest, and Alexander, the next oldest, had marched out together but not in unison, their footprints scattered. Myshka, on the other hand, had taken pains not to disturb the snow but to walk as precisely as he could in his older brothers' footsteps. He had always believed it was bad luck to be the first to disturb virgin snow.

"Who told you to do it?" Nefski asked calmly, his arm about her rigid shoulders. He could feel her trembling; her arms and neck muscles were going into spasm, her skin covered in goose pimples. Nefski shifted his arm down about her, gently rubbing her buttock. "There's no need for all this, eh, Alexsandra? It only causes trouble for everyone."

She lowered her gaze to the windowsill. Nefski told her brusquely to look up, ordered her to look out through the frost-edged glass, down at the prison yard, at her three brothers, and she knew Nefski had done such things many times before. The officer was now pushing the brothers against the wall, his boots kicking theirs as far apart as possible.

"Well?" Nefski asked her. "Tell me a story, Alexsandra. A true story." Her face was white as the snow, and taut, the blood draining from her cheeks.

"You look kosher," he laughed. "Well—?" The officer down in the quad looked up at Nefski, and the colonel lifted his finger. The officer roughly jerked Michael away from the wall, turned him about, and ordered him to look up. He seemed confused.

"Well, I'm waiting," Nefski told her.

Tears were streaming down her face.

"The oldest one," Nefski said. "Ivan. Did he—?" She waited for him to say something else, but he didn't.

"You see," he told her, "you have brought it to this. *You.* You and your brothers. Traitorous Jews. All of you. But I will spare them, Alexsandra—if you tell me what I wish to know."

"Neskazhi im!"—"Don't tell them!" It was Ivan screaming up at her, his voice barely audible from behind the high, closed windows. The officer shouted, his voice echoing from the stone walls. A guard stepped forward, driving the Kalashnikov's butt into Ivan's stomach. As Ivan fell, the officer kicked him hard on the back, keeping him down in the snow.

"You bastard!" she shouted at Nefski.

Nefski opened the window and made a sign to the officer, and a squad of six of the nine guards marched Alexander and Myshka back toward the cells. The officer had drawn his pistol. Now Nefski knew that Alexsandra finally understood her lover's name wouldn't protect her—or her brothers.

"She's tough," Nefski said to Ilya in mock admiration, while lighting a second cigarette from the first. It was starting to get dark, the jagged ice at the confluence of the Amur and Ussuri rivers now silhouetted like black daggers as it broke up the dying sunlight. The officer in the courtyard, his foot still on Ivan, looked up at Nefski again, waiting.

"Well?" Nefski asked Alexsandra. "What's it to be?"

She said nothing, her gaze below transfixed, her knees shaking.

Nefski dropped his hand. The officer fired at point-blank range. She screamed, hands leaping to her face, then turned to attack Nefski, but Ilya held her, dragging her back into the chair. Nefski turned his back on her and walked to the window, smoking his cigarette. Two guards entered to return her to the cell.

"Next time," Nefski told her without turning around, "it will be the second oldest, Alexander, and then Myshka."

With her screams reverberating down the stairwell, she was taken away. Ilya asked Nefski when they would try again with Alexsandra. Nefski said nothing.

"Do you think she'll crack?" Ilya asked him.

"Possibly." He paused to draw heavily on the cigarette. "There's more than one way to skin a cat."

CHAPTER TWENTY-THREE

DAVID AND HIS driver, Parkin, had arrived in Bouillon, where Lili's parents lived, only minutes before the first salvo of long-distance Russian SS-11s crashed into the ancient town. The SS-11s, designated "rockets" by NATO, rather than "missiles," with their nuclear warhead connotation, made a strange shuffling noise in the air. The first rocket had exploded high up on the spur of Ardennes woodland upon which the ancient castle of Bouillon sat, overlooking the confluence of the two flood-swollen arms of the Semois River that embraced the ancient Walloonian town.

David had come to tell the Malmédys about Lili, but within minutes, people were rushing for shelters, Parkin and David finding themselves separated, calling out, agreeing to meet back at the Humvee parked outside the Café Renoir. Soon they lost sight of one another, Parkin finding himself carried by the crowd into a shelter holding about sixty people. Mostly locals, they went out of their way to make Parkin feel welcome, telling him, as if it were somehow a comfort, that the Russians launched their rocket attacks only in bad weather when Allied bombing of their launch sites was limited, and that the Russians were not really trying to hit Bouillon but the Fabrique Nationale small-arms complex north of Liège and Allied supply depots that had been identified by SPETS dropped behind Allied lines into the Ardennes. The CEP—circular error of probability—one of the elderly Bouillonese told him, was plus or minus two hundred meters, "well over," the man explained to Parkin slowly in English, "how do you say, monsieur—over 'alf a mile, eh? Bah! The Russians cannot hit anything."

"Then, monsieur," said another elderly gent, "why are we in here?"

They had to remain in the shelter for over an hour, and with the sharp splitting sounds of wood exploding in the Ardennes and the earth-shuddering thumps of hits on Bouillon, Parkin, pushing his schoolboy French to its limit, asked if anyone knew of Monsieur Malmédy and where he lived.

"*C'est moi,*" came a friendly voice in the crowded shelter. All Parkin could see was a beret and a hand. There followed a rattle of French that Parkin didn't have a hope of understanding. He was grateful his French was so poor. He had no desire to tell the old gentleman. That was Lieutenant Brentwood's job, and Parkin was praying Brentwood had made it to a shelter.

When the "all clear" sounded, even before Parkin helped the frail Monsieur Malmédy up the stairs to street level, they could hear a commotion. People were pouring out of the shelters, but suddenly all movement seemed to cease, many standing with mouths agape—like stunned mullet, thought Parkin. A huge cloud of dust and smoke obliterated the castle, its eastern ramparts no more than an avalanche of smoking rock and debris that had cut a great swath out of the forest beneath the castle, some of the rubble having taken out a dozen or so trees and houses along the esplanade. Fire trucks were already screaming across both bridges, and over the river they could see trees near the railway station aflame, despite the drizzling rain. Parkin looked about for the Humvee, relieved to see it still there, but Brentwood was nowhere in sight. "Bloody hell!"

"Pardon?" asked Monsieur Malmédy.

"Where are the other shelters?" Parkin asked him, gesticulating back to the one they had just emerged from, but Malmédy was unsure of what he meant, another man helping out, pointing to the white office building off to their right. Parkin indicated to Malmédy that he should follow him. Malmédy hesitated.

"Lili," said Parkin.

"Ah!" the old man happily exclaimed, and graciously motioned Parkin to go before him.

Bloody hell, thought Parkin. He thinks I'm taking him to Lili. Parkin looked about for Brentwood but couldn't see him. Surely he couldn't be far from the Café Renoir. Policemen were already on duty on the nearest of the two bridges, stopping outgoing traffic from the old part of the town to allow an ambulance, its siren blaring, to pull out of the congested line leading from the rail station.

CHAPTER TWENTY-FOUR

DEEP IN THE Montana missile silo, it didn't matter whether it was night or day. Only the clock told Melissa Lange and her co–team member, Shirley Cochrane, that it was 1730 hours. Having received the command, Melissa sat in the high-backed, red upholstered chair, slid it forward on its glide rails and buckled up, waiting for Shirley. When Melissa heard the click, she began the litany. "Hands on keys. Key them on my mark. Three—two—one—mark." Both watched the clock, its long, white second hand having passed zero and now sweeping to ten seconds before 1731.

"Light on," confirmed Shirley. "Light off."

The second ten seconds passed, both women tense.

"Hands on keys," instructed Melissa.

"Hands on keys," came Shirley's confirmation.

"Initiate on my mark. Five, four, three, two, one. Now, I'll watch the clock."

"I've got the light," said Shirley. "Light on. Light off."

"Release key," ordered Melissa.

"Key released."

They waited for the launch code to come in, their one-crew key-turn having initiated only one "vote" in the launch process. The ringing, indicating "launch message coming through," sounded like an old telex chattering inside a metal box. They were now on "standby," requiring another vote from another LCC—launch control center—in order to go to "strategic alert," the yellow lights changing to white as they moved from the "key release" waiting mode to "launch-fire-release" mode, after which the five nuclear warheads would be sent streaking toward their targets, their "infinity" delay shifting to a ten-second delay from target, each of the two women praying for the ILC—inhibit launch command—to be activated instead of the "valid" word/numeral message for Armageddon.

They began to relax, waiting for the instructor to call it off and tell them it was a drill. Suddenly there was a high-pitched electronic tone and a man's even, modulated voice above a sizzle of static. "Charlie . . . Tango . . . Papa . . . Sierra . . . Oscar. Stand by. Message follows." Then came the repeat, "Message follows."

Both women, heads bent, pencils poised, waited, then they began to copy. "Victor . . . November . . . Uniform . . . Oscar . . . Charlie . . . Tango . . . Hotel . . . X-ray . . . Sierra . . . Papa . . . Papa . . . Lima . . . Two . . . Seven . . . November . . . Foxtrot . . . Echo . . . One . . . Lima. Acknowledge."

"Copied," said Shirley, her voice without a quaver. "I see a valid message."

"I agree," confirmed Melissa. "Go to step one checklist. Launch keys inserted." Both women unbuckled, went to the midpoint "red" box. As Melissa and Shirley each took out her respective round, red-tagged brass key, their eyes did not meet. Both returned to their consoles, flipped aside the plastic safety cover, inserted the keys, and then buckled up once more in their seats. "Ready," said Melissa.

"Ready."

"Okay, hold it!" said the instructor. "It's a drill." Melissa felt her whole body sag, then she sat up briskly again so as not to show it.

"Shirley," said the instructor. "What's the matter with your chair? You wasted three seconds back there."

"Don't know sir. Strap won't reach . . ."

"Give it play. Let the strap run back and pull it right out again. Just like you do in your automobile."

Shirley gave the strap more play. This time the buckle clicked in.

"Damn belt," Shirley complained to Melissa as the door of the silo elevator shut silently and they began to rise. "Happens to me all the time."

"I've had the same problem. Something wrong with that seat," said Melissa. "The guide rails. Don't worry, they'll fix it. Wasn't your fault. You were cool as a cucumber down there."

"Oh yeah?" said Shirley, slipping into her cheeky Harlem accent. "Were you?"

Melissa thought for a second, wondering if the elevator was bugged. Would they do that? She looked across at Shirley and shook her head.

Shirley burst out laughing. "I wet my pants, honey."

They rode the rest of the way in silence, relieved the drill was over but still too tense to come down from the adrenaline high.

As the air force van slowed to drop them off at their shared bungalow, Shirley's boyfriend, a junior lieutenant from the silo complex HQ, was waiting in his car, its exhaust blowing clouds of steam high into the frozen air, and Melissa could feel the steady thump, thump, thump of the stereo as she got out of the base van, the frigid blast of air hitting her like a sheet of ice.

"Hi," she heard Shirley call out to the boyfriend. "Come on inside!"

He shook his head, sliding the window down a fraction. "Kiloton's in there. Doing some repair work. Didn't think I should go in. Anybody knows you gave me a key—"

"Well," said Shirley, walking over to his car, "you can come in now, can't you?"

He looked anxiously at his watch. "We're gonna miss that movie."

"Okay," Shirley called out, "give me a couple of minutes."

Already inside, Melissa saw the jack-of-all-trades repairman known on the base as "Killerton." He turned around, his bodybuilder's torso threatening to burst the coveralls, a clump of chest hair so prominent, it made her look away.

"Didn't think anyone'd be home," said Killerton, grinning, his smile immediately suggestive, a shock of black hair as dark as that on his chest, Melissa noticed. Melissa shook the snow off her boots, still shivering and not knowing quite what to say to the repairman, not that there was anything unusual about him being there. Base personnel often requested repairs, and the workmen were issued a key. Happened all the time. She didn't have to say anything to him. Just fix the damn ceiling tile and roof.

"Requisition," said Killerton, holding up the pink slip from his toolbox for Melissa to see.

Shirley came in, snowflakes racing after her. "Hi, Killer. Didn't see your truck."

"Round the back."

"You fix that sucker?"

"Workin' on it. You got a leak, all right, coming right through the flashing." He indicated the spot with a full-sized hammer that looked like a toy in his hands.

"Uh-huh," commented Shirley, uninterested, taking off her parka.

"Can't see it from there," he said, looking over at them.

"Well, I tell ya, Killer," said Shirley, "I'm not into roofs, man." She disappeared into the bathroom. "Show Melissa."

"Don't bother," Melissa said quickly. "I'm not into roofs either." Shirley was calling out from the bathroom, " Lissa—you and Stacy coming to the movie?"

"Rick's probably still on his solo."

"So? Give him a call. If you two are still talking, that is."

Melissa didn't answer, and out of the corner of her eye she could see Killerton with a grouting gun, testing the nozzle against his hand, wiping the putty off on his coveralls as Melissa dialed Stacy's bungalow. Outside, the wind was picking up, throwing peppercorn-sized snow hard against the panes. No answer from Stacy's bungalow.

"He's not there," Melissa told Shirley.

"Come with us, then."

"No, thanks. Three's a crowd. I don't think your beau would appreciate—"

"*Beau!* Honey, he'll do what he's told or else."

"No, thanks. I feel zapped anyway. I'll wander down to the PX later on. See you there."

Shirley was out of the bathroom, walking back to the door and pulling on her anorak. "Well, rug up, honey. Freeze your butt off out there."

"I will."

" 'Bye."

The moment the door slammed shut, Melissa wished she'd gone with her.

"I won't be long," said Killerton.

"Fine."

Melissa sat down and switched on the TV, but the repairman's presence made her feel uncomfortable. Although he seemed to be patching the leak, smoothing it off, Melissa felt he was watching her. She was starting to get annoyed, but it was really her own guilt for having requested base repairs in the fight with Stacy. She should have left it for Rick to do instead of being petty about it.

"Worse then I thought," said Killerton. "Wood's rotten in here. Wormed right through."

"Oh?" said Melissa, uninterested, but adding politely, "Thought it'd be too cold for them."

"Sure, now it is, but summertime it's hotter'n a pistol out here. No, this is old damage. I'm gonna have to fill in more holes than I thought."

Melissa said nothing and changed channels. A commercial for "Rocky Mountain Bottled Water" blurted out, with a jingle she despised.

"The war's the best thing that ever happened to 'em," said Killerton.

Melissa looked over at him. He was reloading the caulking gun with a new tube, but did it with such dexterity and long experience, he didn't even glance at it, looking at Melissa, explaining, "War's kicked the ass out of all the Europeans. Destroyed fuckin' Perrier, and now with most of our water poisoned—hell, Rocky Mountain can jerk us off any way they like." He was still smiling and she was flustered. The bad language was nothing she hadn't heard before, but he seemed to be throwing it down like a gauntlet—to see how she'd react.

"Feeling pretty thirsty myself," he said.

"Would you like a Coke?" she asked, for want of anything better to say.

"Beer if you've got it."

She went over to the kitchenette, took a Coors from the fridge, and passed it to him. Still looking at her, he tore the tab off with his teeth.

Revolting, she thought—a big, hairy adolescent right out of *Animal House*. It was the kind of comment David might have made. And Rick. It was about the only thing Rick and David had in common—a disdain for the gross macho bit. Yet, try as she might, she couldn't deny in her a sense of danger, of excitement, around Killerton. With a man like this, she knew you could let yourself go completely. Mind you, it could never be a permanent thing.

She heard the click of the toolbox.

CHAPTER TWENTY-FIVE

WHEN PARKIN FOUND him, David was all but unrecognizable, covered in the chalk dust from the direct hit on the castle high above the town. With only his eyes visible beneath the chalk, Brentwood would have looked comical had it not been for the broken child in his arms. He walked straight past Parkin and Monsieur Malmédy toward the first aid post set up by the Café Renoir, the child's head, her spine snapped, lolling like a rag doll, apparently without a scratch on her, the muck and stench of body fluids causing the tiny dress to cling to her matted hair, her eyes wide open, fixed in horror. When David placed her down, taking off his tunic to cover her crumpled body, he tried to shut her eyes, but they wouldn't. He drew the battle tunic up higher to cover her face. Old Malmédy, Parkin saw, was in tears as Brentwood lowered his head for a moment—to compose himself, to pray, or both—Parkin didn't know which—only that when the American straightened up, he looked different. It wasn't simply that now his tunic was off, the clean, pressed army shirt and lieutenant's collar bars were in such sharp contrast to his bedraggled vaudevillian appearance moments before that they made him look fresher than others who had been in or near the shelter that had taken the side blast of a near hit. The difference in Brentwood's appearance was in his eyes. They were the eyes of an old man in a young body, not wearied by age, but the determined steel blue of a man who had at one stroke lost all illusion about the fairness of life—a man who, to Parkin, looked resolved.

"What a bastard!" said Parkin, looking down helplessly at the tiny form covered by Brentwood's tunic. Brentwood said nothing, his eyes not moving from the girl's body, but if there was compassion in them, it had become subsumed, his look, Parkin thought, more that of a surgeon who, along with the recognition of the tragic, seemed to be standing in judgment not only of those who had done this terrible thing but of himself, of his own behavior, his competence, of how he might have prevented it. And now he had to tell the old man who was already in tears over the young girl that *his* daughter, too, was dead. He put his arm about the old man, and instantly Malmédy knew it was terrible news.

As Parkin watched them walking down the street, seeking a moment of quiet amid the cacophony of the rescue now near fever pitch, he saw the old man stop, burying his head in his hands, unable to go on, and Brentwood standing with him, holding him for Lili.

Before they left Bouillon, David tried to phone Captain Smythe, but all lines were down in Bouillon following the rocket attack, and he had to wait until he reached Namur.

While welcoming Brentwood's change of heart, Smythe felt obliged to tell David that it was by no means a "foregone conclusion" that he would make it into SAS.

"Why not?" asked David. "I qualified as a marine, didn't I?"

"Well, yes. But I think you'll find our Special Air Service training is somewhat different. Tell you the truth, quite a few of our Red Berets and your Navy Seals have tried and failed. It's a very concentrated training course for what we have in mind."

"What's that?"

"Can't tell you that, old boy. 'Need to know.' If you pass the course, you'll find out."

Brentwood was irritated. Here he was volunteering, and *now* Smythe was telling him he mightn't be good enough. And how, he wondered, could this joint British-U.S. force possibly be tougher than the U.S. Marines? What was so special about SAS training?

"Have you ever heard of Brecon Beacons?" Smythe asked him.

"No," responded David. "What are they?"

"Mountains," said Smythe. "In Wales." The only thing David could remember about Wales, he told Smythe, was the Prince of Wales—and an old movie where coal miners, black with soot from head to toe, came home up a hill, singing.

"Ah!" said Smythe. "*How Green was my Valley?* Walter Pigeon. Well, I don't think you'll find there'll be much time for singing."

Smythe's remark, David Brentwood was about to discover, was a classic case of British understatement.

It was Christmas Eve, snowing heavily in Washington, D.C., and Gen. Douglas Freeman's plane at Andrews Air Force Base was delayed once again, the general standing impatiently inside the hangar as the de-icing trucks rolled out and sprayed the wings once more.

After his briefing with the president on the Korean situation, Freeman had immediately asked for the best pilot available to fly him to Honolulu, where they would have a brief refueling stopover, then on to Japan and Seoul. They had assigned a major from Andrews' military air transport squadron, a man, they said, with more time on 747s than any other officer on duty that day. But at the last minute, Freeman, in his usually gruff and straightforward manner, asked his G-2, Colonel Norton, whether the major assigned had had any combat experience.

"General. These people are on the Air Force One flight crews. And they're selected to fly the president. They can fly anything from a Tiger Moth to an F-18."

"Norton," Freeman said exasperatedly, his athlete's bulk impressive even in his "incognito garb," as he called the business suit and matching serge coat. "I took you on as my G-2 because you were smart enough to spot those Soviet T-90s in the reconnaissance photos didn't have extra fuel tanks strapped to their backs. That gave me the opening to go full steam ahead for Warsaw even though we were low on gas and the fat was in the goddamned fire, Soviet artillery pounding us left, right, and center. I also hired you then because you gave me straight answers and were willing to risk my displeasure with bad news. Now, if we're going to keep getting along, Jim, in Korea, from here on in, you'd better tell me everything I want to know without any farting about. Otherwise we're never gonna get those Chinks' asses back over the Yalu, where they belong."

"He's had no combat experience, sir."

"Then, damn it, I want someone who *has!* And I want him *now!* I don't want to go flying in there on a wing and a prayer with someone driving this thing who hasn't seen a Flogger coming up his ass at Mach 2 through the blind spot."

"Yes, sir, but we will have fighter escorts from here right on through to Seoul. Course, that doesn't invalidate your point. I'll get someone with combat experience."

"How many fighters'll be flying escort?"

"Twenty, sir. F-15s, Hornets . . ."

"What?" bellowed Freeman. "That's not an escort, that's a goddamned invitation. Draw the enemy like a bear to honey. Fewer aircraft around me, the better I like it."

"Yes, sir," said Norton, saluting from habit, even though the general was in civilian clothes.

"We own the Pacific from here to Japan, don't we?" asked Freeman.

"With the exception of the Russian subs, yes, sir."

"All right then, let's keep the bulk of the fighters away from me. Japan to Korea's a different story. It's catch as catch can across the Sea of Japan. So here's what we do when we enplane from—where will it be—Hiroshima?"

"Possibly, sir, or Matsue, if the weather's bad on the east coast."

"Well, wherever—when we leave, send fighters ahead on a northwesterly course. We'll go a few minutes later with only three fighters escort, maximum. If the Russkis do know anything about me coming—which I sincerely hope they don't—they'll go for our big fighter formation while we slip into Seoul. And they'll get their tails shot off."

Norton, anxious to draw another pilot from the duty roster who had combat experience, nodded quickly in agreement to the general's diversionary plan. It was typically "Freemanish"—deceptive but also putting himself in danger with little protection. All Freeman cared about was the importance of the presidential order to get to Korea as fast as possible and revive America's military fortunes there. If he didn't turn things around there, the entire Asian theater would collapse and give the Russians' Far Eastern Command an unprecedented opportunity to direct all the forces it was holding in reserve against a possible American attack from Korea toward Vladivostok, toward the Aleutians—to hit America's "back door."

"Besides," added Freeman, "if this play actor they've got impersonating me in Brussels does his job well enough, damn Russians won't even know we're coming and we can just fly across under the normal patrol umbrella of the Sixth Fleet."

"Must say, General, that sounds like a much better way of seeing the Sea of Japan—with the Sixth Fleet below us."

Freeman frowned, but Norton wasn't sure whether it was something he said or whether the general, whose pride kept him from wearing eyeglasses for his myopia, was squinting, having difficulty making out the approach of Lieutenant Harlin, the new press aide, Freeman's regular press officer having been left in Brussels to help coordinate the impersonation/deception plan.

"Jim, when we reach Japan, it's no longer the Sea of *Japan* we're going over. It's the *East* Sea. Our South Korean allies are very touchy on that particular point. They wouldn't give you a stick for a Nip. Historical enemies. Hadn't been for Korean Admiral Yi in the twelfth century sinking all the emperor's ships in the Tsushima Straits, they'd all be eating sushi in Seoul. Poor bastards. And that's another thing, Jim. I don't want any member of this flight—fighter pilots included—to leave the air base in Japan—wherever it is we land. They start eating all that raw fish crap, next thing we'll have half of 'em down with the Johnny runs."

"Yes, sir. Talking of Japan, it's been suggested by the State Department that a visit to the emperor wouldn't go astray in the interest of interallied—"

"Goddamn it, Jim! I can't go giving an order for everyone to stay put while I go out and eat seaweed with the emperor. Besides, what if somebody recognized me en route—never mind this Wall Street garb they've stuck me into. It'd compromise the whole operation. Besides, only emperor I wanted to see was Douglas MacArthur. Then he went and screwed it all up. Gave them brand-new factories—put them years ahead of Detroit, which is why the automobile industry in this country is a basket case." Freeman paused. "You don't agree?"

"Never said a word, General."

"I can read it all over your face. Well, I'm no racist bucko. I'll fight and die with those people. What they did for us in the early months of the war when our perimeter 'round Pusan shrank till we didn't have a pot to piss in was magnificent. Magnificent. But—" for a moment the general moved closer to the colonel, eyes intense "—I'll tell you this, Jim. If there's anything left of a command in Korea and I do push Premier Lin Zhou's boys back across the Yalu and the Tamur, I won't be giving Beijing new automobile factories so they can pull another economic 'miracle' on us. Hell, I'd give 'em democracy, too, but they'd have to rebuild from the rubble."

Norton felt a flush of alarm—the "rubble" in Japan's case had come from an atomic bomb. "You don't mean you'd drop the bomb on the Chinese, General?"

"When are those jokers going to have my plane ready?"

"Excuse me, General." Freeman turned to see his press aide and the U.S. Navy pilot, name tag "Maj. F. Shirer."

"You have combat experience, Major?" asked Freeman.

"Yes, sir."

"Where?"

"Aleutians, sir. Pyongyang."

"Pyongyang?"

"Yes, sir. I flew off the *Salt Lake City*."

"Cover!" said Freeman. "For my choppers?"

"Yes, sir," answered Shirer, adding in a tone that spoke of pride with a flush of uncharacteristic immodesty, "Led the wing in twice."

"That where you got that Navy Star, Major?"

"Yes, sir."

"Well, hell, son, what are you doing here?" There was a sudden tension in the air, Norton knowing that if the general thought for a moment anyone was goldbricking, he'd just as soon shoot him.

"Beats me, sir," Shirer told him honestly. "Apparently I'm a replacement for one of the Air Force One teams. Told me they wanted someone with combat hours, though why they chose—"

Freeman extended his hand. "I've got a more important job for you than ferrying the president around."

The young press secretary shot a worried glance at Norton as if there might be some hidden microphone or reporter in the hangar, despite the fact that no one from the press would have been allowed anywhere near Andrews if there'd been even a suspicion that Freeman was in town.

"What's the mission, sir?" asked Shirer, barely able to contain his excitement at the possibility of returning to active service, maybe even the Aleutians.

"Back to Korea," explained Freeman, beaming. "As my pilot."

Shirer hesitated. "You mean—a 747?"

"That's right."

"Yes, sir."

Norton tried to send an eye code to Shirer to the effect that it wasn't just anyone who got the job of flying the legendary Freeman back to the scene of his first glory. But the truth was that Shirer had had enough honor since he had come to Washington. What he wanted was combat. Instead he'd be jockeying the big, slow 747. If a fighter was a sports car, the 747 was a Mack truck—fully loaded. Besides, it wouldn't take him anywhere near Lana. He also didn't like the general calling him "son." Though only in his late twenties, it wouldn't be that long before they'd be retiring him from fighter duty.

"Shirer," said Freeman, "if you don't want it, say so. But before you do, remember this. I'm directly responsible for implementing the president's orders. Now, I don't care what you think of me, but the mission is nothing less than to initiate a decisive action to win the war for us in Asia. If my hunch is right—it'll be a commuter ride from here through Pearl and on to Japan. And it should be a breeze from there to Seoul. I'm not supposed to be here—but in Europe. All our indications are that our ruse is working, so there shouldn't be any trouble. But there could be Red Navy units with surface-to-air missiles, and if any shooting starts, I'd like a veteran at the wheel."

"I'd be honored to go, General."

"Good man! See him aboard, Jim."

"Yes, General."

The young press aide was now alone with the general. Freeman shook his head, grinning, watching Shirer heading out through the bluish-white veil of snow toward the aircraft. "He's about as happy to be flying that big bird as I'd be seeing the emperor."

"Yes, sir," agreed the press aide, Harlin, eagerly. He had still not recovered from being assigned to the general's staff—overawed by the general's reputation and the scenes it evoked—of the general shooting his way room to room through the Great Hall of the People of Pyongyang, looking for his nemesis, General Kim.

"Know why he'll do it?" said Freeman. "Because he's a soldier. He's a warrior, Harbin."

"Yes, sir," said Harlin, too awed to tell the general it was "Harlin," not "Harbin."

"I want you to take some notes, Harbin," ordered Freeman. "Pass 'em on to Jim Norton soon as you finish."

"Yes, sir. Shoot!"

Freeman raised an eyebrow and looked down at the young aide, offering him a stick of gum.

"No, thank you, sir."

"Last chance you'll have between here and Korea. We're going to be at the front, Mr. Harbin, not sitting on our butts in Seoul in that sewer staring up at the big board." He meant the subterranean HQ operations-shelter complex beneath Seoul. "And at the front, a Commie can smell a stick of gum half a mile upwind. Now, first thing I want you to put down on that pad of yours—distribution, all commanders down to battalion and company level—is that I don't want anybody pulling back from anywhere. The second thing is—you getting all this, Harbin?"

"Yes, General."

"Good. Second order is that ammunition is not to be wasted. At present we have an effective ammunition usage rate of twenty—thirty percent tops. This constitutes a seventy to eighty percent consumption rate—fired in panic and it's got to stop. My G-2'll want to see all AURs—" The press aide stopped writing.

"Ammunition usage reports," explained Freeman. "And if anybody's just shooting for the hell of it, he'll have to answer to me personally."

"Yes, sir."

"Course," said Freeman, smiling, "an order like that's impossible to police, but I want our boys to get the general idea. *Capiche?*"

"Yes, sir."

"We're in a winter battle," Freeman went on, his voice rising above the wild spitting hiss of the de-icing sprays. "Those Nangnim Mountains are going to be rough. Peaks well over six thousand feet. Next order is, I want hot food chuted in and chopper-dumped wherever possible. Though, of course, that won't be possible at the front."

"Yes, sir."

"Next thing. Memo to the entertainment officer in Seoul. I don't want any Communist propaganda film shown in any unit—and that includes hospital units in Seoul." The press aide was nonplussed. He doubted very much whether entertainment officers would ever do such a thing, even if they were KGB plants, which you couldn't discount, given the paranoia sweeping the States in the wake of the poisoned water crisis and other sabotage.

"By that," Freeman explained, "I mean that I don't want any goddamned Hanoi Jane movies. Got it?"

The lieutenant, in his early twenties, wasn't familiar with the actress's name. "Are they bad movies, General?"

"*Bad!* Harbin, the only goddamn picture I want to see *Ms.* Fonda in is a cartoon of her ass being blown to pieces by one of those guns she sat on in Hanoi when she was calling our boys war criminals! And another thing. I don't want any *MASH* reruns. You know what I'm talking about—old, funny Hawkeye with all the jokes about the futility of war and the mad American generals. If it wasn't for mad American generals like MacArthur and Ridgeway, there'd be no funny Hawkeyes in Hollywood. They'd all be munching rice, Harbin, and a lot of South Koreans would now be fertilizing the paddies of the North with their bones. Trouble is with *MASH*, it was an antiwar film against Vietnam policy set in Korea, but our boys won't make that kind of distinction, Harbin. Too young to remember Korea. I don't want them sabotaged in the rear by those long-haired weirdos that did us in over Vietnam. And I'll tell you another thing, Harbin. North Vietnam's one of the poorest, most oppressive countries in Asia. That's why there's no *MASH II*."

The hapless press aide was glad to see Colonel Norton returning from the 747, informing Freeman, "All set to go in twenty minutes, General. They're sending a crew bus to take you out rather than an official car—case there's some press hanging around the—"

"Never mind that, Jim," said Freeman. "Nothing wrong with my legs. Let's go, Harbin. What's the flight schedule, Jim? How many hours?"

"Twenty plus, sir, allowing for refueling in Hawaii and Japan."

"Forecast?"

"Snow from here to the Midwest, General, but then clearing up as we get to Hawaii. From then on, it gets better."

"Good. Harbin!"

"Yes, sir."

"Notice you don't use a plate between those note pages."

Harlin didn't know what to make of it and looked over to Norton for help, but the colonel's head was down against the fine-grained snow that was bouncing off them like uncooked rice.

"Piece of aluminum," explained Freeman, striding ahead. "Don't use cardboard. Plastic if you like. But never write any of my orders down without a separating pad between the pages. You put the top ones in the burn basket as a matter of course, but more than one sergeant I've known has been reading his CO's confidential memos, holding the second page up to the light. That happens in my command and you've got a free ride to nowhere. Understand?"

"Yes—yes, sir," answered Harlin.

"Don't worry about it," said Freeman. "But you see, son, any fool can figure out the big plans. Only have to look at a map. It's the details, Harbin. The details. That's what wins or breaks the day."

"Yes, sir. I'll remember."

"I know you will. Now, you just relax. We're gonna have that big bird all to ourselves. Coca-Cola machines. Everything. More electronics on that baby than you can shake a stick at. Next thing you know, we'll be in the land of the rising sun. Ever been to Japan, Harbin?"

"No, sir."

"Beautiful country. That right, Jim?"

"Sure is, General."

"You eat sushi, Harbin?"

"Ah—" He thought the general had said "shoosh."

"Raw fish," explained Norton.

"No—I—I don't believe I have, General. Didn't have any of that in Idaho."

"Just as well. Mightn't be here today if you did. Goes through you like crap through a goose. Sucks all the energy out of your legs. That right, Jim?"

"That's right, General. Though I must say I've never had any trouble with—"

"Don't contradict me, goddamn it!"

"No, sir."

CHAPTER TWENTY-SIX

"DO WE KNOW for certain?" asked President Suzlov.

Soviet head of KGB Vladimir Chernko was equivocal. "Not absolutely, Premier—I mean Mr. President." Despite his support of *President* Gorbachev during the latter's years of decline, Chernko had always found it difficult to address subsequent leaders as "president" rather than the old pre-Gorbachev "premier." "Our agent, one of the best in Brussels, said the car was unmarked—a Mercedes en route to the airport. No fanfare, no motorcycle escorts. But a glimpse of Freeman stepping out. It's Freeman's style, President."

"What?" challenged Suzlov. "To slip out in the middle of the night? Hardly, Comrade. I thought he was a prima donna. Likes to be seen."

"Unquestionably, Comrade President," said Chernko. "Publicly—and I suppose for that matter, privately, but he's no fool. He is the most brilliant tactician the Americans have. Anywhere. A master of the unexpected. Everyone thought this would be a war of high mobility and technology. That the so-called technological imperative would dictate strategy. But this Freeman has obviously mastered more than technical manuals. His grasp of tactics and of tactical details is legendary among his troops. We know now that the Pentagon thought he was mad when he presented the plan for Pyongyang—an airborne assault. At night—precisely when the American and South Korean forces were in full retreat. Therefore it is logical in my opinion that they would shift him back to Korea now the Chinese have crossed the Yalu. He knows the country."

Suzlov remained unconvinced. "Yes, Comrade Director, but another of your agents is reporting that Freeman is still in Europe—going between Brussels and the front. He may be a first-rate commander, Comrade, but he's not a magician."

Suzlov turned away in his swivel chair, banks of white phones behind him, and looked over at the picture of Lenin. "He can't be in two places at once. And why would the Americans give him a new command when his offensive against us is going so well in Europe?"

"Their supply line from the French ports to our Polish/Russian front is now over seventeen hundred kilometers, Mr. President. It's true they have aerial superiority and their armored divisions have moved within striking distance of Minsk, but we are having increasing success where it ultimately counts—with our submarines. In the Pacific and the Atlantic, they're about to turn the tide."

"Are you that confident, Comrade?" asked Suzlov while studying Lenin's photograph as if he had never really seen it before.

"Yes," came the reply from Director Chernko. "If our submarines continue to stop the supplies, we will win. The mathematical equation is simple—no supplies, no advance. Meanwhile we are also reinforcing our supplies along the Trans-Siberian to Khabarovsk and Vladivostok. And now China's entry has diverted what would have been NATO supplies from America to Korea, this takes even more pressure off our western front. If the Americans are beaten in Korea, we'll be free to move our Sino-Soviet divisions for a final push against the Aleutians. It's no wonder Washington is sending this Freeman back to Korea."

"Perhaps," responded Suzlov, "but you can never be sure what the Chinese will do. They will make peace and war when it suits them. Our situation will not influence them either way. They are strictly allies of convenience. You know this. If we falter anywhere in the Eastern Theater—they will cross the Amur into *our* territory and gobble up what they can. Look at Khabarovsk. Sabotage is already taking place there and we can't seem to stop it."

"We will," Chernko promised him. "But back to Freeman. It makes sense for the Americans to give Freeman the Korean command. The snow is deep in Western Europe, and neither side, apart from the air forces, will be making much of a move until the spring. It is an ideal opportunity for them to recall their senior commander for 'consultation.' We also do this when—"

Suzlov turned abruptly away from the table, and began pacing down past the long, baize-topped table where the STAVKA high command sat during the long day and night sessions in the enormous complex of the Council of Ministers building. Suzlov was considering the number of fighters the director was requesting, based on air force estimates of what Chernko's plan would need. Most of them would probably be shot down by either American or Japanese fighters. The bulk of the Soviet fighters might evade radar on a low run in from the Russian airfields at Vladivostok, but the rotodomes of the American Hawkeye electronic surveillance planes from the U.S. carriers in the Sea of Japan would pick them up before they intercepted Freeman's plane. If indeed it *was* Freeman who had left Brussels en route to Washington, D.C., and then possibly on to South Korea.

To make it more difficult for Suzlov, the distance, he discovered, between Vladivostok to Seoul was twelve hundred kilometers. MiG Flogger C interceptors with a combat radius of twelve hundred kilometers would need drop tanks, thus slowing their speed significantly, to say nothing of their maneuverability—at least on the way in. Still, the target, Suzlov had to admit, was irresistible. If they could get confirmation from their Japanese agents of Freeman's arrival in Japan, and attack him en route to Korea, his death would be a stunning victory.

America would be devastated by the loss of her most able field commander, and at a time when she desperately needed him, if her troops in Korea were not to suffer another humiliation at the hands of the Chinese-NKA legions. And the psychological effect of Freeman's death in Europe would be almost as dramatic, and help tilt the odds in favor of the Soviet Union.

"If we are to do it," said Suzlov, "we must have the best. All volunteers."

"That doesn't necessarily bring us the best, Comrade President."

"Oh?" said Suzlov, looking genuinely surprised. The president turned back to his desk and globe, contemplating the Korean Peninsula. It had been a constant thorn in the Soviet side. First it was Kim Il Sung using millions of rubles in foreign aid to build towering bronze statues of himself all over Pyongyang, and his son, Kim Il Jong, determined to keep the "dynasty," as Gorbachev had once referred to it, going. And now there was talk that General Kim, hero of the North Korean invasion of the South, once in disgrace due to the success of Freeman's Pyongyang raid, was now back in command of all North Korean forces along with Zhou Li, supreme commander of the PLA's northern armies.

Kim was no more likable, in Suzlov's opinion, than Kim Il Jong and Co., but at least he was convinced that for North Korea, allegiance to Moscow was as important as allegiance to Beijing—unlike Il Jong and Il Sung, who had been stunned by Gorbachev's criticism of their self-glorification. Freeman's death would also have the advantage of impressing Kim that allegiance to Moscow was not, as Beijing not so subtly charged, "less important" because of North Korea's closer proximity to China. It would demonstrate that in matters of technology, the kind of technology it would take to kill Freeman, the Soviet Union was light years ahead of China.

"Very well," said Suzlov. "Go ahead, but only if we get *positive* confirmation of Freeman arriving and leaving Japan."

Chernko rose matter-of-factly, thanking Suzlov but careful not to be effusive, too ingratiating—it wouldn't do for Suzlov to get too big for his boots. Besides, Suzlov had not impressed Chernko by his willingness to accept Chernko's statement that volunteers are not always the best. They were, of course—provided basic military criteria were met—but Chernko's comment that they weren't always so had been calculated to give him leverage against another member of the STAVKA, Marchenko, another comrade who was getting too big for his boots. In return for Chernko not ordering the Far Eastern Air Force Command at Khabarovsk to assign Marchenko's son, Sergei, to fly on the top secret and highly dangerous mission, the director knew that he would incur an implicit, yet clearly understood, IOU from Marchenko Senior.

Or so he believed.

In Khabarovsk, Gen. Kiril Marchenko strolled with his son Sergei outside the hardened shelters of the fighter squadrons. At six feet, the general was half a foot taller than his son, and in his general staff uniform, looked more impressive. He was conscious of the fact that throughout their relationship, his rank had intimidated Sergei, but he doubted that this still held true, now that his son had become one of the Soviet Union's most decorated fighter pilots. The general would have preferred to be inside the base HQ in the warmth of the operations room than strolling outside, but he did not want to be overheard. This was as much a family matter as a military one. Pulling up the collar of his greatcoat, his breath steaming in the Arctic air that had swept down from Siberia, he gazed up for a moment at the stars, their brilliance in the clear air astonishing after the pollution of Moscow. "You should have had more sense," he told Sergei.

"I'm a man," replied Sergei unapologetically. "It isn't exactly unnatural."

"I'm not talking about *that*," said Kiril. "Of course a man gets lonely. Needs the company of—I understand your feelings." He hesitated, then added, ". . . Especially after your experience in the Aleutians. A close brush with death often does that to a man. Stirs up the blood. This is quite normal. But a Jew? You know how they are, no matter what they say. Even that fool Gorbachev understood that much. Why do you think he let so many of them go?"

"Then why are you so worried?" retorted Sergei. He felt good—a combination of his status as an ace, the tailored dress uniform under the greatcoat, the weight of the coat, made by one of the Jews from the autonomous regions, fitting perfectly, as did the boots that crunched the hardened snow beneath him. All of this gave him a consummate feeling of well-being, of power. He remembered reading in his father's library, when his father had been chief censor and therefore the best-read man in the USSR, a book by the Englishman Orwell, in which the Englishman had written of similar feelings—about his mounted policeman's uniform when he served the British Raj in Burma. Of how the uniform, the riding pants, the boots, spurs, and the riding crop had given him, too, a feeling of pleasure and power.

Following the surge of confidence he'd experienced after shooting down the American Tomcats in the Aleutians, Sergei had worn the uniform with special pride. And so now, next to his father, whom he had always held in awe, he felt a rush of equality.

"I told her nothing of military operations here," he told the general. "I'm not that stupid."

"It's not what you told her," retorted the general, "but playing in the muck puts you in a vulnerable position."

"You mean it puts the family in a vulnerable position."

"If you wish to put it that way. Yes. Besides, she could have slipped you poison—anything."

Sergei laughed and, seeing how it infuriated his father, rather enjoyed it. "Poison?"

"Or some filthy disease," snarled the general.

"I use precautions," said Sergei. "I'm not a moron. Besides, poison's only for the Politburo." Sergei sensed his father stiffen beside him, but the general kept walking, the snow crunched harder. "You miss the point entirely, Sergei. You know she's been arrested as a saboteur. Her brothers also."

"That's not my affair. Am I supposed to run a security check on every peasant I—"

"You're supposed to use your judgment. You might be a fighter ace, but you've obviously a few things to learn about women. About living with your two feet on the ground. She's using you, no doubt, and her arrest could place you in a precarious position." The general stopped for a moment, began to speak, then walking on again, announced abruptly, "It would be unwise of you to see her again or have anything to do with her family. Keep away from Jews."

Sergei said nothing.

"Well?" pressed the general.

"What?" Sergei challenged him. "Do you want me to sign an affidavit?"

"I want you to assure me, here, now, that you'll not see her again."

Sergei turned to head back toward the fighter hangars, his father following.

"The question's academic, isn't it? I doubt the Committee for Public Safety will release her." There was a sarcastic edge in his use of the KGB's official title. "I assume you've made sure of that."

"Don't be insulting!" said Kiril Marchenko, looking at his son angrily. There was a long silence as they continued walking, the only sound that of their boots, now out of step, in the snow. "Colonel Nefski," began the general, "is in a difficult position. If these saboteurs aren't caught and they cut the Trans-Siberian, our garrisons out here would be seriously—"

"I know that," said Sergei impatiently.

"Your own squadron will feel the effect, too," the general continued. "Not only from the railway delays but the munitions being made out here."

"We've already had problems," said Sergei.

"Oh—" The general slowed. "Nefski never told me that."

"Some of the Aphids," said Sergei.

"What are they?"

"Air-to-air. They appear not to have exploded on the target range—though it's possible they could have gone into the ocean. It's difficult sometimes to—"

"You see," said the general, seizing the opportunity. "This is *precisely* what I mean, Sergei. This mission against the American general, Freeman. Imagine if, after all that trouble, a rocket didn't—'' He stopped. ''You haven't volunteered, have you?''

''Of course.''

Kiril Marchenko had said it before his professional obligation had had a chance to override his feelings as a father. ''Then—'' he said, ''I'm proud of you.''

Sergei said nothing. They were approaching the control tower, a dark obelisk in the sporadic moonlight that was shining through wisps of stratus, the air redolent with pine, and in the distance somewhere a convoy, the faint slits of its air raid headlights approaching the base like some strange, segmented yellow snake weaving through the forest. The saboteurs, Sergei remembered, had also cut the Khabarovsk and Volochayevka roadway.

''Would be nice,'' said Kiril Marchenko, changing the subject, ''if you wrote your mother more often.''

''Yes,'' said Sergei, ''I mean to but—''

Kiril held his gloved hand up. ''I know. I was the same. But I told her I'd order you.''

Sergei couldn't see his father's face clearly but sensed the attempt at good humor.

''Is she all right?'' asked Sergei.

''Thriving. She's soon to be promoted—head of chemical defense for all of Moscow. The first woman. It's quite an honor.''

''You think it will come to that?''

''No,'' said the general. ''The Americans don't have the stomach for it. Not after they've seen what we've done with our sleepers in their own country—their water supplies and the like. It's the one great advantage we have over them, Sergei. One must admit that for all his childish idealism, Gorbachev did at least make it easier for Chernko to flood the United States with our agents. Happily, it's never been the other way around.'' The general paused for a moment, looking about to see whether any of the air traffic control sentries were nearby, lowering his voice. ''But if we're attacked with it, we'll use it. Suzlov won't hesitate.''

''Neither will the STAVKA,'' put in Sergei. He said it without rancor but as a matter of fact.

Kiril saw a guard at the door, silhouetted against a faint glow from the officers' mess. He called out to the man, reminding him it was an air raid precaution violation and to have the shutters drawn securely.

''Sergei, I wouldn't be surprised if Comrade Nefski gives

you a call—to warn you off this woman. Try not to be rude. It won't do you any good. Just accept you've made an error." The general hurried on. "You can find another outlet for your passions—you understand, eh?" He slapped Sergei on the back. "Find a good Russian girl or one of the brown-skinned ones, eh?" He paused at the entrance to the mess.

"My plane leaves in half an hour." Sergei still said nothing. It was Sergei's worst failing, in his father's view. On the battlefield his son had distinguished himself more than once, but he had retained a childish propensity to sulk. Or was it only with his father that he behaved so? "Look," said Kiril. "A man must be sensible about these things. If you need more money in order to—"

"Huh—so I can buy a woman?"

"If necessary, *yes*," said Kiril Marchenko. "If you go to a clean place, at least you know what you're getting. You're not the first soldier to—"

"I don't need money," said Sergei. "I have enough." His father hadn't even used her name. Again there was a long, awkward silence between them. Finally Sergei murmured, "Don't worry. I'll be careful."

"Good," said the general. They hugged.

"Write to your mother."

"Yes."

In the officers' mess, Sergei was flipping through a finger-worn copy of a German pornographic magazine, lingering over a blonde, tarted up in a top hat and tails, no shirt—her long, red-nailed fingers clasping the silver top of a long walking stick. Sergei and his wing man, Boris, were trying to discover whether the blonde's attributes were natural or silicone-assisted. Such procedures were rare in the Soviet Union but apparently quite common in Germany.

"Our women have bigger breasts than that," said Boris.

"And bigger bottoms," countered Sergei.

"So what's wrong with that?" parried Boris. "I like something you can grab on to."

"All I want to grab," put in the ground crew captain, "are enormous, great, pendulous—"

"*Mayor*—Major—Marchenko!"

"Da?"

"Telefon."

When Sergei heard Nefski's voice, he was immediately on guard, at once struck by his father's warning that his association with the Jewess was bound to incur a warning from the KGB to stay away from the Yevreysk autonomous region.

"Major. We believe you know the girl Alexsandra Malof?"

"Yes," Marchenko said, then, as he was wont to do in a dogfight, seizing offense as the best defense, added, "She's a Jew."

"Ah—now, there you are. You see—" The KGB colonel seemed to be talking to someone else at the other end, then came back on the line. "—I was just telling my assistant, Major, that you are just like your father. A man who gets straight to the heart of things."

No, thought Sergei, I am not like my father. I won't do a dance around it. The Jewess was the best lay he'd had during the entire war. Besides, what could Nefski do to an air ace? It would make the local KGB boss very unpopular, not only with the STAVKA HQ in Moscow but with all the propaganda cadres throughout the sixteen military districts and the four air armies.

"I would like to talk to you," said Nefski, his tone upbeat, casual.

"Yes?" said Sergei guardedly, waiting.

"No, no," said the colonel. "Not on the phone. Let us have a meal—dinner—at the Bear Inn?"

Marchenko knew the place in Khabarovsk. It specialized in Yakut food.

"What is there to talk about, Comrade Colonel?"

"Let's talk."

"I can't tonight."

"I realize that," said Nefski, Marchenko surprised that the colonel apparently knew about *"Operatsiya otmorozhennaya"*—"Operation Frostbite"—the planned intercept of the plane that reportedly would be flying the legendary American General Freeman across the Sea of Japan to Korea. But then, Sergei told himself, he should have guessed that Nefski would have spies everywhere—probably knew what the base commander had for breakfast.

"Tomorrow night then," said Nefski congenially, "when you return."

Marchenko knew that what Nefski meant was "*if* you return." Or had he merely guessed that Sergei had volunteered to go on the mission? No, Sergei concluded, the colonel would *know* not only that he had volunteered but was also leading the mission.

"Major? Would sixteen hundred hours be satisfactory?"

"Yes," agreed Marchenko.

"Good," said Nefski. I hope you understand we have no objections to our men in uniform going out with the Jewish faith. Such prejudice is against Soviet law."

"I know," said Sergei pointedly. It wasn't that he loved Alexsandra. He didn't. She was merely an attractive brunette, her figure enough to satisfy even his ground captain's more outrageous fantasies. It would be easy for him to ditch her—there was a lot more pussy around Khabarovsk. Besides, being an ace meant having the highest pay scale of any field combatants—he could buy what his uniform and medals couldn't attract. No, what he objected to was the politicos like Nefski telling him whom he could screw and whom he couldn't. The odd thing, however, was that Nefski's tone, despite his parroting official policy of nondiscrimination against minorities, made it sound as if the colonel didn't really hate Jews. Which was unusual.

CHAPTER TWENTY-SEVEN

DURING THE RETREAT from the frozen jumble of ice that was the Yalu River, its chopped-up appearance due to sections refreezing after American 105-millimeter artillery shells had holed it, the Third Infantry Division, under Gen. Arthur C. Creigh, now in full retreat from the river, was encountering the worst Korean winter for the past seventeen years. Medics were carrying their morphine ampules in their mouths in order to keep the morphine warm enough to pass through a syringe.

Many of the wounded, waiting in the heavy snow for the "khaki angels," the helo Medevacs, died before the choppers could reach the besieged Changsong Road that lead back from the river toward the MASH units of Kusong. Many of the wounded, covered with snow, slipped into the warm sleep of hypothermia as plasma froze solid, drip pouches split open, and the men still able to march discarded everything nonessential, including mess kits, using their helmets instead. Others ate the freeze-dried emergency C ration as it was, unable to get hot water except for rare moments when a tank, or rather those tanks still moving, could provide the heat from their engines.

While the freeze-dried food kept some of the troops going, many of the wounded, who normally would have survived the relatively quick Medevac, ate the food, using snow to wash it down, and in doing so, reduced vital body heat before the consumed food had time to do any good. Since coming under heavy fire from the Chinese artillery, much of which had been carried piece by piece by the Chinese and Korean infantry to the ridges overlooking the road, Creigh's division had suffered over four thousand casualties.

At 1400 hours the snowfall swallowed up the sun, thereby limiting the vital air support that had been coming in from the carrier *Salt Lake City*. It gave the Chinese perfect opportunities for ambush and close-in fighting, for which they had been especially trained. By 1630, the divisions' casualties had climbed to over five thousand, making it—apart from the mass U.S. surrender on Corregidor in World War II—one of the worst disasters in U.S. military history.

As fresh Chinese and North Korean divisions continued to pour across the Yalu, General Kim's North Korean regulars formed the eastern arm of a pincer soon to be completed by an artillery-supported right hook of four Chinese divisions—over sixty thousand Chinese and North Koreans in all—closing on the beleaguered Americans.

The next morning, December 25 in Korea, Christmas Eve in the United States, millions of viewers across America were riveted and sickened by astonishing clear TV-satellite-relayed pictures from the Changsong "gauntlet," seeing haggard, hollow-eyed American infantrymen, many too weak either from exhaustion, wounds, or both, struggling to fight off repeated Chinese attacks, which at times cut the road into segments in which they hoped to annihilate the U.S. troops, the fighting often hand to hand, after which the remaining Chinese, cannibalizing the retreating GIs' equipment, re-formed for yet more attacks on the flanks of the demoralized and retreating American army.

In all the television footage, however, one shot, a lingering pan of a quarter-mile section of road that had been white but was now red with American blood and littered with American dead, was the picture that traumatized civilians back home. About the road, brown boils of uprooted earth marked the spots where shells from the Chinese artillery had bracketed the retreating Americans. And now, in this war, the taboo that had been so long and meticulously observed right up to and including Vietnam—never to show a dead American's face on film if possible—was broken. The taboo had not been violated through any willfulness of field reporters but because of the sheer efficiency of the electronic media whose signals were received in *real* time only seconds after the action had taken place. What, at first, viewers assumed were long shots of crumpled clothing turned out to be close-up photos of dismembered American soldiers blown apart by the Chinese artillery and high-velocity close-in weapons fired only seconds before.

Throughout the television coverage, one of the most persistent comments concerned the bravery of the television cameramen who, though their pictures often shook violently from time to time, more from the pressure waves of the few remaining American 105s and mortars than from fear, kept filming some of the worst of the fighting. Even the older generation of civilians at home who, though too young to have remembered the Vietnam War, had seen footage of it later on, had never seen such carnage.

What the U.S. media didn't know, however, was that North Korean General Kim, whose favorite expression at Panmunjom during the prewar days was "Be careful, you Americans, or you will end up like Kennedy. Shot like a dog in the street," had issued orders, with threat of severe punishment if not obeyed, that enemy TV cameramen and crew were not to be harmed wherever possible.

"They are your allies in the struggle against the American warmongers," Kim had explained to his comrades. "The way to defeat Americans is to show what is happening to their children. They are a weak people. They will cry for armistice as they did when our forefathers defeated them over fifty years ago. Remember, Comrades, American television was one of the most decisive strategies of our comrades in Vietnam. Show them American casualties and the antifascist youth of America will clamor for their brothers' return. This is particularly true of the American bourgeoisie—the middle class. Show them how we are cutting the Americans to pieces and there will be mass demonstrations in the streets to bring their sons home."

* * *

When the first reports, both visual and decoded military traffic, of Creigh's retreat first reached Douglas Freeman, his plane, en route to Korea, was approaching Hawaii, and against all normal safety procedures, he not only refused to leave the plane while it was being refueled but ordered all thirty electronic warfare and other console operators to stay aboard as well. The situation in Korea was too critical for anyone to leave the plane, Freeman having decided to immediately issue orders for Creigh to stand and fight.

"Not a matter of heroics, Jim," he told Colonel Norton, "but if this casualty rake keeps up, the entire division'll be wiped out before they get anywhere near Kusong. That's over forty miles away. My God—what's the matter with Creigh?"

Norton handed him a sheaf of "eyes only" transmits from Creigh's retreating HQ, the messages routed via Seoul.

"Sir," one of Freeman's aides cut in, "we've got reports here from General Waverley, Two Brigade commander in Creigh's outfit. He doesn't come right out and say it, but you can read between the lines. Waverley's saying Creigh's stressed out!"

"*Stressed out!*" bellowed Freeman. "Goddamn it! I'll give him stress." He stood up from his seat in the plane's forward command booth. "Riley!"

The radio operator came running down through the "canyon" between the two rows of consoles.

"Yes, General?"

" 'Top secret,' priority rush to General Creigh, Second Infantry Division, Korean Northern Command. If you can't pinpoint his position and beam it down, funnel it through Seoul, but get it there."

"Yes, sir," said Riley, flipping out his notepad.

"Message reads," began Freeman, glowering as if Creigh, a popular commander by all accounts, was standing before him, Freeman starting to pace up and down the aisle just beyond the radio control like a caged bear. "Second Division is to cease retreat immediately. If you are incapable of command, you should transfer all authority at once. Repeat 'at once.' Shoot any man refusing to fight. I accept full responsibility. Freeman, C in C Korea. Message ends."

"By God," said Freeman, turning to address the two lanes of operators. "Stressed! That's just a fancy word for funk. Word gets out about Creigh shitting in his pants, we'll have desertion on that road.'' His voice was rising. ''We'll leave more than blood on that road, gentlemen. We'll leave American honor.'' He paused—Norton taking the opportunity to follow the radio operator down through the canyon. ''Now,'' continued Freeman, ''I want everyone here to remember that. I don't ever want to hear 'stressed out' in this command—goddamn pansy excuse for not working hard. Not doing your job. Do I make myself clear?''

There was murmured assent.

''Do I make myself clear?''

''Yes, sir!'' came a chorus.

Down by the radio console, Norton stood behind the operator and spoke in a quiet, even tone, to Riley, who was feeding the message into code pretransmission. ''Change the first part of the message, Riley,'' Norton told him. ''Replace 'if you are incapable' with 'if you are *incapacitated*.' ''

Riley looked up worriedly at the colonel.

''Just do it, son,'' said Norton. ''If it hits the fan, I'll take the flak.''

''Yes, sir.''

CHAPTER TWENTY-EIGHT

IN THE HALLS of the Admiralty in London's Whitehall and in Brussels HQ, a crisis of another kind was building, one of whose consequences, if nothing was done about it, would be infinitely more terrible than those facing the Americans in Korea. The operations board told the story in cold, unemotional figures—the rate of Soviet submarines sunk in the Atlantic had fallen off drastically, and the Allied convoys from the United States and Canada devoted to maintaining the rollover necessary to resupply Allied Europe were being sunk at a rate greater than that which had occurred in the early months of the war. For NATO's C in Cs, the danger, suspected earlier, was now being confirmed with yet another convoy of fifty ships having suffered over sixty percent losses barely a hundred miles north of the Azores. How the Russians submarines were doing it, neither Admiralty in Whitehall nor Norfolk, Virginia, knew, but the mathematical equations gave them the stark warning: If rollover faltered any further, then not only would Europe face the possibility of being starved into submission through lack of conventional munitions as well as food from America, but this lack would force the Allies to the weapons of last resort, which might be the last of everything.

But if in Whitehall the growing fear of the Allies was evident in the cold statistics on the computer screens and by the tiny models representing the growing number of convoy ships sunk, then for the Allied submarine commanders like Robert Brentwood, a thousand feet or more beneath the surface of the Atlantic, the danger took on an infinitely more palpable, if invisible, reality.

CHAPTER TWENTY-NINE

The Hawaiian Islands

THE FIJIAN TRAWLER MV *Vanuatu* was manned by East Indian Fijians with long memories of Colonel Kabuka's coup d'état of 1987 when the Fijian-run military overthrew Her Majesty's duly elected government in the South Seas island. Indian journalists were imprisoned, and the ever-present hostility of the native Fijian population against their fellow East Indian citizens was as palpable in the balmy air as the humidity that hung so oppressively over Suva Bay. Paradise had lost its innocence forever after the coup, and into the void created by the condemnation issued from Her Majesty's government, the Russians had come, bearing aid. In return, the Russians received not only fish treaties but also the right to visit and use Fijian port facilities for repairs to the huge Soviet trawler fleet whenever "necessary."

At one stroke the Soviets in the eighties had extended the KGB's and MVD's intelligence-gathering facilities halfway around the world to the South Seas—hitherto the American navy's domain.

And so it was that the MV *Vanuatu*, ostensibly a Fijian trawler but in reality under subcontract to the Russian merchant marine, operating between the Ellis Islands group and Hawaii, was in Honolulu when Freeman's 747 landed. Still, the Indian operatives aboard the trawler wouldn't have learned of his presence but for one of the civilian ground crew from Honolulu's airport grouching in the Reef Bar about missing the first round of poker because he'd had to work overtime "juicing up" some bigwig's "flying lanai."

"Some politician's freebie," suggested one of the players, another mechanic, making like a high roller, ordering mai-tais all round.

"Nah," said the airport mechanic. "Wasn't politicians. They hit the tarmac soon as they land. Suck in their gut, leis all around them, and big smiles for the *Advertizer*. These guys wouldn't even leave the plane when we were pumping 'er full of Avgas."

It wasn't much to go on for one of the *Vanuatu*'s crew sitting at the bar, knocking back his fourth Bud, but it was enough for *Vanuatu*'s skipper to pass it along via "fish talk." This innocuous plain-language transmission, full of information about sea conditions, movements and depth of schools of fish, was relayed from one trawler to another as far as the South Korean and Japanese trawler fleets plying the Tsushima Straits off Japan's southern island of Honshu. By the time Freeman's plane reached Tokyo's Narita Airport—Osaka ruled out because of fog—a South Korean trawler, manned by North Korean illegals, all with bona fide ROK papers, had sent a fake SOS of predetermined coordinates. The rescue hovercraft of the Japanese defense forces, taking the message as a genuine distress call, ended up on a wild-goose chase and assumed the boat had sunk when they reached the area and found no sign of the vessel.

The coordinates, a number-for-letter code, alerted Soviet operatives from Japan to Vladivostok and Khabarovsk that the Americans' VIP plane was at Narita.

In order that there would be no possibility of either Soviet or Chinese radar-guided, surface-to-air missile batteries along the

Yalu and Tamur firing at the Soviet mission's aircraft as they headed south, a secret message in "four group, number-for-number" code went out from STAVKA Moscow HQ to Far Eastern TVD HQ Khabarovsk—for repeat to the Soviet Embassy in Beijing. The message, mainly for the benefit of the Chinese, was to inform all AA batteries that in the next twenty-four hours, Soviet fighters would be in Manchurian air space and were not to be fired upon.

The message was intercepted by U.S. intelligence satellite K-14 in geosynchronous orbit over the South China Sea, but as the STAVKA's code had not been broken, the number series transcript of it was filed—to add to the voluminous piles of other intercepts, which included everything from military traffic to civilian traffic between the United States, Canada, and Asia. Even if the code had been cracked by U.S. intelligence, the chances of it being brought immediately to SACPAC HQ in Tokyo were fifty-fifty due to what insiders habitually called the PHS, or Pearl Harbor Syndrome, referring to the avalanche of information which might contain what you want to know but which, even with computers working flat out, takes hours, often days, to process.

"I assume we don't have to stop at Matsue?" Freeman asked Norton as their car drove across from the secluded VIP lounge at Narita to the Boeing. "We can go straight through to Seoul."

"Yes, sir, and in the morning we fly up to Pakchon—it's only about thirty miles from the front."

"Front the front! It will be the front if Creigh doesn't pull himself together."

As the car drove across the runway, a dull, thudding sound came from underneath as the clacking of the tires on the cement seams was muffled by the car's heavy armor-plated chassis. "Those fighters. Remember to have them go off a half hour before us."

"It's all arranged, sir. Don't think there'll be any problem. Overcast above the Sea of Jap— sorry, sir, over the East Sea. That'll help hide the big bird. And so far, security seems to be holding up." By way of underscoring his point, Norton reached forward and took a copy of *Stars and Stripes* from the pocket by the jump seat. "Here's a photo of you inspecting the forward troops around Warsaw. You were in Washington at the time." The headline ran,

FREEMAN CROSSES BORDER—TAKES BREST DRIVES ON TO MINSK

The look-alike, Freeman had to admit, was very convincing and well rugged up, the military scarf speckled with snow, bundled high against the cold—and close-up shots.

"Yes," agreed Freeman, obviously pleased, if not by the deception, then by the paper's announcing to the world at large that his American-led NATO armored column had succeeded in breaking through and were now engaging the Russians on their own soil. Nevertheless, he uncharacteristically intoned a caution. "But can we hold them, Dick?" He paused and put down the paper. "By God, I told my men I don't want to ever hear we're holding anything, and last report I get is we're grinding to a stop, 'consolidating,' because Russian subs have been chopping up our Atlantic supply line. We've gotta have more gas, Jim, more food, munitions—more of everything before those bastards in Moscow can organize a counter attack. More battles in history have been lost by overextended supply lines than for any other reason."

"The Russians are stuck, too, General. Snow is neutral."

"The hell it is. For the Russians it comes with mother's milk."

"Maybe, sir, but the fact of the matter is, they *are* digging in for the moment."

Freeman nodded, pulling up his coat collar and tightening his belt as he walked unhurriedly in the pouring rain to the plane. "Stuck! But for how long, Jim? Russia's vast, all right, but their supply problems are still not as rough as ours. We can blow up their rail tracks. They fix them. We blow them up again, they can use horses to haul supplies if necessary. But we have to cross an ocean." Deep in thought, the general walked up the stairs to the plane. "You know the greatest surprise in this war, Jim?"

"What's that, General?"

"All the *experts* said that there would never be trench warfare again because it would be a war of mobility—the fastest-moving war men had ever seen. Fact is, soldiers have never been worn out physically and mentally as fast before—all because of this mobility. At this point in history, both sides are exhausted." Colonel Norton thought it impolitic to remind the general of what he had said earlier about stress being an excuse for cowardice. Geniuses, he figured, had the right to be inconsistent.

"We've got to surprise them, Jim. Somehow we have to—"

"Merlin?" proffered Norton, referring to the plan the general had been working on, a plan so secret that only he, Norton, and his G-2 knew about it.

Freeman shook his head. "Our boys aren't ready yet, Jim. God knows I'm not known for overcaution, but we'd only have one shot at it. Besides, it's a last-ditch scenario. Don't want to use it until I absolutely have to. First let's try to untie this logjam in Korea, beat the Chinese and North Koreans back over the Yalu. If we do that, we can take pressure off our boys around Brest while our jokers figure out what the hell is going on with our convoys. Something screwy going on with the Russian subs. Well," he sighed, "at least the Russians don't seem to know I'm over here."

"No, sir. Flying over the East Sea's going to be the most restful part of the trip."

"Good. I sure as hell could use the sleep."

As the general buckled up, the Boeing's jets screaming into high pitch, Norton was called up to the communications console. Moments later, he walked back through the eerily lit alley of winking consoles and computers and handed Freeman a top secret message of unconfirmed gas attacks by PLA—Communist Chinese—forces against several South Korean positions across the Yalu.

CHAPTER THIRTY

THE TWIN-FINNED MIG 29-A, NATO designation Fulcrum A, was not only top of its class; some NATO pilots believed it to be the best fighter in the world, smaller than the Tomcat, more powerful than the F-18. In ready rooms all along the NATO front, Allied pilots held that, were the Soviets allowed time to produce enough of them, the Allies would no longer have the edge in the European war.

Sergei Marchenko, holder of the Order of Lenin, Hero of the Soviet Union, and Distinguished Flying Medal for his actions both at Fulda Gap at the war's beginning and later over the Aleutians, where his MiG-27 Flogger D had downed, among others, Frank Shirer's F-14 Tomcat and where, in turn, Marchenko himself had been downed, snatched from the freezing Bering Sea with only moments to spare, was known by sight to all civilian and military personnel at the huge Khabarovsk air base. Yet he was not liked—there was a hardness about him that was off-putting—a brutal streak, some said. But as a pilot, it was said he had no equal.

In a world of high-tech millisecond avionics, Marchenko's fame—his ability to make split-second decisions and his extraordinary skill at handling the Fulcrum—had spread throughout the armed services. Not only was he recognized as a natural in the air, but it was common knowledge that despite the best possible connections in Moscow, he had proven himself as an ordinary soldier in the blood and dust of the *boynya*—"abattoir"—of Fulda Gap, where the sun itself had been obscured by the massive clouds of exhaust, dust, and shellfire from the massed American and Russian armor locked in battle. And even those who saw the killer too often in his eyes acknowledged that, unlike the sons of other important men, he had not placed himself within the highly protected walls of the

Kremlin, in the STAVKA's HQ as an officer, but had volunteered for frontline duty in the Far Eastern TVD. Despite this, he remained a loner, occasionally sociable in the mess and ready room, but always holding something in reserve. The cold, hard streak, which some claimed verged on the sadistic, didn't show itself, however, until he was in aerial combat.

Among the ground crew he was known as "*Nemignuvshiy*"—"No Blink"—a reference to the story that had been passed on from his training days after he'd moved out of the two-seater L-29 jet trainers at the Yuri Gagarin Academy, qualifying for MiG-21s at the Gagnon Higher Aviation Academy. They had been readying for an air race at the end of the course to test them before they could go on to fly the top-of-the-line fighters. The test, in MiG-23s, involved a low-level half roll and loop, then a return to level flight over the academy's airfield prior to receiving the coveted wings to go with the green "CA" shoulder boards. Before the race, the pilots, six of them including Sergei Marchenko, had walked, as was customary, through the maneuvers on the chalk lines outside the academy's glass-and-cement tower. Even then one of the instructors had remarked on Marchenko's total concentration while the other cadets occasionally glanced at one another, to see how the others were doing, indulging in a joke or two as they slowed the walk to avoid near misses.

The six went up, moving off two at a time, the MiG-23s' Tumansky R-29s on full afterburner, swing wings at sixteen degrees, the MiGs gaining altitude, retracting landing gear, extending the dorsal fin and spreading wings to forty-five degrees. The fighters formed a six-plane perfect diamond, performed one thundering low-level pass over the field, separated, and climbed for the ten-thousand-foot ceiling, the training video camera in each plane, mounted beneath the sight for later replay, already whirring, the instructors in the tower listening closely to the chatter for any sign of hesitancy. All six MiGs then came in for the low roll under Mach 1 but in excess of six hundred miles per hour, where a split-second mistake would put them into the ground.

They came out of the half roll in unison and were into the second half of a loop. There was a cry from one of the pilots at the apogee of the roll. The instructor's shouted correction from the tower came too late—the MiG-23 a ball of fire in the birch trees on the eastern edge of the runway. In that moment, as the videotapes of the remaining five planes later showed, only *one* pilot, Sergei Marchenko, hadn't looked down at the crash but, in that instant, had exerted maximum throttle—and won.

Zipping up his G suit, Marchenko said nothing as the other pilots on the mission talked animatedly among themselves, most, he noticed, strictly observing the ritual of zipping up either right or left boot first. To Marchenko it didn't matter. Their rituals to him were those of juvenile superstitions, of talismans, lucky numbers, obsessions held as tightly as American baseball players who, an instructor had once told him, often favored the same pair of socks or undershirt as being "lucky" for their game. Marchenko viewed such rituals with the same contempt as he did belief in God. It was all voodoo. The only belief one could rely on was the belief in oneself, in one's own precision and ability—the best talisman being the sure knowledge that you could do it—and win.

Marchenko saluted his ground crew captain, the man barely visible in the dim red night light by the plane's ladder, and lowered himself into the Fulcrum's cockpit, pulling on the skull cap, followed by his dark-visored helmet, and a metamorphosis took place. Man is a natural killer, his father had told him. Regrettable but true. The best warriors knew this. Caldwell, the Australian ace who in World War II shot German pilots in their parachutes after he'd let one go and seen the German kill his best friend the next day, knew it. And so did the great American aces of the Vietnam War. There was no glamour. There was only precision and death. In the Fulcrum his precision and the cruel beauty of the Mikoyan fighter met and fused as one.

He could perform a hammerhead stall/tail slide under a mere three thousand feet, then go straight, and he meant *straight*, into an eighty-five degree climb, the combined eighteen-thousand-pound thrust of the twin Tumansky R-33Ds shifting the metallic, honeycombed, and plastic composite machine from "reduce thrust" to "idle," back to "flat out," without the engines so much as missing a beat. For Marchenko, the Fulcrum's thrust/weight ratio, greater than one, was *velichestvennoe*—"sublime"—and it made the Fulcrum not only a superb fighter but an ideal interceptor as well.

His Fulcrum, a large 9 painted on the starboard jet's box intake, with its slogan "*Ubiytsa Yanki*"—"Yankee Killer"—next to the blue-beige winged insignia of the Mikoyan-Gurevich design bureau, rose with the eight other MiG-29s into the zero visibility above Vladivostok, crossing the Soviet-Chinese border, heading south over China's northeasternmost province of Heilongjiang.

En route to the planned intercept of the American-fighter-protected 747 believed to be carrying the American general Douglas Freeman, strict radio silence was observed. No active radar, which might be picked up by U.S. fighter cover over the Sea of Japan, was permitted. Only passive radar could be used to receive advance warning of the American presence.

The American fighters, Marchenko knew, would no doubt be doing the same, but once contact with them was made, six of the Fulcrums would peel off to the southeast to engage the largest group of the American fighter cover. The remaining three Fulcrums, Marchenko leading, would ignore all else, staying low, in the sea scatter, in hope of hiding themselves from American radar, their sole target the largest blip recorded by Vladivostok Control, the latter coordinating the Soviet-Chinese ground radar network as well as the offshore buoy-mounted radar.

Once they picked up the 747, Vladivostok Center would send a burst transmission, vectoring the 747's position relative to the Fulcrums. Only nearing the vectored point of intercept would the MiG-29s' look-down, shoot-down radar, with a range of sixty-seven miles, be turned on for the attack.

Climbing, then diving at Mach 2.8, over three thousand kilometers per hour, loaded with six pylon-mounted Alamo air-to-air missiles apiece and fully drummed thirty-millimeter gun beneath the left wing, Marchenko's Fulcrum and the other two following him in arrowhead formation would close the sixty-seven miles to the 747 in two minutes, plus or minus fifteen seconds. Only then, Marchenko had told the other two pilots, would each plane's IRST—infrared search and tracking—dome, mounted high on the starboard side of the Fulcrum's nose, be switched on to pick up the 747's exhaust lest the Boeing's formidable jamming capability scramble any of the Fulcrum's avionics, including the multimode nose radar and the Sirena 3 radar warning receivers.

It was 0957 and eleven seconds when Vladivostok's Ground Station Four on the Jilin Province–USSR border reported a cluster of aircraft rising from Matsue, Japan, heading across the East Sea at twenty thousand feet and traveling at Mach .9. The operators opined that though these aircraft were traveling at only seven hundred miles per hour, they were possibly a fighter umbrella protecting a larger blip traveling at Mach .7, accompanied by three smaller aircraft farther south of the first group, EIT plus or minus fourteen minutes.

The nine Fulcrums peeled off to engage, not doubting for a moment that what Ground Radar Four had seen were American fighters going slowly to keep pace with the Boeing 747. What they did not realize was that the burst message they received from Vladivostok Control was immediately picked up by two of the fifty-man 747 crew manning the consoles aboard the big 231-foot-long Boeing jet and that via satellite bounce, the positions of both groups of Fulcrums, the six coming straight for the American fighters and the three others "on the deck" staying on course for the 747, were being plotted by the Americans.

Then, for both sides, the fighter pilot's nightmare happened: The first crack, then rumble, of one of several electrical storms fractured the air above the Sea of Japan with a "splitting" that began to play havoc with the sophisticated avionics of both the hunters and the hunted. The only hope was that in between electrical surges, a quick fix on the opposition might be possible.

Aboard the Boeing, commander of the aircraft, Frank Shirer, was immediately alerted to the presence of Bogeys, the battle staff correctly assuming, and he concurred, that the six Soviet fighters—too fast to be Chinese—were peeling off to engage the F-14 Tomcats farther north while three who'd been trying to hide in the scatter were the "strikers," now climbing, fast, toward him, while the bigger American formation would have no choice but to engage the six Fulcrums.

"Damn it!" said Shirer, glancing over at his copilot, "I wish to hell I was in two oh three—my old F-14. I'd give those bastards a run for their money."

Without any armament, the electronics of the 747 having taken up all available space, Shirer felt naked. Then it started to rain—"like a cow peeing on a flat rock," announced Freeman.

"He's cool," commented the copilot as Freeman left the cabin.

"He's not driving," said Shirer.

In the rear of the 747, Jim Norton looked ill. He tried to hide it, but he was a white-knuckled flier at the best of times, and the storm was terrifying. "Jim," said Freeman, "I ever tell you 'bout the time I was in Louisiana? Bunch of us on leave, dressed in civvies, went into this greasy spoon. Bill Fryer was with us. You know Bill. Hundred and first Airborne."

"No," said Norton, and he didn't care.

"Well," said Freeman, "this white waiter ambles up, takes one look at Bill, and says, 'We don't serve coloreds here.' Everyone's struck dumb, 'cept Johnny Morgan—my G-2 at the time. Quick as a flash Johnny looks from Bill Fryer to the waiter and says, 'But he's a *king*.'

" 'No shit,' says the waiter, and toddles off. Manager comes down, and now Bill Fryer's sitting there like he's King Farouk and we're all going along with it—kowtowing, 'Your Majesty' this, 'Your Majesty' that. Manager's as obsequious as a pimp on a slow day . . . apologies galore . . . so's the waiter by now. What can they do for us? et cetera, et cetera. So we stay and have a big meal. All the time we keep up the act, treating Bill like he's a goddamned royal." The 747 lurched violently. Norton closed his eyes. "Well," continued Freeman, "just as we're about to leave, the waiter comes down with the bill, all smiles, looks at Bill Fryer, and says, 'We ain't never had a king here before.' Know what Bill Fryer says? 'No shit!' "

Norton shook his head.

Freeman laughed so loud, Norton felt obliged to offer a weak smile, convinced by the turbulence and the oncoming Soviet fighters that it might be the last joke he'd ever hear.

CHAPTER THIRTY-ONE

FROM THE TRAIN, David Brentwood looked out on the rolling green hills of west England's Herefordshire. He thought it the most beautiful country he'd ever seen. And as the train passed on through Hay-on-Wye over the English-Welsh border, winding its way between the brooding black mountains deep into Brecknockshire toward Brecon at the foot of the two windswept mountains known as the Beacons, slowly and inexorably, everything changed for David. It was as if he had been in this place before. It wasn't only the smell of the fresh winter air, the earthy dampness that reminded him of the wet winters in the Pacific Northwest in Washington and Oregon, but the wild beauty of the place. The wind-riven hillsides of flattened grasses spoke to him, as they did to few others on that train. Though brought up by his mother in the Protestant faith, which viewed God in deeply personal ways, David could not believe as she did. The suffering of children, the death of Lili—how could there be any good in that? "We all have to die," his mother would say. "The timing and circumstance of it, David, are only things *we* fret about so long as we see this life as all there is." Was this war all there was? he wondered. If so, then winning it seemed more important than ever before, for in mourning Lili's death, he'd realized in a way he never had before how short life really was. It had been a thing his parents and grandparents had always told him—an old person's cliché, repeated to the young so many times, it became nothing more than a bore, because inside him there had been the secret belief of all youth that they would not die—at least not before their time, a time which in their own minds was always secure and far in the future.

For a moment he had doubts about volunteering for the SAS force. If this life *was* such a transitory thing—why bother? Because, he answered himself, corny as he knew it might sound to others, he believed it was right to fight evil. If you didn't, then people like Lili, Melissa—damn her—would live in a far worse world, a world where there could be no honor, no love, only subservience to the kind of brutality he'd seen as a child the day the newscasts had shown the Communists crushing the movement for democracy with tanks in Tiananmen Square.

As the train carrying him, Thelman, and the other ninety-six volunteers who had been interviewed for the SAS training program pulled into Brecon, David looked up again at the grass-covered sandstone slopes, the sweeping line of the high hills broken now and then by woods of gnarled trees deformed by the wind, and cottages that had looked picturesque from the distance but which now appeared to be deserted and run-down. High above the three-thousand-foot Beacons, buzzards circled, ever patient, waiting, he presumed, for any of the black-faced sheep grazing on the steep slopes to fall. Still, the scene did not depress him, and inhaling the fresh mountain air, he closed his eyes, the better to impress it upon his memory as a new beginning, a place that, whatever happened, would always be close to his heart. Perhaps it was not so much the place at all but that it was a *new* place where he might regain the old surety of action he'd known before the nerve-shattering experience of Pyongyang and Stadthagen. A new beginning.

"You okay?" asked Thelman.

"Fine," said David. It was the first time Thelman had seen his old buddy of Parris Island days smile since they'd left France aboard the overnight Hovercraft, the Channel still blocked by the massive explosion that had closed it in the first weeks of the war when a SPETS cell, one of them posing as a cross-channel truck driver, had set off the bomb that had collapsed the two main tunnels, concussion killing most of those in transit, the North Sea pouring in and drowning the rest.

"Nice little town," remarked Thelman. "Somebody told me Wales was full of slag heaps."

"Well they're not here," replied David. He had no inkling that within forty-eight hours he would hate the place, cursing the moment he had agreed to "try out," as the English Captain Smythe had so casually put it. Yet the beginning of his time at SAS gave no hint of how quickly he would feel he'd made a mistake, for at first it wasn't at all like Parris Island or Camp Lejeune. Indeed, when he first stepped out of the train, he and all the others had been struck by an angelic singing, male voices in a harmony he wouldn't have believed possible outside of the Mormon Tabernacle Choir—voices raised, singing ancient Welsh hymns. It *did* sound like *How Green Was My Valley*.

As David looked around at the other ninety-odd volunteers, he saw unit badges from every kind of regiment, including several Dutch and German troops, sappers to engineers, even a Seabee, and at least six men from the Coldstream Guards, all brought to a standstill by a chorus they could hear somewhere beyond the station. Even Thelman, though an avid fan of what David's father, the admiral, would have described as "moron thump," stood on the station platform, listening in rapt attention.

"Concert in town?" one of the volunteers asked the SAS regimental sergeant major who turned up to greet them.

"No," the RSM replied, his quiet Welsh accent surprising to David. "Cymru versus the Barbarians." Thelman and Brentwood looked at one another in bewilderment.

"Football!" interjected a captain called Cheek-Dawson, wearing the coveted beige SAS beret with the blue-winged dagger above the emblem "Who Dares, Wins." "Welsh against the English," he explained. "The singing you hear, needless to say, is coming from the Welsh supporters. If they lose, I daresay we'll hear a pretty decent requiem."

"Ah," said one of the sappers, a Hispanic American, name tag "Bartroli." "Soccer, right?"

"No, no, man," said the RSM, his tone good-natured but intent on correction nevertheless. "Not that sissy business. This is rugby."

"More like American football, right, Sar'Major?" said Cheek-Dawson good-naturedly.

"Without the ruffles," replied the RSM.

"Ruffles?" challenged Thelman.

"All that padding."

"Wonder you don't kill yourselves then," retorted Thelman.

"It happens," said the RSM. "All right, lads—into the trucks with kit. Reception at Senny Bridge in—" he glanced at his watch "—half an hour. Fourteen hundred."

Thelman reminded Brentwood of the joke they'd heard at Parris Island about the first intake of women into the Marine Corps getting it all wrong when the female DI said she'd give them twenty minutes to get ready for *kit* inspection . . .

Brentwood fell silent, remembering the last time he'd heard the story was from the British sergeant who'd been murdered along with Lili on the train to Liège.

An Australian listening in to the joke as the trucks pulled away from Brecon station laughed so loud, Thelman thought he'd fall off the tailgate.

"Heard the one about the kangaroo and the priest?" asked the Aussie.

"No," said Brentwood. The Aussie was talking to them as if he'd known them all his life. He didn't get to tell them his joke, however, as they were passing the football ground, and a surge of Welsh patriotism, mainly the voices of old men—most of the young ones having been drafted—filled the truck with such emotion that men who'd never heard of rugby were moved.

"You play that in Australia, don't you?" asked David.

"Yeah, but Australian Rules mainly," said the Aussie.

"Australian rules?" put in Cheek-Dawson with good cheer. "I should have thought that an oxymoron."

"What d'ya mean?" said the Aussie. "Moron?"

"Ah—I meant a contradiction in terms," explained Cheek-

Dawson, "You know—Australians and rules? No offense meant."

The Aussie grinned. "None taken, mate. The name's Mick. Mick Lewis. They say that with a name like that, I'm half-Irish and half-Welsh. But I can't sing a bloody note."

The first hour was like that—informal, the distinction between officer, NCO, and other ranks not paid anywhere like the attention it received elsewhere, particularly in the British forces, where class differences readily became recognizable to even the most recent arrival from overseas. It was different, too, from Parris Island, which surprised David and Thelman, and no doubt many of the other American recruits. No DIs screaming hysterically at you, treating you like dirt even before you got off *their* bus. And David couldn't imagine a regular British officer elsewhere joking with the Australian—there certainly wouldn't have been any apology so readily offered.

Shortly after 1400, they arrived at the SAS HQ at Senny Bridge, eight miles west of Brecon, the headquarters having been moved forty miles west of Hereford on the English side because of Soviet rocket attacks. The Brecon Beacons were covered in deep, fast-moving shadows and then brilliant sunlight. "A dabbledy day," said the RSM as he jumped down from the jeep leading the three-tonners, and looked up at the jumbled sky. "All right then, lads. Columns of three. Tallest left and right—smallest in the middle. Shake a leg."

Major Rye, an officer in his midforties with slightly graying hair and a broad, friendly face, dressed in beret, camouflage-pattern battle dress smock and trousers, came out to welcome them. They were all volunteers from every branch of the services—their reasons for volunteering as varied as the men themselves, some bored with life in the line regiments, which, because of the slowdown in supplies occasioned by convoy losses, were now forced to dig in and wait. Others no doubt were escaping domestic entanglements of one kind or other, and some had volunteered because they, as young men, some of them children at the time, had been electrified, as was the whole world, by the riveting spectacle of the first SAS public appearance. There had been rumors that an elite force, called the Special Air Service, had existed, but the first time the world knew the rumors were right was on May 6, 1980, in London in "Operation Nimrod." The SAS counterterrorist team, covered head to toe in what was to become their telltale black uniform, wearing CS gas masks, which also protected their identity, attacked and, with astonishing speed, ended, in front of the world's TV cameras, a six-day, twenty-one-hostage drama in the Iranian Embassy. The attack, combining sheer-cliff mountaineering abseiling, stun grenades, and perfect HK MP5 submachine-gun kill shots at close range in crowded rooms, was so fast, the Iranian terrorists literally didn't know what hit them.

Though this constituted the first public view of the SAS, the Special Air Service had already been operating for over thirty years, ever since being formed from an "odd-bod" collection of commando enthusiasts who wreaked such havoc behind the enemy line in the Western Desert, destroying over 380 of Rommel's German aircraft and vast quantities of oil and ammunition, that Adolf Hitler issued a personal order to the Wermacht regarding the SAS that "these men are dangerous. They must be hunted down and destroyed at all costs."

After the Second World War, the SAS had carried on its covert service of British foreign policy, involving them in everything from the Malayan Communist emergency to joining the West German counterterrorist CSG-9 in the hostage-rescue attack against the hijacked Lufthansa airliner on the airstrip at Mogadishu in Somalia. The fierce gun battle there lasted for more than seven minutes, but the success of the operation—only one hostage was wounded, and not fatally—was due once again to the extraordinary speed and accuracy of the assault, during which every terrorist aboard was hit in the first bursts of the commandos' gunfire. And then there were the audacious and devastating night raids in the Falklands War, and later deep inside Iraq, against Saddam Hussein's airfields.

CHAPTER THIRTY-TWO

OVER THE SEA of Japan, Shirer nosed the 747 down toward the thick cumulonimbus at fifteen thousand, seeking protection of zero visibility against the three breakaway fighters, the 747's over-the-horizon radar showing the Bogeys were now only sixty miles away, active radars on and coming in arrowhead formation for interdiction at a thousand miles per hour—almost certainly MiG-29 Fulcrums.

Shirer knew the F-14 Tomcats that would try to protect his 747 were good—on afterburner, over a hundred miles an hour faster than the Fulcrums—but, as an ace, he also knew the old rule still held: With the gizmology being more or less equal, over sixty percent of all kills in dogfights went to only the top six percent of pilots.

As the 747 entered the cloud in the pitch darkness, the three Fulcrums now only forty miles away, Shirer called through to the COMCO—countermeasures control officer. "Compute distance from Vladivostok to here and back. Approx."

The COMCO's Cray computer had it in four seconds. "Return journey plus or minus one thousand miles, Captain. I say again 'miles.' "

As if reading Shirer's mind, the officer had already computed the Fulcrum's combat radius of plus or minus eleven hundred kilometers against the distance from Vladivostok, and the arithmetic projection was clear: The Fulcrums could make it to interdiction and back to Vladivostok, but it would leave them little time for the attack. Their wing commander must certainly have taken this into account. COMCO's conclusion, quickly relayed to Shirer, was that the Fulcrums were probably hauling drop tanks for extended range.

Even so, Shirer knew that during an attack, the Bogeys would, at some point, have to jettison the drop tanks, even if they hadn't used all of the fuel from them, in order to reduce weight and so engage the Tomcats at maximum speed. This would force the Russians' fuel consumption to jump to eighteen times normal "suck-through" rate. In four minutes on full war power, each Fulcrum would guzzle more than thirty percent of its entire fuel load.

Shirer flicked on his mike. "Freedom One to Angel Leader. Do you read me?"

"Angel Leader," acknowledged the Tomcat pilot. "Go ahead."

"Fire Fox One at each Bogey. Repeat, fire Fox One at each Bogey."

The RIO—radar intercept officer—behind the pilot in each Tomcat wondered what in hell Shirer was up to. Very soon each of their Fox One air-to-air radar-homing Sparrow missiles would be ready, the fast-closing Fulcrums within range, but why, they wondered, fire now—allowing the Bogeys to have at least ten to fifteen seconds to "jinx" their way out of it, particularly when the Fulcrum was so highly maneuverable?

But orders were orders, all three RIOs in the Tomcats going to "warning yellow, weapons hold" status, each of the RIOs straining to hear the tone alert—a low growl in their earpiece telling them the missile was fully armed and ready for launch.

Back in the general's compartment, Col. Jim Norton was ill, the 747 continuing its hair-raising forty-degree dive, buffeted by so much turbulence, the whole plane seemed to be rattling to pieces, Norton convinced his stomach was now in his chest—or was it the other way around?—blocking his breathing. Glistening in the redded-out combat lighting of the aircraft, the droplets of sweat on his forehead looked like hundreds of tiny rubies.

"Now, don't you worry about it, Jim," Freeman assured him. "That boy up in front is gonna put this bird down in Seoul in no time."

Norton couldn't speak, unable even to articulate his terror, the veins in his hands standing out like dark strings as he clenched the armrests, eyes discombobulated, mouth parchment-dry, his heart thumping rapidly, doubly mortified at exhibiting such fright in front of Freeman, and painfully conscious again of the great and terrible divide between a çivilian aircraft and a military one. Here the noise was at once thunderous and screaming as it fell through the blackness, the nausea, indescribable in its clammy dizziness, overtaking him in a suffocating net.

"Fix your eye on something middistance, Jim," Freeman instructed him. "Helps keep your balance."

It was the stupidest goddamn thing the colonel had ever heard Freeman utter—there *wasn't* anything fixed! Everything was spinning out of control. Christ! He wished the general would just shut up and let him die.

In the Tomcats, the radar intercept officers got the tone alert.

"Master arm on," announced the Tomcat leader. "Centering up the T. Bogeys twenty-one miles. Centering the dot . . . Fox One, Fox One!"

The next rush of conversation between the Angel pilots and their RIOs surged with static and was full of overlay so that it was difficult for Shirer to know exactly who was speaking. Battling with the yoke in heavy turbulence at ten thousand feet, he heard his copilot yelling, "There they go!" the exhaust of the 524-pound American missiles lighting the clouds nearby in a momentary and astonishingly beautiful peach glow, and then six seconds later, a fast, broken chorus of "Good kill! Good kill! . . . Shoot him! . . ."

"Haven't got a fucking tone . . ."

"Shoot him . . . Shoot . . .!"

"Christ!" said Shirer's copilot, seeing a blip on the Boeing's radar screen disintegrating. "They got one of ours!"

Shirer was fighting to keep the Boeing in the steep dive, slipping farther away from the point of intercept, the babble of the Tomcats now interspersed with Russian: " *'Unichtozhit'! . . . 'Unichtozhit'!"—"Finish him off! . . . Finish him off!"*

"Lock him up! Lock him up!" a Tomcat pilot was yelling to his RIO. Then "Good kill! Good kill!" the RIO yelling, "Bogey missile . . . two o'clock high . . . two o'—"

"Jesus! . . ."

Behind Shirer, at the consoles, chaff and wide infrared-band flares were being jettisoned to confound the Fulcrum's missile, which the COMCO saw wasn't aimed at the Tomcats but was streaking toward the 747 at over twenty-one hundred miles an hour.

The console operator, his body at a down angle of thirty degrees, face bathed in perspiration, fought with everything he had to maintain control of the scrambler beam he was "coning" in on the incoming missile; any wider cone and he would interfere with the avionics in the Tomcats. The Russian missile, a quarter mile away, curled hard left and exploded, an amber blossom on the 747's console screen. Seconds later the shock wave and debris hit the Boeing, and Shirer saw the warning light for the starboard two engine flashing, its intake fouled, temperature soaring. He shut it down but still kept diving, hard to port, down toward the sea. As long as there were Bogeys in the area, he wanted to get down low where the Boeing's upward-looking radar could pinpoint the attackers for electronic countermeasures but where the Fulcrum's downward-looking radar would be confounded in an electronic haze of sea scatter.

"Bogey contact!" Shirer heard from somewhere high above him in the night sky. "Judy at ten o'clock. Splash!" It told Shirer that one of the two remaining Fulcrums was down.

"One to go!" came an exhilarated cry.

"Angel Leader to Angel Two. That's it. Break off . . . Let him go."

"Aw, shit!"

"Let him go!" repeated the Tomcat leader. "Cover the big bird. That's our job."

"You see any eject?" asked the second Tomcat pilot.

"Negative."

Sergei Marchenko didn't know who the pilot of Freeman's Boeing was, but whoever it had been, he knew his business. The Boeing was lost, and all that he was getting on his radar screen was the leaping "frying" static of sea clutter, like a television set gone haywire, and in the dogfight he'd used up so much fuel, he knew it was *opasnoe delo*—"touch and go"—as to whether he'd make it back to Vladivostok, let alone Khabarovsk. And he suspected that one of the Tomcat's rotary-barreled twenty-millimeter cannons might have taken a chunk out of the fuselage covering his nose landing wheel. There was no warning light on, but air speed indicated there was a drag somewhere, and even if the hydraulics hadn't been hit, the Tomcat's short burst had made a hole somewhere—big enough to slow him down.

He punched in the coordinates for Vladivostok return, the computer telling him he'd be on empty fifty to a hundred miles before, depending on headwinds. He jettisoned his remaining 101 R Alamo air-to-air missile, which made him 350 pounds lighter. Fate willing, this might just do the trick. Alert, yet fatigued from the combat in which he had downed one of the F-14s, he thought for a moment of Alexsandra, of her long, dark hair, the slow way she unpinned it before they made love. If he got back, he was going to see her again—and to hell with Nefski. There was nothing gentle about his desire for her, no sense of protecting her from Nefski or himself, only the sheer drive, after having cheated death once more, to have her with all the force he could muster. But first he'd have to fill out a *zayavlenie o poteryanom imushchestve*—"lost-property report"—explaining, on the prosaic gray form, why he'd dumped millions of rubles' worth of air-to-air radar-homing missile. Well, he asked himself, what did they want? A top ace in Far Eastern Command or an easily replaceable missile?

As the Boeing 747, still 170 miles away, below the radar screen, approached the South Korean east coast, F-16s were leaving Taegu in the south to look for it, while in Seoul, the aides of Freeman's hastily assembled advance staff waited anxiously for word of whether or not the 747 had made it—and if so, whether the general was still alive.

Shirer maintained total radio silence as he continued over the sea, beginning his climb off Yongdok to cross over the six-thousand-foot-high hump of the Taebaek range, then descending, still on three engines, over the western lowlands, out over Inchon, using up gasoline, fuel gauges showing a leak in the left wing tanks, the gas vaporizing, streaming along on the port-side fuselage.

Shirer wanted only enough kerosene left to land and was too careful a pilot to consider himself as good as home as he let the Boeing's nose dip, then lift, as he approached Kimpo Field, the "foamed" airstrip rushing at him in the night like a long streak of shaving cream, neither ground control, Shirer, nor his copilot able to tell from visual flyover whether the landing wheels were fully extended, the warning lights blinking but erratic.

His handling was as perfect as a pilot could make it under the conditions, but not until after he heard the banshee scream of the engines as he applied the brakes—enough to control the skid in the fire-retardant foam—then shut the engines down, was he satisfied.

Freeman was the first man in the cockpit, wearing a broad grin. Shirer was slightly disappointed—the least the general could have done was to have been as scared as most everybody else on the plane.

"You said you missed combat flying, Major," Freeman said. "Hell, I bet that's the best damn sortie you've flown!"

Shirer smiled politely and felt the general's firm congratulatory handshake for a job well done. "By God," said the general, "I'm going to recommend you and your copilot for a decoration."

Shirer knew immediately it was one of those moments that

might never come again. ''General . . . sir. May I make a request?''

''Shoot!''

''Well, sir, I know I've been seconded to fly Air Force One VIPs, but—''

''Permission denied, Major,'' said Freeman, but without rancor, and as dispassionately as his gratitude for Shirer's outstanding flying would allow. ''You ordered those Tomcats to fire missiles when the enemy was barely in range. Why was that?''

There was a spurt of air traffic control talk from Kimpo tower and Shirer hit the squelch button, shrugging with professional nonchalance. ''Thing to do, General. Figured they must be carrying drop tanks, given the return distance to Vladivostok, and before they'd go into action, they'd drop 'em. Those tanks weigh you down a ton, General—reduce speed down to—well, like I say, I figured if we got away a few Sparrows at 'em, they'd have to start maneuvering pretty damn quick, otherwise they'd be blown out of—''

''So you forced 'em to drop the tanks?'' cut in Freeman. ''Dump a whole bunch of fuel—reduce their attack time to hell and gone.''

''Yes,'' said Shirer matter-of-factly. ''That was the idea. Why do you ask, sir?''

Freeman shook his head, but it was a gesture not of incredulity but of admiration. ''Shirer, you realize how many 747 jockeys would have thought of that? And as fast as you did? Only a combat pilot—look, I'll give it to you plain and simple. I know you're not as happy on board this airborne bunker as everyone here thinks you are, right?''

Shirer's answer was tight with passion. ''Sir, I wasn't trained to run away from MiGs. My job—my whole reason for—sir, my job's to splash 'em. That's what I'm paid for—not to—''

''You're paid to do what you're told. Request for retransfer to fighter command denied. If everything suddenly goes to hell in a handbasket and the president has to go up in his Taj Mahal, I can't think of a better man to be driving it.''

Shirer's jaw clenched. ''Yes, sir.'' Shirer saluted Freeman, who returned the salute and moved out of the cockpit, Colonel Norton standing outside by the first console with a goofy grin, in stunned wonder at his deliverance. He hadn't stopped shaking but was looking about the plane as if seeing it for the first time, as if God had descended. Aides from Seoul HQ were now pouring into the aircraft. Suddenly Freeman turned back to look at Shirer, still strapped into the pilot's seat, his shirt soaked with sweat. "Major?"

"Sir?" Shirer's tone was militarily correct but bordering on "carrier sulk," the kind of pretantrum dog-in-the-manger mope that carrier pilots went into when the deck boss, for whatever reason, grounded them.

"How long do you think it'll take them to fix this bird up?"

"No idea, General," said Shirer, indicating the copilot, who was in dreamland over the possibility of a decoration from the legendary Freeman. "Ah—" began the copilot, "ah, three to four days, sir—if we're lucky. Maybe more. There's the engine, leaking gas, wing patch—"

"All right," said Freeman impatiently, holding up his hand to thwart the copilot's apparently endless list, and looking back now at Shirer. "If we can get you a fighter, you can keep your hand in until this bird is ready." Shirer's face was transformed—a schoolboy flush.

"Now, just hold your horses," Freeman warned him. "First I need to know—" He stopped. "Goddamn it, *I'm* the Supreme Commander Korea—" With that, he shouted above the bevy of aides. "Air Force liaison?"

"Me, sir. Richards."

"Richards! Doug Richards! By God, I thought you were dead. Someone told me you got an assful of shrapnel up around Nampo."

"Just half an assful, General." Loud laughter filled the plane.

"Well, Richards, can we get a Tomcat, F-16—anything fast enough for this gentleman? And I don't mean those ladies around Itaewon Barracks."

"Think I can dig one up, sir—a plane, I mean."

"Good. Because this man wants to shoot Communists. Doesn't like the idea of being fired on without being able to fire back. Reasonable enough, seems to me. And by God, we can help him partway at least. Flew cover for us at Pyongyang!"

"In that case, I'll guarantee it, sir," said Richards. He called through the narrow passageway to Shirer. "See me after debriefing, Major."

"Yes, *sir*!" said Shirer, even though Richards, a captain, was a full rank below him. Making their way out of the plane toward the gangway, Colonel Norton thought it prudent to remind the general that his impetuous ad hoc order to let Shirer get his hand back into fighters might not go down well with the Pentagon brass who'd had him transferred for Taj Mahal duty.

"Hell, Jim," Freeman responded, "don't be such an old woman. I know it's a risk. Could lose him. But if we don't let a man like that fight—he won't get the shame of turning tail out of his system. I know exactly how he feels. It's everything to a warrior. That was his job. His raison d'être. He gets a crack or two at those Commies over the Yalu the next few days—he'll be back to his old self. Come back and drive this monster without resentment. Method in my madness, Jim."

"The president," said Norton, "has specifically ordered us not to antagonize the Chinese. I mean, that goes for our pilots as well as our men on the ground. We're only supposed to push them back to the Manchurian border and that's it. Not to go over the Yalu."

"And let 'em shoot at us with impunity from the other side?" said Freeman, shaking his head with incredulity. "No, Jim. Last time we tried pussyfooting around with those sons of bitches, we had our boys freezing to death all along the Yalu—facing Chinese regulars—thousands of the bastards—sitting across the river, and we couldn't fire—by *presidential decree*. And our boys died—by the bushel. No, Jim—" He caught his breath in the icy blast that funneled its way up from the tarmac as they started down the steps. Freeman buttoned up his coat and saluted the assembled dignitaries below. "Don't worry, Jim. It'll be all right. We are going to launch air reconnaissance patrols *in force* across the Yalu. *Purely reconnaissance*, you understand. Course, if any Son of Heaven shows his ass, we're gonna shoot it off. Jim, we've got to maintain the Yalu as a moat—if they get close to us . . ." He stopped as he saw the provisional president of South Korea, Rah, moving forward to greet him.

Freeman was all smiles and diplomacy, thanking the president for his personal greeting, and genuinely touched that he had come out himself, but Freeman was really only interested in General Kim: the commander in chief of the NKA army now recouping and massing troops behind the protection of the North Korean–Chinese border along the Yalu and Tamur, and attacking, mainly at night. The most forward American line, he was told, had collapsed and was now no more than a series of outposts, while General Creigh continued to fall back to Kusong, with over 70 percent casualties. It had been the worst American retreat anywhere in the war.

"Tomorrow morning," the South Korean president was

informing the general, "we have arranged an official reception—"

"Mr. President," Freeman interjected. "I thank you kindly, but I'm afraid I won't be able to attend. I'll send a representative, of course, but I'll be heading for the front."

"But, surely," began President Rah, "the general will need to rest—"

"With all due respect, Mr. President, my boys aren't resting on the Yalu front. My place is with them. I thank you all the same. And Mr. President, I've been told by President Mayne to convey his best wishes to you and Madame Rah."

"Thank you, General. Of course I—"

Freeman's car had arrived.

As regulations demanded, the 747's debriefing was attended by Shirer, the copilot, and all console operators, as well as by Jim Norton, who joined in watching the Boeing's infrared video replays of the attack with a strange combination of relish and exhilaration that owed as much to the safety of the underground bunker they were viewing it in as to Norton's euphoria at having come so close to death and surviving. Though he would have been loath to admit it, he had never experienced such a high.

"There they are," said one of the console operators through the haze of tobacco smoke. "You were right, Freddie. MiGs—definitely Fulcrums." Another fighter was blurred by the heat wash of the missile it was firing. Shirer noted "1931 hrs" registered in the bottom right-hand corner of the video frame, the time the copilot had told him a missile was inbound.

"Hold it!" Shirer called out. "Can you run that back?" The hazy number on the fuselage under the Fulcrum's wing was due not only to angle of the 747's camera but to the fact that the MiG had been on full afterburner, further blurring the image. But running the frame back, freezing it, and going in with the zoom, you could see it was number nine—Russian Cyrillic lettering next to it: "*Ubiytsa Yanki*'."

"What the hell's that?" asked one of the operators.

"Number nine, you hayseed!"

"I know that. I mean that other crap—Jimmy?"

Jimmy, one of the 747's four Russian-speaking intercept operators, had nodded off but said he couldn't see because of the guy in front of him. They ran back the video. He walked up close to the screen.

"Come on, Professor!" someone urged. "I'm thirstier than a—"

"Um—means 'Yankee Killer'!"

"That fucker's mine!" It was Shirer's voice, unusually profane.

"Bit late, Major," someone hollered. "Probably home now in Vladivostok giving the missus a bit of surface-to-surface."

"Well," put in Richards, the liaison officer, "there's a good chance you'll see him if they send fighters back across the fortieth parallel, old buddy."

"Or if old Freeboot sends *you* across," said someone.

"Can't do it," countered another operator. "Not allowed."

"Says who?"

"Says the prez. That's who."

Shirer glanced at Richards through the flickering light cast by the video. "You serious, Captain?" he asked. "I mean about it being possible we'd run up against that MiG again?"

"Hell, yes. If you're on the eastern corridor patrol. From Kimpo here to Wonsan, over on the east coast, then the high-altitude run over Vladivostok. They don't like us taking snapshots of 'em, mind. Scramble every time."

"Thought you weren't supposed to cross the Yalu."

"Well, it isn't the Yalu, is it?" Richards smiled. "I mean, it's out to sea a bit, right?" His hand was making a sideways-slipping motion. "Anyway, on occasion we get to fire a few bursts 'fore we head home with the recon shots."

"That all that happens?"

"Sometimes we mix it up." The two men were silent for a moment, the operators cheering the explosion of one of the Fulcrums. Richards waited till the hurrahs died down. "Shouldn't let it get personal, though. That's dangerous."

Shirer said nothing. Someone trying to kill you—whether you were in a 747 or anywhere else—was about as personal as you could get."

"Look," said Richards, "I don't know how you'll react to this, but that number nine. We've run into him before. He's taken out three of our guys already. Our computer intelligence, enemy base/pilot profile, has him down as an ace."

"Where'd he get his kills?" asked Shirer. "Western Europe? Or Eastern Theater?"

"Both. Why?"

"Because I've seen that slogan once before. In the Aleutians. I splashed him."

"Well," said Richards, "I wouldn't put too much on that.

I mean, the Aleutians comes under Eastern Theater, all right, but I'd guess 'Yankee Killer's 'bout as common as 'Commie Killer' on our birds. What was your guy flying? The guy you took out in the Aleutians. A Fulcrum?''

''No.''

''Did he eject?'' asked Richards.

''Don't know. Didn't see.''

''Could be the same guy,'' conceded Richards. ''He sure as hell would've needed a new plane—right?''

''What's his name?'' asked Shirer. ''From the printout?''

''Number nine!'' Richards called out to the sergeant in charge of the debriefing records. ''Fulcrum out of Vladivostok. Got a handle for us?''

''Hang on a jiff,'' replied the sergeant. ''Yeah . . . Mar—''

''. . . chenko,'' said Richards. ''Yeah, that's right. Marchenko.'' He turned to Shirer. ''Ring a bell?''

Shirer shook his head. ''We didn't have time to swap autographs.''

Richards laughed. ''Well, ole buddy, you see him again, make sure you do. Tattoo the fucker.''

''I will.''

Richards added a cautionary note. ''Be careful, though, Major. Whoever he is, he's no slouch.''

''I know that—if he's the same guy who gave me a bath.''

''Then you're one-all,'' said Richards.

''No,'' answered Shirer. ''He damn near got me tonight.'' Shirer made a face. ''What's that damn smell?''

''*Kimchi,*'' said Richards. ''Sour cabbage. Koreans love it. You'll get used to it.''

''Don't plan on being here that long,'' said Shirer.

CHAPTER THIRTY-THREE

AS SERGEI MARCHENKO'S bullet-splattered Fulcrum came in, its braking chute deploying less than a hundred feet from the runway, puffs of steam could be seen, caused by the friction of its front and two side wheels coming in at over a hundred miles an hour onto the icy runway.

The ground crew were already calling Marchenko *''Kot''*—''Cat.'' Nine lives. Not only had he and his aircraft once again escaped injury, this time from the burst of American gunfire from the Tomcats escorting the big 747, but his fuel gauge was registering empty when the ground crew rolled it into the hangar. His ground captain was already on the phone, telling Khabarovsk's KGB chief Nefski that Marchenko had survived but that he was lucky—the ground captain estimating the Fulcrum probably had no more than twenty liters of fuel left. He was mistaken—there were only ten gallons remaining. And so it was that as he stepped out, exhausted and disappointed that he had not *ne ulovil*—''bagged''—the American general, Marchenko's legend, with one more F-14 to his credit, grew even more.

Nefski wasn't pleased about the new accolades for the ''Cat.'' It might make it more difficult for the KGB ace to convince the fighter ace that he should assist them in suborning his girlfriend, Alexsandra. Moscow had called Nefski yet again, within an hour of Comrade Marchenko's departure, pressing him for more information about the sabotage ring Nefski was sure that Alexsandra's brothers and she were involved in at the Khabarovsk munitions factory. But Nefski, like Marchenko, was not a man to panic under pressure. In any case, he was encouraged by Marchenko's honoring his agreement to dine with him at the Bear Inn.

One look at the menu and Sergei Marchenko wished he hadn't come. It was all stodgy, fatty-sounding fare, what Marchenko called "Eastern Siberian"—by which he disparagingly meant anything east of Lake Baikal. The big favorite apparently was pigs' trotters done with a variety of Buryat sauces with exotic names, most of which sounded to Marchenko as if they might be prepared solely to cover the lack of meat.

"If you wish," Nefski said, "you may order the *vyrezka svininy*—pork tenderloin."

Marchenko scanned the menu. "There isn't any."

"Ah!" Nefski said knowingly, and snapped his fingers. A waiter scurried over, his drooping walrus mustache so prolific that in the dim candlelight, he appeared to have no mouth.

"André," began Nefski—and Marchenko burst out laughing, not bothering to hide his contempt for the provincial snobbery that would pretend to have a genuine French waiter in Khabarovsk, the fighter pilot's laughter puncturing the respect shown the KGB chief. Nefski's smile was a forced grin. "You don't like pork tenderloin?"

"I love it."

"Well then, be glad you're not a Jew like that little whore of yours."

"You're jealous."

"Not at all. I've released her from prison—for the time being. Give her a taste of how it can be for her if she cooperates."

Marchenko was unimpressed. What Nefski no doubt meant was he'd released Alexsandra hoping she'd lead him to whatever he thought she was involved with. Obviously she hadn't led him to anything.

Nefski poured the vodka and raised his glass, its oily liquid turning to amber in the candlelight. "To Mother Russia!"

"To Mother Russia!" said Marchenko. It was as natural a toast as "Next year in Jerusalem" would be to Alexsandra.

"Tell your little Jew girl that if she doesn't tell us who's involved with the sabotage ring, we will put it about how her family changed its Jewish name to ingratiate themselves with the Soviets. And how now that Mother Russia is at war, they have turned on her—how they seek to stab her in the back—and that—"

"You've already put that about," said Marchenko contemptuously. "That won't budge her."

"I'm not finished," said Nefski, "but it's interesting you

say it won't budge her. Your tone suggests she *should* be budged."

"I don't approve of sabotage, no, but—"

"If you don't approve, it's your duty to help. Tell her if she doesn't cooperate, I will have her entire family—grandparents, everyone—all sixteen of them—shot."

Marchenko laughed. "You invite me so you can have your pigs' trotters and ask me to pass on your threats. Why don't you tell her yourself?"

"Because, Colonel, we have another message for her. If she doesn't cooperate, we'll arrest *her* again and put her in the *tranzitnaya kamera*—holding cell. Not one of her own, you understand." He poured another vodka. "The holding cell is a mixed mag—common criminals, rapists—all three sexes. I'm sure you can inject more concern about that than we ever could." Nefski raised his glass again. "Mother Russia!"

Marchenko pushed his glass away, his tone low, angry. "Leave her alone."

"When she tells us what we want to know."

"Perhaps she knows nothing."

"Don't be stupid, Marchenko. She's a dirty little Jew. All the Jews know something. They cling together like maggots in our belly. We have to shit them out." He smiled. "Except the ones we want to keep for our amusement, of course." Nefski paused. "Honestly now, Colonel—would you marry one?"

"That's not the point."

"Ah ha—"

The waiter returned, the tenderloin surrounded by small baked potatoes and fresh sautéed greens, the bread so fresh, it was still warm from the oven—a long French loaf. Marchenko was astonished.

Nefski was already attacking the pigs' trotters, slicing off the crisp bubbling fat, consuming it quickly, washing it down with more vodka, and adroitly mopping the fat that dribbled over his bottom lip. "Look, Comrade, I'm not going to fuck around with you any longer. I try to be nice, but being an ace has gone to your head." He jabbed his fork, laden with fat-soaked bread, toward Marchenko. "We are fighting a war down *here* as well as you are in the air." He gobbled the bread and downed another vodka. "I heard you missed the American?"

"There'll be more."

"You come to the point readily," said Nefski, turning full onto him.

"How do you mean?"

"There won't be any more opportunities for you if you don't convince her to spill her guts." Marchenko sneered with derision at the threat, though his reaction was mitigated somewhat by the tenderloin—done to perfection, the best he'd ever tasted.

"Oh—" said Nefski, with his interrogator's unnerving ability to predict his victim's next response. "You think you are so important I wouldn't dare? That Daddy would protect you?" He stopped eating for a moment and wiped his mouth, using his thumbnail to push a small sliver of bone from his teeth. "Listen, Colonel Hero, I, too, have connections. If push comes to shove, we could all get bruised, but comrade Chernko swings more weight than your father any day of the week. Are you so stupid not to know that? A fighter pilot is important, but if the rail lines and munitions keep getting hit, your fighter pilots'll have no gasoline with which to fly." He pointed his knife at Marchenko. "Besides, I don't have to bother with any of this official nonsense, crawling around, cap in hand, like we did for a while in Gorbachev's time. That's all finished, my friend." He tore off another piece of the baguette. "You know about Lieutenant Yablonski?"

"Never heard of him."

"No, because he wasn't around long enough, that's why. Transferred here from the Western TVD. We asked him to help us, too, when he was here. He didn't."

"So?"

"A truck. The brakes failed one night. On the base."

"You threatening me?"

"I'm telling you a story," said Nefski, mopping up the residual fat.

Marchenko fell silent, took another vodka, and smiled. "What if I told you I'd been wearing a tape recorder?"

Nefski belched and wiped his mouth again with the stained napkin. "Don't be childish, fighter man. You're out of your depth. Completely." He turned to Marchenko. "It is the first thing we check."

"You're bluffing."

Nefski sat back and opened his jacket to reveal a small black box, covered with perforated black leather like a transistor radio, less than half a cigarette pack in size. "Mike detector," he explained. "Standard equipment. As necessary to us, Comrade, as oxygen to you when you fly. *If* you fly again." Nefski closed his coat and resumed eating. "I've tried to be nice to you, but always you want to play the big man. So now I'm telling you, hero pilot. I give you forty-eight hours. If that little cunt of yours doesn't start telling us what we want to know, I'll let her loose among the other scum. They'll fuck her dead and you won't fly again. *Ever. Ofitsiant!*—Waiter!"

"Sir?" The walrus was by his side.

"Telefon!"

Next minute the waiter was frantically unraveling a phone cord like a man readying to abandon ship. Nefski pushed the phone toward Marchenko. "Call your base commander. Tell him I want to talk to him." Nefski was still chewing, staring at Marchenko, daring him.

Marchenko dialed, and when the base commander came on, his tone was terse, clipped, authoritarian, asking Marchenko what he wanted. Nefski grabbed the receiver, identifying himself brusquely to the commander, then held the receiver far enough away so that Marchenko could hear as well. The change in the commander's tone upon hearing Nefski had been instantaneous. Marchenko was disgusted. The man was senior fighter commander TVD, yet his tone was cloyingly subservient. Nefski smiled and spoke brusquely to the commander, "I want you in my office within half an hour."

"Yes, Colonel," came the response. "Of course, I'll—"

Nefski put down the receiver and stared at Marchenko. "And I want that slut talking in forty-eight hours." With that, he left.

Marchenko sat, the vodka cupped in his hands, his eyes fixed on the little oily sea inside the glass, and waited for what he thought was Nefski's final insult: leaving him to pay the bill. When it didn't come, he called over the waiter to hurry it up, but the walrus informed him, "Monsieur, there is no bill for Colonel Nefski's guests."

"Oh," Marchenko said, feeling momentarily like a naive schoolboy, and grabbing his cap and coat, made his way out into the blinding snow. He hailed a troika—more of them about now that gas rationing was even more severe than normal. With the harness bells jingling, the outer two horses' nostrils flaring, the steam of their breath almost instantly frozen to icicles, Marchenko sat back into the troika's deep embrace, pulling down his cap, and the collar of his greatcoat and the rough serge blankets up about his ears. As the shushing of the snow, like the threshing of wheat, cut through the silence of the dark streets, the old, grizzled driver, his beard a clump of watery ice, snapped the whip, driving Marchenko fast toward the Jewish sector.

CHAPTER THIRTY-FOUR

"THANK YOU ALL for coming," said SAS Major Rye, his voice surprisingly soft, so much so that Brentwood, in the third row of the platoon, could barely hear him. "As usual, we like to bring you in on a Monday," Rye continued, "so those who won't be staying with us can rejoin their units next weekend."

The Aussie put up his hand.

"Yes, Mr. Lewis?" asked Rye quietly.

The Australian was as surprised as everybody else that the major knew his name straight off. And *Mr.* Lewis! "Stone the crows." said Lewis. "You blokes don't waste any time."

"What's your question, Mr. Lewis?" asked Rye politely.

"You mean the course is only a week long?" asked the Aussie.

"No," replied Rye, again not as if he were answering an NCO or "other rank" but speaking to Lewis more as an equal, a member of the same sports team. There were obviously no "Lords" and "Others" entrances to SAS cricket grounds.

"The course," explained Rye, "normally takes several months. Naturally we've had to streamline this to a matter of weeks because of the difficulties over the water, but most of you have already gone through some sort of specialist training—in part. I do emphasize *in part*, however. As a prerequisite for volunteering for SAS tryout, you must have all seen action and be considered mature. We are not looking for, nor do we want, young men who either have not been under fire or who have what we deem to be romantic notions of combat. In all, our screening process allows us to reduce the course to five weeks, including a 'sort out' first week." He paused for more questions.

"Sir," Thelman asked, "are we being trained for any specific missions?"

"Yes and no."

"That's bloody helpful," said Lewis. The major had no difficulty hearing, even if he spoke softly.

"It means, Lewis, that if you and your colleagues succeed, you will form a pool—or I should say add to a pool, albeit a relatively small one—from which we can draw from time to time should we receive specific requests. But as it is a small pool, and only those of you who pass tryout will learn the organizational structure necessitated by our limited number, we are rather particular about what requests we respond to. In short, if we think they can be handled by line regiments, we say so. Our intention here, quite frankly, is to be the unit of last resort. We do what others say can't be done or is overfraught with risk. We do not counsel immodesty, gentlemen, but I think it fair to say SAS has a long, and I believe distinguished, tradition. You'll hear more of that as you proceed—*if* you proceed." The major paused to make sure everyone was giving his full attention.

Lewis didn't understand some of the words the major was using, but most Poms, he concluded, were like that—all sounded like they'd swallowed a bloody dictionary. Anyway, Lewis got the general drift.

"One of the things we'll be looking for in the first week," continued Major Rye, "is what we call 'crossover ability,' Our basic unit is a four-man one in which each man is a generalist but also a specialist in a particular field so that should you be on a sticky 'op,' you will have the ability to step into one another's shoes as it were. And quickly. First week, however, will be devoted to weeding out those of you who are not up to it. You will discover this yourselves. I want it clearly understood that there is absolutely no stigma for failing SAS's first phase. You've been chosen because you're the best in your own regiments, but we do aspire to the *very* best, and physical fitness forms the basis, though by no means all, of the criteria."

Rye paused, his gaze casual yet at the same time searching. "One more thing, chaps. If and when you return to your units—after this week or later after you've served with us and can no longer 'cut the mustard,' as our American cousins would say—we do expect absolute secrecy about SAS methods and organization. If you do not keep it to yourself, we will kill you. Sar'Major?"

"Sir!" responded the RSM, saluting briskly and turning the platoon. "Platoon—dismissed!"

* * *

"Charming!" said Lewis, while making up his bunk, David Brentwood and Thelman taking the second and third tier respectively. "Bloody charming. Well, I'll give the old bastard one thing—he gives it to you straight." The Aussie drew over the blue military blanket, tucking it tightly beneath the mattress. "Still, can't be too bad. I've done Canungra."

"What's that?" asked Thelman, folding his kit bag. "Aussie dope?"

"Oh, spare me," said Lewis, pulling out his khaki T-shirt and socks from the chocolate-colored bag. "*Canungra*. In Aussie. Jungle warfare school. Don't you blokes know anything? It's a real bastard there, I'm tellin' ya." Lewis dropped his blanket. "Snakes this fuckin' long and this small. One bite and you're a goner—'less you got the old razor and Condies crystals into the wound."

"Don't see any snakes around here," said David.

"Eh, don't come the raw prawn with me, mate. You know what I mean. These bloody hills are nothin' compared to jungle. Got nothin' but a few bloody sheep on 'em. Could *run* over 'em."

Which is precisely what Lewis and the other ninety-seven volunteers did the next morning—without breakfast. At 5:00 A.M. Loaded up in the freezing darkness aboard the three-ton lorries, the trucks dropping them off at quarter-mile intervals between Senny Bridge and Brecon on a twelve-mile front, each man having been issued a waterproof storm suit, regulation SAS Bergen rucksack loaded with twenty-five pounds of bricks, a ten-pound rifle, a map of Brecon Beacons national park, compass, and, yelled out to him by the RSM, a six-digit number for the latitude and longitude. Instructions: to reach an abandoned chapel at Merthyr Tydfil—fifteen miles from the Beacons as the crow flew but much longer up the Beacons' north face and down the southern side. The only other order given them before they left was not to make notations anywhere on the map—an enemy could use the pencil marks to back-plot. They were to reach Merthyr Tydfil by 1400 hours. Any later and they were out.

In the pitch blackness of that morning, it was minus five degrees when each of the ninety-eight men began his private trial, heading across rain-swollen creeks and sodden, slippery slopes up toward the Beacons. For the first two hours, many of the men made good time, but by 0900 hours, the crest of the Beacons buffeted by sixty-kilometer-per-hour winds and aswirl in a snowstorm, several men were wandering blind. By noon only seventeen had made it to Merthyr Tydfil: most of these, troopers from the Coldstream Guards regiment. Twenty-odd more, a number of them close to hypothermia despite the storm units, straggled in around 1300 hours, all totally exhausted and near frozen because they had not packed the storm suit properly in the rucksack, preventing zippers from being fully closed, allowing the rucksacks to become sodden, the damp transmitted to the storm suits.

Small details, but SAS Captain Cheek-Dawson knew they could be deadly mistakes on an "op," and none of them escaped Cheek-Dawson's eye or that of the RSM.

David Brentwood staggered in at 1340, only twenty minutes to spare, Lewis fifteen minutes behind him, and Thelman barely making it, falling against the chapel door, followed in by an angry flurry of snow. Cheek-Dawson was looking disgustingly dapper in full battle dress, patiently waiting. As Lewis flopped to the floor, it was several minutes before he could speak. He nudged David. "When did Lord Cheek get here?"

"Ten forty-five," said one of the engineers. "He and one of the Scots Guards."

"Bullshit!" said Lewis. "Must have got a ride."

The engineer shook his head. "No, he was dropped off from the truck just before me. Bugger kept me going—yelling at me, 'Come on, Swain. Put your back into it—come on, Swain. No loafing,' Real pain in the bum, I can tell you."

"That your name?" asked Lewis, barely able to prop himself up on his elbows. "Swain?"

"Yeah, mate. Why?"

"How the hell can they remember all our names?"

" 'Cause they bloody like us," said Swain.

"They do their homework," said another man, eyes shut, stretched out on the cold, dusty floor of the long-disused chapel. "Know us all better'n our muvvers, they do."

"I'm starving," said Lewis. "Opened me bloody pack and you know what I found?"

"Bricks!" said Brentwood.

"Yeah," said Lewis. "Fuckin' bricks—and they number the bastards."

"That's—" Thelman began, but had to stop for lack of wind. He looked close to total collapse, his bloodshot eyes in stark contrast to his black skin. He accepted the water bottle offered him by the RSM and continued his explanation. "They number the bricks, a guy told me, 'cause they have to account for them."

"That's right," said a cockney accent, the man wearing a Coldstream Guards patch, which surprised Thelman. He'd always thought, from their pictures, that the tall, bearskin-hatted Guardsmen would speak in an upper-class accent. "See," continued the Guardsman, "Ministry of Supply's very touchy about losing bricks."

There was a ripple of tired laughter.

"Sar'Major?" asked Cheek-Dawson, hands akimbo on his battle dress smock. "How many still out?"

"Six, sir."

"Very good. Call the Back Markers on the blower and let them go in and round them up. They don't find them by fifteen hundred hours, better call Brecon police station, army, and air force mountain rescue."

"Yes, sir."

Professional pride counseled against calling in army or RAF mountain search to help the Back Markers, but Cheek-Dawson was obliged to do so, two men having died from exposure several months before.

The six men who were still out, it was understood by all, would be returning to their regiments, as would anyone else who wandered into the disused chapel after 1400 hours.

When the final tally was in, forty-three out of the ninety-eight volunteers had already failed phase one and would be returning to their units.

"Not bad, Sar'Major," said Cheek-Dawson cheerily, his bonhomie somehow making the musty-smelling chapel even more depressing and cold.

"Just over half made it," said the sar'major.

"Quite."

"Jesus!" Lewis told Thelman, who had made the silly mistake of taking his boots off. "At this rate we'll all be dead by sunset."

David agreed. He was astonished—that was the only word for it—at the sudden change of weather and drop in temperature on the Brecon Beacons and at the equally sudden hatred he now held for any lyrical notion he'd had about Wales. Wales was where you died, and you'd volunteered for it. Everyone, he noticed, was complaining bitterly of hunger.

"Righto, chaps," said Cheek-Dawson. "You've not done too badly, given the rapid change in weather conditions. Now, all hand in your maps and then we'll have a spot of lunch."

"That's bloody more like it," said Lewis. "I'm for that."

"Good man, Lewis. We like initiative. First in line then. Map?"

Lewis unzipped the chest pocket that served as an extra thermal layer, extracted the folded map, and handed it to Cheek-Dawson. The RSM had poured two cups of steaming hot coffee.

"Oh dear—" said Cheek-Dawson. "Oh *dear*."

"What?" said Lewis, alarmed, turning back from watching the coffee, face tight with hunger and fatigue.

"No lolly for you, old chap!" He meant no candy—no prize.

"What you bloody mean?"

"Look!"

Lewis did look, at the map, now unfolded and spread out on the table. Suddenly he remembered the warning about not marking it up with starting coordinates, et cetera, lest the enemy, as Cheek-Dawson had cautioned, could backtrack on it. He peered closely at the map. "Hang on. Here—let me have a gander." With this, Lewis bend down, looking closer at the map. At that moment another man, one of the missing, collapsed in the doorway. Two men lumbered to their feet, went over, and dragged him in.

Lewis was still staring at the map. "There's no bloody writing on it. Look, not even a pencil impression." He held the map up like holding a sheet to dry. " 'Ave a look."

Cheek-Dawson turned him about to face the class, prostrate before him. "Anyone see it?"

Everybody gazed up at the map, some of them looking like stunned cows, still not recovered. There *was* no writing on it, just as Lewis had said.

David Brentwood reluctantly put up his hand. Poor old Lewis looked as if he'd collapse if they didn't give him something to eat soon. "Folds," said David. "You can see the square where the map's been folded and pressed down."

"Top of the class, Brentwood. Folded *square*!" said Cheek-Dawson, taking the map from an incredulous Lewis. "Enemy interrogator sees that he'd know precisely the grid you started from. Reduce his search pattern by a factor of ten at least. And you *and* your group would've had it."

Brentwood pulled out his map. "I did the same thing," he said, looking up at Cheek-Dawson.

The officer smiled. "So did I—first time out. Don't do it again. Keep folding it different ways—confuses the dickens out of them—*if* you're caught!"

"Can we eat now?" said Lewis unrepentantly.

"Of course," said Cheek-Dawson. "Then after lunch you lot take a stroll down to Abergavenny. We'll pick you up there with the lorries and take you back to Senny Bridge. Everyone clear on that?"

"Why can't we go back now?" asked a Coldstream Guard.

"Yeah," added Lewis.

"Lorries are tied up, I'm afraid," answered Cheek-Dawson. Besides, a stroll after lunch'll do you good. Otherwise you'll get sleepy."

"Where is this Aber—"

"Aver*gavenny*," said Cheek-Dawson, noting the Coldstream Guard's name. Anyone who couldn't get a verbal instruction right the first time could put a troop, or an entire SAS squadron of seventy-two men, at risk. Foreign-sounding names were no excuse. Scotland and Wales were full of them.

"It's just east of us," continued Cheek-Dawson. "Follow the road. It's clearly marked."

"How far, sir?"

"Oh, what is it, Sar'Major—twenty-three, twenty-five miles?"

" 'Round that, sir."

There was a surly silence in the cold chapel.

"Right you are," said Cheek-Dawson. "I'll not hold you up any longer. You can have lunch. Pipes are frozen—no joy with the taps, I'm afraid, so you'll have to do the best you can on that score." He handed the map back amicably to Lewis and headed for the door with the RSM toward their Land Rover outside.

"Where's bloody lunch?" asked Lewis, joined by a discordant chorus.

"In the bag," said the RSM, pointing to a kit on the only table in the hall. "Where'd you think?" With that, he and Cheek-Dawson left.

Lewis opened the kit bag and staggered back. It had been tied tightly so that only now could they smell it. It was full of dead rats—and a note: "You must learn to live off the land, but we'll give you a head start this time. From now on you'll have to fend for yourself."

One man began throwing up. Thelman said he felt sick. So did David. One of the Brits, a sapper, rose and kicked the table leg. "Fuck this for a lark! I quit!"

David rose slowly from the floor, every muscle and tendon in his body throbbing with pain, made worse now because of the cold, the temperature in the disused chapel only a degree or so above the minus five centigrade outside. He was looking back at the last man who had come in—someone said the man was so cold he was turning blue—and all David could see was the blinding snow of Stadthagen, the dogs chasing him, the guards screaming, and the cold, so cold it was unimaginable. "All right," he called out to several of the troopers at the back of the chapel. "Take turns cuddling up to him. Thaw him out or we'll lose him."

"That Cheek-Dawson," said Lewis. "He's a fucking sadist." David knew it was just as tough in the U.S. Special Forces—no doubt to separate the men from the boys when everyone was exhausted, cold, morale at rock bottom. Yet for David, this was worse than anything he'd seen in Special Forces. Intellectually he understood, but emotionally he was furious. But "fury just fucks your mind," a black instructor had wisely told him at Camp Lejeune. "Fury gets you nowhere, man, clouds your judgment," when judgment was already clouded because of the cold, hunger, and resentment. David walked over to the table and called out, "Anyone got a knife?"

Several hands went up.

"Lighter—matches?" he asked next.

"Yeah. I got one."

"All right. Let's get the fire going."

"Where? There's no grate, no stove."

"Tear apart the altar rails," David said, pointing to the front of the chapel. Stick by stick."

"Christ, there'll be trouble for that," said someone.

"You want your meat raw?" David asked. There was a loud crack—a plank coming away.

"All right," said David, turning to the two men with the knives. "Start skinning." One man came forward, the other not moving, shaking his head, his mouth twisted in a mask of repulsion. "I—I can't."

Brentwood walked over to him. "Listen, chief—you want to eat or not?"

The man shook his head.

"Then you'll starve. Give me the knife." He turned to Lewis. "Aussie, take this guy and a few others outside, tear off the guttering. Water'll be frozen in that. We can melt it over the fire."

"Okay, Davey boy," said Lewis. You're the boss. Come on, fellas—get the lead out."

"Who's that?" asked Cheek-Dawson, now sitting in the Land Rover parked a quarter mile down the road out of sight, listening to the parabolic mike feed on the Land Rover's radio. "That the American chap—Brentwood?"

"Yes, sir. Didn't say much before. You think he's a goer?"

"The point is, Sar'Major, can he hack phases two to six? This is kindergarten."

"True enough, sir."

"Well then—shall we join them?"

"Very good, sir."

When Cheek-Dawson reappeared with the RSM, everybody stopped what he was doing.

"Enough for two more?" asked Cheek-Dawson.

"No problem," said Lewis. "You can start if you like, Captain."

Cheek-Dawson didn't hesitate. Pulling his SAS dagger from its scabbard, he pulled the rat from its spit, sliced a piece off, and, using the dagger as a fork, raised it to his mouth, blew on it to cool it, then began to eat.

"True what they say, Captain?" said Lewis with relish. "Taste like chicken?"

"Taste like rat, Aussie," said Cheek-Dawson. He turned to Brentwood. "Course, you made a bad mistake with the fire, old boy."

"Oh?" retorted Brentwood. "You couldn't see it, could you? We jerry-rigged a canopy, blackened out the windows. You couldn't have seen it. Besides, it's snowing. So what's the beef?"

"The rat's the beef," said someone. Brentwood ignored it, waiting for Cheek-Dawson's response. He had him cold. Didn't he?

Cheek-Dawson took another slice and began to chew it, pulling a long, stringy piece from his teeth, balling it up and popping it back into his mouth. "Smell, old boy," he said, looking straight at Brentwood while still chewing. "Smell it for bloody miles."

"So what would you have done?" asked Brentwood, bristling at the criticism.

"Cold, old boy. Can't go pratting around with ruddy great

fires, can you? Might as well send up a ruddy great flare—tell 'em where you are."

"You wouldn't eat it bloody cold," said Lewis. "Pull the other one."

Cheek-Dawson walked over to the bag, pulled out a rat, threw it on the table, beheaded it with his dagger, and bisected the rest, pushing one half forward, silently cutting up the remaining half.

"Jesus!" someone said. Cheek-Dawson kept chewing, wiping the blood from his lips. He waited.

"Can I borrow your knife?" It was Brentwood, looking straight at the Englishman.

"By all means, old chap," said Cheek-Dawson, handing him the SAS dagger.

CHAPTER THIRTY-FIVE

HEADING OUT FROM the Murmansk sub pens on Kola Peninsula, an Alfa 4, the fastest nuclear-powered attack sub in the world, passed beneath the Stednaja Nuclear and Conventional Weapons Arsenal. The Alfa 4 was one of the *zolotaya ryba*, or "golden fish," so-called because it was the most expensive sub ever made in the Soviet Union.

Diving as soon as she could, she set her course along the relatively shallow seven-hundred-foot dip in Scandinavia's continental shelf. No longer patrolled by NATO AWACs since the Russians had overwhelmed the Norwegians, the shallow exit was as safe as the Alfa could hope for before reaching the deeper waters that lay off the continental slope west of the North Cape. Once it had reached a point four hundred miles south, the Alfa, under the command of Nikita Yanov, would be in the six-thousand-foot-deep Norwegian Sea and then, turning to the southwest, would head for the sector of the Spitzbergen fracture zone, toward the Pole, searching for American Sea Wolfs, the 360-foot-long U.S. nuclear attack and ballistic missile subs that moved from station to station within easy striking distance of the Soviet Union.

For the Sea Wolfs, the distance from the deeps around Spitzbergen to Moscow was farther than from some sub pens on Scotland's west coast, but Yanov knew, as did all Soviet sub captains, that though Moscow was closer to the Scottish sub pens, the *zhostkie*—"hard"—strategic targets for Americans—the big sub bases on the Kola Peninsula—were much closer to the Spitzbergen Trench. Still, Yanov and his crew knew there was another reason for the lurking Sea Wolfs. The main incentive for the Americans to head high into the Arctic was not to hide their ballistic missile subs in the protection of deep water but to seek the protection of the ice cap. Of course, it was possible to blast the ice cap first, then send in depth charges and acoustic homing ASW charges, but such tactics were the theoretical dreams of the experts ashore. The reality was that blowing holes in the ice would make such a noise that before the Alfa's antisubmarine missiles could reach the target, the enemy, alerted by the tremendous explosion of the ice blowing up, would have already begun countermeasures. No, Yanov knew that the only way was to find them as quickly as you could *under* the ice, and destroy them there.

It took skill and some luck, but Yanov had something else to help him: the benefit of the Soviet Union's unprecedented developments in submarine warfare. Even the U.S. Navy had admitted that the Soviets' increasing speed, higher reserve buoyancy, and titanium hull on the Alfa heralded an astonishing advance in Soviet submarine warfare capability. It was even more impressive given the fact that contrary to what many NATO commanders believed, the Soviet Union had not stolen most of her advances from the West but developed them herself. The exception was the spectacular KGB coup in obtaining Western technological breakthroughs in sonar detection and in "quietening" the sub's prop—an intelligence coup made possible through the secrets sold to the Soviets by the Walker family spy ring in the United States.

Yanov took particular pride in the fact that, compared to the 360-foot-long, 42-foot-wide American Sea Wolfs and the Soviet Union's *tyfuns* or "typhoons"—at twenty-five tons, the biggest subs in the world—his Alfa, at twenty-nine hundred tons and only 267 feet long and 31 feet wide, was so sleek, it was like a shark among whales.

Yanov's Alfa, built in the Sudomekh Shipyard in Leningrad, had already proved herself many times. Yanov glanced at the three red combat efficiency stars mounted above the planesmen in Control. One of the stars, with the black letter "T" printed on its white center, was for torpedo excellence, the second, with "EM" at its center, was for propulsion efficiency, and the third, a red star within the four black lines, testified to superior antisubmarine warfare, awarded to Yanov personally by the Northern Fleet commander.

Most impressive of all, above the three stars was the gold-ringed white circle which contained the blue and white naval ensign of red star, hammer, and sickle. This told anyone who saw it—and they could hardly miss it in Control—that Yanov's submarine had been acclaimed "Outstanding Ship of the Soviet Navy." This was the reward for Yanov's sub having sunk twenty-three NATO merchant vessels, each over fifteen thousand tons, and for the destruction of two NATO nuclear submarines, one a British Trafalgar, the other a French Rubis.

It was an enviable record, but one that Yanov was not satisfied with. What he wanted, what he yearned for—so much that it invaded his dreams—was to sink an American sub, and not just any American sub, but the best they had: a Sea Wolf II. Yanov's progression from *Kapitan* to *Kontra-Admiral* would then be guaranteed.

The war, while bemoaned by so many others, had been a godsend for officers like Yanov—a chance for him to cut out of the herd before he was too old. If you retired from the submarine service as a *Kapitan* these days, you'd stay a *Kapitan* forever, as there were over eighty attack submarine captains alone vying for Admirals' Row.

Yanov ran a check of his "sticks," including the high-frequency mast, the park lamp DF loop, and the search-and-attack periscopes. The cluster of five sticks atop the Alfa's streamlined sail was similar to that of the Victor-class nuclear subs, but there any comparison ended. Alfa wasn't only the world's fastest attack sub, it was also the deepest-diving, its titanium hull capable of withstanding the enormous ocean pressures to a depth of three thousand feet. In addition, the Alfa's twenty-one-foot-long, twenty-inch-wide torpedoes, fired from the Alfa's "covey" of six tubes, mounted forward, could reach forty-five knots, faster than most American subs.

In addition to all this, the Alfa carried two-to-fifteen-kilohertz low-frequency towed sonar arrays and a markedly improved Snoop Tray radar. But technology aside, his Alfa,

Yanov knew, had another distinct advantage over the Americans—one that not even Yanov's colleagues in the other Alfa had. It was the experience of his forty-five man crew. Yanov's crew had logged more time in Arctic waters than any other attack submarine in the Soviet navy. They were ice-trained, Yanov's sonar operators having become extraordinarily sensitive to the sounds that emanated from the proximity of unseen but huge subsurface ice, creating the impression that an enemy sub was nearby when in fact it was not. But if you fired at that noise, you gave away your greatest weapon: your silence. And every enemy ship within a hundred kilometers would hear you and come homing in on you.

CHAPTER THIRTY-SIX

AFTER LUNCH, CHEEK-DAWSON rapped the bare table for attention. "All right, chaps—I've got an announcement. Bad news, I'm afraid. Sar'Major's just received a radio message that the lorries aren't at Abergavenny. Some cock-up at the regular army motor pool apparently. Always happens when you deal with outsiders. Let this be a lesson. We can only rely on ourselves."

"You mean we have to walk all the way back to Senny Bridge, sir?" asked a sapper. "That's fifty-odd mile."

"Yes," said Cheek-Dawson.

"Gawd blimey," muttered one of the cockneys. "That's diabolical, that is. Bloody diabolical."

"You still plan on staying with the group?" Thelman ribbed Lewis.

"I know what SAS stands for," said Lewis. "Special Army Sadists."

"You told us that before," said David.

The Australian stood up. "Sir?"

"Yes, Lewis."

"Lot shorter back over the hill."

"The *Beacons*?" a cockney voice shouted. "You're off your Uncle Ned."

Cheek-Dawson's expression was fixed on Lewis. Finally he nodded, then shifted his gaze to the rest of the volunteers. "The member from down under has a point, gentlemen. Tougher going—but half the distance. That right, Sar'Major?"

"Easily, sir."

"Very well," announced Cheek-Dawson enthusiastically. "It's back over the hill, then."

"Very nice, Aussie," said the trooper next to him. "Well done. Bucking for sergeant?"

But Cheek-Dawson noted the trooper's mock derision of Lewis was only that, mock—nothing mean about it. And if it's one thing the SAS, rated higher by NATO than the U.S. Seals or even the Israeli commandos, had learned during its long and distinguished commando years, it was that, contrary to the public's *Dirty Dozen* view of such groups, a convivial sense of humor was essential.

As the men rose, checking their "Bergens," as they'd already begun calling their SAS rucksacks, Lewis, tightening his straps, suddenly experienced a surge of intuition about where they were going. The rats were the clue, he told Brentwood. "The tropics!"

"You daft?" asked a Tommy. "Why 'ave they got us in bloody Wales then?"

"Because," retorted Lewis, "they're bloody comedians, that's why. Like to watch us suffer. Besides—doesn't matter *where* they train us. It's *how*, right? Now, the rats—"

"Rats are everywhere," said the Tommy. "I don't think even Cheek-Dawson knows where we're going."

"Yeah," agreed Thelman. "You heard him last night. Said we're 'on call.' "

"Not so fast, Thelma," said Lewis. We haven't qualified yet."

"You know what I mean, Aussie."

"You tryin' to tell me they've got no idea where we'll be going?"

"I didn't say that," answered Thelman.

"There you are then. I tell you it's the tropics."

"A quid says you're wrong," challenged the Tommy.

"You're on," said Lewis. "That's a quid gone west, mate." Lewis looked around. "Anyone else?"

Cheek-Dawson was standing by the door, opening the rucksack and counting out the requisite number of bricks, the sergeant collecting the first batch of those men who had failed and who would have to be taken back to Senny Bridge by the Land Rover. Buckling up the rucksack, Cheek-Dawson called David Brentwood over. "Your service record says you're para trained."

"Yes, sir."

"HALO as well as regular?" By HALO he meant high-altitude, low-opening jumps—high-altitude to avoid AA and radar detection in free fall, low-altitude-opening for steering to a pinpoint landing. It was the kind of thing sky divers did, except they didn't carry the enormous load commandos were required to. The difference was like that between one man swimming in a pair of trunks, the other in full gear and rifle.

"Only regular chute training," replied David. "At Camp Lejeune. With Thelman. No HALO."

"Not to worry. Shouldn't take you too long once you've had the basics." He paused, shifting the weight of his pack. "If you're game."

"When do we start?" said Brentwood.

"I admire your confidence," replied Cheek-Dawson, zipping up the nylon storm suit. "But you have a few hoops to pass through yet."

David said nothing. The truth was that, despite his bravado in front of Cheek-Dawson, he had a blister on his left heel that was about to burst. If he was to get back over the Beacons in the snowstorm, with a windchill factor of at least minus ten, it'd be a pure case of mind over matter. When Cheek-Dawson opened the door, flurries of snow flew through, stinging his face.

"If this is phase one," said Thelman, slinging his rifle, "I'd hate to think what the next five are like."

"So would I, mate," said Lewis. "And it's not five more."

"Thank God," said Thelman.

"It's six!" said Lewis.

Cheek-Dawson looked back at the fifty-five men who had earned the right to more pain. "First man back gets free beer!" he announced heartily.

"That's me!" shouted Lewis.

"Oh *ja*?" It was a West ranger commando. "I was the champion drinker in my Einzelkämpf unit."

"Einzel—*what*?" said Lewis, winking at Brentwood and Thelman. "Sounds like a flamin' disease!"

"You want to bet on it, Aussie?" asked the German.

"Aw, don't waste your dough, Fritz. You'll need it for an oxygen bottle." There was some hearty laughter despite the impending trek.

"Never mind," said the German in correct, if heavily accented, English. "I will bet you twenty marks."

"All right, Fritz," rejoined Lewis. "But let's make it real money. Dollars. U.S."

Gambling was strictly against Queen's Regulations, but Cheek-Dawson and the RSM were quiet on the matter. What Major Rye had in mind for this lot—those who were left at week's end—would require more than top physical fitness. Their morale, as the U.S. Marines were fond of saying, would have to be "outstanding," and if a wager here and there helped, so be it. Some of them would never get to spend it.

By 2200 hours that evening, Major Rye watched them straggle in after the killing pace set by both the German ranger and Cheek-Dawson, who had led most of the way as well as checking for stragglers. Rye noted there were seven more, three U.S. Marines and four British, who decided it was too tough for them. Rye spoke gently to the seven, as he had to the "cot cases" brought in earlier by the sergeant major in the Land Rover. Rye not only thanked them all for coming but spoke individually to each man as he signed out, asking the failures what they thought had been the hardest part of the trek for them and telling every one of them that they were welcome to reapply for SAS at anytime. Confidentiality, he told them, would be assured. Apart from their respective commanding officers, as far as their regiments were concerned, they had merely been seconded for other duties for a week. Major Rye then told them he had failed in his first attempt. It softened the blow visibly.

"What did *you* in, sir?" asked Lewis, out of breath but with his usual bluntness intact.

"Cross-country march," answered Rye without hesitation. "Full pack and weapons. Somewhat heavier than you're carrying now, I should add. Forty miles—rough terrain. Timed us at twenty hours."

"When do we do that, sir?" asked Thelman.

"Oh, early on. Phase two."

"Stone the crows!" said Lewis, but before he could say any more, Cheek-Dawson was telling the forty-eight men remaining that in half an hour's time, he wanted them in four-man troops, or "fire teams, as you Americans call them." Two men were assigned to be on the "blackboards" as each of the eleven four-man troops was to submit a plan of attack against the hypothetically heavily defended chapel at Merthyr Tydfil, whence they'd just come. Apart from judging initiative and organizational abilities on short notice, the purpose of this exercise was to have each group's plan "rubbished" by three regular SAS NCOs from the air services' oldest regiment: the Twenty-second, based in Hereford. In the main, this consisted of picking the plans apart and ridiculing each group's suggestion as either "daft" or "bloody stupid," while the men were mentally and physically exhausted, many of them disoriented by the sudden shock of the total immersion of the Beacons "caper," as it was known in SAS. If they couldn't stand having, in the lexicon of the SAS, "the piss taken out of 'em," then they were dropped. In SAS's experience, bad temper was as fatal to an operation as bad planning. A line unit could put up with misfits, but misfits in the SAS had to "fit" together.

"You owe me twenty dollars," the tall German ranger said, approaching Lewis, Brentwood, and Thelman, the four of them forming one of the four-man troops.

"What's your name, sport?" Lewis asked the German.

"Wilhelm Schwarzenegger."

"Yeah, well, listen, Willie. I'm a spot short now. Fix you up on payday."

"*Ja, ja.* Sure, no problem."

"Hey—you any relation to Arnie?"

"Who?"

"You know, old Arnie Schwarzenegger. Used to be a big movie star years ago. Muscles like chickens' insteps."

"No. I do not think so. Maybe way back."

"So, Aussie," David interrupted. "How we going to take the chapel?"

"Ah," said Lewis, putting his rifle on his bunk and then walking back to the group. "Like Willie here says. 'No problem.' Piece o' cake. Bracket the bastards with a mortar, and while they've got their noggins down, move in. Not too wide a front, though—we'd end up shooting one another."

"*Lewis!*" Everyone stopped talking, the regimental sergeant major's voice echoing, bull-like, through the barrack.

"Yeah?" said Lewis.

"Yes, *Sergeant Major*!"

"Yes, Sergeant Major?"

"In this regiment you may hate your mother, you may not pay your taxes, but you are *never*—I repeat *never* to be out of reach of your weapon. Do you understand?"

"Yes, Sergeant Major."

"Carry on."

Sheepishly Lewis walked over, got his rifle, and returned. For the first time since he'd met him, David Brentwood saw that the Australian was embarrassed—though he wasn't at a loss for words. "Old fart! I'm never out of reach of my weapon."

"You were then," said Thelman.

"I mean my cock, Thelma!"

"Jesus, you're rude."

"Okay," said David. "What size?"

"My cock?" said Lewis. Wilhelm was shaking his head.

"The *mortar*!" said David. "Can't be too heavy. Eighty-one-millimeter weighs a hundred pounds, shells around fifteen. Not very effective, Aussie. Most we could carry is six rounds."

"I meant a light job," explained Lewis. "Sixty-mill. Fifty-pound barrel. Rounds weigh in at less than ten."

"You must be joking!" said one of the SAS NCOs wandering among the groups. "Snowing to beat the band and you're talking about mortars! You'd get moisture in the barrel and—poof! Unless you're a good infielder, mate, you'll end up with your family jewels blown across five acres."

"We're not that stupid," said David. "We'd make sure the barrel was—"

"No?" cut in another NCO. "You fire a mortar round and next minute you'd be on their infrared scopes. Big blobs against the snow, you'd be. You blokes might as well hang out a shingle—tell 'em where you are."

"Stop screwing around with mortars," said the British NCO. "Go in fast. Don't give 'em time to think China!"

"We have any artillery backup?" asked Thelman.

The British NCO exchanged an incredulous glance with one of the American NCOs. "Pathetic, isn't it? Absolutely pathetic!" He squatted down next to Thelman. "If we had artillery that close, you ning-nong, we wouldn't need Special Air Service, right? Christ—what did you blokes have for lunch? Fairy floss, was it?"

Thelman glowered at the British NCO. David quickly cut in. "You're assuming they've got infrared scopes," he put to the NCOs.

"What we're assuming," said the British NCO, "is that you blokes don't know your ass from a hole in the ground. *Artillery!* Jesus! Self-reliance, amigos—that's what it's all about. No one else there but you."

As the two NCOs moved on to the next group, Thelman was still steamed. "What the hell's fairy floss?"

"Candy floss," said Brentwood.

"Yeah," said Lewis encouragingly. "Don't let 'em get to you, Thelma."

David snapped his fingers. "I've got it!"

The NCOs turned around.

"Tell them to surrender," David explained. "Give 'em two minutes. Tell 'em we've got the place completely surrounded. Bluff. It's worked—"

"Oh," said the British NCO, his voice dripping with sarcasm. "Oh, that's brilliant i'n'it? Got your Berlitz tape with you, have you, Brentwood?"

"No," said David steadily, "but one of us would speak the language."

"My," said the British NCO. "Would 'e now?"

"Yes," chimed in Aussie. "SAS troop of four always has one man who speaks the lingo of the opposing force."

"And who told you guys that?" asked the American.

"No one," replied Brentwood. "But Aussie has a point. Seems your recruiting offices placed a lot of emphasis on a second language."

"Yeah," said Aussie. "Dave's right. Your bloke was very interested in knowing I spoke Malay."

"So," continued David, "I figure there's one guy in every troop who—"

"Do you now?" cut in the British NCO.

"Yes."

The American NCO couldn't contain a smirk, and his British colleague gave in. "All right, Sherlock Holmes, you're right. But how do you know what language you'll be using?"

"You find out that by asking the other three in the troop whether they speak a foreign language."

"Carry on," the Brit said, and walked over with the American toward Cheek-Dawson, who was picking the plan of another would-be fire team apart.

"I told you," said Lewis, looking around triumphantly at the other three in the group. "The bloody rats. We're being trained for the tropics. My Malay!"

"How about Fritz here?" asked Thelman, indicating Schwarzenegger. He speaks German as well as English. Right, Fritz? Could be we're going to Germany."

"Aw, rats!" said Aussie dismissively, not noticing his pun. "Old Freeman's lot 'ave gone through Germany like a packet of salts. It's Malaya. Southeast Asia, boys. Communist insurgency. I can smell it. Hell, that's where the SAS cut their teeth. Fighting the Commies in Malaysia."

"I say it's Germany," said Thelman. "Flushing out SPETS maybe?"

"No way," retorted Lewis. "Absolutely no way."

Brentwood was feeling the blister thawing out, hurting like hell. It told him that he wouldn't make phase three, and he was struck once again how sometimes such small things could change your destiny. "Look," he told the others. "Four of us came together by chance. First, only two of us are probably going to make it through the course. They're the odds. And those two'll end up in another group of four. So we don't know where anyone's going. So let's drop it."

Schwarzenegger nodded. "Good point, Brentwood. *Ja!* Good point."

"Yeah, Dave," conceded Lewis. "Guess you're right. Hell—I don't think even old Cheek knows."

But Brentwood's real reason for not wanting to speculate was that Schwarzenegger's mention of SPETs reminded him of Lili.

CHAPTER THIRTY-SEVEN

TIME TO THINK. It was something that Ray Brentwood, ex-commanding officer of the guided missile frigate USS *Blaine*, had plenty of time for—ever since that misty early morning in the Sea of Japan, in the very first attack on an American naval ship in the war, when he was engulfed in flame, the Exocet slamming into the *Blaine* forward of the bridge.

At San Diego's Veterans Hospital, the so-called "restorative" operations were over, but despite laser "weld" plastic surgery, the tight, polished-skinned ugliness of "burn unit" surgery remained. It was so severe that, upon meeting him, people made a point of chatting with him and looking at him longer than they normally would any other acquaintance in order to prove to him and to themselves that it didn't really matter—when it did. Beth and the children had been the least of his worries, as it turned out. At first he'd been afraid that John, four, and Jeannie, seven, would, albeit unintentionally, shy away from him. But they, like Beth, adapted faster than Ray thought he had any right to expect. The worst of it for the children wasn't the long trip down from Seattle to San Diego Veterans—they welcomed these—but the teasing by other children. The "Frankenwood" jokes. Who was it, Ray wondered, who had said children had become more sensitive in America because of the experiences of so many minorities in the melting pot? It was a lie. Children—no matter what their nationality—all lived in the same country in childhood. It was the world of survival of the fittest, the most natural instinct to pick on the weak.

Even so, for Ray Brentwood, his children's burden at school, caused by his disfigurement, was not the worst of it for him. Much more damaging for the family as a whole was the undeniable fact that Ray Brentwood, captain, U.S. Navy, had been fished up out of the water by rescue craft while many of his crew had perished aboard the frigate, fighting the fires that had finally been extinguished.

Ray had gone over his testimony to the naval board of inquiry a million times. He remembered one moment he'd been standing on the bridge. There was an explosion of glass as the missile had hit, and then he'd been thrown back. The second officer, or was it the third?—covered in blood—was screaming something at him, and the next thing he remembered was thrashing about in the water. The crucial question for the board, and for his peace of mind, which had never been answered, was: Had he been pushed over by the officer of the watch or somebody else who had thought the ship was irretrievably lost? Or had he quit the ship voluntarily?

In vain, his court-appointed lawyer searched for testimony that would answer the question, but all the others on the bridge were dead within minutes of the missile hitting or had died shortly thereafter before any exonerating testimony could have been collected. The fact that the *Blaine*, one of America's top-of-the-line Oliver Hazard Perry fast-guided missile frigates, was the first ship hit in the war had made it the focus of enormous public attention. The navy was reluctant, "in the extreme," as the prosecuting lawyer had advised the board, to lend any solace, even the merest suggestion of it, to any idea that a captain could abandon his post under duress.

The Brentwood case wasn't simply a matter of naval PR for the Pentagon but was seen as a crucial case not only for the navy but for all the services. With thousands of young officers raised in peace, not having received a baptism of fire, it was considered vital by the chief of naval operations that benefit of doubt, which might properly be extended in a "civil mercantile marine situation," should not be extended in the case of Capt. John Raymond Brentwood, USN.

Ray Brentwood was then named an "interested party" to the inquiry. It was an innocent-sounding phrase but one that spelled terminal paralysis, if not outright rejection, for the hopes of advancement in any career officer. The decision of the inquiry was to "immediately relieve" Captain Brentwood of his command over the *Blaine*, which was now being virtually rebuilt from the hull up where the Exocet had blown a bank-vault-sized hole in her forward section. Brentwood was now dubbed "Lord Jim" after Conrad's character who had deserted his ship and passengers during a typhoon only to arrive in port on another vessel to find his had weathered the storm after all. Ray Brentwood was also told unofficially that he was "damn lucky" not to have been court-martialed. The scuttlebutt had it that two things had saved him from this. First, his family connections—that is, string pulling by his father, retired Adm. John Brentwood, Senior, now serving on the New York Port Authority as director of convoys, and by his younger brother, David, one of the heroes of the Pyongyang raid.

Second, it was rumored that the navy, because of the increasing convoy losses due to the unexpected successes of the renewed Soviet sub pack offensives in both the Atlantic and the Pacific, needed anyone who could tell a bow from a stern. The first part of the scuttlebutt, about his family connections, was untrue. Adm. John Brentwood was the last man to interfere, to pull strings for kin. He abhorred it, fought it all his life. The second part of the scuttlebutt was correct—the U.S. Navy *was* desperate for trained men, if not to man new ships, then to train younger men who would. And it was this fact upon which Ray Brentwood, now released from the Veterans Burn Unit and waiting at home in Bremerton, Washington State, had pinned all his hopes. Either that or, as his wife Beth had suggested, he could opt for early retirement because of his facial disfigurement.

"Retire to what?" he'd snapped. "Who'd have me anyway?

The sea's the only thing I know anything about—only thing I care about."

"How about the family, Ray?"

He'd turned on her, the bright sheen of what had been his cheeks stretched tighter than usual over the reconstituted jawbone they'd wired together for ten weeks—all his nourishment had had to be taken by straw. "You know what I mean, Elizabeth. I *am* thinking of the family."

He walked away from her and looked out from the living room of their bungalow toward the clutter of gantries, gulls, and noise of traffic below, the latter's diesel and gasoline fumes so thick that only now and then could he hope to catch a whiff of the sea. Thank God the burn hadn't taken away his sense of smell. "If they'd only send me to sea again, I—" He spread his hands in utter frustration. "Goddamn it! I have to get back my pride. A coast guard cutter, patrol boat—anything! All I need, Beth, is a command again."

He sat down on the love seat, tossing his cap on the coffee table, running his fingers through his hair, which by now had all returned except for a mangy patch above the left ear. He was glancing anxiously at his watch. In ten minutes—three o'clock—Washington said it would ring with the Pentagon's decision. "Make a difference to the kids, too, wouldn't it? To say I had a command again."

"Yes," said Beth softly, "I guess it would. But you'd still be away from us." He looked across at her. Her love was genuine; he could see it in her eyes and it constantly amazed him. She saw right through him, right to the heart, to his desperate longing for things as they used to be and knowing they couldn't be the same ever again. It was *she*, he remembered, who had made the first move in bed on his return from the hospital. Before they had begun, he had asked her to turn off the lights.

"No," she'd replied, her hand cool, calmly stroking him over the hard, unfeeling scar, looking only at his eyes. "I love you," she'd said. "You understand, Ray? I love you." He'd cried and she held him and he wept like a child. "There's plenty of time," she'd assured him, and at once he'd felt humiliated—as low as he'd ever been—and grateful, and angry that he should be grateful, and overwhelmed because she meant it.

The phone rang. She looked at him to answer it. "You take it," he said, not wanting to grab it—sound as if he'd been anxiously hovering over it all day.

"Hello? Yes, he's here. Just a moment please." She placed her hand over the mouthpiece and held the phone out to him. "I think it's the Pentagon."

She waited as he spoke, biting her nails. Damn it! Why couldn't he ever give any indication of what was being said? The old navy macho cool.

"Yes, sir," was all she heard him say, his tone neutral. "Yes, sir. I understand—yes, sir." He put the phone down slowly.

"*Well?* Tell me!" said Beth.

"Hi, Mom!—Where are you?" It was Jeannie, home from school. Then they heard John.

"Quickly," Beth urged Ray.

"Wait till the kids simmer down," he told her.

"*Ray*. Tell me!"

He looked down at his cap. "They've given me a command. Don't know what yet. Have to report to San Diego in forty-eight hours and—"

"Hi, Dad!" Jeannie called out, then stopped, letting her school bag slide to the ground. "What's wrong?"

"Nothing," said Beth quickly. "Your dad got one of those darn gnats in his—straight in his eye. Here—" She handed Ray a crumpled Kleenex.

"Ah," said Ray, turning around to face Jeannie full on. "Little buggers—'scuse me—little beggars. So tiny you can't see 'em. Flew right into me." He blew his nose, then suddenly clapped his hands. "Hey! How about we go out for Chinese?"

"Thought the Chinese were fighting us?" said Jeannie.

"Not these Chinese," said Beth. "We've been eating there for years."

"They could be spying on Hood Canal—watching Uncle Bob's ship . . ."

Ray had developed a particular sympathy for outsiders since his days in the confinement of the burn unit. "They're not spying, for crying out loud. Hell, if they were spying—"

"How about all that water poisoning stuff and . . ." continued Jeannie.

"Hey, Tiger!" said Ray, seeing Johnny walk in. "Are you ready for liberty?"

John hadn't seen his dad in such a good mood since—he couldn't remember when. "Yes sir!" said John, saluting.

Ray straightened and returned the salute. "Very good, officer of the deck. What'll it be? Chinese or hot dogs?"

Jeannie knew John would opt for hot dogs if she didn't move quickly. "Chinese cookies," she said. "Yummy."

"Yeah, Chinese cookies," said John enthusiastically.

"Very well," said Ray. "Now, all hands hear this. Liberty boat departs in exactly—" he glanced at his watch, frowning authoritatively "—ten minutes. Go!"

When the children had left the room, Beth ran over and hugged him. "I'm so happy for you . . . I . . ."

He said nothing. He couldn't.

"So they didn't tell you what it is?"

"Not on the phone, no. But he did say it would be a command. Ten to one it's a PT boat. I don't mind. They're fast, Beth, and they carry a wallop. I don't mind at all." He closed his eyes and hugged her. "Thank you."

"Uh-oh," called out Jeannie. "My little cooing turtle doves."

Ray batted her with his cap. "Where'd you hear that, kid?"

"Old movie at school. W. C. Fields. You know him?"

"Wasn't he some admiral?"

"Oh, Daddy!" Without further ado, she turned to her mother. "Mom, can I tell you what happened at school now?"

"This is an equal employment facility," said Ray. "Shoot."

"Guess who won the spelling bee."

"Oh, Jeannie!" said Beth. "That's great, honey."

"Hey, hey," said Ray. "Atta girl. Give me the killer word."

"Uh—let's see—"

Beth was bursting with it all. She hadn't seen the family so exuberantly happy since—

"Cacklebladder," said Jeannie.

"What in hell's that?" asked Ray.

"Right!" put in young John.

"It's when spies pretend to kill someone but they don't really," Jeannie explained.

"That's dumb," said Johnny.

"It is not dumb. It makes the other guys think the guy is really dead when he really isn't."

"What for?" said Johnny combatively.

"To fool them, silly."

"That's dumb."

"It is not. Besides, you're too young to—"

"All right, all right," said Beth, moving in to referee. "No arguments. Let's go or we don't eat."

Heading out to the car, arm in arm, Beth was laughing.

"Cackle—what was it? I've never heard of such a word. Have you?"

"No," said Ray. "It's all they're hearing at school now, I guess, with all this espionage business. God knows it's real enough."

"You mean you've never heard the word?" asked Jeannie.

Ray turned, surprised. "Nope. Never. I'm not a spy. I'm a sailor, Jeannie."

"Yes," said Beth, and for a second they savored everything that meant—before the kids started fighting about whether it would be chop suey or chow mein.

Ray's fortune cookie told him "Your expectations will be exceeded."

"A destroyer!" said Beth, reaching over and holding his hand. "Or maybe—"

"Shush!" he told her. "Don't tempt fate." Then smiling, lowering his voice, "Besides, Jeannie might be right. The cook might be listening."

It was the fortune cookie he was thinking about two days later when, after a night during which he'd been too excited to sleep, he reported to San Diego and, in the gray morning light, passed ships from a carrier in for refit to a missile frigate like the *Blaine*—was it the *Blaine*? He looked more closely through the maze of electrical cables and oxyacetylene torches. No, it wasn't.

It was muster, and ship's companies were quietly, quickly assembling on deck for morning assignments by the time he reached "vessel designation IX-44E," the USS *Grace*.

It had to be a mix-up. He saw a sailor in oily overalls coming down slowly along the pier, against which the low tide was slopping, the smell of the intertidal life all but lost under the stench of oil-fouled water. He hated the smell of diesel and considered that the greatest single advance in the modern nuclear navy was doing away with the fume-laden, oil-fired steam propulsion of the old days.

"Sailor?" he called out to the man in the overalls.

The sailor stopped, should have saluted but didn't. Instead, he looked affronted, staring at Brentwood's face angrily. "Yeah?"

"You tell me where the *Grace* is?"

"You're looking at 'er." With that, the sailor walked on farther down the pier. Ray felt his stomach go to ice, the enormity of the disappointment hitting him with the speed of a rushing locomotive.

The *Grace*, a surface vessel, was designated IX-44E. "IX" indicated "unclassified miscellaneous," "44" indicated "sludge removal barge. Self-propelled." He didn't know what the "E" stood for. Dazed, as if he'd been poleaxed, he walked down the bowed plank onto the creaking apology for a deck. It was all wood—old wood—wood that looked as if it had been cut from waterlogged trees eons ago. And grimy. It was 115 feet by 27 feet—or so the lone sailor aboard, who was awakened, cursing, told him.

"What's the ships complement?" Brentwood asked, his voice strained, barely audible.

"Twenty—ah, maybe twenty-two, Captain."

"You mean you don't know?"

"Think it's twenty-one. Sir."

"Propulsion?"

"Ah—this here barge is self-propelled, sir. Not pushed."

"I know *that*. But what pushes it, sailor—an eggbeater?"

"Ha, ha—no, sir. We got a GM 8 down below."

"Horsepower?"

"Couldn't tell you that, Cap'n. Two shafts, though. Yes, sir—one of the boys told me that." The man frowned, looking deeply troubled. "I think it's two."

Ray Brentwood, ex-commander of the fastest guided-missile frigate in the United States Navy, took a deep, long breath and immediately regretted doing so. All he could smell was thick, sinus-plugging diesel. "How many officers?"

"Uh—never had one of those, sir. You're the first."

"Who's been in command then?"

"Uh—Petty Officer Beamish, sir. He's ashore with the rest of the guys. They come on around ten."

"What's your name and rank?"

"Able Seaman Jones, sir. Guys call me Jonesy."

"What are your duties, Jones?"

"Uh—now, *that* I can tell you, sir. See, we go out, suck up any oil that's leaked from the bilges in transit up and down the coast. Then that derrick there in the middle—"

"Midships," said Brentwood, appalled.

"Yeah, well, we lower the suction hose down over the A-frame and *slurp!* Up she comes. Then we trundle back here to port and dump 'er in that old scow—the *Elaine*—up yonder by the big . . . carrier there—*Salt Lake City*. Sometimes folks up the coast see a bit of oil and give us a call, so we go and mop 'er—''

"It's filthy!" said Brentwood.

"Well, Captain, diesel's dirty stuff. Course, sometimes we get a few eggheads—uh, sorry, sir—I mean, ocean scientists down from La Jolla and we let 'em hang some stuff off the stern. They keep track of the oil spills, see? Like every oil cargo is different, sort of—"

"Isotope stamping," Brentwood cut in. "It's called fingerprinting." It was a long-standing pollution control device to track down whoever flushed oil from bilges in transit up and down the coast.

"Yeah, I reckon that's what they do," said Jones.

"What's the 'E' stand for?"

Jones's gaze followed Ray Brentwood's finger pointing at the designation IX-44E in faded paint on the barge's port side.

"Oh yeah. That's 'E' for 'experimental.' "

"You mean the oceanographer's stuff?"

"No, sir, I mean this is the first self-propelled sludge-removal barge in port. Used to just push 'er around with a tug."

"Jesus!" said Brentwood, and right then and there he decided he was going to resign from the navy. If they thought they could push *him* out quietly with this insult—the bastards were right.

What saved him, changed his mind, was Robert Mitchum, an actor his dad used to like, whom he'd seen in an old late show one night watching KVOS-TV out of Seattle. Mitchum was playing the part of a destroyer captain in World War II being hunted by a sub, and the destroyer had been hit. It wasn't out for the count but was well on the way. "Old Bob," as Ray's dad used to call Mitchum, as if they were brothers, ordered everybody to abandon ship except essential crew. The officer of the deck had the job of making up the list of the nonessential personnel and had put down the garbage baler's name—a low-IQ eccentric who was in charge of garbage disposal.

"Old Bob," sleepy-eyed, had said no—the garbageman had to stay. Everybody disliked the man because he stank and had a weird passion for his job. But "Old Bob" told the OOD that the man's dedication to "baling"—compacting garbage, making sure it sank out of sight instead of breaking up and acting as a trail for the marauding sub to spot and follow—could save the ship. Ray remembered that on this foul-smelling, misty wharf, and what his father had always told him—to swallow his pride and think of the navy, that it was bigger than any individual. Had to be.

Ray ordered the lackadaisical Jones to round up the vessel's "full complement" by 1000 hours or he'd fine every man jack of them. They were going to scrub her down—stem to stern—and the engine room, crammed box that it was, was going to be so clean that any one of the ship's company could eat their dinner off it. Was that understood?

"Yes, sir," said Jones, saluting and wiping dirty hands on his dirty dungarees.

As Ray Brentwood watched him walk up the gangplank along the wharf, he felt the barge shift and strain against the hawsers. The tide was coming in. He saw a forlorn-looking sea gull perched atop the grease-stained derrick well forward of the wheelhouse, the latter looking like a box plonked on a slab of tired wood. "Well, bird," Ray told the sea gull, "I don't think *Grace*'ll win the war—running up and down the coast sucking up bunker C—but at least we can give the lady a little respect."

In all the annals of war, never had a man so unwittingly belied the role of the vessel under his command—sludge-removal barge IX-44E—propelled.

The gull rose, squawking, depositing on Brentwood's cap what the *Grace*'s captain took to be appropriate comment on his career prospects.

CHAPTER THIRTY-EIGHT

BESIDE THE CRACKLING warmth of the Oval Office fireplace, the president of the United States felt cold.

With the chiefs of staff, press aide Paul Trainor, and National Security Affairs adviser Harry Schuman sitting on the white leather lounge chairs behind him, he read the message that had been relayed directly to him by the U.S. trade legation in Taipei:

POISON GAS USED BY PRC FORCES AGAINST ROK POSITIONS NEAR MANPO ON YALU STOP POISONOUS GAS NOT YET KNOWN FOR CERTAIN BUT HAS BEEN CONFIRMED AS NERVE GAS TYPE SIMILAR OR IDENTICAL TO THAT USED IN NINETEEN EIGHTIES IRAQ/IRAN WAR STOP OBVIOUS DANGER IS THAT IF BEIJING HAS AUTHORIZED USE AGAINST NKA WE MUST ASSUME THEY AND/OR NKA GENERAL KIM WILL NOT HESITATE TO USE AGAINST US FORCES IN KOREA MESSAGE ENDS

Mayne stared into the fire as he finished reading the message and saw the red coals collapsing as he imagined ancient Pompeii must have disappeared in Vesuvius's molten sea of lava. "Has Freeman been told?"

"Yes. Mr. President," answered Army Chief of Staff General Grey.

"What's he doing about it?" he asked General Grey.

"Only thing he can, sir," replied the chief of the army. "Making sure each man has CBW clothing and masks."

"How about Europe?"

"We're doing the same thing there, sir. So are the Russians and Chinese if our intelligence reports are accurate."

"Those dumb bastards!" said Mayne, his right hand massaging his forehead, the message from Taipei dangling from his left hand like a white flag.

"Mr. President," said Air Force General Allet. "We can't say for sure that Beijing ordered the use of the gas. It could have been a local decision by one of the commanders. Might have panicked when he saw ROK forces coming at him."

"Good Christ!" said Mayne, turning away from the fireplace. "Well, let's find out."

"We can't get through to Beijing on normal hookup, Mr. President," General Grey informed him.

Mayne was incredulous. "Why, dammit?"

"Several microwave relay stations have been knocked out."

The CNO—chief of naval operations—Admiral Horton, held that the question of who authorized the use of gas was more or less an academic one, "now that the 'genie,' " as he put it, had been let out of the bottle. "No one's going to care who started it, Mr. President. Point is, what're we going to do about it now?"

"Warn them," said Mayne. "Beijing *and* Moscow. That this is a no-win situation—for all of us." Mayne caught the quick glance between Admiral Horton and Harry Schuman, his National Affairs adviser, who shifted his cane uncomfortably from left to right, a sign that his usual southern aplomb had been undone.

"Well?" demanded Mayne. "Isn't it? A no-win situation?"

"Mr. President," answered General Grey, moving forward uneasily in the plush lounge chair, "the army, marines—and the other two services all have supplies of Sarin and VX nerve gases, despite the agreement to reductions signed by Bush and Gorbachev. It was clearly understood by both sides it could never be a total ban, when at least fourteen other nations had similar chemical and biological weapons, including Libya, Iraq—"

"So? We get the message through to Beijing and Moscow—through Geneva if necessary—that we can play this game, too. God knows we don't want to, but if any U.S. troops are attacked with gas, then we'll retaliate in kind. We couldn't pin this goddamned water poisoning that swept the country on them for lack of evidence, but this is clear-cut, gentlemen. And as Churchill told the Nazis: 'We didn't ask that the rules of the game be changed, but if they want to play rough, we can play rough, too!' Agreed?" He waited impatiently for the consensus.

"Afraid not, Mr. President." It was General Grey again who dared broach the harsher reality.

"What in hell do you mean, General?" asked Mayne, tapping his breast pocket, as if looking for his reading glasses, and asking his press aide to bring him a glass of water, a sign for Trainor to get the ABM—antiballistic missile—as he called the migrane medication, often having told Trainor in lighter moments that migrane is like an ICBM: if you didn't start defensive measures quickly, you'll lose.

General Grey was now sitting uncomfortably on the edge of the lounge seat, hands clasped but looking directly up at his commander in chief. This was no time, he decided, to play pussyfoot or to assign blame. It was the moment for an unsparing truth—not known by the American public at large and not even by many senior officers.

"Sir," Grey began, "the treaty between Gorbachev and Bush was unable to cover all kinds of chemical agents—only those known for sure as potential weapons at the time. Later the British were the first to notice a problem—a new type of chemical called PFIB. I believe its chemical name is perfluoro—"

"I don't want a lecture, General. Just give me the bottom line."

"Well, sir, this PFIB is ten times more lethal than hydrogen cyanide—easily deliverable and thermally stable. Make the damn stuff by superheating Teflon. Problem is, it permeates our gas suits, which are essentially activated-carbon based. It's only a fairly recent development—the PFIB, I mean. But even against the known nerve gases, VX for example, our M 17 respirator isn't very satisfactory."

"Satisfactory?" said Mayne angrily. "You mean the damn thing doesn't work?"

"Uh—providing the concentrations aren't too high, it's—"

"You're telling me the damn thing doesn't work!"

"Mr. President," interjected Admiral Horton. "General Grey is pointing out, sir, that the CBW suits we have for our troops are markedly inferior to those of the Soviets. As with their space program, it's one area that they've been remarkably—"

Mayne was stunned by the information Grey and Horton were giving him. He looked at Air Force General Allet and Harry Schuman to contest the issue, to tell him they were wrong. But it was Schuman who delivered the final blow. "Mr. President, I'm afraid they're correct. There's been a lot of intense interservice rivalry on this one—as with so many contracts." Schuman turned to the chiefs of staff. "Am I right, gentlemen?"

There was an uncomfortable murmur from the leather lounge, the three chiefs of staff of what they believed was the most powerful nation on earth caught out like guilty schoolboys.

Schuman continued. "We do have some better suits—the MCU-2P has very good visibility. Trouble is, it has what they call a butyl-rubber nylon hood. It's like a sauna. Impossible to fight in in certain situations, and besides, we haven't nearly enough to—"

"Mr. President," cut in Grey, bridling at the prospect of the army taking the full rap. "We had to decide where best to spend the money. Especially after the Gorbachev-Bush love-in. CBW defense has not been put on high priority, not only because of the competition for sophisticated defense of ICBMs allowed by the treaties but because, quite frankly, we put our faith in the Triad—bombers, subs, and our land-based ICBMs. Nuclear forces. Now, we do have most of our M-1 tanks fitted with good antigas air-conditioning units, and they're pretty safe, but for the infantry—you see, sir, a drop of VX anywhere on the skin can kill you. It's very difficult to design a suit—one that you have to actually fight in—to satisfy the—"

"Then how come the Russians have done it?" shot back Mayne.

There was silence, until Admiral Horton spoke. "Because, sir, the Soviets've put a hell of a lot more of their GNP into defensive capability—CBW defenses in particular. Moscow had miles of tunnels built in the Cold War and also utilizes its extensive subway system as a shelter network. In that regard they're like the Israelis. I mean in how they've prepared for it. Israeli defense forces've run gas drills every day since the Iraqis bought the eighteen-hundred-mile-range Chinese East Wind missiles capable of delivering CBW warheads. Soviets have the same kind of drills—as often as we have fire drills. The Russians might be backward as hell in making shoes or running a consumer economy, but not in CBW warfare. They're infinitely more prepared than we are."

Mayne walked over to the Oval Office desk, his back to the chiefs, and took the three headache pills lying on his blotter, swallowing them in one gulp before returning, glass in hand, to the fireplace, aware that there had been a subtle but terrifying shift in the conversation. One minute they had been talking about Teflon-produced gas, combatants in chemical/biological warfare; now the three service chiefs seemed to be talking about the vulnerability of the American population at large and not only its soldiers. "You're telling me," said Mayne, "that not only are our boys equipped with inferior CBW suits but that those to be used for the civilian population are just as bad?"

Admiral Horton was staring at the fire, Air Force General Allet carefully flicking off a piece of invisible fluff from his knife-edged trousers.

"I think," put in Harry Schuman, grasping his ornate cane in both hands, "that what the chiefs are saying, Mr. President, is that we have *no* civilian CBW contingency plan to speak of."

"That's not correct," put in General Grey quickly. "Every city has emergency plans for—"

"Yes," rejoined Schuman, "for earthquakes, fires—but we've no comprehensive CBW strategy or protective clothing. Correct?"

"Essentially that's—"

"What the hell does that mean, General?" pressed Mayne,

"have we or do we not have effective CBW defenses for our civilians?"

"We do not, Mr. President—except for you and your battle staff in Washington should the occasion—"

The commander in chief took another long draft of detoxified water. "Well, gentlemen, we screwed up on that, wouldn't you say?"

"Yes, sir," replied Grey. "But there's nothing we can do about it now except try to stop them using it on us. If they attack us with gas, we'll lose."

"Not necessarily," cut in Admiral Horton. "A CW attack won't affect our subs at sea or even our surface vessels. Wherever possible, our ships have undergone 'contoured refit'—got rid of sharp-angled pockets in the superstructure. All the vessel has to do is head into the sea and it in effect washes itself down. That goes for nuclear radiation or CBW attacks. We just seal 'em up and they can continue to fight in that condition. With air conditioners and filters—"

"You can't seal a carrier, can you?" challenged Mayne acidly. "If you want to use aircraft."

"Well, that is an exception, Mr. President."

"A rather large one, I would have thought, Admiral." The CNO did not respond.

"I trust the logic of this situation hasn't escaped you," pressed Mayne, throwing the remaining water from his glass onto the fire. The coals sizzled for a second but then just as quickly were flaring again. "The situation, gentlemen, is that because we don't have any significant CBW defensive capability, we would have only one alternative if so attacked. Nuclear war."

"God forbid, Mr. President," said General Allet. "But the air force is ready for that."

"*Are* you, General? Well, I'm not!" replied Mayne.

The elderly Schuman used his cane to help drag himself forward and up out of the lounge. "Mr. President, none of us, in a sense, is ready for a—uh, nuclear exchange."

"Let's call it war, Harry, shall we?" said Mayne icily.

"Very well, Mr. President. But if Moscow was to use such a weapon—and I must tell you that Moscow is surely now aware of Beijing's action against the ROK forces—I'll give you any odds that their advisers will see the sudden window of opportunity they now have—namely that this is one area in which they are unquestionably superior to the United States."

"Suzlov's not that mad," retorted Mayne, but it was said more with hope than conviction.

"You might be correct, Mr. President," said Harry Schuman, "but Suzlov's not the only one running the show now. His chiefs of staff, including Chernko, are no doubt pointing out that while nuclear arms destroy everything, chemical/biological weapons destroy only the people—and leave everything intact for the victors. All they have to do is wait till the gas does its job—dissipates—then they move in. And Suzlov's generals have much more say in making policy these days, Mr. President, than we do with you. I'm not complaining about that, but that is the fact of the matter. Remember, too, we're now on Russian territory. For them, the temptation is much stronger than for us. It's one thing for us to sit thousands of miles away, across the Atlantic, but with NATO forces on their front lawn and Freeman on the Chinese-North Korean border, I must concur with General Grey. However distasteful it is, Mr. President. If we can't win a chemical war, we will have to be prepared for a nuclear war."

"Yes," said Mayne, "but if that starts, who stops it?"

Harry Schuman sighed heavily, both hands resting on the silver knob of the cane. "Mr. President—contrary to those on the extreme left who are always talking doomsday, I believe that it is possible to contain it. One or two air bursts on Soviet territory—Siberia—will demonstrate the point adequately."

"No!" said the admiral, his tone tense with urgency. "Sir. If we're talking about it, risking a nuclear war because we have to, then our first shots should at least hit vital military targets. The Kola Peninsula, for example. One air burst there could knock out three major military bases, including one SSBN base. Hell, one burst over Siberia, unless it hits an ICBM site right in the middle of the bull's-eye, will only kill a few reindeer and wipe out a village or two in the boonies. And what in hell do we think they'd be doing in the meantime—in Moscow? No—the way we do it, Mr. President, is to launch an ICBM, land-based or sub, and not have it head for some outlying area that Muscovites don't give a damn about but aim for a highly strategic target. That'll show 'em we're not fooling around. If we have to do it—we should go for a hard military target. The bigger the better. Not a wild shot somewhere in the boonies."

"The admiral's quite right, sir," said Air Force General Allet. "If we're going to use the stick—might as well show them we can put our missiles where it hurts them most."

"Why not Moscow then?" asked Mayne.

"Because they'd all be in the shelters," explained General Grey.

"Yes," confirmed the chief of naval operations. "They'd be down there well out of air burst range. Many of the deep tunnels are nuclear-repellant. Superhardened."

"Perhaps," said President Mayne, "we could give them a message some other way. Any suggestions?"

"Not at the moment, sir," answered Grey.

"Then put your backs to it!" enjoined Mayne. "Meanwhile I want you to send the word out that no commander is to use any chemical or biological weapons without my personal directive."

"Sir?" said Press Secretary Trainor. "We could have a problem with Doug Freeman on this. He's a brilliant field commander, but if the Chinese pour everything they've got into North Korea, he might be tempted to cross the Yalu, use 105-millimeter A tips."

"Goldarn it!" said Mayne, turning on Grey. "General! You tell Freeman that he is *not* to cross the Yalu. He is to stay this side of it and do what he's damn well told."

"Yes, sir."

Mayne leaned forward, shaking his head, letting a pencil he'd been twirling fall from his fingers. "What a mess!"

"War usually is," commented Harry Schuman. The president could feel the migrane getting a stranglehold on him, despite his preemptive strike.

CHAPTER THIRTY-NINE

IT WAS BITTERLY cold, the Yalu River taking on a strange, ethereal blue though it was still an hour till sundown. Despite the piercing cold and the exposed forward position of Outpost Delta, Norton felt much more comfortable in the hills overlooking the Yalu than he'd been in the claustrophobic warmth of the Boeing. "They won't try gas here," he proclaimed confidently.

"What makes you think they won't?" pressed Freeman, looking down through Delta's field scope, moving it through a 140-degree arc west to east over the valley below where the ground tumbled away to flats a quarter mile from the frozen river and the wild, snow-covered mountains of Manchuria beyond. "You think they're more afraid of us than they are of the ROK?"

"No, sir," answered Norton, "but they're too close to us, sir. Up here the major says the wind can change because of that valley below quicker than you can blink."

Freeman was worried. Delta had barely been blooded and morale was rock-bottom all along the Korean front, following Creigh's humiliating defeat.

"Jim," said Freeman, still looking through the scope, "you know the prime tactic of the Chinese infantry?"

"Let's see if I can remember my little red book," said Norton. "When the enemy attacks, withdraw. When the enemy withdraws, attack. Always seemed pretty much like common sense to me, General."

Freeman stood up from the scope, hands on his hips, resting on the two leather holsters. "Yes, I know. . . . And put the door back on the house when you leave." He turned to Norton. "That was old Mao Cow Dung's way of teaching his peasant army not to act like occupiers when they went through a village—get the people's backs up and they turn against you instead of helping you. Often used a door for a table in a village—only damn thing big enough. You're right, though—most of it's pretty much common sense—at least when you're not in the thick of battle." Freeman squinted, for though the sun was starting to dip down to the mountains behind him, there was a glare coming from the broken china of white-covered peaks beyond the Yalu as the mountains of Manchuria reflected the sun's dying rays. "*But* some of their tactics aren't so obvious, Jim. Ever figure out why they attack en masse?"

"Logistics. Plenty of 'em, I guess. One man's there to pick up another's rifle if they haven't got enough arms. Don't pick up a dropped weapon, you could lose it—especially in the snow."

"True," answered Freeman, still looking at the mountains, trying to detect anything that might signify the Chinese positions. It looked snowbound and deserted. "Attacking in numbers like that also panics defenders," said Freeman. "Unless they're veterans. But the main reason, Jim, is that the Chinese infantry commanders, more than any others, want to close with Americans more than with any other army. Want to get as many men in and around our positions as they can."

"With our firepower, General, seems a pretty crazy tactic."

Freeman said nothing for a moment, looking through the scope again. "Know what they used to say at the movies when I was a boy, Jim?"

"What's that, General?"

Freeman swung the scope to the northern sector of the field of fire overlooking the valley and the big bend in the river. " 'Too quiet.' And that's what I'm feeling now. Too damned quiet." He turned about and briskly drew Delta's HQ bunker curtain aside. "Major? How long you say it's been since the last engagement?"

"Yesterday morning, sir. About 0500. Nothing since then. Not even sniper fire." The major emerged from the bunker, pulling his collar up against the wind that was blowing snow off the crests of the hill. "You figure they've gone back to Beijing, General?"

"The hell I do. Those rice-eating sons of bitches are over that river dug in. Something's brewing. I can smell it."

"Maybe they're going to hit us in another sector, General," proffered the major. "Now they've pushed Creigh back and driven a wedge between First Army in the west and Ten Corps further east. Maybe they're moving west to reinforce the wedge—spread it out between us."

"I haven't seen any sign of them moving, Major," replied Freeman.

"Not in daylight, General. Chinks are night birds."

"Intelligence," put in Norton, "haven't reported any movement west."

"Intelligence!" snorted Freeman, his breath steaming in the air. "That's cold comfort, Jim. Intelligence, with all that damn satellite gear, didn't see any of them when they first hit us. They came over that river and were butchering Creigh's men before he knew it."

"I realize that," said Norton, "but the intelligence boys were having trouble with their thermal sensors then, General. Sometimes when the weather gets—"

"They had trouble with their sensors, Jim, when our boys were hit in the middle of the night at the beginning of this war by two Chinese divisions. By God, we flew over the Changsong Road yesterday. Creigh didn't even have time to bury his head. Littered along the highway like—" He turned to the major. "I'll tell you the first thing we're going to do here, Major, is mount reconnaissance patrols in this area—right across the front. Day and night until we find out what the hell those bastards are up to. I don't want another Chinese breakthrough here. And another thing, Major. I want all cooking fires put out. C rations only. And a forty-eight hour ban on smoking. And start digging "Z" turns and star trenches—put all the dirt at the end of the trenches, not over the top, otherwise the Chinks'll see the fresh soil. It'd stand out a mile in this snow. Right now my hunch is those Sons of Heaven are sitting around and having more than a political meeting. They're dotting their maps with our positions for a night attack, making sure they know where we all are so they won't lose their way in the razor wire."

Gazing across at the now ice-blue fastness of Manchuria, Freeman shook his head, not at something seen but, as Norton could tell, out of respect for his enemy. "Say what you like, gentlemen, those bastards are geniuses at burrowing under the earth." He paused. "Ever been to China, Major?"

"No, sir."

"I was there in the nineteen eighties—before Tiananmen. Went to see the clay warriors they dug up in Xian. Full-sized—all in full battle order. They'd been there thousands of years—longer than the pyramids—and nobody knew about them till the nineteen seventies. Completely hidden. Imagine—an entire army! Emperor Qin wanted his army to guard him in death. Hadn't been for some peanut farmer kicking up a bit of clay with his plow, they'd still be hidden. No wonder we can't spot the tunnels from the air. It's a contest who is better digging tunnels—Chinese or the Vietcong.''

Jim Norton rolled his eyes at the major. Freeman was good for a half hour on tunnels anytime, day or night—the ingenuity of construction, the ammunition dumps built off to the side, the traps for the unwary. Happily for Norton, the general's lecture on the enemy's art was interrupted by the rolling thunder of the sonic boom from four F-14s thundering high above the bleak white humps of the snow-covered hills that tumbled down toward the flats in front of the Yalu.

By the time the jets had passed overhead, the Delta HQ major had been called in by a signal corpsman with an urgent transmit from Seoul. Freeman stood watching the fighters' contrails as they went into a tight bank to the northeast following the snaking line of the Yalu to the Tamur and the Sea of Japan. ''Might be Shirer up there, Jim,'' said Freeman. ''Beautiful things, aren't they?''

''Yes, sir, but I'm just as happy to leave them to the flyboys.''

''Well,'' commented Freeman, as the Delta major reappeared, ''We'll be off. Strategy's straightforward enough. Change your internal placements, mortars, machine guns. . . . That attack yesterday morning was probably just a probe—to pinpoint your positions. You shift things about like I told you and we'll give 'em a big surprise when they come up this hill again.'' The major was looking worried, preferring that the general had said *''if''* the Chinese came up the hill again. The men's morale was bad enough after Creigh's humiliating withdrawal without confronting them with the prospect of another battle.

''You and your boys are going to have to hold these ridges, Major—till we can mount a counterattack. Chinese get up here with their artillery overlooking the next valley, they'll make mincemeat of us. That's what happened to Creigh—so I don't want anybody falling back. Understood?''

''Yes, General.''

As Freeman and Norton walked down from the snowy crest toward the snow-covered, sandbagged chopper pad, the rotor slap of the Black Hawk was already fibrillating the air, curling up snow on the rim of the hill. The general heard a voice complaining above the roar of the motors. "Yeah, well, shit, man. Freeman's same as Creigh. Won't see 'im do it."

Freeman stopped, turned back into the trench, walked around the Z bend, and found himself looking at a dozen or so bleary-eyed and unshaven GIs. "What won't you see me do, soldier?"

There was silence.

"What won't I do?" repeated Freeman.

A GI, using his rifle like a staff, hauled himself reluctantly to his feet, his voice low, almost drowned by the sound of the chopper. "Sorry, General—"

"Won't see me doing what, soldier?"

Norton saw the soldier visibly gulp, trying to find the spittle to answer Freeman.

"Well?" bellowed Freeman.

"Taking out a patrol—" answered the soldier. "Sir."

Freeman was sniffing the air like a bloodhound. "Who's wearing fairy water?" The GIs looked at one another, perplexed, several clearly frightened, a few not giving a damn, leaning sullenly against the trench. Behind the general, Norton was making a quick pantomime for the GIs—as if he were applying deodorant beneath his arm.

"Ah—me, sir," said one of the younger, more hapless GIs.

"By God!" said Freeman, "I oughta have you skinned. You know how far a Chink can smell?"

No one answered.

"From here to Beijing. You're endangering the safety of the whole position. A position taken out, soldier, will break the whole line. A line breached and you could cost a battle—a war. You understand?"

"Y—yes, sir." The private saluted.

"You bury that fairy stick right now and wash out your armpits," growled Freeman. Freeman saluted, turned to go, stopped and asked them, "Why haven't you shaved?"

"No hot water," said a private. "Sir."

"Since when does one of my soldiers need hot water to shave?" Freeman challenged derisively. "Where the hell you think you are, soldier? At college?"

"No, sir."

"You shave that fuzz off. That goes for all of you. Understand?"

There was a murmur of "yes, sir"s. No one was looking at him. His anger seemed to sear them. As he stalked off toward the helo pad, Norton increased his pace to keep up. Going down the hill, Jim Norton tapped the general before they got too close to the chopper for Freeman to hear him. "General, sir?"

"*What?*" Freeman shouted above the noise.

"Sir—the deodorant stick—fine, sir. They needed to be told about that. But the shaving, sir—" Norton said nothing more, his tone carrying implicit criticism.

"Damn it, Jim! Their morale's rock-bottom. They start to lose respect for themselves, their appearance, the next is a slide into lack of self-confidence. No matter what the weaponry, Jim, you know well as I do, low morale loses wars. Good God, if Vietnam didn't teach us anything, it taught us that."

"I realize that, sir," replied Norton, his voice rising to overcome the chopper, one hand holding on to his helmet. "But you told me once the Chinese have a thing about facial hair, remember—any body hair, other than where it should be. See it as the sign of a barbarian. Barbarians scare them, you said, General."

Freeman grunted. "You're telling me I overreacted?" Before Norton could answer, the general waved to the chopper pilot to shut her down—he was a stickler for setting the example about not wasting gas or anything else at the front. Creigh had lost over a hundred tons of supplies, along with howitzers, which hadn't yet been replaced. Besides, he didn't want the Chinese picking up too much of the blown snow from the chopper's wash—to better pinpont Delta.

"Yes, sir," Norton told him straight, uncomfortably but fearlessly. "You did overreact, and you said if ever you did, I had your permission to—"

"Yes, yes," said Freeman grumpily, walking away from Norton and the chopper pad, hands clasped behind him, head bowed, trudging below the line of the hill. It reminded Norton of a painting he'd seen of Napoleon on the eve of the battle for Austerlitz.

When Freeman returned from his solitary walk, his hands were on his holsters. "You're right, Jim. I did overreact, but—" he sighed, looking over at the ice-blue hills "—those men in there think I'm a damned coward." He looked at Norton. "A goddamn yellow belly!"

"No, sir—I'm sure—"

"Higher up the totem pole you get," confided Freeman, his gaze taking in the long, frozen snake of the Yalu, "more you lose touch. Commander's got to lead, Jim. This whole front is moribund. You could smell it in there—that wasn't sweat, that was the odor of fear. Creigh's defeat has passed through the whole front like diarrhea. That'll get more men killed than Chinese bullets." He cast his gaze in the direction of the scattered American positions on the hilltops to the west. "By God, that's what's wrong here, Jim. It's a defeated army."

"Well, maybe now, sir, but when we counterattack—"

"With what?" Freeman growled. "Troops with that kind of morale won't do it. Hell, why should they? Creigh gets *stressed out* and runs. Leadership's gone."

"Sir, they know you were at Pyongyang, that—"

"No, Jim. That was last season. Old coach like me knows better than that. All they see now is someone flying around in this eggbeater giving 'em the old rah! rah! rah!" He was walking away from Norton again. "No, Jim, it won't work. This team won't attack on the basis of my old win. Last year's pennant. Besides, Chinese weren't in the game then. Our boys have got goddamned dragon disease."

Freeman was staring ahead, but Norton could see it wasn't the North Korean fastness that arrested him, but memories.

"When I was a youngster," Freeman confided, "my parents would take me into 'Frisco to see the Chinese New Year celebrations. I remember the very sight of a dragon in Chinatown was more terrifying to me than anything else I could think of. Fire coming out of its nose, damned thing snaking all about. These boys are scared shitless of the Chinese. See it in their eyes." He turned around to Norton, gloved hands on his holsters one second, right arm sweeping toward the Yalu the next. "They don't need me for strategy here. Blind man could figure out the attack plan in five minutes. There's the Yalu—beat the bastards back. Any first lieutenant worth his Sam Browne could figure it out. What we need is esprit de corps. And fast! That's why they haven't been sending out enough patrols up here to get the information we need. You can't fight an enemy if you can't see—" He stopped. There was fire in his eyes that Norton knew was unstoppable. "You know," Freeman raced on, "why the Chinks want to get so close to us?"

Freeman answered his own question. "Because, Jim, they know we won't call our artillery down on our own men. They're frightened of our artillery. We're the best and fastest in the world at setting up and bracketing an enemy attack. We can rain down 105-millimeters on them within ten minutes of an attack—sooner if we're already in place. You know what they do if we close with them—hand to hand?"

Norton didn't have to answer.

"That's right," said Freeman. "They'll bring down fire on their own men. *That's* why they want to close with us. And the sooner they do it, the less time we have for our artillery to break up their attack. And once they close, they'll use our boys—those that are left alive—as hostages against our artillery." He paused, his breathing slowed as if by will. "That's why we've got to beat them to the punch. Find out exactly where their assembly areas are and bring air support and artillery down on their rat tunnels before they can move out." In the fading light—there was still a quarter hour to sunset—he called out to the Delta major.

"Yes, General?"

"You're a witness," Freeman informed him, his voice lowering so as not to be overheard by the men. "I know why the Chinese haven't attacked in the last twenty-four hours, and now I know why it's too damned quiet, Jim."

The major looked at Norton, but the colonel was as perplexed as he was.

"NKA have already used it on their own people. Those bastards have withdrawn across the river because they're going to use gas." Before Norton could respond, Freeman raced on. "Jim, this is an order. First whiff you get, you have 'weapons release' from me as CIC Korea to reply with 105-millimeter atomic warhead artillery. You hear that, Major?"

"Yes, sir, but hell—"

"Major, I want eight men, grenades, and a squad automatic weapon."

"General—" began the major, alarmed.

"That's an order, Major. Now!"

"Yes, sir."

Norton spoke quietly. "Sir, Washington'll have my hide if anything—"

"Jim, I want it known that I'm taking out a patrol. And I mean, I want every son of a bitch from here to Seoul to know. I want them to know that their C in C isn't afraid of some rice-picking comrade. And I want that nuclear artillery release written down on a message pad so I can sign it in front of you and the major. And send it in plain language to Seoul HQ. I want those Commie bastards to intercept it." The general lowered his voice, glancing about to see whether any GI was nearby. "Jim, you and I know that those CBW zoo suits they've issued aren't worth a pinch of coon crap. And the Commies know it. Christ, this weather's perfect for it. Goddamned visors on our suits'll steam up for a start. If I had my choice, I'd rather die in two minutes in the open from a gas attack than shit myself to death for ten inside one of those damned contraptions. Now, you make sure you get a Kraut car up here—on every battalion front within the next twenty-four hours. If their spectrometers signal CBW presence, you let loose with those 105 A tips. There won't be any time to screw around. Then I want you to Flash SACEUR Brussels HQ and tell them that Operation Merlin is to go."

"Yes, General." Freeman signaled the chopper pilot to start her up as Norton, using his thigh as a table, wrote down the order to have a Kraut—German-made Fox NBC—nuclear biological/chemical—weapons reconnaissance vehicle—moved up immediately from Kusong to Delta. After the general signed it, Norton held out his hand. For an embarrassing moment the general thought it was for his pen. Then he realized Norton was saying good-bye. Freeman shook hands, Norton asking, "I suppose there's no way I can talk you out of this, General?"

"Course not," said Freeman, grinning. "You know better than that."

"Yes, sir." Freeman smacked Norton affectionately on the shoulder. "God go with you, Jim."

The colonel tried to answer but couldn't. Instead, he saluted, then turning to the major, gave him the second copy of the message for transmit from Delta Outpost HQ to Seoul, lest the chopper be hit in transit. Lowering his head, left hand holding his helmet down, Norton ran to board the chopper.

As the Black Hawk took off in a bluish-white swirl of snow, Freeman turned and saw eight white figures—the GIs in their white camouflage overlays—straggling out from the trench.

"You boys volunteer?" asked Freeman as he clipped on the grenades and took the squad automatic weapon and pack from the major.

"You kidding, General?" replied one man, but there was a new tone—a respect that Freeman knew would spread like wildfire down the line as the reconnaissance patrol left.

"Major!"

"Sir?"

"It wasn't a '*peanut* farmer,' but it was a farmer."

It took a second for the major to remember the general's story about the Chinese farmer who discovered the massive Chinese army underground. "You ever miss anything, General?"

"Very little, Major. Very little." Then Freeman walked to

the front of the section, to take the "point." "All right, boys. Follow me."

In the chopper, Colonel Norton was gripping his seat tightly, but added to his fear of flying was the haunting, terrible response of the Chinese general Lin Biao, who, when MacArthur had once threatened the Chinese Red Army with the A-bomb, had replied, "So we lose a million or two."

CHAPTER FORTY

IN SEOUL, OR what was left of it after the pulverizing it had taken during the NKA invasion of the South, and again when the Americans, breaking out of the Pusan-Yosu perimeter, had counterattacked before being bogged down by the massive intervention of the Chinese, there was no hesitation in sending the choppers loaded with atomic-tipped shells to the forward positions overlooking the Yalu. News of the Chinese's use of nerve gas had sent a shiver down the spine of every Allied commander from the Yalu to the Russian front outside Minsk. And the failure of enough supplies getting through the Soviet sub packs only fueled the apprehension of frontline commanders, as presidential adviser Schuman warned, that the Russians, seeing a brief window of opportunity, before the Allies could build up enough support for the final push into Russia, might strike with CBW weapons of their own all along the NATO front.

In Beijing, China radio was broadcasting charges that the "ultimate degradation of bourgeois capitalism" was evident in "Washington's criminal use of chemical weapons from napalm to the gas supplied by America to the ROK lackeys and pirates" who had, "on the orders of Washington, attacked the freedom-loving people of the People's Republic of China with nerve gas."

* * *

As Kiril Marchenko stepped out of his Zil limousine for the emergency meeting of the Politburo and presidential advisers in the Council of Ministers Building, snow had stopped falling, but one glance at the heavy, metallic-colored sky told him it was only a brief lull in the latest Arctic storm sweeping down from Murmansk to Moscow and on to the Polish plain.

As President Suzlov moved from his desk to the conference table of his enormous office under the gaze of Marx, aides carried piles of the red-striped green folders of war reports, distributing them to the Politburo and STAVKA members, less than half of whom had been able to make it on such short notice. Marchenko was worried by the implacable expression worn by KGB chief Chernko, who he noticed had been seated immediately to the right of the president. Both Suzlov and Chernko were quintessential *apparatchiki*—''bureaucrats''—efficient, cool, but, Marchenko thought, lacking the human dimension—a deficiency evident in Chernko's argument that a gas attack was now *''sovershenno mozhnym''*—''quite feasible''—against the NATO front, given the strong prevailing southwestward flows of Arctic air that wouldn't endanger Soviet troops.

Suzlov opened the emergency meeting to questions, a meeting that Marchenko quietly noted to his aide didn't have enough members present to constitute a legal Party quorum. Marchenko, already leaning against the highly polished table, his reflection melting like all the others into a blur of khaki and red collar tabs of the general staff, asked, ''Mr. President, I wish to point out that whether a southern wind—''

''South*west*,'' put in Chernko pedantically but without the slightest malice.

''Southwest, then,'' continued Marchenko. ''The supposition that this will protect all our troops from the gas is rather hypothetical given—''

''I can assure Comrade Marchenko,'' Chernko cut in, but was himself interrupted by Suzlov.

''Let Comrade Marchenko finish.''

''Thank you, Mr. President. As I was saying, no matter that the prevailing winds at the moment may favor our deployments across the Brest front. This does not take into account local conditions—local eddies—which could engulf some of our forward units. My wife, who, as you know, is comrade in charge of Moscow CBW defenses, is very concerned by this. We have seen in Moscow that the existence of internal heating and certain structures produces totally unexpected results. Windy places where you would expect— The point I am making, Comrade, is that it's very unpredictable."

"I'm sure," replied Chernko dryly. "But we aren't concerned with very many buildings on the front, General—yes, yes, a few cities perhaps, but we must surely look at the macro situation, Comrades." He made a face of grandfatherly regret. "Admittedly, a few peculiar local air currents, conditions—whatever you wish to call them—may interfere with some forward troop deployments, but on the whole, the Allies would suffer a crippling blow all across the front of the attack."

Marchenko seemed to Chernko as if he was about to cut in again, and so Chernko avoided his gaze, addressing the rest of those present, as if even those absent from the empty chairs were listening. "And one thing in which I'm sure that Comrade Marchenko's wife would concur is that our chemical/biological warfare suits, as well as our shelter defenses, are *far* superior to those of the enemy—with the possible exception of some recently issued to a few German regiments. But as a part of the *whole*, Comrades, this consideration is nothing. What we have here is not only the chance to stop the Allied invasion dead in its tracks but to buy us vital time for our submarines to cripple Allied resupply. Indeed, far from defeat, Comrades—" Chernko was looking directly at President Suzlov now "—I see the very definite possibility of victory. Comrade Marchenko isn't taking into account the fact that within America, my agents and SPETS cells, long in place and recently activated, have created havoc. *Now*, Comrades. *Now* is the moment."

"You don't think," asked Suzlov, "that the Americans will retaliate with chemical weapons?"

Chernko shook his head. "No, Mr. President. As we know, the great weakness in the democracies is that they have to talk about everything for a month—Congress checking with their constituencies—before they decide which toothpaste to use."

There was some laughter, but Marchenko was shaking his head, telling Chernko, "Then, Comrade, you haven't got a clear grasp of America at war. She is slow to respond at first—yes. But once in gear, her production capacity is enormous. And in crisis, Americans empower their executive to act swiftly if need be. As—"

"Comrade General," responded Chernko, "I agree wholeheartedly with you, but I tell you they are not ready for *this*. The logistics of warhead conversion to chemical warheads on their missiles is no small thing, even for the Americans. And in two weeks it could all be over. But we mustn't give them any longer. This is why we have called this meeting."

"It's those damn Chinese who got us into this," interjected General Arbatov, in charge of Moscow missile defense. "If—"

"*Ifs* are quite pointless now," put in Chernko sharply.

"Yes," said Suzlov quickly. "Comrade Chernko's quite correct. Who started it—the Chinese or the North Koreans—though I suspect Beijing—is of no account. The fact is, gas is being used. In any case, Beijing's charging the Americans with it anyway. China radio broadcasts tying it in with napalm are very clever, for what are fuel air explosives like napalm if they aren't chemical?"

"But surely, Mr. President," said Marchenko, "we cannot equate fuel air explosives with gas. Napalm dissipates."

"So does nerve gas," Chernko replied challengingly. "But it is something, Comrade, that radioactivity doesn't do!"

The murmur of approval told Chernko he'd made a telling point.

"This is true," Marchenko conceded, "but you are assuming that the Americans won't answer a chemical attack with nuclear weapons."

"They won't fire nuclear weapons first," said Suzlov. "Ever since Hiroshima, the American presidents have made a fetish out of not being the first to fire a nuclear weapon. Public opinion in America will not allow Washington to press the button."

"What about their submarines?" asked Admiral Smernov.

"Of course, this is a risk," said Chernko. "So is getting up in the morning. It is war, Comrades. And here again—thanks to the expertise of Comrade Marchenko's wife, and others like her in the Moscow Defense Brigade—we have not only a sustainable chemical defense plan for our capital, but a nuclear one as well. New York has no such comparable defense."

"Everyone would get mugged on the way to the shelters," General Arbatov commented.

There were a few snuffles of restrained amusement.

"Yes," said Suzlov, "if they had enough shelters—which they don't."

"Well put, Comrade President," said Chernko. "The point is that Americans have no shelter systems anywhere as good as ours. They know this. Oh, the American public have it in their heads that because we've had lineups for bread, we're as inefficient in everything else. They do not realize, as their scientists do, how sophisticated our space and missile developments have been. But *Washington* knows. It also knows we're far better prepared for nuclear defense than they are. Far better. This is deterrent enough for them."

Suzlov nodded. "Are we preparing our people for this?"

Chernko deferred to the junior Politburo member in charge of the propaganda ministry.

"Comrade President," the radio and TV chief began. "We are showing as much footage as we can of the Americans using gas against their own people. The Chicago and Los Angeles riots have been particularly useful, plus the recent footage of American troops in the Philippines using gas to defend Clark Base against demonstrators. And, of course, a lot of riot control gas from South Korea. We have so much to use, it's difficult—"

"Thank you," Marchenko interceded, not because he thought it was inappropriate to use such footage but because he wanted to point out that after Gorbachev's brief fling with *glasnost*, the Russian people would surely be alert to the distinction between canister tear gas and nerve gas.

Here the Minister for Propaganda fairly bristled with pride. "We have skillfully spliced the film of the American police in riot control using the gas with casualties from the Bhopal chemical disaster from the American plant in India which killed hundreds, and also other footage of American marines firing canisters—"

"So you not only have tear gas clouds fired by Americans," interjected Marchenko, "'but nerve gas victims as well? Is that correct?"

"Yes, Comrade."

"Can you match color, locale, such things . . ."

The minister for propaganda couldn't suppress a smile at the war minister's naïveté on such technical matters. "We have the best Canadian documentary techniques, Comrade, and West German technology to implement and splice."

Marchenko, bottom lip protruding, nodded approvingly. He wasn't one to hold grudges, and he had to admit that Chernko and the Propaganda Ministry had done a fine job in presenting their argument. The propaganda minister added that they were getting much mileage from footage of the "yellow rain" defoliants the Americans had used in Vietnam together with napalm victims, American peace activists, and "brushed-up" footage of an American actress in Hanoi, complete with Vietcong pith helmet, denouncing American fliers on Hanoi radio as war criminals.

Marchenko himself had a sudden and, he thought, convincing argument for Chernko's position. "Of course, if the Americans fired chemical weapon missiles in Europe, the West Europeans would be furious. The danger is obvious—any winds that carry the gas to the Allied front will certainly sweep further west over Germany."

"Exactly!" said Chernko, seizing the moment. "Comrade Marchenko is exactly right on this point."

Suzlov had said little, and now all eyes were on him. He was a man who had risen to power on Party consensus, and in a sense, a decision on chemical warfare was not more or less important than any other requiring Party solidarity.

"We will come together again, Comrades. I want a full vote. It must be unanimous."

"I can assure you, Mr. President—" began Chernko.

Suzlov interrupted. "That the comrades not here will concur? Are you so sure, Comrade? Personally I find your argument a strong one, but it must be unanimous from every STAVKA member. This, I insist, must be on record." He looked at his watch and announced, "Given the urgency of the matter, Comrades, we will meet here again tomorrow evening—midnight. Waiting thirty hours will not scuttle your plan, Comrade," Suzlov assured Chernko, "and it will give our other comrades time to attend. How long would it take to launch the gas attack if we give it unanimous approval?"

"Within the hour," said Chernko. "Our frontline commanders are already on standby."

"Then we can't wait thirty hours?"

Chernko knew bureaucratic immovability when he saw it. And Suzlov wouldn't move until he got unanimous support. "Yes, Mr. President. We can wait thirty hours."

"Good. Then notify all members we'll meet here tomorrow. Twenty-four hundred hours."

"Yes, Mr. President."

Suzlov nodded and walked back to his desk.

"Do you think we'll get unanimous support tomorrow night?" asked Marchenko. "That's if we can get a forum."

Chernko's smile was like that of an alcoholic asked if he could manage another drink. It was a smile that told Marchenko all the KGB's IOUs and power would be used to make sure that everyone who should vote, would. He wondered how much pressure the KGB chief at Khabarovsk, Colonel Nefski, was applying to his son, who apparently was persisting in his liaison with the Jewish woman.

CHAPTER FORTY-ONE

SONAR MAN EMERSON wasn't sure he liked the blue glow of the sonar room forward of *Roosevelt*'s control. He was used to working in the redded-out subs, and in his view, the argument that blue light around the sonar consoles made it easier for the operators to see the blips on the digitized display screen was debatable. "Different strokes for different folks," as he had told the chief of the boat. The chief suspected, however, that Emerson's quandary over the light was really a cover for a much larger concern—namely that this was Emerson's first trip under the ice.

It was, for operators, like moving to a different neighborhood. Lying in bed at night, you knew it was traffic outside, but familiarity with the different sounds took time to get used to. Unfortunately, the war didn't allow you much time to learn—especially given the rate of sub sinkings and "sonar operator stress syndrome," or "SOS," as it was known among the operators. Many had spent up to sixteen hours at a stretch on seventy-five-day war patrols as the Soviet subs lay in wait in the deep ocean ravines of the mid-Atlantic Ridge. It was these ravines, sounded and plotted by prewar Soviet oceanographic "research" ships, that had proved such a boon to the new Soviet sub offensive. No matter how good the NATO warships' depth and profile sounders were, many of the ravines' profiles were so jagged, often near upwellings and other thermoclines, that probing sonar signals were merely scrambled. Such sonar profiles revealed nothing more than the tops of the mountain ranges that formed the Atlantic range.

Despite the hours off watch that he had devoted sitting listening to the *Roosevelt*'s "library"—tapes of enemy noise signatures and the types of sea noise—to fine-tune his ability to distinguish between background sea clutter and heavy concentrations of Arctic phytoplankton, Emerson still felt uneasy about this, his first long war patrol in the high Arctic.

While the rest of the crew actually felt safer below the roof of frozen sea, the constant grinding of the pack ice was particularly disconcerting for a sonar operator, the noise having a tendency to "bully" out all other sounds—a fact that Soviet subs had taken advantage of, using their big cargo ships' prop noise to drown out that of their subs as they broke out of their home ports just before war had officially broken out.

Adding to Emerson's apprehension was *Roosevelt*'s mission to remain as an undetected submarine launch platform for the forty-two warheads atop the six Trident missiles—"the weapons of last resort." *Roosevelt*'s greatest defense, its silence, meant eschewing its active sonar, whose outgoing noise pulses would give its position away as well as pinpointing the enemy's.

This meant that unless Emerson received a specific release order from either Captain Brentwood or the officer of the deck to go "active," all he could do was to stay in the passive mode. However, in passive there was no time/space ratio during the duration between an active sonar's pulse and the return of its echo.

In short, it would be impossible for him to tell accurately how far away a noise source was, or in any ice-free zone, whether it was on the surface or submerged.

Experienced sub hands often made fairly accurate guesstimates of the distance, but this was based purely on experience, not formula. The fact that survival at sea was as much art as science had been brought home to Emerson during the Russian cruiser attacks against the American subs early in the war. Captain Brentwood's advice to a colleague had once saved that man's sub and his crew when, acting quickly in an evasive maneuver, he had simultaneously ordered that the bodies of two men who had died due to flooding caused by a previous depth charge attack be cut up and blown to the surface in several of the torpedo tubes along with diesel oil and assorted garbage, convincing the Russian sub chaser that they'd done their job.

Emerson's sense of responsibility, the knowledge that he could mistake a "biological" noise, such as the sudden turn of a tightly bunched school of fish, for an attacking sub, weighed heavily on him. It would mean life or death for the entire crew, for if he didn't identify an enemy sub quickly enough, there'd be no time for Brentwood to get a fish off. And yet if he mistakenly identified a noise as a sub when it wasn't and Brentwood fired, then at that very moment of the torpedo's release, any enemy sub listening would hear the high-pressure ejection and the cavitation of the torpedo's propeller and would know exactly where the *Roosevelt* was.

The responsibility on Emerson was made worse by the crew's well-intentioned assurances to him that now they were under the ice, he wouldn't have to worry about CVs—surface vessels. Oh no? Emerson thought—what if he heard a sudden crackling noise? Would it be the sound of a Soviet sub "ice-picking" through the twelve-foot-thick ice cap to fire a cruise missile? Or would it be simply the ice pressure sounding off as great bergs, calved off one section of the ice pack, came up against another ice sheet? If you got too close to the sound layer, next thing you might hear could be a "triple": three enemy torpedoes vectoring you even as you dived.

Emerson devoutly wished they were back in the good old plain dangerous North Atlantic and not up here in the depths of the Greenland Sea.

To make matters worse, Emerson could hear a crew member, a new planesman, being reminded by one of the chiefs that beneath the sea, sound traveled in excess of 3,000 miles per hour, compared to the mere 760 miles per hour in air, the sound in the seas racing through the more tightly bunched molecules of water.

But now at least the *Roosevelt* was traveling at ten miles per hour, and quietly—courtesy of her anechoic sound-absorbing paint and her antivibration quotient engines. Furthermore, Emerson took some comfort in knowing that because of the slow speed, it would be more difficult for the enemy to pick up even the noise of her pumps, which had to be kept on constantly in order to cool the sub's nuclear reactor, which provided not only the superheated steam for generators to drive the prop, but power for everything else aboard the sub.

It was at that moment, two hours into the dogwatch, that Emerson, while watching normal "pop bottle fizz," electronic particles jumping in uniform sine waves on his sonar computer, heard the sound of what he thought must be massive schools of shrimp "clacking," bearing one six three degrees.

From the size of the blip and the direction, he guessed it was about ten miles from Molloy Deep, and worked back the vectors. It was also at this moment that Able Seaman Arthur G.

Leach, a steward, was changing the bed linen on the executive officer's bunk in the relatively tiny stateroom. Seeing a Walkman on the bed, he bent over, picked it up, and for a moment, seeing no one was around, slipped on the earphones and pressed the button—some old pop singer called Buddy Holly was singing a peppy song called "Peggy Sue." Leach hadn't heard the song before, but it had a nice, peppy beat to it, 'bout some guy head over heels in love. Kinda mushy but catchy, reminding him of his high school dates.

After finishing the linen change, emptying the wastepaper basket, and putting the Walkman back on the captain's bed, Leach headed down toward the galley for a coffee break. He walked behind the serving counter, took a mug out of its antiroll hole, and lifted the three-quarter-full Silex pot of coffee out of its antiroll cradle.

Then it happened.

Whether the thing that started it was Leach still moving to the beat of the song he'd just heard, or, as he was to claim later, there'd been an alteration made in the trim of the ship which had caused the ship to yaw slightly, the fact was it happened. Some said it was a spot of butter on the galley's decking that had probably caused him to lose his footing.

Other than Leach, the first to hear, or rather to "see," it was Emerson in the blue glow of the sonar room one deck above. Suddenly he saw the steady hiccuping of "ice grind" and shrimp clacking interrupted by a burp: a rounded sine wave on the trace at zero seconds—which told him immediately that it had come from within the sub. He pressed the button for officer of the deck in Control.

"Zeldman, OOD." Emerson could tell from Zeldman's relaxed tone that they hadn't heard it in Control, but even now he knew that the low-frequency thud in the one-hundred- to six-hundred-hertz range was radiating out from the hull at over three thousand miles per hour.

"What have you got?" asked Zeldman easily.

"Noise short, sir. From the sub."

"Christ! How long?"

Emerson had already run back the tape. "It was one point two two seven seconds duration, sir."

"Where in the sub—any ideas?"

"Galley maybe—short in one of the pumps. Insulation shot—I dunno for sure."

"Hold on!" Zeldman said, pressing the intercom for the chief of the boat. "Chief—we've got a noise short. Take a party of six quickly—quietly—for a visual check. I'm calling all compartments now."

"We're on our way, sir," said the chief. Next Zeldman pressed the engine room intercom. They reported nothing wrong. He went to the next most likely possibility, the galley, a bread mixer or some other piece of equipment that may have shorted out or not been seated properly before someone had had a chance to switch it off.

"Galley, Seaman Leach."

"We've had a noise short—any of those mixers been on?"

"No, sir—ah, sir . . ."

"Yes?"

"Uh, sorry, sir. I dropped the coffeepot. Sort of busted against the bulkhead, I guess."

"*Busted!* Must have exploded for sonar to pick it up on the passive. Now, tell me straight, sailor, and don't frig around. Did it *kind of bust* or did it explode? Was it full or empty?"

"Uh . . . it was kind of full, sir."

"Don't you touch another thing. Stay right where you are."

"Yes, sir. Sorry . . ."

Zeldman had already turned to the diving officer. "Take her to two thousand feet." It was approaching their crush depth.

"Two thousand, sir," said the officer of the deck, the order repeated again by the planesman, who gently pushed the control column forward as a pilot would in a shallow-angled dive. They'd been running near the surface, hiding in the ice clutter, and if the angle of dive was too acute, too fast, the stern of the 360-foot sub was in danger of slamming hard up against the ice, creating an even bigger noise short.

"Watch the bubble," Zeldman heard the diving officer caution calmly in the background. Zeldman shot a quick glance at the chart, at the same time instructing the diving officer to call the depth.

"Three hundred feet . . . three fifty . . . four hundred . . ."

Zeldman quickly computed a new course away from their original tack, and the moment the diving officer informed him they were at two thousand, he ordered, "Change of course. Steer zero five two."

"Change in course. Zero five two."

"Speed ten knots."

"Speed ten knots."

"And if any other son of a bitch makes a noise, I'll have his guts for garters." No one spoke until Zeldman, leaving the redded-out Control, walked forward into the more comforting blue glow of the sonar room. But he knew the psychological effect of the color change was merely an illusion. "Pray to God, Emerson, no one heard us."

"Yes, sir."

But praying was no good. One point two two seven seconds was an age for someone whose digitized innards registered a noise lasting only milliseconds. The Russian Alfa had seen the *ikota*—"hiccup"—clearly on its sonar screen, and in any case, even if the operator had not actually seen it, a tone alarm on the console would have alerted him to the incoming noise short cutting into the otherwise steady pattern of incoming sine waves.

Captain Yanov ordered the Alfa to alter course, heading straight along the noise source bearing, and ordered all torpedo tubes, which were situated forward, ready for action. He did not want to switch on his active pinger, for this would alert the other sub, nor did he wish to increase speed too quickly, for even though his was the quietest class of Soviet submarine, his cooling pumps did not make him inaudible, and all they had was a heading, a bearing on the noise, no measure of distance. Yet he had no intention of losing the sub, whose distance, despite the lack of any accurate electronic means of measuring it without using an active pinger, was estimated by Yegor Petrov, his best sonar operator, purely on the basis of his long experience in the Arctic, as being probably plus or minus fifteen kilometers—nine miles—from them.

Yanov looked down at his chart overlay covering the Spitzbergen Fracture zone. "Any of our subs in the area?" he asked his OOD. "Apart from us, that is?"

Officer of the deck, Ivashko, had already anticipated the captain's question, checking their position against the colored strips of the other Russian Hunter/Killer patrol routes. "Should be no interdiction with any of ours, Captain. Spitzbergen Trench is all ours."

"Then he must be American or British," said Yanov. "Could it be," he asked Sonar Operator Petrov, "they've found a soft patch in the ice? Run out their trailing antenna and taken in a VLF signal from their headquarters? Or possibly a location check to headquarters? A transmit? Or a noise short from the surface. Maybe not a sub at all. One of their ASW choppers smashing through the ice to dunk a listening buoy?"

"No," said the sonar operator, doing his best to contain his amusement at the captain's hypothesizing. Yanov was undoubtedly a great captain—the sonar operator had no doubt of this, otherwise he would not be commander of an Alfa—but the control room officers never understood the nuances of the passive arrays. "No sir," he repeated. "Nothing from the surface—besides, radio muster for all Allied ships is 0800 hours, sir. It's 0500 now. Given the frequency, I think someone dropped a wrench or something."

"What would he do?" mused the Soviet captain. "If he knows he's given off a noise short?" He turned to the sonar operator. "Petrov, you think he knows?"

"If he doesn't, Captain, his sonar man was asleep."

"I'd go deep," said OOD Ivashko.

"Yes, of course," concurred Captain Yanov. "But will he hover? Or keep going? It's too deep to sit on the bottom."

"If he hovers, Captain," answered the OOD, "and he thinks he might have been heard, then he must expect his pursuer to reach him sooner or later—if he stays on the same heading. If I were him, I'd keep moving, slowly, zigzagging, backtracking."

"Which direction?" asked the captain.

"It's an east-west trench," said Ivashko, thinking aloud. "If he runs south or north, he's going into shallow water. No one likes that."

"Ah, but canyon walls would help him, eh, Number One? A lot of sound comes off canyon walls. Right, Sonar? Deep feeders, rock falls, noise from ice running down the cliff faces, scuttling, and bouncing off. A canyon wall can bury a lot of other sound."

"Even so," said Ivashko, "I'd shy away from the canyon walls, Captain. The racket from them could smother his passive arrays as well as hide him. He'd be running deafened by canyon noise."

The captain conceded the point. "Yes. Personally I would go up closer to the ice, away from the canyon. There you have the ice noise, but can reel out your passive array well below you. You would still pick up the ice noise, but it's much steadier than in a canyon. It's a static you can recognize. Right, Petrov?"

Petrov gave a conditional nod, the kind that irritated Ivashko. Damn sonar men always thought they belonged to a higher priesthood to which mere mortals such as officers of the deck neither had access to, nor aptitude for.

"Then," said Captain Yanov, "I think it's time to release a Jonah." This was a quiet, buoy-girded, tear-shaped container of approximately 156-liter capacity, about half the size of a

44-gallon drum but designed to create the least possible resistance as it quietly moved through the water. Inside, "Jonah" was intricately designed to contain microtape and speakers with a mechanical timer of ten minutes to two hours duration.

Once released from the hull, powered by a quiet battery-run plastic prop and preset to travel to a point approximately two-thirds along the bearing of a noise short, the tear-shaped container would rise until it was approximately three hundred feet below the surface. In this case, within three hundred feet of the ice.

Here, activated by its timer, it would emit a powerfully amplified sound—usually that of a whale. The sound waves racing out from the Jonah would deflect off the Russian submarine as well as off the American. But because the Alfa would be farther away from the Jonah, the noise source, Jonah's sound, reflected off the American sub, would reach the Russian sub sooner than the sound from Jonah reflected off the Russian sub would reach the Americans. The Alfa would then not only have the American sub's heading but also, because of the time lapse between the emission of the sound from the Jonah and its echoed return, the Alfa would now also know *exactly* how far away the American sub was.

It would be toward this position that the Alfa would now head, not at flank speed, lest its pumps be picked up, but at fifteen knots until it was within torpedo range. But this would only work if the enemy kept proceeding on its last known heading. To be absolutely sure where it was and to verify that it was still within the Alfa's torpedo range, a second Jonah would be released. This noise box, again with a preset capacity of between ten minutes and two hours, would emit a much different noise, the sudden whoosh of a torpedo launch. Once this was picked up by the American captain, he would have to make a split-second decision either to make an evasive dive, hoping to shake off what he would believe to be an attack of metallic homing torpedoes, or to fire his own Mark-48 radar homing torpedoes to hopefully intercept the more quickly fired Russian torpedo.

Captain Yanov looked at his watch. The American could have increased speed, pulling away from the Jonah. He checked with Sonar. "Anything on screen?"

"Nothing but shrimp and ice, Captain."

"Stand by to release the second Jonah," ordered Yanov.

"Standing by to release second Jonah."

"Release!"

"Released, sir."

"Torpedo room ready?" said Yanov, bending low, his finger still on the intercom button.

"Ready, sir."

It would be another fifteen to thirty minutes before the second Jonah would be far enough away from the Alfa. If the bait of the firing torpedo sound was taken by the Americans, the Alfa would be far enough back not to be caught in the pressure of the Americans' exploding torpedoes, the Alfa nevertheless still in torpedo range itself. In any event, if the Americans fired, the Alfa would have an exact fix on them. Using the noise of the Americans' torpedoes exploding around the torpedo-sounding Jonah, the Alfa would then race forward at full speed, approaching fifty miles an hour—slow, stop, fire its tubes. And wait.

"If he fires," instructed Captain Yanov, "It will likely be one or two of his forty-eights. Range forty-six kilometers, twenty-five meters a second. Wire trailing until it's radar homing takes over. And so if he fires, we go immediately to attack. Flank speed. Understood?"

"Understood," confirmed the torpedo officer. "We're ready, Captain."

"Good," said Yanov. He then turned to the officer of the deck. "*If* we fire—we'll wait five seconds to clear, then go to maximum depth. Understood?"

"Understood, Captain."

"Good."

CHAPTER FORTY-TWO

THE WHITE COTTAGES of Scotland were tiny dots far below, the weather outside the Hercules fine but windy. Inside, however, all David Brentwood and the other twenty-seven SAS trainee finalists were aware of was the thunderous roaring and vibration of the engines.

"Remember!" shouted the SAS sar'major. "You aren't jumping to entertain the crowd at a county fair. Civilian jumpers don't have full military kit on their back, so in order for you to maintain starfish posture, you must, I repeat *must*, control turns and cross tracking by keeping all extremities extended in starfish pattern until three thousand feet, when your chute will open automatically.

"Do not, repeat do *not* 'grab air' unless as a last resort. Wait until you are *positive* something is wrong with your automatic altimeter release before you attempt to open it by hand under your belly."

The danger was that trying to grab air directly in front of the helmet in order to maintain stability while using the free hand to pull the reserve chute's grip could send you into a "tumble," like a plane out of control—during which arms and legs could become entangled by the chute's cords.

There was a loud whine and the ramp was going down, yawning over the purplish blue of Scotland's western Highlands, the glens between the hills no larger than the size of a penny from eleven thousand feet.

The red light went on.

"Stand up!" shouted the sar'major. "Goggles on."

The stick of twenty-nine men, seven groups of four, the basic SAS unit, with Cheek-Dawson leading, was about to go out for their first HALO.

For Brentwood, Lewis, Thelman, and Schwarzenegger, who

were in the same four-man unit and who had stayed together through the grueling ''three'' and ''four'' phases of SAS training, the high-altitude, low-opening jump was almost a relief. Anything was a relief after phase two's killing forty-mile, full-pack, cross-country march—each man alone, with full seventy-pound pack and weapon, having to complete the forty miles in under forty hours.

''Thought Scotland'd be covered in snow in early January,'' shouted Lewis.

''Scottish people like being different, Aussie,'' said the German. He pronounced ''Aussie'' with a slow deliberateness that belied his alertness and agility in training.

''East Africa!'' said Aussie, looking down at the wild folds of Scotland. ''That's where I've seen hills like that before.''

''Thought we were going to Southeast Asia,'' Thelman ribbed him.

''Well, somewhere in the tropics,'' said Lewis. ''Wanna bet?''

''No thanks.''

The sar'major felt good about the group, as he'd seldom heard them talk with such easy banter before their first HALO, even when they'd done regular para jumps before. The camaraderie came from the special cohesiveness formed among the four men who were theoretically leaderless but who had a group confidence that had grown steadily after the exhausting ''sorting out'' hardships of the first few weeks.

''Green light. Go!'' called the NCO, tapping the first man as he went out, looking like a combination of some great bird of prey and a stuntman going for a belly flop. The difference was they were now in full battle kit and would reach 120 miles per hour in the first sixty seconds of the free fall until their chutes would open automatically—they hoped—at three thousand.

Cheek-Dawson, the first out, immediately slid off to the left to avoid the possibility of midair collision with the men in the stick coming after him. He did not expect them to keep any kind of tight formation in this early jump but was mainly concerned with seeing that they kept their starfish stability as they dropped toward the purple smoke spiraling up wispily from around the landing zone. He saw the third man in trouble almost immediately, and going into a slip roll, gaining speed, he glided laterally; reaching the man, he kept four to six feet away from him, taking his left arm, the man almost in a tumble. His Bergen pack, though tight enough, had not prevented a dangerous shift of weight on his back. Once he had got the man's starfish under control, Cheek-Dawson gestured to him to keep his arms fully extended.

Cheek-Dawson moved on to the next man he saw wobbling, one of Brentwood's group, he thought—the German. Twenty-six seconds had gone, and by the time he had assisted the German, it was forty-seven seconds—twelve seconds till the chutes would automatically open.

He looked over the stick of men who now looked more like a scattered flock when he saw the first man he'd helped get steady going into a tumble. The man's left hand shot out in front of his helmet to grab air in an effort to steady himself while pulling the manual release with his other hand. Two things happened simultaneously. The man's chute opened and he tumbled into the cords, and Cheek-Dawson immediately went into a fast lateral slide with ten seconds to go.

It was too late for Cheek-Dawson to help. Despite the express-trainlike roaring of the wind rushing past his ears, he nevertheless heard the crisp snap of his chute opening at three and a half thousand, suddenly stopping him, the other man's chute a Roman candle, its black silk a streamer.

Second on the ground was David Brentwood. He saw Cheek-Dawson swiftly and expertly folding his chute while he, David, released the parachute harness and ran over to the fallen man. The man had struck soft moorland, but his head had burst like a coconut, a hairy mash splattered on the turf, the man's body strangely flat—an illusion created by the fact that hitting the ground at over one hundred miles per hour, his body had penetrated six inches into the turf, every bone broken.

"Brentwood!" bawled out Cheek-Dawson.

"Sir?"

"Go and fold your chute, man. See it for bloody miles!"

The only thing David could think of was that this was only their *first* HALO. There would be two more "daylights," this same day, and then a night HALO, from twenty-five thousand feet. Full kit and oxygen masks.

CHAPTER FORTY-THREE

AS THE IX-44E sludge-removal vessel—''self-propelled''—putt-putted out of San Diego harbor, the carrier USS *Salt Lake City* towered above the tiny vessel like a skyscraper, and even the men on the hangar deck one story below the flight deck looked toy-sized to Brentwood, while the carrier's anchor chain alone would have sunk his barge. One of the sailors high up on the hangar deck, holding a bucket, gazed down at the small slab of wood that was the barge's deck and at the butter-box wheelhouse. Mockingly he saluted the tiny apparition. There was a roar of laughter from the carrier, made louder by its echoing off its enormous steel sides, as Ray Brentwood and his nine men—the other two of the crew of eleven in the engine room, or rather engine cubbyhole—returned the salute. Brentwood's face was flushed—hot with embarrassment as more and more of the carrier's sailors and yardbirds working on the great ship lined up stem to stern to watch the joke sail by. One of the *Salt Lake City* crewmen, part of the one-hundred-chef contingent aboard the five-thousand-man carrier, grabbed a loud-hailer, calling out, ''Don't you go bumpin' into us, now!''

''What is it?'' hollered another man. ''Smitty, you drop that garbage overboard?'' It was light relief for the men on the carrier, who were in for refit after the *Salt Lake City* had been attacked a thousand miles north of the Hawaiian Islands en route to launch carrier-based attacks against the Russian-held Aleutian Islands. More islands had fallen to the Russians as they drew ever closer to Unalaska's Dutch Harbor. Two Black-jack Tupolev X bombers, swooping in low on afterburner at 1.4 Mach, had released their sixteen tons of ordnance, including a cluster of air-to-surface Kingfish 6 missiles.

Two of the 10,600-pound missiles, coming in at the *Salt Lake City* at over 790 meters per second, had been shot out of the air by the carrier's Phalanx radar-guided .50-millimeter-machine-gun batteries firing dense sprays of high-velocity depleted-uranium bullets. Two of the missiles were struck at three hundred meters from the ship, exploding, raining white-hot debris onto the sea; the fireball from one, streaming from a hundred-pound fragment of the missile's midsection, kept going, hitting the carrier's island, wiping out PRIFLY control and demolishing the backup "ops" board. Seven sailors had been killed outright, eight others badly burned.

Of the remaining two Russian missiles, one was taken out a mile from the carrier by a five-thousand-pound Sea Sparrow, though it was the men on the .20-millimeter, fifty-round-per-second Vulcan antimissile gun batteries festooning the carrier's side who claimed credit for downing the missile.

The remaining Kingfish was a dud, but unstopped, did the most damage of all, its 10,600 pounds, traveling at seventeen hundred miles an hour, striking the carrier's starboard side above the waterline on the starboard quarter with the impact of a heavy-haul locomotive hitting a metal garage door, the missile disintegrating, and though not exploding, tearing through ten bulkheads, the resulting shrapnel killing 117 men and injuring scores of others, leaving a gaping, jagged-toothed hole twenty feet long and fifteen feet high. The friction of the impact started several fires, one of which, its flames shooting up air-conditioning ducts, ignited three Grumman Intruder bombers. The resulting explosion killed fifteen men and destroyed over $170 million worth of airplanes and spare parts as well as scorching the forward starboard side of the hangar, the fumes from the paint downing several maintenance crews and getting into the pilots' ready rooms sandwiched between hangar and flight deck.

It was little wonder then that the crew, now safely back in port, thought that a little levity at the expense of IX-44E—sludge removal—was in order. But for Ray Brentwood and his hapless crew, it was a humiliation that not even the gregarious and convivial Seaman Jones could forget or forgive.

Shortly, a deck officer aboard the carrier came down to the edge of one of the lower loading flight decks, ordering the jeering crew back to work, and when they had gone, in the worst humiliation of all, the officer cast a brief, pitying glance in Brentwood's direction before disappearing from view.

The IX-44E started to buck in a chop coming in from the direction of Point Loma, a chop that would not even be discernible to the dozens of warships and the carrier high above, flying the pennants of battle honors won.

While the warships' crews were readying again for war, Ray Brentwood had the decidedly dull and uninspiring task of plowing up the coast fifteen miles off the beach, where a hysterical member of the La Jolla chapter of "Environmental Watch" had reported another "massive" oil spill.

When they got there, Seaman Jones estimated it was an "iddy biddy" spill of no more than a hundred gallons, probably burped out by one of the warships or one of the coast-plying cargo vessels. The barge nudged about in the increasing swell, its very motion seeming to Brentwood as resentful as the harsh coughing of its engine, while the flexible polyethylene hose that served as a boom trailed off the stern with all the enthusiasm of a sullen snake, flopping into the water to contain the rainbow-streaked chocolate-mousse oil that stained the cobalt blue of the sea.

"Down with the hose!" ordered Brentwood, then seconds later, "Suck 'er up!"

"Oh, sweetheart," murmured one of the crew.

"What was that, sailor?" snapped Brentwood.

"Nothing, sir."

"Then get to it. I want all of it."

"Oooohh—" groaned an oiler. "He wants all of it."

"C'mon," said Jones. "Poor bastard's already had the shit kicked out of him."

"Yeah—well, Jonesy, he's still alive," said the oiler.

"Not sure I'd wanna be," said the winch operator. "With that kisser."

"Yeah, he's still kicking, ain't he?" added the oiler. "Hell of a lot of guys from the *Blaine* were deep-sixed. He got off."

"Shut up," said Jones. "He'll hear you."

"So what!"

"Come on!" called out Brentwood from the wheelhouse. "I want it up before it goes to a tar ball." If the oil did coagulate and sink, it would be pushed up later on the beach by the tide, and over the next few days he'd have every retiree in La Jolla going into cardiac arrest and calling their congressman, never mind the poor bastards on the west coast of southern Alaska and British Columbia, where one of the Russian subs had sunk both a huge freshwater carrier and oil supertanker, spilling millions of gallons. They'd be cleaning that up for years.

It was this thought that started Ray Brentwood wondering,

as he knew they had been in Ottawa and Washington, how the hell the Russian subs had gotten in so close to the coast without detection. Sure, there had been a lot of surface interference, gale conditions, but still, the SOSUS hydrophone arrays on the sea bottom, monitored by the Canadian navy out of Esquimalt on Vancouver Island, should have picked up a sine wave or two of the sub's cooling pumps. Of course, once they'd sunk the tankers, the subs had had no trouble getting out under the cacophony of torpedoes exploding and ships going down, such noise completely overwhelming the SOSUS network, providing cover for the Russian subs to hightail it out of the area at maximum speed, the noise of their cooling pumps, racing flat out, lost in the death throes noise of the dying tankers.

"There y'are, sir," said Jones. "Got 'er all in the tank."

"Very well. Up hose."

"Up hose!" mimicked the oiler. "Christ, think he was still captain of a missile frigate or something."

"Well, once a captain, always a captain, I guess," said Jones.

"Of this bucket?" sneered the oiler. "Shoot—he might as well've stayed home, played in his friggin' bathtub. He's not gonna impress anybody down here with all his orders."

"So why don't you put in for a transfer?" asked Jones, though knowing that none of them would get it. IX-44E was the bottom of the barrel. To the navy, they were all losers on this barge.

Aboard the *Roosevelt*, sonar operator, Emerson, didn't have to tell Zeldman about what he'd seen on the screen, as the listening sonar was on amplification in the control room—everybody hearing the telltale whoosh of a torpedo being fired.

"Incoming!" shouted Emerson. "Submerged hostile, by nature of sound. Bearing zero four seven."

"Battle stations!" ordered Zeldman, the yellow chime alert already pushed, its soft-toned urgency filling the sub. "Speed?" asked Zeldman, pressing the captain's cabin call button.

"Forty-five knots," replied Emerson.

It was almost faster than the *Roosevelt* could run.

"Hard right rudder to zero three five degrees," ordered Zeldman.

"Right rudder to zero three five degrees," came the confirmation, even as the *Roosevelt* was turning, its rudder control and trim closely watched by the diving officer.

"Bearing. Mark!"

"Zero four seven," came the response from the fire control party.

"SA tube one, fire MOSS."

"SA tube, fire MOSS."

A light tremor passed through the *Roosevelt* as the mobile submarine simulator shot out from one of the two five-degree-angled starboard abaft tubes situated below and abaft the sail, the simulator traveling at over forty miles per hour on the same course as the attacking torpedo and emitting an identical noise signature to that of *Roosevelt*.

"Forward tubes one, two, three, four, ready with warheads." As he spoke, Zeldman could hear the easy, metallic slide and click as the Mark-28 wire-guided radar-homing torpedoes slipped from racks to tubes, the latter's "lids" closed, the rope-hung "WARNING WARSHOT LOADED" signs now slung from the spin wheel lock on each tube.

"Tubes one, two, three, four loaded, sir."

"Warheads armed."

"Warheads armed, sir."

"Very well. Stand by."

Three flights down, the torpedo room's chief petty officer was watching the enlisted men carefully. Since the bigger and much heavier Trident II D-5 ballistic missiles had been put aboard, replacing the Trident I Cs, and upgraded Mark-48-C torpedoes had been introduced to *Roosevelt*, the firing orders were at times quite different from those of the *old* Sea Wolf routines, and this was no time for a mistake.

"What's up, Pete?" It was Robert Brentwood, looking somewhat disheveled, eyes still blinking, adjusting hurriedly to the redded-out control.

"Under attack, sir. Torpedo on zero four seven. Speed fifty-four knots."

Brentwood looked at the computer for distance and estimated impact time but wanted the sonar team's independent assessment as well. "TTI, Sonar?"

"Time to impact six minutes, sir."

"How long's the MOSS been under way?" asked Brentwood.

"One minute, sir," answered Zeldman. "Live ones in the tubes in case the MOSS can't fox 'em out of it."

"What've we got in forward tubes?"

"Mark-48-Cs, sir. Wire-guided, radar-homing."

"Very well," said Brentwood, pulling down the flexi-cord mike, informing the ship's company, "This is the captain. I have the con. Commander Zeldman retains the deck."

Zeldman saw they were at two thousand feet, just above the sub's "crush depth," though this was always a "safe-side" depth, a sign to discourage any recklessness or undue risk taking. The Sea Wolf, he knew, could dive deeper, but then the digital readouts would go from green to red as they entered the danger zone.

"We have a new contact," said Emerson, and Zeldman was immediately by his side.

"Where?"

Emerson pointed to the top of the three sonar screens in series. "First contact, zero speed. New contact bearing zero four two. First contact seems dead in the water."

"Jesus!" said Zeldman, turning to Brentwood. "Captain. First one must have been a feint—or a dud. Either way, he suckered us."

Without a word of reproach or the merest suggestion that Zeldman should have waited a bit longer before deciding to release the MOSS, Brentwood turned his attention to the tracking vector to see if the Russian torpedo was changing course, curving away toward the simulator Zeldman had fired. Maybe the Russian fish was a "line-of-sighter," its computer nose not radar-homing but merely compensatory, set to adjust its heading according to Sea Wolf's speed and heading but not an electronic lock-on. But then Sonar reported a blip coming through the subsurface shrimp and ice clutter, the blip now being received aboard *Roosevelt*, the Russian torpedo's active pulse shooting ahead, the torpedo homing in on the bounce-off from the target.

"TTI?" he asked Sonar again.

"Five minutes, forty seconds, sir."

"Definitely a homer, then," said Zeldman. It was his way of suggesting they should fire their warhead torpedoes now.

Brentwood was thinking so fast that a dozen images simultaneously jostled for attention in his brain, the most bothersome that of the Soviet captain firing at such long range. Surely the Russian must know a Sea Wolf would hear his torpedo coming and immediately change course to avoid—

"He mustn't be homing on our hull," said Brentwood suddenly. "SOB's locking onto our prop signature."

"If he'd been close enough for that, sir," suggested Zeldman, "we would've been hit by now."

Damn it, Zeldman was right. It had to be hull lock-on, the surface area of the MOSS too small, not giving off the same echo as the Sea Wolf's larger displacement hull. The only chance was for the Sea Wolf to go to maximum speed, despite the increasing noise her pumps would make, and try to outrun the Russian torpedo. But no sooner had Brentwood given the order for burst speed than Emerson reported two other torpedoes racing for them in "fan" formation, one fired to intercept at a point forward of the Sea Wolf's present position, the other aft of it.

Brentwood knew he could turn tail and run—and the geometric and trigonometric vectors spewing out of the computer told him that even if the Russian torpedoes were of their fastest class, with a maximum range of thirty-five miles, the *Roosevelt* might be able to evade the middle of the three torpedoes. At this point he still had a five-mile head start. But it would be, as they'd said at Balaclava, "a close run thing." It would mean he couldn't weave but would be committed to a straight-line retreat—not only directly from the approaching middle torpedo but also in front of the Russian sub. And if the Russian was faster than the Sea Wolf—though only the Alfa class was—then the Russian would outrun the *Roosevelt*. But then, if the Russian was an Alfa and fired another one at closer range, even the Sea Wolf's burst speed would be unable to evade him.

"TTI five minutes," reported Emerson.

"All right," replied Brentwood. "Switch on our active. Let's try to see what he is. Might as well use it—he knows where we are anyway."

But even as Emerson pushed the button and heard the distinctive ping of the active pulse passing out from the *Roosevelt*, he felt guilty, that he was betraying her, so ingrained was the operator's code of silence. It was as if a priest had been ordered to break a sacred rite, the Sea Wolf's mission to listen only on passive—not to betray their lethal load by making their own noise. It was a catechism drilled into him from his very first days in Bledsoe Hall in Groton. But if Emerson had doubted the order, Zeldman didn't. Brentwood's decision to go active was the right one. With its awesome missile load, the *Roosevelt* couldn't preserve America's nuclear sea-strike capability if it couldn't survive.

"TTI four minutes thirty seconds," said Emerson. The

MOSS was long gone, out of play, none of the Russian torpedoes curving off to go for the bait. Now the pongs—the echoes of *Roosevelt*'s active pulses coming back at over three thousand miles per hour—were registering in high-pointed sine waves on the computer screen that Emerson had now linked to the "Chinese library." This was the sonar operators' name for the library of "ping/pong" sounds that, taking into account water salinity, thermal inclines, hot vent upwelling, temperature, and currents, sought to match sound peak ratios to hull size.

"Looks like a small one to me, sir. A Hunter-Killer. Plus or minus four thousand tons." Brentwood could now see the digitized speed readout, an estimate that the active pulse made possible. Emerson was shaking his head in disbelief. He'd never seen a sub coming in at them at over forty-three miles an hour. It was at once terrifying and awe-inspiring.

"Goddamn it," said Zeldman. "An Alfa."

"TTI four minutes," said Emerson, his voice now tauter than before.

Still watching the sonar screens, Brentwood informed the firing control and tracking party, "Target designations as follows. Bravo, Charlie, Delta—three fish. Got it?"

"Target designations Bravo, Charlie, Delta."

Brentwood shot a glance at the Russian's incoming vector. It had changed slightly to zero four nine. "Bring the ship to zero four nine."

"Zero four nine, sir."

Four seconds later, *Roosevelt* was on the zero-four-nine heading, the new vector for target Bravo. Brentwood called for the range, then announced, "Angle on the bow—starboard one seven. Firing point procedures. Master one zero. Tube one."

"Firing point procedure master one zero. Tube one," came the confirmation, immediately followed by, "Solution ready, sir. Weapons ready. Ship ready."

Brentwood was watching the bearing. "Final bearing and shoot. Master one zero."

The bearing and speed of the target were confirmed, and Brentwood heard the firing control officer take over. "Stand by! Shoot! Fire! . . . One fired and running."

"Shift to zero zero five," Brentwood ordered as the *Roosevelt* was brought about onto the vector for the second torpedo.

"Zero zero five, sir."

"Very well. Fire two."

"Fire two . . . Two fired and running, sir."

"Shift to one seven three."

This took a little longer as the 360-foot-long *Roosevelt* turned through almost 180 degrees in an east-west semicircle to bring her on line with target Delta, the third torpedo fired by the Alfa, clearly meant to interdict aft of her should she try to run that way.

"Easy—don't want to stretch the wire," Brentwood heard the diving officer say, referring to the wire that the Mark-48, the top of its line in the U.S. torpedo arsenal, would trail behind it via which the torpedo would receive fire control and tracking party guidance until it got close enough to the target for its radar-homing computer to take over.

"On one seven three, sir."

"Very well. Fire three."

"Fire three . . . Three fired and running, sir."

Zeldman was now ready for the order to turn and run and go deep, but it wasn't given.

Instead Brentwood ordered, "Diving officer, we're going up. Take her to three hundred feet. Maximum angle thirty degrees."

"Take her to three hundred—slowly," said the diving officer. "Minimum incline. Don't snap the wire."

The diving officer repeated the instructions, but the man on trim and one of the planesmen couldn't believe their ears. And it got worse, though it wasn't evident at first, because the direction in which they were going was taking them away from the Alfa toward the northern side of the Spitzbergen Trench. It was at eight hundred feet, *Roosevelt*'s up angle increasing beyond ten degrees in a slight upwelling current from the sea bottom, causing Zeldman and Brentwood to hang on to the scope island's rail.

The diving officer held on to the roll bar above him, closely monitoring the planesmen. "Watch the bubble . . . watch the bubble. . . ." he advised, fatherly, calmly. "Slow her down. . . . Don't want to slam up against the ice. That'd be a 'short' to write home about."

What the planesmen couldn't figure out was why in hell Brentwood would take them off to the shallow waters on the north shoulder of the deep trench, the seabed sloping gently away to the top of the trench.

"Three hundred feet, sir," reported the diving officer.

Suddenly everything was blurred—instruments, tightly secured as they were, rattling like cutlery. Then the shock wave grew in intensity, the sound of the explosion that had occurred several miles away, but not close to the Alfa sub, now shaking *Roosevelt* violently.

Either the Mark-48 from the *Roosevelt* had taken out the first torpedo fired by the Alfa or the latter had taken out the first "fish" fired by the *Roosevelt*. In any case, the Alfa's first torpedo was no longer a threat to the *Roosevelt*, and the *Roosevelt*'s first fish had not sunk the Russian.

"Holy livin'—" Emerson began. He had never seen anything like it on his screen, the explosions creating a frenzy of lines that made no sense. "Overload," he said in an understatement that was lost in Control crew's attempts to keep the *Roosevelt* steady.

"Zero speed," ordered Brentwood, and only now could Emerson see his three sonar screens returning to something like normal. The muffled sound of the pumps that never stopped could now be seen registering on the "hash" of ice grind and clacking shrimp.

"*Kuda on ushol?*—Where's he gone—Petrov?" Yanov asked his sonar man. Their screen, too, was fuzzy. "Where's the bastard—"

The sonar operator was still getting "flood-over" from the explosion of the first torpedo that the Alfa had fired at the American. Or was it sound wave residue from one of the Americans' torpedoes? Then came a second explosion, as loud as the first, but again, it barely shook the double-bottomed titanium hull of the Alfa, the sub merely yawing slightly in the concussion waves.

"He'll dive to near crush depth," predicted Yanov.

Brentwood was waiting. It would be another four minutes before the last of the three torpedoes he had fired was due to make impact with target Bravo. With two fish exploded, he could only hope his third would be lucky. He was also wondering if he'd done any damage to the Alfa through concussion, though he knew that unlike the Sea Wolf, whose hull could be ruptured even if a torpedo didn't actually hit it but exploded some meters away, an Alfa was more resilient to being punctured by the massive pressure waves, its state-of-the-art double titanium hull the envy of every other submariner.

"TTI for target Delta," cut in Emerson, picking up a trace, "three minutes."

"Perhaps we should have fired another one," said Zeldman.

It wasn't a question—more a suggestion—and the only time Brentwood had ever heard his executive officer even slightly nervous, except possibly when Zeldman had confided that Georgina Spence had proposed to *him* rather than he to her.

"No, Pete, we did all right with three. We fire another one now we're in cover of ice grind, we negate us being up here. I'm banking on them thinking we've gone *down*, deep into the trench to hide, looking for somewhere to hole up. Let Ivan think we've gone deep under the sound smother of the explosions. He'll be listening for us away down there, and we're up here only three hundred feet from the roof—nice and cozy in the ice clutter and—"

He never finished. Suddenly *Roosevelt* yawed violently, hard left, then right, and she was sliding, the control room crisscrossed with the hissing spraying of leaks that suddenly exploded into vapor jets under the pressure of 187,000 pounds per square foot.

"Flooding in the engine room, flooding in the engine room . . ."

"See to it, Chief!" called Brentwood. "Where's the Alfa, Sonar?"

"Don't know, sir . . ." called Emerson, his voice rising, scared.

"Keep it down," Brentwood counseled him. "Watch him. Find him for me, son."

"Yes—yes, sir."

Behind him, Brentwood could hear the damage reports coming in on the intercom as Zeldman tried to steady the motion of the sub via trim and rudder control. Amid the chaos Emerson realized that the *Roosevelt*'s third torpedo hadn't knocked out the last of the fish fired by the Alfa but must have been thrown off course, its thin control wire to *Roosevelt* inadvertently severed in the sub's turn as they'd headed up. The result was that the *Roosevelt*'s third torpedo, away and running, its radar-homing head now uninhibited by wire control, had probably overshot the oncoming Russian torpedo and zeroed in on the Alfa instead. Either this, or the Russian torpedo homing in on *Roosevelt* had exploded against subsurface ice, creating the concussion now causing the leaks which were not only flooding the engine room but which were making it impossible to see in Control.

Emerson heard a tentative cracking sound, and in a sudden, gut-wrenching moment, was sure they were breaking up until the sensors, at least those that were still in operation, told him it was the ice above that was fracturing and breaking up from the thwacks of the explosions. But then he felt the sub sliding—backward down the slope.

For a split second Brentwood was tempted to order the engines near full power but resisted creating a giveaway vibration that would give the Alfa, if the explosions had not got her, the *Roosevelt*'s precise position on the shelf. Hopefully, though, the Alfa was well away by now, hunting for him somewhere in the deep of the Spitzbergen Trench.

Watching his men running fast but each man clearly knowing what he was doing, he took a momentary pride in how well they had been trained, as within minutes the fierce spray of water that had seemed like an ice-cold steam shower in Control was subsiding. But then he felt the sub still sliding, almost imperceptibly to start with, but gathering speed like a heavy trunk on an incline of gravel. It stopped, slid a little more, and halted again. It was difficult to tell exactly just how far they were from the edge of the slope where it plunged away in the sudden drop into Molloy Deep that was fifteen thousand feet straight down.

Emerson, switching to earphones because of the noise of the hissing water, tried to gauge how far they were from the edge by the sound of what seemed like rock debris tumbling down the slope, scraping the hull, then suddenly disappearing on the sound curve. He figured they were less than four hundred feet from the drop-off.

Brentwood was already getting the good news that the leaks had been stopped in the engine room and that now everything seemed secure—the reactor seemed fine—when a damage report told him that a number of hydraulic lines had been severed so that ballast tanks couldn't be blown—to evict the water with air and thus make them lighter. It meant the sub couldn't rise. "And the integrity of the safety hatches," as the video display informed him, had been breached.

No one spoke for several minutes as the full implications of their situation sunk it. They had evaded the Hunter/Killer only to—

"Sir!" It was Emerson, excitement jolting him out of the sudden gloom.

"Who do you mean?" said Brentwood sharply, injecting a shot of discipline after the chaotic moments occasioned by the blast of the explosion. "Do you want me or the officer of the deck?"

"Sorry, sir. OOD."

"Very well."

"Mr. Zeldman, sir. She's breaking up."

"You sure?" said Brentwood.

"Yes, Captain—it's—"

"Amplify," ordered Brentwood. There was the most awful sound Brentwood had ever heard coming in from the hydrophones and filling the *Roosevelt*—a sound like a great whale groaning in agony.

"Her bulkheads," said Zeldman. "They're giving way."

"We got her, sir," said Emerson, exultant, looking around at the faces clustering anxiously around him.

"Or is it a feint?" asked Brentwood.

"Emerson?" Brentwood repeated. "What do you think?"

"I . . ." They could see the doubt taking over his face. "I—I'm not sure, sir."

"Keep listening."

"Don't think it's a feint, sir. That groan—I mean, the amplitude is too—"

Brentwood felt someone bump him and looked sharply at the men gathered around the sonar. "What the hell is this—the county fair? Everyone back to his post."

"They're going down, sir," said Emerson, more confidently now. "Think they're goners."

"Like us," said someone in Control. Brentwood looked about, ready to tear a strip off the sailor, but said nothing. Naval officers were supposed to be able to handle the truth with aplomb.

"Yes, sir, they've definitely had it," said Emerson triumphantly. "I've got distance as well as speed, sir. It's no feint this time."

He seemed to be right, the groaning of the Alfa's hull testimony to the brutal fact that, double titanium hull or not, every sub had its crush depth, and the Alfa was now well below hers—over six thousand feet below, the sound of crunching steel that would soon be squashed flat rising up from the deep like the death throes of some great leviathan dying the most horrible death a sailor could imagine.

"Go to screen," ordered Brentwood. "Take it off amplify."

"Yes, sir." As Emerson reached for the knob, there was a last sound, a high-pitched scream, that, though obviously from some of the electronic equipment rather than the bone-crushing sound of metal being crushed, sounded eerily human, like a newborn, and for a moment Brentwood thought of Rosemary and the child she was carrying.

CHAPTER FORTY-FOUR

"KOREA!" PRONOUNCED LEWIS, upon looking down from the Hercules ramp at the moonlit snow blanketing the Scottish highlands that were flitting like white islands through churning cumulus over twenty-five thousand feet below. "I knew it. They're sending us to bloody Korea."

The red warning light came on and the SAS troopers stood up, lumbering slowly forward, weighed down by HALO packs, oxygen masks, infrared-goggled helmets, and the SAS weapon of choice—the U.S. Ingram MAC-11—Military Armament Corps—submachine gun, Lewis making it clear to anyone who could hear him above the Hercules' sustained roar that he certainly hoped this would be the last "bloody night HALO" they'd have to practice.

"It is," responded Cheek-Dawson, his face all but invisible in the green/black camouflage paste and helmet sprouting bracken as he checked that each man had spat in the infrared goggles to help prevent condensation and that they had all checked their wrist altimeters—in sync with that of the Hercules.

"Remember the drill," the sar'major told them, his voice tinny through the hailer. "When you land, unhitch but never mind the chute. Won't have time to drag in, fold, or bury it this time. You must expect patrols both inside and outside the drop zone." Lowering the megaphone, the sergeant major looked about. "Aussie!"

"Sar'Major?"

"If a flare goes up?"

"Take off the IF glasses."

"Correct. Now, we have fifteen minutes to take out a divisional HQ. Target, this man." He took a blowup of an Asian-looking officer and held it high, with Cheek-Dawson shining his flashlight on it. "Brigadier general," said Cheek-Dawson. "Insignia—epaulets and shoulder tabs, yes. But the face, gentlemen. Go for the *face*. Remember it." He then passed it around.

"I dunno," said Lewis. "They all look the same to me. What do you reckon, Fritz?"

The German looked at the photo.

"No, Aussie. I think the nose is very definite. You see—and the jaw is—"

"Stone the bloody crows, Fritz," said Lewis, winking at Thelman and Brentwood. "Just a joke. Strike a light—you Krauts take everything so seriously?" Lewis turned his head to Cheek-Dawson. "What's after this, sir?"

"Through the house once more for final selection to the squadron." It wasn't so much a house but a canvas mockup of an enemy's divisional HQ near Hereford, complete with booby traps.

"Whole squadron going, sir?"

"Can tell you that much, yes. All eighty of us—providing we get asked. Apart from that, as you know, our job is to keep fit, on standby."

"You have any ideas, sir?" pressed Lewis.

"Sorry, Lewis, I can't be of any assistance to your bookmaking prognostications, but you know the drill. SAS security's so tight—has to be—that we'd only be told forty-eight hours in advance in any case. That's why we have you cover the field. You're supposed to be ready for anything. Right, Sar'Major?"

"Right, sir."

"You will lose a lot of money if it is Korea, eh, Aussie?" teased Schwarzenegger.

"Aw—shuddup, you Kraut!"

Four of the eighty men were killed during the jump, one in a tumble, one whose emergency chute failed, and two who overshot the zone, going down in one of the lochs, drowned before they could get out of the harness with the 110-pound battle packs weighing them down in the frigid water. Cheek-Dawson took it harder than anyone but was determined not to let it show. They had lost a dozen men in accidents, either going over the Brecons or on the Hereford forced marches and in the jumps. But it had to be done if you were to be the best. Nevertheless, he was growing as impatient as the rest of them for a mission, though here again, he couldn't let on. And so it was with a sense of both exhilaration and measured apprehension that, upon returning to the base, he received the news from Major Rye that Operation Merlin was on.

"Run-through time?" asked Cheek-Dawson.

"Twenty hours," said Rye. "Enough?"

"If we have all the maps, paraphernalia, et cetera," said Cheek-Dawson.

"We do."

"Good show. First briefing early morning?" asked Cheek-Dawson, though it was already near 10:00 P.M., well after lights-out.

"Yes," said Rye.

"Very good, sir. Good night."

"Good night," said Rye, but first he would have to write letters immediately to the families of the four men who had died that night. Contrary to what was generally thought, Rye did not find the task particularly onerous. It was one of the few times when he could talk quite unsentimentally about brave men. Besides, because he was constrained by SAS security requirements, he could give no hint of where they had been or where they would have been going, and this allowed parents and loved ones to gain some solace by thinking the men had already partaken in a highly secret operation and had therefore been killed on "active service"—which was technically correct.

CHAPTER FORTY-FIVE

ROSEMARY SPENCE WOKE up from a fitful sleep of storms and monstrous waves and of men cast upon an angry ocean that was at once majestic and terrifying in its power. But Robert was nowhere among the men she saw passing her in the dream, but could be seen on a distant pebbled shore, the shore pounded so incessantly that the moment she woke and found Georgina by her side, she still felt bound to the far-off island, the pebbles—as in *Dover Beach*, which she'd been discussing with the sixth form the day before—still roiling in dreadful unison as they were sucked out and flung back by the surf—every pebble in the dream a lost soul, as insignificant to the sea as a grain of sand.

"You all right?" asked Georgina, holding her sister's hand.

"I—" Rosemary began, and fell back exhausted onto her pillow. "I'm sorry. Was I making a racket?"

"Not really," said Georgina, "but I could hear you from my room. Sounded like a nightmare." She paused. "Robert?"

"Yes," answered Rosemary, still finding it difficult to tear herself away from the dark yet transparent symbolism of the dream. "Isn't the first, I'm afraid. I worry about him all the time these days." She looked up at Georgina. In the quiet of the room, it was as if the two were meeting in a place where they had never been before, but now, each confronted by her own fears—Rosemary for Robert and Georgina for Peter Zeldman—it was a place they both knew the other understood. Until this moment, they had carried their own fears stoically, and in silence, but in the sharing of them now, there was a mutual understanding and compassion that neither had felt for the other since their childhood.

"You dream of Peter very much?" Rosemary asked.

"All the time. But it's all so terribly vague in my case. I think it might help if I could remember the details after, but I can't. I try. Sometimes I don't even realize I've had a dream about him until later in the day. Then something—I don't know—something quite unrelated, it seems, will remind me of it."

"Do you think of him being on the submarine?"

"No—at least I don't think so. But it's always a very confined space. I do know that. Like a cave, the entrance closing."

Rosemary shivered. "It's always the same island for me. And ice as far as I can see, and the closer I get, the further it recedes, the more I hear the surf crashing on a beach—a cruel, hard beach of stones." Quite unknown to herself, Rosemary's hands were moving protectively over her stomach as she was talking.

Georgina squeezed her hand. "I won't be foolish and tell you you shouldn't worry about the baby. I guess every mother does. But try not to fret too much, Rose."

Rosemary didn't answer. It was the first time Georgina had called her "Rose" in years.

"Oh Lord," said Rosemary, "how can they do that—go down there for weeks at—"

"*Months*," said Georgina.

"Oh, thank you," said Rosemary in mock reproach. "You're a great help." It eased the tension and they began to laugh, and soon the laughter had turned to tears and they were embracing.

"What a pair of ninnies," snuffled Rosemary. "Really—they're probably telling obscene jokes and drinking cocoa."

"Coffee!" corrected Georgina, wiping her eyes.

From the hallway, Richard Spence saw them, thought of going in, but instead withdrew, walking softly back to bed.

"Richard—what's the matter?" asked Anne, her voice dopey with the sleeping pills she had found necessary since young William's death.

"Nothing," he said, and switched off the light, but he lay awake; the sight of his two daughters so close together filled him with a warmth he hadn't experienced in years. Yet he felt it shot through with his own fears about his son-in-law and his doubts about the advisability of Georgina marrying young Zeldman. Anne continued to be all for it, but the war situation was so grave, and getting worse each day, that Richard wanted to spare Georgina whatever angst he could. Most people, he believed, including Anne, simply didn't realize how bad it really was in Europe. Unable to be supplied with as much as they needed because of the Soviet sub offensive was bad enough for the NATO forces, but now it was widely reported that more and more Soviet subs, like those which continued to attack American West Coast shipping, were still getting through the SOSUS network.

As he drifted off to sleep, Richard Spence said a prayer for "the two boys" and for all those other men who went willingly, and not so willingly, down to the sea in ships, and he sought comfort in the words of the ancient Anglican prayer for "those who go down to the sea in ships: We give thee humble thanks for that thou hast been pleased to preserve through the perils of the deep. . . ."

CHAPTER FORTY-SIX

SONARMAN EMERSON WAS not the first aboard *Roosevelt* to detect the deadly danger they were in. This unhappy distinction fell upon Seaman Leach, the steward and cook's helper.

The cook had been trying to cheer up the crew by telling a story about how he used to play his "date line trick"—confusing new shipmates by serving a breakfast twice a day whenever the sub crossed the date line.

But the story fell flat after *Roosevelt*, her starboard ballast tanks ripped open as she lay bottomed and still taking in water, sat stranded, unable to rise. Leach grunted. No one had said a word of reproach to him about the exploding coffeepot that had started the chain of events that now left the Sea Wolf trapped, its escape hatches inoperable and several hydraulic lines severed, the diving plane fixed in an "up angle" but the sub unable to rise the three hundred feet to surface, a ruptured ballast tank completely flooded. Leach couldn't bring himself to look straight at any of the men as he doled out scalloped potatoes and green peas and steak, limiting his line of sight out of shame to their name tags and dosimeters on their belts. It was because of this hangdog expression, unable to look any of his shipmates in the face, that he was the first to notice the danger.

Everybody else had been too preoccupied with their individual jobs, and besides, no one had noticed because they were working in the much dimmer light of the sub's emergency battle lanterns until the blown circuits could be fixed. The men in most trouble, he noticed, were those from the engine room, which, along with Control, had experienced the worst flooding.

By the time he'd finished serving, Leach felt ill, and breaking out into a sweat, despite the chilly fifty-five degrees of the sub, he went to crew's quarters, slid into the six-by-three-by-two-foot slot that was his bunk, and pulled the two-foot-high curtains shut.

The man below him thought he heard a whimpering sound, and when he asked Leach whether he was all right, Leach said he was fine, but his voice was strained. Now and then he could hear the hesitant but persistent tapping throughout the ship as the various department chiefs supervised timber reinforcements against the leaks, tightening C-clamps on the joints and trying to reinforce the big flange joint in the engine room. There were already over nine hundred gallons that had poured in in just over a minute. The sound of the tapping, monitored by Emerson, wasn't too loud and wasn't standing out from the ice clutter. In any case, some of the men argued there was no point in worrying about making sound as they had no choice but to try to mend the damage and extrude the water as quickly as the damaged pumps would allow. Either that or let the sub fill slowly and drown like rats. But soon Leach couldn't stand the noise any longer.

The blue curtain across his bunk space swished back and he dropped down in his underwear, teary-eyed, looking at the other six men in his section. A chief petty officer, passing through, immediately sensed something was wrong, the tension fairly crackling in the air. "What's going on?"

Leach was zipping up his fly. "Permission to see the captain!" It wasn't so much a question as a demand. Before the chief could say anything, Leach bellowed, "Please!" in a tone at once so pleading and threatening that the CPO knew the man was literally on the edge.

"Sure—Leach, isn't it? Sure, I'll take you up."

"Wait here," the chief told Leach, who had seemed to calm down a little on the way to Control. The chief pulled back the curtained door of Control. Inside the redded-out room, Robert Brentwood was surrounded by ship's charts, the chief engineer, and several other technical officers. The chief knew it was the wrong time to interrupt—Brentwood's face lined with the strain—but the chief's expression spoke volumes, clearly conveying the message to the captain that they had a possible Section Eight on their hands. Besides which Brentwood had made a point of being "accessible" to his men's concerns. Brentwood saw Leach wild-eyed, nodded at the chief, and invited Leach aft of Control. Closer now to Leach, Brentwood could see what he took to be the classic signs of claustrophobic panic. It was unusual but not unknown among submariners; sometimes even the toughest among them caught "coffin fever" after extreme stress.

"What can I do for you, Leach?" Brentwood asked, trying to strike the right attitude between concern and the obvious need for expediency.

"Sir, I dropped the—" He stopped, looking down, his chest heaving.

Robert Brentwood thought of his earlier days in the navy, of how it was for all young men, of how it might be for his son—if they won this war—to have to face a moment of devastating truth. "Listen, sailor, any one of us could have dropped a clanger. It was an accident. A serious one. You know that. Everyone aboard does. Can't be undone. You look at it straight in the face, resolve to do better, and go on. But you don't roll over and die. That's no good to us—it's no good to you."

There was silence, apart from the cautious tapping throughout the sub and the oppressive smell of diesel oil, which Brentwood hated with a passion and which was seeping out from some of the severed hydraulic hoses. "Listen, son. First time I was in Bledsoe—in the tank—we had a flange ring separate. Out shot a wall of solid water. Never seen anything like it. Every time I tried to get near it, it just kept pushing me back. Couldn't see a darn thing."

Leach was still looking down at his feet.

"But I finally made it. Know what happened?"

Leach's chest seemed to collapse, then suddenly heave again. Robert put his hand on the man's shoulder. "CPO was yelling at me to stop picking my nose and get in there—the whole ship depended on me. So I had to grit my teeth, charge in, and get the monkey wrench on. Turned the damn thing counterclockwise—opened her up further. I tell you that water was roarin' in like Niagara, but I could hear the chief above it all right. Face redder than a fat admiral. Purple! Said I was a 'disaster'—said a few other things, too, which I won't repeat." Robert grinned. "I thought my life was over—career down the tube. But I got through it. We'll get through this one, Leach. No one bought it, did they?"

"How we gonna get up?" asked Leach.

"I'm working on it," said Brentwood. "Now, if you'll let me get back to the blueprints and—"

"We're all going to die."

Robert nodded. "That's a possibility, Leach. But right now

let's stow that where it belongs. You and I have to get to work and—"

"Radiation," said Leach.

Brentwood shook his head. "Listen, Leach, if that's what's bothering you, you can relax. Reactor room officer and his boys have been over the coffee grinder with a fine-tooth comb. Not even a hairline fracture. Even if there was, we've got the outer shield. They build them tough in Groton, Leach. So that's one thing you can't blame your—"

"*Their* reactor, sir," said Leach. He was now looking up directly at Brentwood. "I've been watching the men's dosimeters as they've come through the chow line. Color change's hard to pick up under the different lighting in the sub."

Brentwood felt his stomach tightening. Instinctively he bent his neck to look down at his own belt dosimeter. There was only a slight change—if any—that he could notice.

"It's not all the men," said Leach. "Not yet. But it's only a matter of time."

"What the hell do you mean?"

"That Alfa, sir. We all heard it going down. Split wide open—their reactor squeezed flatter'n a pancake, I reckon."

Robert Brentwood's tone changed utterly. "Who have you noticed? I mean, which men—"

"Guys from the engine room mainly—where there was a lot of flooding—and in the torpedo room. A lot of leakage in there, I think." He hesitated. "As well as Control."

"You told anyone else about this?"

"No, sir." Leach's confidence was growing in direct proportion to Brentwood's discomfort.

"Well, hold your horses, Leach. We'd better have a good look at everyone's dosimeters before we rush to any conclusions. We'll do another shield check just to make sure. If it's here, we'll seal it."

"If it isn't, sir?"

"Then you're correct, Leach. We're in a lot of trouble." Brentwood made to go but stopped at Control's curtain and looked back. "I won't cover this up if it's true. But I want you to keep quiet until we're sure. Understood?"

"Yes, sir."

"Very well," said Brentwood, and with that he knew that a load had fallen from Leach's shoulders—onto his.

When he reentered Control, the chief engineer was poring over the blueprints of the ship—for its size, it was the most complicated of any vessel ever designed, more intricate than the space shuttles. "Captain?"

"Yes, chief?"

"RRO wants to see you down in the reactor room."

"Very well. You come up with any ideas about how we're going to refloat this baby, Chief?"

"Not so far, Captain."

"Any way we can get that ballast tank self-patching?"

The chief shook his head. "No hope there, Captain. God-damned cave-in. Hole's too big. Drive a truck through it. Damn lucky the pressure hull's intact."

As Brentwood walked down through Sherwood Forest, aft of the sub's sail where the six fifty-seven-ton Trident D-5 missiles stood, a row of three towering either side of him, resting in their forty-two-foot-high, seven-foot-wide tubes, he could hear the steady wash of the forty-ton ventilator like a gentle breeze through a copse of birch. Droplets of condensation beaded the tall, chocolate-colored tubes as if they were sweating, enough deadly power in their forty-two warheads—each reentry vehicle with a six-thousand-mile range and independent navigational equipment—to take the three hundred kilotons to within a circular error of probability of plus or minus two hundred yards from a target.

And yet, trapped beneath the ice, what good were they unless *Roosevelt* could rise and break through? To make matters worse, the 114,000-pound D-5s were heavier than the old 68,000-pound C-5s, meaning the sub was even more firmly weighed down on the shelf than she might otherwise have been.

When he reached the anteroom of the reactor, Brentwood took off his shoes, slipping on a pair of the yellow felt-lined plastic bootees so that any odd piece of radioactive dust that he might conceivably pick up would remain in the reactor room when he changed back to his regular soft-soled deck shoes. "What have we got, Leo?" he asked Lieutenant Galardi, who, despite his white coveralls, looked more like the family dentist than a reactor room officer. He was also a man of few words.

"Captain, we've been zapped and it's not coming from this baby. That goddamned Alfa we sank tore apart—including her reactor. With everything else going on, only a few boys have reported it, but soon, as we get normal lighting back, everyone's going to notice they've got a dose of gamma radiation."

"How big a dose?"

"Not exactly sure." Galardi paused. "I'd like to call in all dosimeters, if that's okay with you."

"Go ahead. What are we up to now in rads?"

"We've passed Greenpeace recommended dosage," said Galardi, with a rare smile that Brentwood found distinctly unsettling.

"Hell, Leo—even God's passed Greenpeace's recommended dosage. How bad do *you* think it is? I mean, if the rate you've seen so far doesn't decrease, what's the prognosis?"

"If it goes up—"

"Come on, Leo, don't dance. You've always given me straight answers. Let's keep it that way."

"If it keeps climbing, sir, we're all going to lose some hair."

"When will you know for certain?" Brentwood realized he'd left himself wide open for a joke—when your hair falls out—but neither of them was in the mood.

"I'll need a half an hour, Captain. Even then we'd have to hear what the experts in the Oxford Rad Lab say to know for sure."

"Well, Leo, there aren't any of them around at the moment."

"I noticed that, Captain."

Brentwood took off the bootees and glanced at his watch. It was 0545. By 0615 he would have a rough idea of whether Leach's fears were fully justified. "Surely to God it isn't that powerful that it can come straight through the hull?"

"Oh, it's not that," Leo assured him. "It's in the water. The leaks. We're swimming in the goddamned stuff."

CHAPTER FORTY-SEVEN

THE JUMBLED ICE of the Yalu proved better cover than Freeman could have reasonably hoped for, and up close, what had seemed, looking down from Outpost Delta, like chunks no more than three or four feet high were in fact enormous shards of ice over ten feet in height, the moonlight throwing the jagged landscape of the river into sharp relief.

The patrol could easily see their way across. And so, Freeman knew, could the Chinese if they were in the area. He was determined to move slowly, for though he didn't fear land mines—the shifting ice too precarious to plant them due to the changing pressure of the ice—he was nevertheless alert to the possibility of booby traps.

On the point, Freeman would go ahead, checking the immediate area about him before waving on the patrol. High overhead the dot of an eagle crossed the moon's face, passing through the aura of ice needles that was clearly visible as a golden ring. Finally the patrol eased its way off the frozen river toward the black humps of hills that faded into the snow-covered foothills of Manchuria.

All this time Freeman was calmly surveying escape routes should firing suddenly erupt around them, his nose as much a guide as his eyes—alert for the smell of wood smoke, which, while it mightn't necessarily signal an NKA or Chinese position, would warn him of a village where the Chinese might be storing arms and other supplies as a forward base.

There was a sudden ice fall. Freeman flicked off the safety catch of his squad automatic weapon, its triangular box magazine pressing in firmly against his side. But soon all was quiet again, and in another little while they came upon a track, or rather series of tracks, leading up from the river, where the grass in the flood margin had been stomped down, frozen like coarse hair, prone to crack underfoot. Freeman knew he had only two options: to go on where they couldn't help but make some noise or to head back.

It might be, Freeman realized, that there were no Chinese or NKA units anywhere in this section, but with the north-south valleys running down to the river, offering natural revetment areas for armor, the general couldn't believe that the Chinese wouldn't use the Manchurian side as a staging area. And if the North Koreans had successfully dug tunnels all along the DMZ—the last one being discovered in 1990—despite American ground-movement sensors, this area could be riddled with underground supply dumps, the Chinese divisions waiting for the next snowstorm that could nullify U.S. air strikes and blind the U.S. artillery's forward observation posts. He knew that if he were the PLA commander, he'd sure as hell be using the sector.

After Pyongyang, Freeman figured he understood something of Kim's strategy, telling Jim Norton once that Kim was a "Korean Montgomery"—wouldn't move until he had a "four-to-one advantage in toilet rolls." It wasn't his—Freeman's—way, but he knew that it, too, won battles.

Ironically, he felt safe the farther the patrol penetrated the hillocks on the northern side. Providing they didn't find any evidence of Chinese or NKA presence following the last attack on Outpost Delta, his patrol would be left alone. And if there were troops in the area, they would only attack if discovered, unlikely to reveal themselves—saving everything for a surprise attack.

He motioned the squad to stop, waited, and listened some more. He'd known of more than one patrol who, in their eagerness to get the nail biting over with, had kept moving forward without pausing long enough each time. And when you didn't rest, the sound of your breathing, your heart thumping, drowned all other noise—including the enemy's.

Freeman could smell both his and his men's sweat and thanked God the wind was blowing against them from the north.

It was a small thing in the moonglow, a depression no more than a few feet wide and an inch or so deep, but with the intuitive sense of the experienced soldier, Freeman was already leery of it. Cradling his SAW in his left arm, he lay down and crawled within a foot of the depression, its outline like that of a big serving dish. Drawing the knife from his calf scabbard, he gently probed the edges of the depression, the blade sounding as if it were passing through coarse sugar. He waited for the click of metal on metal that would signify a mine. There was none. Instead, the knife was stuck. He waved the patrol back several yards and signaled for them to cover up, helmets down tight, but no chin strap. If it was a mine, nonmetallic or not, and went off, the concussion beneath the helmets would lift the chin straps so hard, it'd snap their jawbones. He tried pulling the knife again, and this time it came out. It was a circular cane-woven dish that the blade had sunk into—the kind he'd seen villagers using, tossing up the rice grain during the harvest, but much firmer than the grain platter he had at first thought it was. As he drew it closer to himself, he saw the black hole that it had been covering and knew he was looking at a tunnel entrance.

Slowly he replaced the cover, then eased his way back through the snow to the squad. Now he knew why the trail wasn't mined—it was a pathway from the tunnel to the river. His whisper was soft, distinct, and as Wezlinski, first rifleman in the patrol, noticed, Freeman's instructions were remarkably unhurried.

"It's a tunnel entrance," he told Wezlinski. "If it's active, we know my hunch is right and we can call down artillery on these gooks." Quietly he turned his arm to see his watch.

"Give me twenty minutes," he told Wezlinski. "If I don't pop back up—or you hear one hell of a racket—then you'll know I've found the bastards. Then you get the hell out of here and zero in the artillery."

He took a handful of snow to moisten his mouth in the cold, dry wind. Next he took out a plastic muzzle protector, slipped it over the end of the SAW's barrel so as to keep out the snow, laid it down by the path, then drew both .45 pistols, checking the magazines. "When I come out," he whispered softly, "I'll stick a glove on one of these .45s. You see it sticking up, hold your fire. If I don't find my way back here or have to come out somewhere else, I'll fire a red flare. That'll give your buddies up in Delta a position for artillery fire. You'll have to move fast back across the river. Understand? Now, synchronize your watch."

"But—" said Wezlinski in amazement. "You aren't going down there, General?"

Freeman tapped him, fatherly, on the shoulder. "Our boys did it all the time in 'Nam. Only way to find out whether it's an old tunnel—or if it's loaded to the gills."

"But, General—" said Wezlinski, his voice tight with fear.

"Why don't we just throw in a bunch of grenades, General?"

"Won't tell us a damn thing, son. Way they make these rat-holes, they twist and turn—got vents in them, blind corners, the whole shebang. Even use bamboo screens across to deflect shrapnel. Like goin' down a mine, son. Got to see it for yourself."

Freeman pushed the SAW back to Wezlinski—the big weapon too unwieldy in a tunnel. He checked the six grenades he had clipped to his belt, took off his helmet, put on the tear gas mask from his pack, and moved toward the hole, a 7-shaped flashlight in his left hand, the .45 from his right holster in the other hand. Wezlinski heard a shuffle of ice as the general slid down into the hole.

When Wezlinski passed the word back, the tail-end Charlie, facing the river, shook his head. "No way you'd get me down there, man," he whispered. "He's nuts!"

Slowly extending his arms out in the pitch darkness, the first thing Freeman noticed was that the tunnel was no more than four feet wide and about six feet high, though now and then he felt his hair brush the ice-cold dirt of the roof so that he was forced to stoop. After five yards—he was careful to keep count—he felt the tunnel veering sharply to the left, then going straight for another two yards before it swung hard left again, then right. He thought he heard something up ahead, stopped, but if it had been something moving, it was gone now.

Then he heard it again. At first it seemed to be going away from him, but then was coming toward him—a faint scrambling. He resisted the temptation to use the flashlight. Then there was a fast rushing movement, a furry rat racing over his feet. He could smell them now—a stream of them.

The fact that the rats had apparently turned back toward him indicated he was coming to a cul-de-sac. He heard another sound: a tinkling. He brought his wrist up close to his eyes so he could read the watch face. He'd been down only three minutes. It had seemed like an eternity. The thought of rats gnawing his face if he should fall turned his stomach.

He waited for ten seconds or so, hoping that his eyes might adjust to any faint moonlight that might be penetrating a vent—if there were any—but if anything, it was blacker than before. He heard the tinkling again.

Up above the tunnel, in the world of moonlight and fresh air, Wezlinski cursed silently to himself. Someone in the squad had broken wind and the odor of putrefied baked beans engulfed him, and he thanked God for the breeze that whipped it downwind toward the river.

CHAPTER FORTY-EIGHT

"OFFICER ON PARADE!" called the SAS sergeant major. "Atten-shun!" There was a crash of rubberized Vibram boots from the eighty-man squadron that shook the hall.

"At ease, gentlemen," said Major Rye. "Gather 'round."

As they all crowded in about the twelve-foot-square table, Cheek-Dawson at the adjacent corner, ready, upon Major Rye's word, to take off the cover, Rye announced, "Another HALO jump, gentlemen. That's why we've been giving you lots of practice up in Scotland. This, however, is not an exercise. Gentlemen, you have been *requested*! Code name for the operation is 'Merlin.' "

There was silence following a few joking comments such as " 'Bout time . . ."—comments that would immediately have been withdrawn had they foreseen what now lay before them as, with a flick of the wrist, Rye and Cheek-Dawson removed the green cloth cover from the model of the mission's target. The scale on the accompanying map Cheek-Dawson was pinning on the wall showed the target was no more than an hour's flight from the Allies' most forward airfields—no farther than the Wales-to-Scotland exercises. But even David Brentwood, who, in the Australian's consistently gregarious presence, had adopted a self-protective nonchalance, could not suppress his surprise. The very air seemed to quiver as the new "Sabre" squadron crowded around the model.

"Son of a bitch, Aussie!" said Thelman. "You've just lost a bundle."

"Bloody hell!" retorted the Australian. "The fix is in."

"It is indeed," said Major Rye, looking up at them. "As

you gentlemen will appreciate, the location of this target had to be kept from you till the last moment. Now, however, the request has come and you have a full twenty-four hours to walk it through. Inch by inch." He paused. "Any SAS target, gentlemen, is important. The very fact SAS is called in makes it so. But I can tell you quite frankly that this is *the* most important in our history. I have it on good authority both from 10 Downing Street and, for you American chaps, from 1600 Pennsylvania Avenue, that if we do not succeed in—" he paused "—in 'adjourning' a meeting which intelligence tells us is scheduled for tomorrow night, the war on the European continent will suddenly shift to chemical and possibly all-out nuclear war."

The red-star-topped Byzantine spires were at once familiar and unfamiliar to every man in the room. While they did not know the names of all its salient features, there was no one who didn't recognize the grim and forbidding grandeur of the Kremlin, the cluster of gold cupolas that were atop the once proud yellow brick imperial palaces and cathedrals of the czar of all the Russias, and amid them, the high, ocher-red walls that now contained the seat of Soviet power. In thirty-six hours, they were told, in the Council of Ministers Building, the Politburo and STAVKA of the Supreme Soviet would meet to put their signatures to what the KGB had already decided—to launch nerve gas attacks against the entire NATO front.

"The three troops of Sabre squadron," explained Rye, "will be designated A for Alfa, B for Bravo, C for Charlie—each troop of sixteen subdivided into your four-man modules. Fluent Russian speakers from among the twelve-man HQ group will attach themselves to any of the troops as necessary during the operation. Lieutenant Laylor, leading A Group, will be the first out of three Hercules we're using for the operation. Group A's job is to establish and provide a perimeter of fire, Group B will eliminate the Politburo-STAVKA, and Group C will provide backup and detonations for retreat and for pickup, which I'll get to in due course. One Hercules per group. Second group, B, I must emphasize again, will concern itself only with getting into the Council of Ministers and eliminating the enemy war cabinet. Those of you in this group may require more of the Russian translators than A or C, but I don't expect there'll be a great deal of time for conversation anyway."

There were a few awkward grunts.

"The objective is simple. Doing it, not quite so easy." He took the pointer. "As you can see, the Kremlin is an odd shape—five sides, none of them the same length—but we are only concerned with the northern triangular-shaped section up here.'' The pointer moved to the top of the map. ''This is made up of the arsenal tower at the top left of the triangle, Trinity Tower and Gate further left, to the west, Spasskaya or Savior's Tower and Gate on the right, on the eastern side of the triangle.

''Whatever you do, try to avoid the onion-shaped domes down here south of the triangle. The domes are not your target. No reason you can't abseil down from them, but this will consume precious time, and we estimate you'll have twenty minutes maximum from point of landing to complete the mission.'' Rye paused. ''Questions so far?'' Everyone's eyes were fixed on the map as Rye waited a few seconds, then continued.

''For the last month, U.S. Second Air Force and RAF have been flying bombing missions out of our most forward airfields around Minsk, hitting Kolomna, fifty miles east of Moscow. This has diverted the mobile SAM and AA batteries away from Moscow as well as drawing off Moscow's fighters. At the same time, we've been flying two or three Hercules—very high, under radar-jamming protection—dropping propaganda leaflets. Usual kind of stuff from NATO Psychological Warfare Unit, telling the Russian population at large that 'while you are fighting the war, your leaders are living in luxury.' The Russians already know that, of course. Personally, I think that this sort of thing is highly overrated and indeed counterproductive, but in our particular case, it does serve a very real purpose. By running these propaganda flights over the central Moscow area on a fairly regular basis, it's caused the Russians, when their radar does manage to penetrate our jamming, to pay less and less attention to the Hercules they're used to and instead to concentrate their mobile SAM sites and AA defense units around outlying industrial targets like the Likhachev Works that once produced Zils and are now busy turning out armor, et cetera. In any event, they're understandably much more interested in having their expensive SAMs and AA batteries engage our bombers, not three transports that have been dropping leaflets over the last few weeks, which we've been using as a decoy for your drop. Even so, once you land inside the Kremlin, you'll be up against SPETs elite guard units.''

David Brentwood suddenly looked across at the major. ''We have any idea how many, sir?'' he interjected.

''Three companies, we believe—in all, plus or minus three hundred men.''

"Whew! That's all right then," said Aussie. "Thought there mightn't be enough to go around."

The major grinned politely but quickly returned their attention to the triangular section—at the Kremlin's northernmost end, which was roughly wedge-shaped—the arsenal that would contain the SPETS on the left-hand side of the wedge, the Council of Ministers where the STAVKA meeting would take place, on the right—in between them, a relatively open section of several acres with some tree cover.

Tapping the open area at the bottom or widest part of the wedge, Rye told them, "This'll be your landing zone. Remember, too far west and you're on the roof of the Palace of Congress. Too far southwest and you're into a thicket of spires. Landing atop the Palace of Congress wouldn't be so bad for Laylor's Troop A. It has a very good overview of the open area below it—the middle of the wedge—as well as a view of the arsenal on its left and the Council of Ministers to the right. But Troop B and Troop C, on the other hand, must avoid wasting time by landing on the palace and having to rappel down. Oh yes—too far south altogether and you could find yourself over the wall in queue for Lenin's mausoleum."

"Have to pay to get in, sir?"

"Well I'm sure," quipped Rye, "that whatever currency was required, Lewis, you'd have it."

Rye turned back to the map. "Before I discuss the job of the other two groups—B and C—a few more points you all need to know."

The major paused to make sure every man of the three-troop squadron was watching him before going on. "The raid, gentlemen, is to cut off the head of the snake. It must be a quick and decisive operation. Very fast, very hard. Now, some of you are probably wondering, why not a bombing run? Good question—easy answer. The Kremlin complex covers well over sixty acres. Furthermore, after the U.S. "smart bomb" attack on Qaddafi years ago knocked out everything else but failed to get Qaddafi, which was the whole point of the raid, NATO HQ, correctly in my view, have shied away from delegating this kind of task to a bombing run. Bombing looks all very impressive from postraid aerial photographs. It appears that you've taken out everything when in fact half of it remains operational. We learned that with the Ho Chi Minh Trail. And do remember, gentlemen— the day after the A-bomb landed on Hiroshima, trolley cars were running in the city. No, the only sure way is to actually go in and do the job on the ground. Then you've got a much better chance of taking them out—whether they're in the upper chambers of the Council of Ministers or in the bomb shelters below.

"Understood, sir," put in the Guards officer, Laylor, in command of A Group. "But if the shelters are sealed off, then even if we get some members of the STAVKA HQ upstairs, what happens if the rest scurry to the shelters before we can—"

"Good question, Laylor—so now we come to Groups B and C." The major was looking around at the eighty men. "Ah, Brentwood, there you are. I do hope you don't object to leading Bravo Troop? You were chosen because of your experience in the Freeman raid on Pyongyang.

"Good. Now, your job is to get into the Council of Ministers—hereafter designated COM—while Laylor's Alfa Group is securing the perimeter. Hit them before they know what the dickens is going on. Remember, they've at least two companies of SPETS billeted in the arsenal just two hundred yards west of the COM. That's in addition to regular Kremlin guards stationed at building entrances, et cetera."

The major turned back to Laylor. "In any event, Laylor, the drill will be that whether or not the STAVKA and other members of the Politburo do 'scurry' to the cellars, your job is to secure a perimeter within which Brentwood's Bravo Troop can 'clean house.' Brentwood, your sappers will plant enough plastique to bring down the entire COM if necessary. Whether the STAVKA are shot or asphyxiated by thousands of tons of concrete coming down on their shelter is neither here nor there to us. Your job is to kill them before they get a chance to unleash all-out chemical and biological warfare on our troops and on our civilians.

"Before your departure, all of you will be doing walk-throughs—many, in fact—of a mock-up of Suzlov's office, et cetera, on the top floor of the COM's eastern wing. Remember, all you are concerned with is the area bounded by the triangle—the Kremlin's northern end. You should land within the triangle—hopefully in the more open space between the arsenal and the Council of Ministers. When you open your chutes at low altitude, even with cloud, your infrared goggles should allow you to make out the landing zone area clearly. For a reference point, look for the line of cannons lined up all along here—the eastern side of the arsenal facing the Council of Ministers. We'll be practicing orientation here, sending you up on the mezzanine and looking down on the model. You'll be issued flares—short fuse—but hopefully you'll have the element of surprise and won't have to use them, as you'd only be presenting yourselves as targets. Most critical phase will be the time it takes the SPETs in and around the arsenal to realize what's going on. But no matter where you land within the Kremlin complex, remember you'll never be too far from your targets. So regroup quickly."

Next Rye turned to Cheek-Dawson, who was designated leader of the remaining twenty-odd SAS. "C Troop under Mr. Cheek-Dawson will surround the Council of Ministers Building, to help Laylor's Alfa Group bottle up the SPETS *in* the arsenal while Brentwood is cleaning house. C will also provide a squad of sappers to plant the time-delay plastique which will bring down the COM, covering its shelters in rubble, should Mr. Brentwood's group not put pay to everyone at the STAVKA meeting. No use doing only half the job. Captain, you'll also provide 'fire teams' of two, no more than four, men to plug any weak holes in the perimeter."

"Understood, sir," said Cheek-Dawson.

"Good. Everyone else—clear so far?"

Rye was wearing such an encouraging smile that for a moment it occurred to the Australian, Lewis, that to anyone walking in, it might seem as if they were merely being briefed for yet another practice HALO jump, except the atmosphere in the room was electric with excitement, laced through with the fear that they were going into the bear's den.

"I'll hand this over in a few moments to Mr. Cheek-Dawson for your detailed walk-throughs, but I do have a few closing remarks. We have—I should say MI5 and CIA have—provided us with enough information to arrange a mock-up 'attack set' in our Hereford house. You will all do six run-throughs—each fifteen minutes maximum—before you take off tomorrow afternoon for our forward airfields around Minsk.

"Remember the whole thrust of your training is that above all, SAS *adapts* to any situation faster and better than anyone else. Apart from those weapons and techniques that you've spent the last weeks honing to a fine point, your greatest weapon will be *speed* and *surprise*. If we had thought we could have relied on any other means to do the job, we wouldn't have asked you. That, indeed, was my first consideration when former C in C General Freeman, who originated this plan and kept it on standby, initially presented it to me in Brussels. And if we thought we could get you in by low, radar-evading choppers, we would have also tried that. But I'm afraid the perimeter defenses of Moscow area simply made that unfeasible.

The only way is to go high and drop you in. So far as getting you out—something I venture a few of you at least are interested in doing—" the laughter was short "—Royal Air Force will launch a Harrier-escorted flight of four Sea Stallion choppers for pickup—" he turned to the map "—here at Naro-Fominsk. It's thirty miles out—closest we can possibly hope to get. But we do have surprise help for you on that score."

"A bloody compass!" called out the Australian.

"A little better than that, Mr. Lewis," replied Rye easily. "Sar'Major will fill you in on that. As far as the choppers go, we would have liked to have used something with a smaller silhouette than the Stallions, but each Stallion can carry enough fuel and can get thirty-five of you out in one haul—providing you can reach them. The fourth Stallion will be manned by American medical personnel. I believe they have everything aboard except the kitchen sink." Another smatter of laughter. "Again, vertical-landing Harriers, the only fighters we can put down without an airfield, will be with them, waiting for you. I won't insult your intelligence, gentlemen, by pretending that even if you reach Naro-Fominsk, the evacuation's going to be any picnic. Within five minutes of you hitting the drop zone, I estimate that all SPETS *outside* as well as those inside the Kremlin will be alerted. Hopefully they will also be confused for a minute or so, at least when you go in, and that should give you a vital edge. Best of luck."

With that, Major Rye let Cheek-Dawson take over. It was unstated, but the men drew confidence from the fact that the spearhead of the mission—the job of carrying out the "flush-out," in SAS parlance, of the enemy commanders from their various offices along the eastern wing of the Council of Ministers Building—had been assigned to a veteran of such a raid: the American, Brentwood, and not automatically assigned, as often happened in line units, to the most senior officer, in this case Captain Cheek-Dawson. Every leader, despite his generalist SAS training, had sensibly been chosen because of his experience as well as SAS training, and not his rank.

"Very nice," said Aussie, looking down at one of the lists of Russian phrases several of the NCOs were handing out. "Very nice—twenty bloody phrases to learn off by heart, but who's the Russian specialist in *our* group, may I ask?"

"Why," said Schwarzenegger, surprised that Lewis didn't know. "I am. I speak Russian as well as German, you know. Many Germans do. It's—"

Lewis turned on him. "You boxhead! You never told me that. Christ—you've cost me a bloody fortune!"

"You never asked me," Schwarzenegger repeated, unruffled. "Besides, I thought you were so sure that we were going to Malaya, then Korea—"

"Ah, piss off!"

David Brentwood didn't join in the ribbing. The full realization of his awesome responsibility was now upon him like a backpack twice the weight of the 110-pound load he'd take with him out of the aircraft. And now, too, he was confronted by the memories of how he had lain petrified in the shelled moonscape during the botched-up drop of the airborne outside Stadthagen: how he had been unable to move, too afraid to move, until the SPETS bayonet appeared before his face and he'd surrendered. Oh, he'd escaped from Stadthagen, all right, but that, like the actions of so many others, had been motivated more by fear of what would happen to him if he didn't escape. Physically he felt fit and ready enough for "Operation Merlin," but that had all been training. Now it would be the real thing—*again*.

Cheek-Dawson was taking the roof off the model of the Council of Ministers, indicating to the sappers the points of the building where charges would exert most stress with the least resistance. The man in Laylor's group passing out the list of Russian-English phrases to be memorized and practiced by morning wondered aloud what the word "Kremlin" actually meant.

"Fortress," Cheek-Dawson answered, without looking up.

"Oh, lovely," said Aussie, "Does that tell you something, fellas?"

"Yeah, long way from Korea, Aussie," commented a cockney, who, turning to his mate, continued, "Poor bugger'll owe over three hundred quid, I reckon."

"Less than that," said the Welshman they called "Choir" Williams.

"How come?"

"Work it out, lad. Fortress an' all. How many you think'll make it in? More to the point, how many of us'll get out?"

"You're a cheery one," said the first cockney.

"Just facing facts, ducky."

Lewis, listening in, depressed by the ribbing directed his way, was suddenly seized with an inspiration. As if in a vision, he rose, took out his ever-ready purple indelible pencil, knowing its imprint on paper wouldn't run in either snow or rain, and, licking it, he wandered about the hall, making bets on how many would make it back. If any.

For David Brentwood, the worst of it was that Thelman, Schwarzenegger, and the Australian, Lewis, along with the other sixteen men of his troop, thoroughly approved of his selection as leader of B Troop. His experience on Freeman's Pyongyang raid now made him feel as he had once at college when, unexpectedly having achieved high grades in several subjects, he was automatically expected to continue to lead the field. Adding to his apprehension was Rye's mention of Freeman in the past tense, as former C in C.

Approaching Cheek-Dawson with a nonchalance, the very pretense so unlike him, it only further fueled his anxiety, he asked casually whether the general had "bought it."

Cheek-Dawson didn't glance up from the model of the Kremlin. Like Gulliver, he was still peering down at the Lilliputian world, making notes on precisely where the charges would have to be placed. "Suspect so, old boy," he answered. "Apparently the general went MIA somewhere up near the Yalu. Chaps at Brussels HQ say it was typical, though. I mean, doing his own reconnaissance. From all accounts, he was some general."

"Yes," said Brentwood with a heartfelt sincerity he doubted anyone else in the room, except perhaps Thelman, who'd also served directly under Freeman, could fully comprehend. "Yes—" David stopped, unsure as to whether he should say, "He was," or "He is." Somehow he had always thought of the general as invincible.

The regimental sergeant major was on the hailer before they were due to leave for lunch and then on to the "house" for the dry run-through with live ammunition and full pack. The RSM was holding an "extra roll" above his head, which he explained would have to be put atop the 110-pound pack that would be carried by each man into the drop zone. There was a collective groan.

"Steady on, girls," he responded breezily. "No need to get your knickers in a knot. You'll like this one." The roll of white plastic was no larger than a tightly compressed hand towel, and, he assured them, no heavier. "This little charmer'll go atop your main pack." With deliberate flourish, he unraveled the plastic along the floor. It was a white plastic overlay, the shape of a boiler suit, elasticized at the waist, a fly running all the way up from the crotch to the neck, where two white cord drawstrings were attached to the hood, its design quite different in its hip and shoulder cut from the NATO winter overlay the men had used on all the HALO exercisés.

"We've already got overlays," said Lewis.

"That's for the attack, Aussie. *This* is standard SPETS overlay issue. Compliments of Captain Cheek-Dawson."

Momentarily Brentwood felt better. It was simple yet quite brilliant. During the withdrawal, it would be pitch darkness because of Moscow's air raid curfews—but there would be SPETS everywhere after the attack. Identification of SAS, if they were dressed as SPETS, would be difficult and might buy valuable time, aiding escape.

"How 'bout me?" It was Thelman, the white overlay a stark contrast to his black skin.

"Yer own bloody fault, Thelma!" shouted Aussie. "Told you blokes to quit suntannin'!"

"Fuck you!" replied Thelman.

"Not to worry, mate," rejoined Aussie. "Put cold cream on. That'll do the trick."

"Smell like a whore," countered Thelman in the same easy, yet slightly forced, banter.

Lewis turned to Schwarzenegger. "Hey, Fritz. Five to two Thelma doesn't make it back?"

"Verrückt!" said Schwarzenegger.

"What the hell's that mean?"

"It means you are sick in the head," said Schwarzenegger.

"All right, all right. Eight to two, but that's it!"

Unbeknownst to any of the troops, including Laylor, Brentwood, and Cheek-Dawson, when the troops filed out for lunch, the sergeant major, with the assist of the other HQ NCOs, moved through the weapons racks with pliers, here and there slightly crimping in the magazines. This would cause those weapons to jam during the dry runs, the troopers monitored via the television cameras. It was a random check to make sure every trooper could clear a jam and, as required by SAS, change magazines on the roll. Not only their lives but the entire mission—and in this case, the entire war—might depend on it.

CHAPTER FORTY-NINE

THE TINKLING NOISE Freeman had heard was that of water at the bottom of a well shaft that formed one of the tunnel's exits—the exit hole in the wall of the well shaft six feet in diameter and a good eight feet above the water line. The exit ladder was a series of deep-set iron handholds.

Moving with extreme caution, he discovered that about thirty feet in from the exit whence he had come, there was another branch of the tunnel leading off to the left, to a large twelve-by-twelve-by-six-foot-high storage room, which, using his flashlight, he saw was packed high to its roof with everything from binary shells, binary mortars, heavy eighty-one-millimeter mortars, AK-47s, stick, HE, and phosphorus grenades, dozens of boxes of belt and magazine .76-millimeter and .50-millimeter ammunition. As well, there was a pile of ingeniously built assault ladders which were made of bamboo and which, with canvas strips for cross struts, collapsed like the supports of Chinese tripod clotheslines into one long, light, and easily portable shaft.

Beside the ladders there was a pile of worn brass bugles and a clutch of starter whistles. Then he discovered the room was connected to others of the same size, several of them bisected by timber supports, seven rooms in all, which seemed to radiate out from the well shaft in a spoke pattern, and which had the smell of acrid cordite that came from wooden casks of gunpowder, refilling jacks, and reloading stampers.

In four of the rooms there were dozens of tightly packed rice bags that had been set on bamboo woven palettes, foot-wide trenches running about them, filled with barbed wire, presumably to dissuade rats and other rodents from getting at the rice. In all, Freeman estimated that the complex of tunnels and rooms held enough ammunition and arms and sundry supplies to equip an attack of at least battalion, possibly regimental, strength—enough for between fifteen hundred and two thousand frontline assault troops.

He was in the fourth big storage room, reached by a thick right-angle bend and over a small pyramid of earthen stairs, more steps on the up than on the down side and leading into a deeper tunnel, the right-angled turn he'd just passed through and the difference in the tunnel levels potential impediments against any attack by enemy troops on the tunnel complex. Only under earth-shattering artillery would these tunnels cave in, and even then it would have to be a pulverizing barrage as otherwise the various levels and cunningly devised exits and entrances would act like watertight bulkheads aboard a ship, preventing any full-scale destruction.

Though he was using the flashlight sparingly, only flicking it on for less than a second at a time to take it all in, his attention was immediately attracted by the large number of binary poison gas shells along with the bugles and whistles. A binary was a "natural" for the Chinese—relatively cheap, using otherwise fairly harmless domestic cleaning chemicals which, when combined, would form the deadly nerve gas.

The bugles and whistles told him the Chinese were massing for a close-quarter attack on the American positions across the Yalu. His greatest wish was to defeat them, but the Chinese and the North Koreans—though the latter's cruelty was an abomination to him—aroused in him the respect of a professional soldier. He held the Chinese particularly in high regard, for not only were they brave, even if they were brainwashed, but they were extraordinarily adept at combining the old with the new, and if they didn't have the new, then improvising with what they had. In this case it was the bugles and whistles, the PLA's answer to the exorbitantly expensive—for them—and often temperamental modern microchip radio backpacks. The battered bugles and whistles not only saved on radio and avoided technical foul-ups so prevalent in frontline fighting, but along with lots of screaming in the last hundred-yard run of a night attack, more often that not, created a dangerous confusion in the opposing ranks. Among fresh American and other Allied troops who had not seen action before, the result was invariably one of panic and on occasion mass retreat.

Entering the sixth of the seven rooms, this one piled high with binary shells, he turned toward a sifting sound and tripped over some kind of wire or cord, the flashlight on, rolling, revealing the room seething with rats, turning in panic in the cul-de-sac formed by the room and trying to race out of it, swarming over him, one attacking his face. There was an enormous crash from a pile of pots and pans, no doubt used for a double purpose: to prepare the rice rolls with which Chinese and North Korean troops could march for days and—again typical of the Chinese—to act as an alarm against any potential pilferer tripping over the cord.

Within seconds, Freeman was on his feet, blood streaming from his face, its warm, metallic taste in his mouth as he moved as quickly as possible out of the room toward the main feeder tunnel of the hub-and-spoke complex, his fingers trailing the double-walled turns toward the well shaft exit. As soon as he reached it, he heard the quick babble of voices, suddenly silenced by the barking of sharply delivered orders—Korean rather than Chinese, he thought—and then shapes appeared, one already on the ladder.

Freeman fired the flare, saw its red light blossom high above the well shaft, then fired the .45, heard the echo of his shot and saw the shape on the ladder fall back without a sound, splashing heavily into the water below, a light hail of dirt and stone splattering after the body.

He heard several shots, and the bullets thudding into the well shaft; then, as suddenly as it had begun, the firing ceased and Freeman knew why. A grenade or any heavy-caliber machine-gun fire could penetrate the earthen wall of the supply rooms and set off the whole complex in a series of gigantic explosions. If he moved fast, he might make it to one of the half dozen or so manhole entrances he'd noticed along the main tunnel about a quarter mile back, where he'd left the patrol.

Gripping the flashlight firmly in his left hand, keeping it low, he used his elbow as a touch guide on his way, the .45 in his right hand. He heard the voices behind him receding, then suddenly, after a turn in the tunnel, they increased, which meant that either they had passed one of the right-angle turns or false earthen walls or were coming in from some smaller tunnel that he wasn't aware of. His right hand struck cool, damp earth, the butt of the .45 poking him in the chest before he realized he'd come up against another abutment in the tunnel. Quickly feeling his way around it, he stuffed the .45 in his waist belt, pulled the pin from one of the five-second grenades, stepped out from the abutment, and rolled the grenade hard back down the tunnel before jumping back behind the wall.

The roar was deafening, followed by screams and a pattering sound as dirt kept falling in the tunnel, the acrid smell of the explosive causing his eyes to water as he moved farther on, away from his pursuers, hearing an AK-47 rattling in the background, the dull thud of bullets and then the sound of footsteps drowning the groans as others kept coming.

Suddenly up ahead of him, about fifteen yards, he saw a shaft of moonlight. It disappeared, but not before he'd glimpsed two figures dropping down softly from it into the tunnel. Without breaking his stride, Freeman pulled the pin and rolled the grenade forward, going down on one knee like an indoor bowler to keep it as centered as possible, continuing his drop and covering his head. There was an enormous purplish-white flash, a whistling sound, and he felt a sting, or rather several, as if hornets had bitten him in several places along the right arm, which had been protecting his forehead, and he knew he'd been hit by shrapnel. But what the shrapnel had done to the two enemy soldiers, both Chinese, was much worse. One lay dead in the glow of his burning clothing while the other staggered about like a drunk, hand clasped to his face. Freeman went to squeeze off two more shots, but nothing happened. His finger wouldn't obey his brain. By the time he'd reached the wounded Chinese, he'd transferred the .45 into his left hand. The man ran at him, stumbling. Freeman fired, the man crashing into him, knocking him against the wall before falling dead at Freeman's feet.

It seemed to take Freeman an eternity to extract his left boot from under the corpse, and finally he was moving again down the tunnel, but something was happening to his vision. He was confused and could hear nothing but the high whistle of the grenade's explosion still reverberating in his ear, drowning all other noises.

Another shaft of moonlight—blurred—and a sparkler, like the kind he'd waved around as a kid. He stopped, shook his head as if this might clear it, and tried to replace the .45 in the left holster until he realized that it was the right holster he needed. Shoving the flashlight in his left pocket and leaning against the wall of the tunnel, he moved his hands as quickly as he could to put on the gas mask against the spitting phosphorus grenade that was now lighting up the tunnel in the dancing, ghostly light. He felt better, clearer-headed, and pulled the headband tight as he raced on through the white, choking cloud, a red-hot needle sensation in his left leg no doubt a fragment of phosphorus burning its way in. He could smell his flesh. Then the smell was gone and he knew that as long as he kept moving down the tunnel, tossing a few grenades back whenever he made a turn, he might just make it to an exit before they did. He felt the gas mask crumpling, like cellophane, and suddenly his feet were gone from under him, the rifle butt smashing bone. Everything stopped.

The reconnaissance patrol now under the command of Private Wezlinski, retreating, as they'd been ordered, after seeing the red flare fired by Freeman, were cut down on the ice, heavy mortar rounds exploding about them, sending great shards of ice-shrapnel whistling through the air, one of which decapitated Wezlinski as a radioman frantically begged air support, screaming that "Charlie" depots had been found by Freeman, who had obviously been too far away from them to return in time and so had fired the flare. Whether or not Freeman had been seen by the Chinese before or after he'd fired the flare and whether or not he'd been killed or captured by them was not known. The only thing anyone could be certain about was that Freeman had found the Chinese.

Even though the LORY—low radioactivity yield—atomic shells were on the way, however, it was by no means certain that they would stop the Chinese. If the Chinese had tunneled in, Seoul knew that with the radiation yield and explosive power of the atomic shells being far less than A-bombs, they would not necessarily thwart the attack—only ten shells being fired initially in an effort to convince the Chinese that if they did not stop using gas, the Americans, though poorly equipped insofar as CBW defenses were concerned, were prepared to escalate to full-scale A-shell attacks.

In Seoul HQ, Col. Jim Norton, his face reflecting the soft hues of the operations board, kept hearing Lin Biao: "So we lose a million or two?" He closed his eyes and prayed it would not escalate out of control—and prayed for the safety of Douglas Freeman.

The 122-millimeter Chinese shells ripping open the moonlit sky over the Yalu were "binaries." These consisted of two harmless liquid chemicals separated by a membrane that, upon rupturing during flight, allowed the two liquids to mix so that when the shells struck the American positions, a deadly aerosol of nerve gas was released.

The gas was not detected by any of the enormously expensive and advanced CBW "Kraut" detector wagons moving up to the Yalu, nor by any of the CAM/Sprites—small, remote-controlled helicopters equipped with laser altimeters and on-board chemical processors capable of detecting gas as close as one meter above ground. Instead the gas's presence was witnessed by a GI at Outpost Delta, who, after seeing all nine men in a section falling after the first explosions a hundred yards to his left, donned his cumbersome CBW suit and ran, or rather waddled, over and used the oldest detector of all, a strip of litmus paper stuck on the end of his knife. As he dragged it through the snow around the corpses, the paper changed color, from a navy blue to a salmon pink. Some of the bodies lay crumpled, arms outstretched, hands, more like claws, stiff, others looking as if they had been tearing at their chests in the final moments of paralytic asphyxiation. The remainder of the bodies were in the fetal position, faces buried in vomit.

The GI, as quickly as the cumbersome suit would allow, returned to Outpost Delta's bunker and informed the major, who in turn donned his CBW suit and went over to verify the GI's report as the Chinese artillery barrage, intermixed with shell flares, continued. As the major headed back, picking his way through craters that moments before had been an outlying network of trenches, the GI began vomiting uncontrollably, tearing at his suit, which, like tens of thousands of others, provided by the lowest bidder, failed to keep out the gas and became his tomb even as the major signaled to Seoul HQ that Delta was under nerve gas attack.

What he did not mention, because he did not know, was that in snow conditions, the dispersal of the gas was delayed more than normal, increasing its persistency and therefore making it even more deadly. The major got the call through to retaliate with atomic shells and died in a violent spasm of diarrhea and vomiting as he in turn was asphyxiated by the gas, only dimly hearing the first atomic shells of World War III whistling through the wintry night into the Chinese artillery positions across the Yalu.

From his tunnel position above the Yalu, General Kim, supreme commander of NKA forces, and his Chinese cohorts reported to Beijing that the Americans were using "nuclear" shells. This information, though encoded for transmission to Beijing, was picked up by Soviet satellite, and Chernko's Sino-Soviet KGB units, already knowing the Chinese code, informed Moscow.

The information convinced Suzlov that seeing Pandora's box had been opened, if, at the meeting that night, the Politburo and STAVKA agreed, he would order a first strike of nuclear, as well as chemical, weapons *in Europe* before the American-Asian policy could be adopted by NATO. And it would not only be atomic shells but missiles—for no other reason than that is what Soviet forces had most of. This, Suzlov told his aides, was a direct result of the cutback of conventional arms during Gorbachev's disastrous tenure, for such cutbacks had meant that without enough conventional weapons to stop NATO's advance, the use of chemical and nuclear weapons became inevitable if the Americans were to be defeated.

Cautious though he was, an *apparatchik* through and through, Suzlov also told his aides that if at the meeting the Politburo and STAVKA endorsed him and decided to go nuclear, he wouldn't pussyfoot like the Americans in Vietnam, who procrastinated—and who could have won the Vietnam War in a day had they had the *smelost'*—"balls"—to drop an A-bomb on Hanoi.

He, Suzlov, would go all out, and with the indisputable advantage his people had with nuclear bunker defenses, he would have the decisive edge.

CHAPTER FIFTY

RAY BRENTWOOD'S IX-44E chugged back into San Diego Harbor as the sun was sinking in a tangerine sky, the great towering silhouettes of the warships even more impressive than when Ray and his barge crew had left that morning. In the distance he could see the sleek, black lines of a fast frigate heading out to sea, her bow slicing the water like a knife, and the phosphorescence of her wake the only visible sign of her progress to war.

As they tied up, Ray took the sample bottle of the spill, as he had done more than a dozen times since his sludge-removal barge had been mopping up small spills here and there up the coast. While the Environmental Protection Agency in Washington wasn't overly concerned with "chicken-shit" spills, as one Washington official bluntly put it, EPA had a master data bank into which all oil companies were required to register their cargo's "fingerprints" in the form of having particular isotopes added to each cargo so that polluters could be identified. But EPA was loath to press either IMCO—the intergovernmental maritime consultative organization—or TOVALOP—the tanker owners' voluntary agreement on liability for oil pollution—to discipline their own members when the oil being spilled by enemy subs sinking Allied tankers was astronomically larger than that of local spills. The problem was that EPA hadn't taken into account what they later dubbed the NP, or "nagging power," of local residents up and down California's more affluent coastline who demanded the names of the offending companies and captains who had vented bilge oil at sea, so that they could be prosecuted to the full extent of the law.

And so it was that once a week, Ray Brentwood took his sample bottles of the spills his barge had sucked up to the harbor pollution control office, where he could clip the bottle into the analyzer, flick on the switch, and wait for any matchup with the EPA's master computer isotope list. When the matchups occurred, the terminal beeped, and like an accusing finger pointing at an overdue library book borrower, it kept up until it had stopped spitting out its printout of the matchup between sample and master list.

This day, however, two of the twelve samples would not match. Ray ran them again, with the same result. Next, he called EPA in Washington, though with the phone networks still in a mess from sabotage, it took him fifteen minutes to get through. Was it possible, he asked, that there was oil not "fingerprinted" with isotopes? The answer was a definite no—*all* refined oil and crude was fingerprinted by law, and supervised by government inspectors.

"Yes," answered Ray, "but was it possible that the government rules and regulations had been relaxed because of the war—to make it easier to move oil more quickly?"

"Hell, no." was the bureaucrat's answer. "Doesn't take any time at all to seed the cargo. A few drops and it's done. If you have two that aren't matching, there must be something wrong with your terminal. If you like, I'll authorize one of our electronic technicians out there to check it out. We've got a couple on the base."

"Yeah, I know them," Ray Brentwood answered. "Thanks."

The technician took ten minutes to tell him there was nothing wrong with the terminal. Ray ran the two samples again in the technician's presence, aware as he did so that the technician, thinking Ray couldn't see him, was staring at Ray's face in the kind of fascinated horror that children exhibited upon first seeing him.

"Still no friggin' matchup!" Ray snapped at the technician.

"Master data bank mightn't have all—"

"Yes it has!" said Ray just as grumpily as before. "Something's wrong."

"Well, it ain't that terminal, man. It's A-okay."

Ray took the two samples down to the privately run yard laboratories and asked the chemical lab technician there if he'd do him a favor and run them through the spectrometer. After what the navy brass had done to him in their inquiry about the *Blaine*, Ray was going to play it by the book, too, and nail the big brass of whatever warship had opened its bilges and caused the ruckus in La Jolla and environs.

The lab technician told him it was his coffee break.

"Look," said Ray, "I'm due back at the ship. I'm in a hurry." The technician couldn't suppress a smile. He'd heard about "Frankenstein's" boat. Not a bad guy, Brentwood, they said, but man, his face was a weapon—should send it into North Korea—get the bastards to surrender in no time.

"Okay," said the technician magnanimously. "Wouldn't want to delay your sailing. What are you on, destroyers?"

"Not at the moment," said Ray quietly. "How long will this take?"

"Whoa there. You just got here, mac. Five minutes. Can you wait that long?" He flashed a friendly grin. Ray nodded. Destroyers? Screw him.

"It's the sulfur content that'll tell us whether it's navy or civilian fuel," said the technician. "Tell you by the smell it's diesel."

"I *know* that," said Ray irritably. Destroyers. Smart-ass.

When the computer slave hooked up to the spectrometer, the printer started chattering and the technician, his hands thrust deep in the pockets of a scummy-looking, acid-holed lab coat, started rocking on his heels, announcing knowingly, "Yep! What'd I tell you? Dieseline. Let's see." He leaned closer. "Sulfur content coming—hmm. That's funny."

"What is?" asked Ray.

"Sulfur content," the technician answered.

"What about it?"

The technician had stopped rocking and was now frowning. It brought a twisted smile to Ray's face. So he was right after all—one of the navy's big ships had spewed out the oil in the sample. Or *both* samples. He'd get his own back.

"Holy Toledo!" the technician said, slipping in the second bottle. It, too, was from a diesel load, he told Ray.

"All right," said Ray. "You have a U.S. Navy master sheet here?"

The technician was running the sample again. "I don't need a U.S. master sheet," he said. He turned around and looked worriedly at Ray. "Captain, that's Baku—prime grade. We're looking at Russian oil here."

"How the hell—" began Ray.

"Submarine grade," said the technician. "This crap is from diesel subs. Two different lots."

"Can't be," said Ray Brentwood. "They couldn't get that close to our coast. Christ, even their nuclear jobs are noisier than ours—in their 'silent running' mode, you can still hear their pumps—come in like a heartbeat on the underwater hydrophones and—" Suddenly he stopped. "Listen—I've got to check something out, real fast. But you sit on this until I get back to you. Understand? If we're wrong about this, we'll get our butts kicked from here to Norfolk."

"What are you going to do?" asked the technician.

"Told you. Gotta sort something out first."

Ray Brentwood was walking quickly down along the docks, turning right at one of the submarine tenders toward where he'd seen five 688 *Los Angeles* attack-class subs tied up. Overhead in the fast-fading twilight, gulls screeched, and the only parts of the subs that were visible were the white depth numbers painted on the rudders, which served as perches for groups of brown, dimly silhouetted pelicans. Now, thought Ray, if only Robert were here instead of flitting around the Atlantic, he'd have the answer to his question. He tried to think back to the conversation he had had with Robert about the subs, but his older brother, like most submariners, had been tight-lipped about even the most mundane matters aboard a sub, and especially about where they went and what they did, the brotherhood of submariners in a nuclear age giving new meaning to the "Silent Service."

"Who goes there?" It was a marine guard, his M-16 looking straight at Ray Brentwood.

"Captain Ray Brentwood."

"Check his ID!" It was another marine approaching from the dark shadow of the sub's sail. Ray put his hand up to turn his ID tag, which had flipped over in the wind.

"Don't move!"

Ray mumbled. A flashlight blinded him. Instinctively he turned away from it.

"Jesus—!" the guard began. Then shifted the beam to the ID tag. "IX-44E," he called out to the other guard.

"Check the board!" said another voice, and now Ray was aware that it came from high up on the sub's sail, from the bridge, the officer of the watch a black dot against the rapidly darkening sky.

"Sir," called out one of the guards. "IX-44E is a sludge-removal barge—propelled. His ID number checks."

"Very well," said the OOD. "What do you want, Captain?"

"I want to ask a question about subs."

"They're very well guarded," said the OOD.

"So I see. Look—it's not classified as far as I know, but isn't it true that a nuclear sub's quieter than the old diesels—or any diesel for that matter?"

"Of course. Most of the time. Why?"

Ray answered him with a follow-up question. "What do you mean, 'most of the time'?"

"Well, cooling pumps on a nuclear sub are going all the time—have to because of the reactor. On a diesel you can shut the engines right down. Go on batteries. No pumps at all. No noise. Then a diesel's quieter than a nuclear."

Ray wasn't aware of saying thank you, though he did, but as he turned back along the pier, his pace increased. Born out of his spite, he now knew the answer to the navy's riddle of how the Russians were getting so close to the convoys, and he was now convinced they were close in off the West Coast—no doubt the East Coast as well. He was running flat out, heart thumping. The diesel boats were the key—the diesels, which in the nuclear age had been relegated to the museums. Hell, the United States no longer had any. But they could carry missiles as well as any nuclear-powered ship. And they were cheaper. He knew that much. For every SSN or Sea Wolf like the *Roosevelt*, you could build half a dozen diesels, equip them with snorkels. The only difference was speed and the time they could stay submerged. But if they were on battery power and shut down the engine, they could drift and you'd never hear them. If the war went nuclear in Europe and the Russians decided to launch, having subs close in to the American coast would have an enormous advantage and—

Breathless, he arrived in the San Diego base commander's office, sweat pouring unevenly from his mottled, burn-patch face, terrifying the Wave secretary on duty, who screamed, bringing two burly shore patrol men in from the duty room.

"I've—got—" Ray began, but had to stop to catch his breath. "I've got to see the base commander. At once—"

"Sure, buddy!" said the smaller, burlier of the two linebackers. "You just simmer down now and come with us."

"*Look!*" said Ray, jerking his arms, but they were locked in the shore patrol's grasp.

"Call the LT, will you, Sue?" said the smaller one. LT was the shore patrol's lingo for "loony truck." With the stress of this war, a lot of the guys and some of the women, too, just plain flipped their lids.

CHAPTER FIFTY-ONE

STANDING BACK TO front with him, Alexsandra felt her hair fall softly across Sergei's chest, her hands plying behind her, cupping him, squeezing him. He felt so hard, he could penetrate steel. Then she would relax her grip, kneading his groin with her clenched fists and turning to face him, would kiss him all over as they fell on the bed. Then suddenly she would sit upright, hair swinging back, her breasts thrusting, nipples engorged like dark cherries, her hands behind her again, pulling him slowly with mounting strength and squeezing it at the same time until he groaned and mumbled nonsensically in his pleasure. Suddenly she was off the bed, getting dressed—his favorite tease.

"Vernis!"—"Come back!"—he demanded, then pleaded.

"No!"

"Yes."

"No!"

"Sandra."

Slowly she advanced toward him.

"Now," he gasped. "I can't stand it any longer."

"It's long enough already," she giggled. She didn't love him, but he was fun. She was sure it had been his influence that had got her released from the KGB jail. If she worked on him, maybe—if God wished—her two remaining brothers, Alexander and Myshka, might be set free. It was a vain hope, she knew, but so long as there was any possibility, she must try—do anything if it would help. It meant that she had to pretend a lot: faking an orgasm for his manly pride when she had wanted to choke him. But after pretending so long, she had begun to enjoy it, and the rougher he was with her as he approached climax, the more she liked it. It helped to rationalize what she was doing. It was God's way, she decided, of helping her get through it.

"Sit on me!" he ordered. "Quickly, quickly!"

As she slid down upon him, the storm outside seemed to grow stronger, uncontrollable, the wind smacking the bare branches of the beech tree against the ancient windowpane, making a scratching noise like a cat trying to get in. His nostrils sucked in her smell as his hands and wrist muscles tensed, his body moving up and down beneath her, her breasts rising and falling faster and faster, her loins pressed hard against his sweat-slicked thighs until she, too, began moaning with pleasure.

Ray Brentwood asked the chief petty officer in charge of cells at the San Diego base, if he, Brentwood, wrote a note, would the petty officer deliver it to either the base commander or the base's director of naval intelligence as soon as possible.

The chief petty officer read it. "You sure about this, Captain?"

"Look, Chief, I'm not nuts. Bit too excited, I guess, when your guys picked me up. That's all. And I hope you're not nuts either, because if you don't get that to someone fast, they're gonna do a Pearl Harbor on you."

"What d'you mean?"

"I mean in forty-one there was a message in the hopper

warning Pearl of an impending Japanese attack—the day *before* it happened. But some jerk back in Washington decided to use Western Union instead of calling it through. I've got evidence here that there are at least two Russian subs close inshore, and I mean *close in*. Closer than anyone believed possible, because all we could think of was nuclear and—" He paused as the CPO, his jaw clenched, looking like he was grinding his molars, read Brentwood's message again. "Chief!" said Brentwood. "You deliver that now and you're going to be part of history. A hero. You don't deliver it and your name'll be shit in every textbook ever written about this war. Course, if you don't do anything about it, we'll all be dead, so there won't be any history for you to worry about anyway."

The chief looked at Brentwood, and then staggered him. "Hell, I can't take it anywhere. I can't leave my post. Hey——I'll use a walkie-talkie link to patrol. Get 'em down here to run it up for us."

Brentwood sat back on the hard cell mattress, letting his head roll against the cold brick. "You keep this up, Chief, and they'll make you an admiral."

The chief of naval intelligence for San Diego base was down in the cells fifteen minutes later. He listened to Brentwood and told the shore patrol to get the lab technician out of bed to verify it. "Drag him here if you have to."

When the patrol knocked on the technician's door, he had just convinced his wife to give him some "relief." He swore a lot when they barged in on him and told him he'd have to go back with them.

"Right now?" he asked incredulously. "Damn near midnight."

"My God!" said his wife. "What's he done?"

"Can't say, ma'am."

"Then you can't take him—if there's no charge."

"It's all right, Norma. I know what it's about."

"What? Tell me."

"Can't tell you, hon," said the technician, struggling to get into his pants and nearly falling. "It's classified."

"What's her name?" called Norma.

When they got him out to the Humvee, it was ten after midnight, and Norma was sure he was mixed up with some other woman. An admiral's wife. He was always telling her he needed "it" more than most men. Maybe she should have let him have his way more often. Lord—maybe it was *drugs*! She phoned her mother.

"What'd I tell you, Norma? I told you. He's a bum. But oh no—you knew better. He's a bum, Norma!"

On the other side of the world, Frank Shirer was flying as left wingman in a finger-four formation of four F-14 Tomcats out of Kapsan Air Base, thirty miles south of the Yalu. He was regretting he had broken one of the cardinal rules for combat pilots in not having a substantial breakfast before going up on the border patrol, but the problem was he had never been a breakfast man—early mornings not his forte. But normally he would have grabbed at least a continental: juice, toast, and coffee. It wasn't enough for a pilot who might have to go into a sustained high G-turn, and he hadn't slept well.

During the night he'd had dreams of the Russian fighters out of Vladivostok attacking the 747 in which he had flown Freeman to Korea. He was also a little nervous and almost regretted—heresy for a pilot—having accepted Freeman's offer of a few days of combat patrol to keep his hand in before flying the repaired 747 back to the States tomorrow. The skills of the fighter pilot never left you, but the sudden switch from the big 747 to a Tomcat was like going from a bus to a sports car, and the morning before, he'd been a little slow as the Tomcat leader's left wingman. He'd been only a fraction of a second late in a breakaway, but a fraction of a second could mean you were dead when you were flying over the "fence"—the Yalu. More and more MiG 29A's had been seen in Manchurian air space—riding range on the other side. And sometimes they looked identical to U.S. planes on the radar. Two F-15 Eagles and an F-16 had been "splashed" off the coast by fellow U.S. Navy fighters because IFF—identification friend or foe—had been made on radar alone.

As a result, the American rules of engagement now stated that all U.S. pilots could not engage before IFF had been established by "visual fix"—a radar blip insufficient to assume a Bogey, or unidentified aircraft, was in fact a "Judy"—an enemy plane. Even the normally swashbuckling Freeman, before he'd disappeared across the Yalu, had endorsed the rule, but the necessity of having to make a visual fix imposed a serious tactical disadvantage on the American pilots. It meant that the long-range missiles, such as the nine-mile-range infrared homing Sidewinder, which needed time—even though this was measured in milliseconds—to lock on to an enemy's exhaust or side heat patch, couldn't be used to anywhere near their full effectiveness. At shorter ranges, the missile could be evaded by the tight-turning MiGs before the Sidewinder had time to "lock on."

For this reason, the Sparrow missile was preferred. Ironically it had a longer range at twenty-four miles than the Sidewinder, but did not require heat exhaust to lock on and could be fired from any angle. But at 514 pounds, it was more than twice as heavy as the Sidewinder, and this meant fewer missiles could be carried.

"Bogeys two o'clock high!" It was the wingman—right side of the finger-four formation of Tomcats—the four blips coming out of the northwest behind and to the right as the Tomcats headed southwest over the Yalu. The blips were fourteen miles away. The Tomcats' leader had a choice to either break left, south, away from the Yalu into the U.S.- and-South-Korean-held North Korea, or to go north for a visible fix, with the possibility of engagement if the Bogeys turned out to be Judys. The Tomcats had already consumed half their fuel.

"Go for IFF," announced the Tomcat leader, and the F-14s turned tightly, pulling seven Gs, Shirer already feeling the effect of his heart literally distending under the pull of the G forces, wishing now more than ever that he'd had the toast. Behind him, his radar intercept officer had gone to "warning yellow, weapons hold" status, his active radar frantically bipping and the Northrop TCS—long-range television camera set—unable to identify the blips because of heavy cumulus, which the blips were now entering.

The four Tomcats had split into two combat pairs, Shirer still on his leader's left and back, covering him, the Tomcats' wings now coming in from the extended, fuel-conserving position to the tight V for greater speed at the cost of increasing fuel consumption. Shirer heard the Pratt and Whitney turbofans screaming as he and the leader went to afterburner.

"Bandits!" It was the leader's radar intercept officer, and now Shirer's RIO was telling him that from the computer-enhanced radar cross-section image, the Bogeys were in fact Russian fighters. "Fulcrums," he advised Shirer, "A's."

Shirer, still close to his leader, saw a puff of smoke, and the two Tomcats broke, leader to the right, Shirer to the left, the Soviet missile passing between them. The next instant Shirer's RIO was yelling, "Tally-ho one! Behind us, behind us!" telling Shirer a Fulcrum had been sighted penetrating their cone of vulnerability. Shirer went into a knife-edged turn and dropped, the Fulcrum passing over him and down, Shirer slowing, hoping to go into a "scissors," trying to reverse the situation, putting his Tomcat behind the Fulcrum.

"Master arm on," said Shirer, readying to fire a Sparrow.

"We're behind him, we're behind him!" called the RIO.

"Centering up the T! Centering up the dot!" said Shirer.

The Fulcrum, on afterburner, was already two miles ahead, still on the Tomcat's radar, the other Tomcats having broken up into individual dogfights with the remaining three Fulcrums.

"Fox One! Fox One!" Shirer announced, then felt the tug on the plane as the Sparrow missile streaked ahead, the Fulcrum now only 1.6 miles away.

"He's climbing!" said the RIO. Then suddenly, "He's gone." The RIO's voice was incredulous. "Shit! He's gone!" His tone was one of utter astonishment.

"Can't be!" said Shirer. "We had a lock on."

"Yeah—but he's gone, man."

Sergei Marchenko was in a near-vertical, eighty-two-degree climb, going "up the wall" on afterburner in the plane that even Western experts acknowledged had "no unnatural positions." After two seconds, he had climbed another two thousand feet.

Suddenly he reduced thrust to idle on the two eighteen-thousand-pound-thrust Tumanskys, bleeding off speed, the plane's attitude a hammerhead stall/slide in the vertical plane—the effect of this on the enemy's Doppler radar calculated to be one of utter confusion, for without relative speed measurement, no target would appear on the enemy plane's screen.

Shirer remembered the Russian maneuver, reduced thrust, went into a climb, broke cloud, and glimpsed the Fulcrum still above him sliding backward into his HUD sight. It was only for a fraction of a second. Shirer's thumb pushed the Vulcan button—the burst only a half second, but in that time, twenty-five of the machine gun's twenty-millimeter bullets hit the Fulcrum's spine, the burst finishing its run in the cockpit, the Fulcrum's Perspex exploding in whitish-green fragments. The Fulcrum kept sliding, tail first, its number nine in front of the box jet intake and the slogan "*Ubiytsa Yanki*"—"Yankee Killer"—seen only briefly before the fighter quickly went into an uncontrolled spin, the big slab tail fins a gray blur, obscured momentarily by the sudden opening of the cruciform braking chute. But now the plane was burning, and in another second the chute was a black smudge against the snow of the Yalu's foothills, the explosion as the Fulcrum hit, a silent orange blossom.

"Good kill! Good kill!" the RIO was shouting.

"Any pilot chute?" asked Shirer.

"Negative," confirmed his RIO. "No chute!"

"Great! Now I can go back to the Bus. By this time tomorrow night, I'll be heading back to Andrews."

The RIO was perplexed; the only "Bus" he knew about was the reentry-vehicle dispenser used on intercontinental ballistic missiles.

By now the four Tomcats were too far apart and their fuel too low after the afterburners' greedy consumption to regroup, and so they made their way individually back to Kapsan field south of the Yalu.

In Washington, President Mayne was sitting quietly behind the Oval Office desk as he and the four chiefs of staff, Security Adviser Schuman, and Press Secretary Trainor listened to the chief of naval operations.

"So, gentlemen," Mayne asked, the migrane that had threatened him thwarted not only by medication but by sheer will. "What to do?"

"Tell the Russians," said the CNO, Admiral Horton, "if they go nuclear, we'll fire everything we've got."

"Don't by silly!" said Mayne.

The admiral was stunned, as were the other chiefs of staff and press aide Paul Trainor, though Trainor, with long experience in front of the press, did not betray his surprise. Adviser Schuman, however, was not surprised and sat holding his cane, calmly gazing down at the plush carpet, observing the intricate design of the new great seal of the United States at war, the eagle's clutch of arrows in the right rather than the left claws.

"The president's correct," said Schuman. "You people were telling us only the other day, Admiral, that whatever their deficiencies, the Russians are infinitely better equipped to have at least a quarter of the population avail themselves of extensive nuclear shelters. We, however, are out to lunch as far as that's concerned, because, as you correctly pointed out, gentlemen, my learned colleagues in Congress have long accepted Mr. Sagan's view that a nuclear war is unwinnable. Never mind the limited radiation yield, for example, on our atomic shells, et cetera. Mr. 'Billions and Billions' and his disciples convinced us that civil defense was futile. Now we're paying the price for our gullibility on that score. And because of that, the only thing we can really threaten them with is our submarine-launched missiles. We have a few ICBMs operational in the Midwest, but communications are so generally fouled up because of continuing sabotage, we cannot depend on any realistic coordinated or widespread missile offense from our land-based silos or from SAC."

"Sir, I think—" began Allet.

"Oh, yes, yes," said Schuman, "you may get a few planes off—providing the SPETS cells in this country, who we already know have used surface-to-air Stinger missiles, don't bring them down as they take off. Besides, it will take only one or two air bursts and the resulting electromagnetic pulse would scramble whatever networks we have remaining. There's not enough sheathed wire in the country to prevent a wholesale screw-up."

Mayne had never heard Schuman use anything approaching foul language.

"No," continued Schuman morosely yet emphatically, using the tip of his cane like an exclamation point. "In the last analysis, we can really rely only on our submarines." He turned to the CNO. "Can we get a message to them about the Korean situation vis-à-vis the use of Chinese nerve gas and U.S.A.-shell retaliation, perhaps tempting the Soviets to go nuclear in Europe?"

Admiral Horton pointed out it would be difficult to raise all of the submarines—as even in the best of circumstances, there were problems with thermal inversions, atmospheric conditions, et cetera, though he conceded submarines would certainly be alert to any massive "nuclear engagement in progress." Air bursts above most targets, especially those on the seaboard such as New York and Boston, and in Europe above such vital ports as Portsmouth and Hamburg, would be picked up all over the world by some sub via the sound channel.

"Then," concluded a somber Schuman, "seeing as our civilian population is without shelters of any kind against an all-out exchange, the only option we'll have if things become unraveled is tit for tat. Instant retaliation—target for target.

The president nodded. They could hear the clock on the mantel above the fireplace. Finally it was Mayne who broke the silence. "Of course, if 'Merlin' succeeds, we might be off the hook—prevent Europe from turning into another Yalu."

The chiefs were split on this. The army thought that if the SAS could eliminate the Moscow leadership, it would certainly buy time. The navy and air force, however, were still worried about the IAL—"independent launch authority"—of Soviet submarines.

"Surely to God," said Mayne, "we must know where most of their subs are and so be ready to intercept any—"

"Most of their nukes, yes, sir," answered Horton. "That is, we can pretty well tell you the general areas where all the nuclear subs are but, the problem is that if this—" Exhausted, the admiral tried to think of the man's name, but the more he tried, the more it receded.

"Captain Ray Brentwood," said Trainor.

"Yes. Well, the problem is, if his hypothesis about two diesel-electrics being close in somewhere on the West Coast is correct, we could be in a lot of trouble. Now that we've managed to repair the severed hydrophone arrays on the East Coast, we've got the situation in hand in the Atlantic. Of course, that's where we've had our greatest concentration of ASW forces because of the NATO convoys. The problem in the Pacific is that they don't have to go through anything like the Greenland-Iceland-UK Gap, where we managed to sink a lot of the Russian subs early on.

"The assumption made by this Ray Brentwood, and I think he's correct, is that the two diesel-electrics unaccounted for probably came out of Vladivostok, snorkeling in bad weather, when it's hard to spot them, even by satellite, and when prop noise is difficult to pick up. Coming down from the Japanese Current into the southbound Californian Current, they'd be able to drift a ways and come in close on battery power. Their silent running, unlike that of the nukes, is really silent. At least with their nukes, our hydrophones can pick up the sound of the pumps."

"How big are these diesel-electrics?" asked the president.

"Assuming these are the ones whose signatures we had prewar but cannot account for now, we'd say they're probably converted Golf V–class diesel-electrics. Around twenty-seven hundred tons—three hundred and twenty-eight feet long. Carrying either one SS-N-20 or two SS-N-8 ICBMs and ten torpedoes. This Brentwood thinks they're probably carrying the two SS-N-8s—each warhead a reentry vehicle with seven hundred and fifty kilotons. Not very fast subs, compared to the nuclear boats—seventeen knots surface, twelve to fourteen submerged."

"But they can fire intercontinental ballistic missiles?"

"Yes, sir. This Brentwood in San Diego thought at first that the oil was accidentally discharged, as an enemy sub wouldn't deliberately leak oil. But now he seems to think it's the old Russian problem. Good at quantity—they made at least thirteen Golf-class subs that we know of. But they're not good at quality. That is, the leaks were probably from either poor design or lines squeezed by the pressure on the hull."

"You think we can find them, Admiral?"

The CNO exhaled slowly. "We can put everything in the area—saturate the coast with ASW. Drop hundreds of active sonar buoys, which will send out pulses, unlike our SOSUS arrays on the bottom. Should be able to get echoes. But we need it carefully coordinated, Mr. President. If we don't know exactly where all our ASW ships are at any moment, one of our ships could mistake an echo from one of our own for one of the Russian subs. One thing I would recommend, Mr. President, is that we shift as many mobile surface-to-air missiles from the midwestern states to the West Coast as possible. Fly them in if necessary on Galaxy transports."

"So that," interjected the president, "if either of these Soviet diesels, wherever they are, do fire, we stand a chance of intercepting them?"

"That's the general idea, sir, yes. But hopefully we can corner them before they get off any shots. If we find them, I'm sure we can sink them—their speed can't outrun us. I've already ordered a cluster of surface-to-air mobiles around San Diego, Bangor, Washington State, and Norfolk sub pens. Brentwood believes San Diego is the target, and I'd go for that. I mean, with their slow speed and limited battery power, they'd have to start up engines if they were to go further north to attack targets up there."

"If these diesel-electrics fire from close in, what's our response time? I mean how long would we have to intercept?"

"Response time would be just about zero, Mr. President—if they're going for targets like San Diego right on the seaboard."

"Has this Brentwood any suggestions?"

"Yes, sir. He wants overlapping Airborne patrols up and down the coast looking for diesel oil patches."

"Have you done it? Sounds like a good idea."

"They're on patrol now, sir," reported Air Force General Allet.

"Will they be able to spot anything at night?"

"Yes, sir—infrared and patch color distinguishers are aboard as well as MAD—magnetic anomaly detectors—and sonar buoys. We've also got the satellites on the job, but unless the subs are near the surface, emitting heat for thermal patches, the satellites are only of limited use in this case.''

''Now, gentlemen,'' said Mayne, ''I don't want any foul-ups here. From what you've told me, we need first-rate coordination between the navy, airborne ASW, and—''

''We're already working on that now, Mr. President.''

''What?'' Mayne's outburst was so sharp that Trainor thought the migraine must be winning the battle. But it was plain anger, straight from the heart. ''Now, don't you boys go jurisdictional on me. There isn't time to play bureaucratic parlor games about who's going to be cock of the walk. I would think this Brentwood is the man for the job. Seems to me he's made some pretty sound deductions so far. He's been in on the ground floor. What say we appoint him?''

There was an awkward silence, ended by Trainor. ''Ah, Mr. President? Captain Brentwood was the commander of the USS *Blaine*.''

Mayne nodded, readily remembering the ship, for it was the attack on her as well as the NKA forces pouring over the DMZ in Korea that had been the flash point that had started the whole war.

''Yes, yes, I know,'' he answered. ''Fished him out when some of his men were still aboard, as I recall. Suspected cowardice.''

''We can't say that for certain, Mr. President,'' began Admiral Horton, ''but I would advise against appointing someone who has been named 'an interested party' in the inquiry that followed.''

''But as I understood it, the evidence was circumstantial,'' replied Mayne. ''That is, he could have been helped, pushed overboard or whatever, by a member of the crew who had every right to do so if he felt the ship was going down.''

''Yes, sir—it could bear that interpretation.''

''Benefit of doubt, gentlemen,'' said Mayne. ''Besides, he followed this oil business with some diligence. I say give him a boat.''

The CNO flushed. Mayne's persistent use of ''boat'' instead of ''ship'' annoyed him intensely, particularly as he suspected that Mayne deliberately used it whenever he was being particularly dismissive of naval tradition.

''Give him a boat and put him in charge,'' said Mayne. ''He's Johnny-on-the-spot.''

The admiral wasn't agreeing or disagreeing, keeping his options open. ''I should point out, Mr. President, that if we were to do this, Brentwood couldn't retain his present rank, and it might send out an ambiguous message to—"

"Admiral!" The change in Mayne's tone was ice-cold. "As your commander in chief, I order you to assign coordination of this operation on the West Coast to Captain Brentwood and to assign him, *without delay*, command of the fastest, most up-to-date ASW ship afloat. Do you read me?"

"Yes, Mr. President."

"I want to know—by dispatch rider, if AT and T can't get this goddamn phone service back in shape—within fifteen minutes the name of the ship to which this Brentwood has been assigned. It's vital he have no bureaucratic hindrance whatsoever—so he'll have to be put in overall command of West Coast naval defense as well. Now, if this means slapping a few more gold rings on his sleeve, do it, and do so without delay. Make him an admiral if you have to." The president turned to Trainor. "Paul!"

"Yes, sir?"

"Have an executive order typed up to this effect immediately. I'll sign so the admiral here can take it with him. And I want it done in five minutes. Get Rosey onto it. She's the fastest."

"Yes, Mr. President."

"Then get me San Diego on the short-wave relay if you have to, and the admiral can inform the base commander there verbally."

"I can't use plain language on the phone, Mr. President," interjected the CNO. "I mean, if the Russians know what we're up to—"

"Have you a verbal code?" asked the president.

"Yes, sir. I can read out a letter-for-word code. Have you a Bible?"

"My glory, Admiral. Isn't that the most logical book the Russians would expect for a letter-to-word code?"

"We don't use the King James version, Mr. President. We use one of the modernized versions."

"Oh, all right," said Mayne. "In that case you're quite safe. No one'll understand it."

While they were waiting for typed authorization, Mayne told the chiefs, "One thing the British won't do is promote quickly in the field. Class system, you see." He paused. "By God, I hope we haven't lost Doug Freeman. Now, there's a general who'd promote in the field. Made a private a captain once in the Dortmund-Bielefeld pocket to get the job done."

* * *

The base commander's office in San Diego was in a flap. "Frankenstein"—he of IX-44E—had suddenly been propelled to no less than admiral.

"Bullshit!" roared the base commander, Adm. Roger D. Rutgers the Second. "Must be a code screw-up," he informed the Wave secretary.

"No, sir. We've had it confirmed."

"Well, I'll be—"

"Sir!" It was the Wave, trying frantically to signal with her eyes that someone was right behind her. "Ah, Admiral . . ." she spluttered. "Sir, this is Captain—I mean—"

"It's all right, Sue, calm yourself," said Rutgers as he saluted and, coming around from his desk, offered his congratulations to Ray Brentwood. Brentwood returned the salute, shook hands, relished it, and wasted no time with small talk. He had a list, a short one, which he presented to Rutgers. Point one—he wanted all commanders of ASW ships in port to report to his office immediately. Two—all ASW ships in port that were seaworthy were to be fully loaded and ready for sea by 0700, only a few hours away.

The base commander pointed out, "with all due respect," which Brentwood knew was without any respect at all, that the large number of civilian longshoremen involved in the loading of stores would have, by union regulations, to be given at least forty-eight hours written advance notice of any such change in the agreed-upon working hours.

"Admiral Rutgers," said Ray Brentwood, "under the power invested in me through the president's executive emergency war order 1347D-5, any longshoreman refusing to load American warships at any time will be shot under the conditions which apply to all alien and/or indigenous saboteurs. And if you don't have the ships loaded, I'll shoot *you*!"

The Wave was speechless.

"In all my years—" began Rutgers.

"Admiral Rutgers, if you don't do what I tell you and get those commanders to my office right now—none of us will have *any* years left."

"*Where,*" thundered Rutgers, barely under control, "*is* your office?"

It was the only time that Ray Brentwood had smiled since arriving in San Diego. "IX-44E."

"What the hell's IX—?" Rutgers asked Sue, so incensed,

he could barely speak. The Wave ran her finger quickly down the long list of auxiliary vessels. "It's—it's a barge, sir."

"A *what*?"

"Barge, sir. Sludge removal." she replied, frightened, adding timidly, "propelled."

"*Propelled!*"

They said Rutgers sounded like a sea lion bull in the San Diego Zoo.

CHAPTER FIFTY-TWO

THE CHIEF ENGINEER aboard the USS *Roosevelt* had managed, by raising more pressure in the lesser-damaged port ballast tanks, to force out more water. For a while, as the sub rose to just over two hundred feet below the ice roof of the surface, it seemed as if, with her "flaps down"—diving planes reversed in the vertical position, ready to "pick" the ice—survival was near at hand. But then she stopped rising, the damage sustained by the ballast tanks under the Alfa's attack too great to allow further lift.

The emotional roller coaster of depression after the near fatal miss by the Alfa's torpedoes, the belief that they were trapped, then the mounting excitement as the ship had slowly risen a little, and then the plunge back again into depression as she lay there, was almost too much to bear. But bear it they did, without histrionics or ill temper but quietly now and bravely, as if all the world were watching when they knew the world was not, that they were alone, each submariner's doubts and fears battened down in the watertight compartments of his soul.

Not one whined about the contaminated atmosphere they now breathed as a result of the radioactive water that had poured into the sub. Depending on where they were in the sub at the time, they had received between 250 and 480 rads, which, in the cold, undeniable statistics of radioactivity, meant that more than 50 percent of these men would die within weeks or months, depending on their individual metabolism. Those who'd received between 100 and 200 rads were already doomed to shorter life expectancy through longer-term cancer, and any children they might have would be subject to the risk of genetic defects, even if old "Bing," as they referred affectionately to Robert Brentwood, could perform the impossible and get them out of the sub within the next few hours. For some, given what they saw as the utter impossibility of Brentwood ever getting them out of it, it was as if the gods were merely playing with them for their sport, for while monitors showed that the steel hatch covers of the missile tubes were unaffected, the escape hatch covers remained jammed shut.

Robert Brentwood and the chief engineer, the pile of blueprints before them, turned pale gray in the reddened-out control room light, as they pored over the sub's intricate systems, Brentwood posing possibilities, the chief listening. But, confronted by the sheer logic of physics, the chief was forced to reject all the captain's proposals as unworkable due to some irreparable malfunction caused by the Alfa's attack, both acutely aware of the supreme irony, voiced disgustedly by the chief, that the only thing still in full working order was "Sherwood Forest" and its firing control system.

"Rifle's in fine working order, eh, Chief?" said Brentwood. "But the rifleman is down."

"That's about it." Behind them, Peter Zeldman kept moving from the red of Control to the blue light of the sonar, everyone in the ship knowing that after the explosions, both enemy air and sea vessels could be moving toward them to investigate. Zeldman stared at the fathometer, willing its recorder needle to move upward from two hundred feet. For one breathless moment he saw the needle registering 199, 198, 197, only to see it fall back to 203, the momentary rise due not to any increase in buoyancy in the sub's ballast tanks, as he'd hoped, but rather to a cold "updraft," or column of water rising locally because of differences in the sea's salinity.

"If I didn't know better," Zeldman told Sonar Operator Emerson, "I'd say some joker was up there trying to get us mad."

Emerson didn't reply. Despite the small cross he unabashedly wore about his neck, he rarely spoke about his religious beliefs, but he believed unreservedly in the goldfish-bowl view of God: that the Creator made the world, put us in to swim, and after that, it was up to the goldfish—that divine intervention came only at the beginning, and all else was a matter of accident in which only a person's will and courage could alter the outcome. If it was their fate to die, then they would all enter God's other domain in which judgment would be revealed. Sonarman Link, Emerson's colleague and backup on the shift, thought all religion "bullshit," and the two were the best of friends, their bond mutual tolerance for each other's "weird" beliefs, and their love, their passion, to be what they were—America's point men in the earth's largest domain.

"Any change in the ice growl?" asked Zeldman.

"Nothing, sir," replied Link, knowing that Zeldman's question was to verify Emerson's evaluation that there was no "singing"—significant sound amid the cacophony of ice growl, shrimp snapping, and other ocean noises.

In Control, the light from the reactor room lit up.

"Con?" acknowledged Brentwood.

"Captain, we have a minor steam leak."

"Can you contain it?" asked Brentwood calmly.

"No problem at the moment, sir."

"Very well," acknowledged Brentwood. "You in foil?" He was referring to the bright silver heat-reflecting suit with air-breathing hose attached, which was required by regulation for any repairs in the reactor room.

"Yes, sir."

"Keep me posted."

"Yes, Captain."

Brentwood turned back to the blueprints of the sub. "Enter it in the log, Pete."

"Yes, sir," replied Zeldman.

Brentwood stood up, ran his fingers through his hair, and, arms akimbo, rotated his torso to rid himself of the stiffness of having been hunched over the blueprints for so long. "Going aft to stretch my legs, Chief. You come up with anything, call me immediately."

"Aye, aye, sir."

What Brentwood meant beneath the mundane exchange was that it was time to "walk through"—to see how each department on the four levels of the sub was holding up. As he passed the galley, he could smell hamburgers frying. "Sliders, Cook?"

"Yes, sir."

"Suits me," said Brentwood easily. Farther on, he saw two stewards coming toward him from Sherwood Forest laden down with bags of onions and potatoes that had been strung up from the maze of pipes that surrounded the six missile tubes. Next, he passed a man coming up from the stern ballast area and noticed the sailor's yellow thermoluminescent dosimeter was missing from his belt. "Where's your TD, sailor?"

The man looked down guiltily, "Sorry sir—loosened my belt on the off shift and—"

"Go get it," said Brentwood, patting him on the shoulder and passing on into the cool, clean, polished smell of Sherwood Forest, the ventilators' fans like a running stream. It made no sense to him but, compared to the rest of the sub, in Sherwood Forest, for all its electronic wizardry, he had the same feeling of tranquillity that he had experienced as a boy in the woods of Washington State and Oregon.

Standing close together against the missiles' firing control panels were two technicians, the first checking the twenty-five rows of circuit indicator lights on one of the tall, blue-gray consoles, the other man checking the first man's every move, verifying the sequence. Another pair were checking the missile tubes' monitors, making sure the humidity and temperature in each of the six chocolate-brown missile tubes were within operational parameters.

As Robert walked down the starboard side, the big white numbers on the chocolate tubes indicating missiles one, three, and five passed him like slow tracer as he kept moving through the "forest" that took up a full third of the sub. His sense of frustration at not being able to get his men out of harm's way, unable to maneuver except for the two paltry five-knot-maximum props set in the after-ballast tanks, while the six multiwarhead missiles were safe, grew until he had to caution himself to calm down. If only they could get to the surface, rising fast enough to smash through sonar-identified thinner ice, they might stand some chance. But unless the sub could rise, the hope of getting the men out, airlifted off the ice to Spitzberg or south to Iceland or even west to Greenland, was just a dream. Realistically, however, Robert Brentwood knew their only prospects now were that the sub would in fact go deeper if any more leaks occurred, and each inch she fell increased the "taffy"—the effect of increased water pressure over her entire hull.

After reaching the reactor room and satisfying himself that the steam leak was in fact minor, he passed on to the engine room, noting along the way that some of the green rubberized tile on the walkway had curled at the edges. It was down here that some of the worst leaks had occurred before the pumps had got them under control. "You boys enjoy the dip?" he asked.

"Yes, sir," answered a ginger-headed young auxiliary room mechanic who looked to Robert Brentwood as if he must be no more than nineteen or twenty—about the same age as Rosemary's younger brother, whose bones now lay scattered somewhere on the bottom of the Atlantic. Brentwood saw the man's dosimeter had exceeded the two-hundred-rad mark, and the young man saw him notice but smiled good-naturedly before turning away, busying himself with the oil pressure gauges.

Robert Brentwood was so moved by the young mechanic's quiet bravery that as he headed back through Sherwood Forest, he took out a Kleenex, pretending to blow his nose, using the tissue as a cover for the overwhelming tears of pride and the sense of honor it gave him to command such men. Seeing another pair of missile technicians working the port-side monitors, he quipped lightheartedly, "Hope you boys aren't getting bored down here."

"No sir, Captain," answered one. "These D-5s are more temperamental. Humidity's—"

It came to him in a flash. He could have hugged the technician—name patch Sayers—except they would have labeled him as a Section-Eight. As it was, the two technicians saw Brentwood do something that no one had ever seen "Bing" do. He began running through the sub, the alternate numbers of the missiles on the port side—two, four, six,—flashing by him. Halfway along, he heard the soft gong: "Captain to Control. Captain to Control."

"How'd he know they were gonna call him?" asked Sayers.

"Don't ask me, man," replied his checker. "Sixth sense. Sub captain's got to have it, I hear."

"Bullshit! No way he could've—"

"Hey, man—watch it. You missed a step. Back up in the sequence."

As Brentwood entered Control, he was told by Zeldman they had a contact.

"Hostile?" asked Brentwood, catching his breath.

"Too far away as yet," answered Zeldman. "The estimate is fifty-five thousand yards. About thirty miles."

Brentwood had always made it a habit to be overly conservative when it came to estimates of contact distances, and decided to act as if the approaching submarine—as it certainly couldn't be a surface vessel—was closer to them.

"What's your guesstimate, Link?" Brentwood asked the other sonarman.

"Well, sir, it's a bit fuzzy, but that may be because some of our sensors were ruptured during the Alfa attack. But it's definitely coming towards—"

"He's gone," said Emerson. "Shut down his active."

All eyes in Control were on the monitor panels. Brentwood seemed as alarmed now as he had been excited when he entered Control.

"Very well," he said, the phrase, and his tone, gathering them all together. He gave orders for the emergency props to be extended from the belly of the sub. If they couldn't rise, they could at least turn *Roosevelt* to face the last-known bearing of the sonar contact, and try to defend head-on, rather than sitting like a sunken log, offering their flank. Next, he ordered all torpedo tubes loaded, advising the torpedo officer to be ready for "snapshot two, one," or informing him, as they were under possible attack, they might have to get a quick return shot away within forty seconds. During this time the torpedo crew would have to flood the tubes, open their caps, and maintain tandem communication with the Mark-118 firing control system.

"Either way, torpedo room," Brentwood advised, "I want you to load one SA tube, one PA tube, with short-range contact fuse fish."

"One tube starboard abaft with contact fish, one port abaft with contact fish," came the confirmation. "Short-range fuse."

"Man battle stations missile," ordered Brentwood, standing by the raised podium of the control room's attack center, his arms folded, the small of his back touching the brass rail that girded the search and the attack periscopes' housing. "Set condition one SQ." They were now on highest alert.

"Set condition one SQ. Aye aye, sir," repeated Zeldman, and upon seeing the various departments punching in "ready," he confirmed, "condition one SQ all set."

"Very well," answered Brentwood. "Neutral trim."

"In neutral trim now, sir."

"Very well. Prepare to spin." Several men in Control looked across at each other in alarm. "Stand by to flood tubes two, three, and four," ordered Brentwood, and they could hear the faint rushing of water filling the torpedo tubes. Tube one already contained the Mark-48 with contact fuse, the remaining three torpedoes now sliding forward from their rail-tracked dollies into the tubes, assuring that *Roosevelt* was now ready to fire at any enemy sub—if that's what the contact had been—which might try to run interference with the missile launch.

Inside Missile Control, the weapons officer was waiting anxiously for the order to complete "spin-up," entering the local orientating corrections into the missiles' computers so as to assure the best possible trajectories for the MARVed—maneuvering reentry vehicle—warheads. But as yet no targets had been given. Given their present location, there were any number Brentwood could choose under the U.S. policy of "counter force," that is, against military targets only, and not cities. It wasn't as if Brentwood didn't have enough to choose from; in fact, the nearest and most worthwhile targets would be the forty high-priority military bases clustered along the Kola Peninsula, but still the designation of targets had not come, and instead Brentwood requested "missile status report."

"Sir, the spin-up's not complete."

"Do as I say!" snapped Brentwood. "Prepare missiles for launch."

"Yes, sir. Preparing missiles for launch."

"Very well. Prepare for ripple fire."

"Yes, sir. Prepare for ripple fire."

All over the ship, men were moving to their firing positions within two seconds of the operator squeezing the yellow handle and the soft but persistent musical gong sounding, the ripple firing sequence they were readying for one that would eject missile six first, then missile one. This staggered sequence would offset starboard and port yawing when water would rush into the four-storied missile tubes after each 114,000-pound missile had passed through its blue asbestos phenolic dome. The dome would shatter first, its symmetrical destruction being achieved by small explosive charges under each dome a split second before the steam pressure expelled whichever missiles Brentwood would select.

"Sir," said Peter Zeldman, "we have no radio message to launch. Have you reason for 'independent authority to launch'?" It was the first and, as it would turn out, the last time Peter Zeldman would ever question an order by Robert Brentwood.

"Don't worry, Mr. Zeldman," Brentwood said, so all of

Control could hear. ''The missiles I select will not have their warheads armed.''

Zeldman exchanged a quick glance with the chief. Was Brentwood cracking up?

Like Zeldman and others, the weapons officer looked worried, too, and it wasn't missed by his assistant, who, with wire trailing from his headphones, was moving back and forth, head bent like a priest at prayer, along the narrow ''Blood Alley,'' the redded-out corridor of high computer banks, where he checked out each missile's status, verifying for the weapons officer that each of the six Trident D-5 missiles was ready to pass through its four prelaunch modes.

''Missiles ready,'' the weapons officer confirmed to Control.

''Very well,'' said Brentwood. ''Prepare for ripple fire.''

While the weapons officer, his forehead beaded with perspiration, waited for the designation of targets, in Control, Robert Brentwood, double-checking the computer screens that all missiles were, as he'd just been told verbally, ready for launch, held his key ready to click into the Mark-98 missile firing control system, the weapons officer waiting below, his black flexihose trailing snakelike behind him from the plastic red firing grip in his hand. His thumb was now on the transparent protector cap, ready to flip it up and depress the red button—six times in rapid succession—the moment Brentwood gave him the order.

''The ice!'' It was a hoarse whisper from the blood-colored face of the assistant weapons officer. ''If we fire—''

''Weapons officer,'' called Brentwood, his voice calm, resolute.

''Weapons officer. Sir?''

''Disarm missiles one and six. Stand by.''

The weapons officer hesitated, but only for a moment. ''Disarm missiles one and six. Yes, sir. Missiles disarmed.''

''Very well. Stand by.''

''What the hell—'' began the assistant WO.

''Be quiet!'' said the WO.

Brentwood turned toward Emerson. ''Sonar—any further contact?''

''No, sir.''

Brentwood knew that if it was a hostile, it would be in torpedo range within thirty minutes. In that moment he envied his brothers and sister, far away somewhere on dry land, solid ground beneath their feet.

* * *

High over the English Channel beneath the heavy throb of three Combat Talon IIIs, the fast upgraded versions of the Hercules, carrying the SAS's Sabre squadron to its mission, the occasional flashes of blue forked lightning illuminated the SAS troopers' blackened faces and their cold-weather khaki/green/white winter combat uniforms. The all-white SPETS overlays were to be used only after the attack, for as the RSM had no need to point out, the overlays would be dead give-aways "if they turn on the searchlights and fire parachute flares."

"Won't be any," said Aussie. "It's a surprise, remember?"

"*If* there are searchlights, et cetera," the RSM happily corrected himself as he walked, or rather shuffled, beneath his 110-pound pack, between the two rows of ten men each which formed David Brentwood's B Troop, the plane carrying A Troop a quarter mile ahead, that carrying C, the same distance behind.

"Wish he'd sit down," said Aussie. "Stop motherin' us. Givin' me the bloody pip!"

"He is conscientious," said Schwarzenegger.

"Hey, Dave," Aussie asked Brentwood, his voice rising above the sound of the engines' rolling thunder. "What d'you reckon? Think there'll be a reception party?"

"We know there will," put in Thelman. "SPETS—two companies."

"Aw," said the Aussie dismissively, "I don't mean them. Bastards'll be asleep time we make the big jump. Well past their bedtime. No, I mean the AA boys. Think they'll be onto us when we make the jump?"

"You're a cheery son of a bitch," said Thelman.

"Not talkin' to you, Thelma. Dave—whaddya reckon?"

"Possible," commented David, who, having been one of those who, picked at random, had had his gun jam during the dry runs through the "house," was now checking his Ingram MAC submachine gun, The nine-millimeter short weapon, which on a quick glance looked like an Uzi, its pistol grip doubling as the housing for a thirty-two-round magazine, had a barrel only half the length of the Uzi, with a folding stock and effective range of fifty meters. This was less than the Uzi's two-hundred-meter range, but in close-quarters "housecleaning," it was considered more than adequate by the SAS troops. And the Ingram's shorter range was more than compensated for by its overall weight of 1.6 kilograms, less than half that of an

Uzi. Besides, the SAS liked the American gun better because it produced a wider spray pattern—much preferred in general housecleaning than in the terrorist/hostage ops, when a wider spray was as likely to cut down a hostage as a terrorist. Above all, in an operation of this type, the American-made Ingram inculcated what the SAS liked best about the American disposition—the desire to get things done quickly—achieving a rate of fire of over eleven hundred rounds per minute, twice the number that the ubiquitous Uzi could deliver in the same time.

"Bad weather is in our favor going in," commented the RSM reassuringly. "Play merry hell with their radar, and no way they'll hear us over all this ruddy thunder. Anyway, these Talon II transports have more electronic countermeasures gear and infrared gear than you can shake a stick at. Besides, we're too high."

"How about the weather over the target?" asked Thelman.

"Clear, so the pilot tells me," answered the RSM. "Don't worry, lads. You're in luck."

"*'You're in luck!'* he says," commented Aussie laconically, throwing his head up, pushing his helmet back against the cargo net, and turning first to Thelman on his right, then Schwarzenegger to his left, and then back up at the RSM. "You going home then after we jump? Return flight, is it?"

"All right," said the RSM. "*We're* in luck. Suit you better?"

"Then, matey," said Aussie, suddenly producing a small indelible pencil, the flash of lightning reflected from the heavy cloud cover illuminating the bizarre contrast between his dark camouflage paint, green khaki uniform, and pink tongue. "Put your money where your mouth is. Come on, you blokes. I believe the sarge. Four to one says there's no reception committee."

"You're crazy!" said Thelman. "Goddamn nuttier than a fruitcake."

The RSM feigned disgust, but whatever else he was, the Aussie was an entertainer. And whether the men realized it or not, by being willing to take wagers about what kind of interference they might expect over the drop zone, the Australian and his outrageous obsession with gambling kept the others—eighteen, not counting the RSM, in Brentwood's troop—from dwelling on their own fears. Even the taciturn Brentwood, the RSM noticed, who had seemed unduly subdued, more so than most of his men and not a good sign in the man leading the troop, couldn't help but shake his head at the Australian's willingness to bet on anything. The RSM flicked the Aussie's indelible pencil. "Where the hell did you stash that?" he asked, for there didn't seem to be a spare centimeter in the 110-pound pack they were carrying.

The Aussie lifted his right magazine pouch, showing a piece of blackened sticking plaster which he'd used to attach the pencil. "All right—step up the ladder," the Aussie called out to them. "Who's game?"

"A quid there are no lights on us," said Cpl. "Choir" Williams, a stout Welshman of tough mining stock who, in addition to his standard troopers' load of eight of the SAS's own '"flash-bang" magnesium stun grenades, was also carrying three French light and disposable Arpac antitank launcher/missile packs.

Hopefully they wouldn't need them, but if they came up against Russian armor during their withdrawal, Rye wanted them to have something other than the normal heavy antitank weapons, given the fact that they were already loaded to the hilt with abseiling—grappling—equipment as well as ammunition and grenades.

"Hey," said Choir. "Are you marking my bet down then, Aussie?"

"Sorry, sport. A quid—hardly worth the trouble. I'm looking to retirement. Minimum bet ten quid—or you Yanks, twenty-five bucks. Aw—I'll be generous. Twenty bucks."

"Up yours!" said Williams. "With brass knobs on."

"Promise?" said Aussie.

"Twenty for me," said Schwarzenegger, "No reception committee."

"Okeydokey, Fritz, you're covered." With that, Lewis licked the indelible pencil and carefully entered the bet on the palm of his left hand.

"What if you lose your mitt?" said Thelman.

"Morbid, Thelma. Very morbid. I won't be losing anything."

The amber light came on and they heard the pilot's voice. "Twenty minutes to the drop zone."

"Right, lads!" said the RSM. "Final check."

David squeezed his canvas side holster until he could feel the Browning nine-millimeter's hard outline. At the same time his left hand, beneath his right, felt the light but strong Kevlar "Sportsman" crotch protector. He was sure that if he was going to be hit anywhere, it would be there. He thought of

Melissa and Stacy and let his memory of Lili evict them from his mind as he flipped up the cover on his compass watch, holding his arm up, the signal for everyone to synchronize. From now on, nine minutes to target, he, not the RSM, was in total command of Troop B.

CHAPTER FIFTY-THREE

PRESIDENT MAYNE'S IDEA of going to Camp David was, as his press aide Paul Trainor knew, militarily unwise. The shelter there wasn't as good as that below the White House, and it was farther from Andrews, where, in the event of a "nuclear exchange," the president would need to go to board NEACP—"Kneecap,"—the national emergency airborne command plane. But politically, the president going to Camp David was a smart ploy. All three evening news networks—despite the lead stories of deepening gloom about the possible escalation of the war in Europe because of "the Korean situation"—showed the president smiling, confident, even relaxed, waving, as he stepped aboard the presidential chopper on the south lawn, heading off to spend the weekend at Camp David. Another bevy of television reporters was on hand to watch him being piped aboard Camp David, it being a naval establishment—the cameras still showing Mayne smiling. Above all, from the moment he left the White House, alighted from the chopper, and entered the bulletproof limousine which soon eased to a stop in front of the Aspen Lodge, he conveyed the impression that the president and commander in chief of the United States had matters firmly in hand.

If things were bad, Mayne had never seen any point in making them seem worse—especially to the public. Accordingly he had insisted that the air force colonel who shadowed him as custodian of the "football"—the black vinyl briefcase containing the nuclear war codes, should it come to that—must not be in service uniform but rather in civvies and should not get out of the limousine until the press were well out of the way.

They had been in the lodge for only two minutes when the phone rang, CNO Admiral Horton informing the president that following the chemical weapons/A-shell "exchange" in Korea, two long-range E-6As—early-warning radar dome aircraft—had already been dispatched, one from the naval air station at Patuxent, Maryland, the other out of Reykjavik, Iceland. The planes were trying to make contact with two Hunter/Killer Sea Wolfs. Neither sub had "clocked in" to SACLANT either at Northwood, England, or Norfolk in the United States, and were presumed either sunk or in deep hiding, lying in wait for Soviet subs in the deeps between the spurs in the undersea mountains running off from the global spine of the Atlantic Ridge.

The plane out of Patuxent, Maryland was concentrating on the HUK *Vermont*'s last reported position; the E-6A out of Iceland was trailing its five-mile-long VLF wire antenna, attempting to contact the *Roosevelt,* which, following the sabotaging of the Wisconsin sub "signal farm," could not be reached and, it was thought, might be hiding somewhere near or in the Spitzbergen Trench.

Approaching the cyclone-fenced compound of Romeo 5A, one of the underground launch control silos in Wyoming, Melissa Lange had two shifts to go before she would take a week's holiday, and she was keen to complete the next twenty-four-hour-shift as efficiently as possible.

Looking smart in her striking blue uniform with red cravat, she scanned the slip of paper containing the day's entry code, placed it in the "burn" slot, where it became instant gray ash, then she entered the carpeted elevator, descending sixty feet.

After punching in the code, she waited for the eight-ton blast door to open. Inside, she saw that her crew partner, Shirley Cochrane, was already readying herself for the shift, pushing her long brunette hair up into a tight, rather severe bun so that it wouldn't get in the way of any of the silo's console switches. Melissa stepped out of the way of the two crew members who were coming off shift. Everything was cordial as usual. Cantankerous types weren't suited for "Ground Zero," "Bullseye," or "The First Good-bye," as the silos were unofficially referred to. You had to be able to get on with people. Of course, there was always the danger of someone becoming distressed because of personal pressures, such as that Melissa was undergoing, rethinking Rick Stacy's marriage proposal after he'd found her and Killerton having it off in the bungalow. Stacy had "forgiven" her, which made Melissa madder than if he'd gone berserk. It was supposed to be nobler on his part, she guessed, showing how "controlled," how "civilized," he was—the kind of cool that had got his promotion to SAC headquarters down in Omaha. But his lack of anger angered her and made her feel even guiltier for the sudden, uncontrollable passion she'd given way to as "Killerton" had wordlessly stridden over from where he'd been fixing the leak, switched off the TV, and quite literally lifted her off her feet, holding her hard up against the bungalow wall, she trying to fight him off until the moment she felt him penetrating her and she yielded—telling herself it was rape, that she had no option. Yet only seconds later, she gasped with sheer pleasure, urging him on. For several moments at a time, he'd pause, fondling her breasts, suckling them with a tenderness so at odds with the brutal fullness of his entry.

Despite the guilt that at times would sweep over her in drowning waves, Melissa was confident she could keep the lid on any personal pressures during the twenty-four-hour shift. If you didn't, you'd be on report—and if you ever did "freak out," your partner's side arm would take care of it.

As Romeo 5A's other shift handed over the two keys, Melissa tried to put Rick out of her mind. The green strategic alert light was already on, and her concentration would have to be total when she and her partner went through all the checks and double safety procedures. For every minute of the twenty-four-hour shift, there was the ever-present probability that one of the sixteen million possible war-order codes might well require them to launch Romeo's cluster of ten ICBMs. Each of the ten missiles carried a three-warhead load of multiple independently targeted reentry vehicles or MIRVs. And each of the thirty warheads carried 335 kilotons. This meant that each of the thirty missiles from the Romeo silo cluster alone carried over twenty-two times the explosive power of the atomic bomb dropped on Hiroshima.

During a newsbreak on ABC, a reporter revealed that the military officer usually carrying the "football" had been in civilian clothes—fueling speculation that the change from military uniform to civvies signaled not a lessening of the world war tension but rather an attempt by the president to *downplay* an escalating crisis.

In response, press secretary Trainor stated there was "no special significance in this," that "as you know, the president doesn't stand on ceremony."

No one believed him.

Over seven hundred miles southwest of Romeo complex, Rick Stacy, in Omaha, Nebraska, was en route to his monitor station, walking through the unimposing front office of SAC HQ.

Pausing to brush the snow off his fur-lined blue parka before passing the bust of General Curtis LeMay, Stacy waited as two bereted guards checked his ID, and only then escorted him down through the "no lone zone," deep underground to the bank of TV monitors and consoles below SAC's command balcony. Here Gen. Walter G. Carlisle sat in a dark, stained leather chair by the yellow phone with which he could order a massive SAC B-1 bomber attack, each aircraft carrying twenty-four ALCMs, each of the air launch cruise missiles dropping from the B-1s' hard points armed with a two-hundred-kiloton warhead. SAC's readiness, however, had been put in some doubt because of the base's vulnerability to electromagnetic pulse in the event of a nuclear air burst above them. For this reason alone, the old prestige of SAC being the foremost defense arm of the United States had long since passed to the submarine fleet. It wasn't only SAC HQ that would suffer an air burst "wipe-out" of all the electronics, including much of the vaunted sheathed circuits for hundreds of miles around. Soviet air bursts could also sever the vital connection to NORAD control deep in Colorado's Cheyenne Mountain.

Stacy and all other operators on duty in SAC had heard of the nerve gas/atomic shell exchanges in Korea and were especially alert. Their readiness was not evidenced in any kind of frenetic activity but, ironically, in a lower-keyed, gentler, and well-mannered approach. It was as if these "electronic warriors," as General Carlisle had called them, were very conscious of being alive at a historic moment in the nation's history as they studiously watched and monitored the six big screens in the soft blue light.

Stacy liked the whole ambience of the place, particularly the smell of Command Center. Apart from its generally calming atmosphere, it always had the pleasant odor of the old movie theaters he remembered as a kid—a polished leather upholstery smell. Normally staffed by eleven men situated beneath the balcony, SAC now had fifteen working the consoles. As Stacy took his position, message lights began streaming in on the blue screen beneath the big clocks marked "Omaha," "Zulu," "Washington," and "Moscow." The message informed them that communications were temporarily down in the Aleutians. General Carlisle did not issue any orders but waited calmly for the explanation. Was it atmospheric in nature or some kind of enemy jamming? Within five seconds the reason given was "ionospheric anomalies." Carlisle asked one of the operators for the computed position of "Looking Glass," the SAC battle command plane. It was reported to be at twenty-three thousand feet above Utah. Carlisle ordered it higher, twenty-six thousand feet, to hopefully get it out of the atmospheric interference.

Stacy was thinking about Melissa. He hoped they could work it out. He took a strange comfort knowing that if they couldn't resolve their problems and she refused to marry him, he would in any case stay on in SAC's HQ, the prime target of the Soviets in any nuclear war, more important even than Washington or New York, because it was a nerve center of America's retaliatory capability. If he died, she'd be sorry. He knew it was childish, but nevertheless it made him feel heroic. More lights signaled a new incoming message.

In Romeo 5A, Melissa and Shirley, checking procedures, were interrupted by incoming letter-for-letter code in groups of five. Both of them buckled up in their high-backed, red-upholstered chairs and slid forward on the glide rails.

"Hands on keys," ordered Melissa. "Key them on my mark." "Three—two—one—mark!" Both she and Shirley Cochrane watched the long white second hand sweep around to 2105 hours.

"Light on," confirmed Shirley. "Light off."

Another ten seconds passed.

"Hands on keys," instructed Melissa.

"Hands on keys," came Cochrane's confirmation.

"Initiate on my mark," said Melissa. "Five, four, three, two, one. Now. I'll watch the clock."

"I've got the light," said Shirley. "Light on. Light off."

"Release key," ordered Melissa.

"Key released."

Now they waited, their one-crew key-turn having initiated only one vote in the launch process. They needed another which would take the litany further. Melissa prayed it was another drill, waiting for the ILC—inhibit launch command—to be activated instead of the word/numeral/word sequence that would give them a "valid" message, taking them closer to "The First Good-bye."

CHAPTER FIFTY-FOUR

"YOU STILL HAVE a contact, Sonar?" asked Robert Brentwood.

"No, sir. He's still hiding in the ice scatter or he's gone away."

"Very well. Angle on the bow?"

"Sixteen degrees, sir," answered Zeldman.

"Very well. Contact fuse torpedo in tube one ready?"

"Contact fuse torpedo in tube one ready, sir."

"Angle on the bow?"

"Sixteen degrees, sir."

"Very well." It would mean that with the sub at two hundred feet below the ice roof, the contact-fused Mark-48 torpedo, leaving it at fifty-four miles per hour, should hit the ice roof several hundred yards away at plus or minus six seconds.

"Fire contact fish."

"Contact fish away." There was only a slight tremor through the sub. In five seconds Emerson and Link turned down the volume, having no intention of being deafened for life. The explosion was loud enough, the sub trembling while the preparation for the missile firing sequence continued.

"Torpedo room, you all ready to go?"

"Yes, sir."

"Sonar, I want you to send out active radar bursts to the surface, ahead of the ship."

The ping of the active mode and the hollow, almost singsong sound of the return echo could be heard by all in Control, and

Emerson and Link could see the "fragged" or fragmented echoes, the middle of the arcs missing or segmented as the echo returned. It told the sonar operators that the sound from the active pulse was not returning in the middle of the band, telling them an enormous hole, hundreds of yards across, had been blown in the ice, the segmentation of the return echoes indicating that some surface ice was floating back into the hole blown out by the torpedo.

The *Roosevelt*'s missile tubes were now open, water rushing in through the narrow spaces between each of the six 114,000-pound D-5 missiles and the elastomeric shock absorber liners that would help stabilize trajectory.

"Sonar to control," came Emerson's voice. "Contact! Bearing two-seven-niner. Distance fifteen thousand yards. Speed thirty knots." It was approximately nineteen miles away. Twelve minutes.

"Con to sonar," said Brentwood. "I hear you." Next he called missile fire control.

"Weapons officer here, sir."

"I want warheads deactivated. I say again, deactivate warhead-arming circuit. Enough gas/steam to clear interface."

He heard the confirmation from the weapons officer. If there was alarm in Zeldman's or anyone else's mind, they did not show it. Everyone was too busy.

"Sonar, sir. Contact confirmed hostile by nature of sound. I say again, *hostile*!"

Robert Brentwood didn't hesitate. He ordered, "Firing point procedures . . ." convinced that it was more than likely that the hostile, whether it previously intended to or not, would now certainly fire its torpedoes within range, interpreting the sound of *Roosevelt*'s icebreaking torpedo as an attack upon it.

If and when the hostile did this, Brentwood determined he would fire four of his Mark-48 wire-guided homing torpedoes at the hostile, hoping to "triangulate" him so that no matter which way he turned, *Roosevelt* would get him. Unless he got *Roosevelt* first.

CHAPTER FIFTY-FIVE

IN THE THREE SAS transports high above the cloud cover, the red "get ready" light came on.

"Stand up!" ordered the jump masters. "Secure oxygen masks. Adjust IR."

Even without the infrared goggles, the troops could see flashes of light, not from the storm, which they were now well clear of, but from the man-made storm of antiaircraft missile and gunfire opening up on the lower-level diversionary F-111—fighter bomber—attack that was under way on the Likhachev Works and the factories beyond. Over Moscow itself, a rain of Allied propaganda leaflets drifted down with the flakes of snow, the people rushing out of their homes, occasionally risking the wrath of the *upolnomochenny vozdushnoy okhrany*—"air raid blackout wardens"—in order to collect the propaganda leaflets. These were prized by the civilian population, whose shortage of toilet paper was the most acute in years—so much so that children fought over the leaflets, not only for their families but in order to sell the letter-sized leaflets for several kopecks, many customers preferring the smooth, albeit print-covered, surface of the leaflets to the coarse *nazhdachnaya bumaga*—"sandpaper"—of the severely rationed Soviet-issue toilet paper.

In the cockpit of the lead transport carrying Laylor's Troop A, the navigator was watching the flicking green bar lines of his computer square moving closer together over the approaching drop zone. He pushed the magnifier button and the lines spread out again to the periphery of the screen. The square looked much larger now but was in fact covering the smaller area of the drop zone and taking into account wind speed and direction, temperature, and humidity in order to allow the troops the best possible chance of landing, not simply in the drop zone of the Kremlin's sixty-three acres but within the bull's-eye of the thirty-acre triangle that formed the northernmost corner.

On the left-hand side of the infrared screen, the copilot could see the long, brutish outline of the arsenal across from the COM, the Council of Ministers, on the eastern—right-hand—side of the screen. The partially treed and opened section, in between them, the designated drop zone. To the south lay the spires of Assumption Cathedral, the Kremlin Palace, and the Moscow River a quarter mile farther south.

In the cockpit the navigator saw the infrared square screen closing on the rough triangular shape. "Now," he said. The pilot acknowledged and behind the flight deck the red light went to green and the eighty SAS troopers fell, black starfish into the night.

For all their practice, the blast of freezing air always came as a shock, the cold hitting their faces with the force of a blow, screaming about their oxygen masks, infrared goggles, and huge backpacks like a wild banshee, each man seeing the others in his troop clearly as white shapes moving against the gray smear of cloud cover ten thousand feet below, as clearly as they spotted the Ping-Pong-ball-sized blots of whitish light to the southeast as reddish-orange bomb blasts ran in strings of explosions, their sound unheard until several seconds later.

The odds were only one in over four million, but a trooper in David Brentwood's stick of twenty, struck in the chest by either a stray machine gun bullet or shrapnel from the air battle miles away, went limp, going into a tumble. Through Brentwood's infrared goggles, the blood sucked out of the dead trooper looked like the spiraling vortex of a tornado. Then the wounded man's weapon load, probably the nine-millimeter shorts, began popping off.

David knew the sound wouldn't be heard, as they were still too high, but if the man's automatic altimeter-release chute controls were damaged, the chute wouldn't snap open at four thousand feet and the man would hit the ground before any of the remaining fifty-nine troopers. David "humped" his back and went into a right-hand downward slide to catch up with him. It was a move sky divers used to form hand-holding circles, but not under the weight of a 110-plus-pound pack, and with the hard buffeting of the Arctic-born air further increased by the corrugated-road like concussions of air caused by the multiple *ack-ack* explosions away to the southeast.

David saw a white blur through his infrared goggles—

another trooper moving in from the other side toward the tumbling man. The white infrared blur was broken by a black patch that David recognized was the bump of the man's colder backpack. Now, at fifteen thousand, both men closing in on him, the wounded man's body kept plummeting, uncontrolled, when, in a move that David right there and then knew was one of the neatest he'd ever seen, the other trooper closed against the tumbling man's body and they became one. The next moment David Brentwood was below them, having overshot, the trooper releasing the wounded man's emergency chute, still clinging to him. David Brentwood was swearing, the mumbled words resounding back at him inside his oxygen mask. The drill wasn't for the trooper to pull the man's chute but to stay with him until the four-thousand-foot level, for while there was lots of cloud cover, one chute opening *before* they all got to four thousand could be a sixty-second giveaway if the big chute was accidentally caught in one of the periodic searchlight sweeps from the city, the beams crisscrossing, bunching, and crisscrossing again, like enormous bunches of white celery, off to the southeast. Thank God, thought David, they would have good cloud cover to six thousand, below which the last weather report said it would be clear.

But now, falling at over 130 feet a second, a glance at his wrist altimeter telling him he was at twelve thousand, with just under eight thousand—fifty-nine seconds—to go before all chutes would be pulled, David saw the would-be rescuer desperately trying to cut himself out of the tangle, but now falling out of starfish pattern and tumbling himself, dangling by one foot from a maze of twisted nylon. Two seconds later, David saw the wounded man's chute "thin" to a Roman candle and lost sight of both of them. Suddenly, frighteningly, everything was black. He had a sensation of hurtling into the stark vortex of some gigantic wind tunnel, his face mask hissing under the onslaught of granular snow, stinging his face and drumming off the IR goggles like hail on a metal roof.

Looking down for the blobs of infrared heat emission they said he should see coming up from the drop zone—particularly from the two domes on the Council of Ministers Building, the smaller one on the western side, the larger on the eastern—he saw nothing. Then suddenly, bursting out of the snow cloud, he could see the two blurred orbs and other traces of heat emission from the roofs of the Kremlin complex, though from the fuzz veiling the infrared, he could tell it was still snowing. On one hand, it would make spot-on landing difficult, even given the relatively large area between the buildings. On the other hand, the snowfall would soften the impact. The real key, however, was whether the SPETS guards would have any forewarning.

He glanced at the altimeter needle, saw it was forty-two hundred feet, a gust of wind pushing him hard left. Quickly he corrected, going into a right-hand drop, and before he was ready for it, he heard the whiplike crack of the chute opening above him, the sudden deceleration, so that now his descent seemed to be taking forever—and he felt that the whole of Moscow must be able to see them—all about him the white blurs of starfish flipping, changing into men. There was another crack, then another—a trooper so close to him that he had thought for a second it was the crack of rifle fire. He had no idea who the two men were who had gone down in the tumble. All he could hope was that the trooper who'd gone to help had freed himself from the chute foul-up and that the other had plummeted to earth either in the trees southward in the Taynitsky Garden or into the river itself—well away from the drop zone.

In fact, both men had come down in Red Square just to the north of St. Basil's, not far from the red-star-topped Spasskaya, or Savior's Gate. One of the two gate guards, hearing a snow-soft thud, moved forward, but unable to see very far in the falling snow and forbidden to leave his post, he rang for two other guards in the warming room beneath the gate's barbican to go and investigate, suspecting it might be a piece of equipment from the snowplow now working the square. The plow's half-slit yellow headlights were barely visible in the blackout as it worked to keep the square as clear as possible for the members of the Politburo and STAVKA for when they left the emergency meeting now under way in Premier Suzlov's office. The plow also had to keep the square clear for the twenty or so T-90 tanks parked in the lot behind the corner arsenal tower, should they ever be needed quickly in the square—loose, unpacked snow particularly annoying to the machine gunners, who, unlike the main gunner, did not have laser sights.

A minute later, one of the investigating guards pulled out his walkie-talkie. "*Parashyutisty!*"—"Paratroops!"—he yelled. "*Parashyutisty protivnika!*"—"Enemy paratroops!" The guards at the Spasskaya Gate alerted the KGB guards officer and the commander of the arsenal SPETS troops. Thirty seconds later, 345 men were pouring out of their barracks within the arsenal, quickly donning winter battle smocks, snatching arms from the racks, the general alarm whooping at all gates, all entrances and exits to the Fortress closing—SAS already landing in the area between the arsenal on the western side and the COM, a half dozen or so running forward from the old Tsar Apartments five hundred yards south, the snow roiling in beams of searchlights that began crisscrossing the sixty-three acres like enormous headlight beams sharply defined in the frozen, snow-thick air.

David Brentwood's MAC 11 was already spitting flame as he, with six other troopers, who he could see were also firing, came down in the large open area between the Council of Ministers on his right and the Church of the Twelve Apostles to the south. Suddenly his face was smacked violently to the left—there was a ripping, tearing sound on his mask, a flurry of some enormous bird, its talons into his neck as he hit the ground. Before he had time to realize it had been one of the Kremlin's goshawks, he heard a tinkle of broken glass somewhere behind him. A searchlight died. Next there was a stuttering burst of AK-47 fire, and David saw two of his troop, snow flicking up about, dead, but not before the SAS troopers from A Troop, landing on the broad, flat section of roof on the Palace of Congress, had killed four SPETS as the Russians emerged from the southern end of the arsenal, trying to make it to the trees in front of the COM. Another SPETS was shot, mistaken by a plainclothes KGB for one of the attacking Allied force.

But if the SPETS had moved fast and were in action within seconds, as became their elite status, then so had the SAS—all expertly trained, in Olympian condition, and superbly practiced in what to do and above all how to adapt with ingenuity as well as rapidity when confronted by a plan that David Brentwood recognized was off to a bad start. The SPETS had begun engaging them, albeit in poor visibility, before a good many of the SAS were even out of harness. But against losing the edge of complete surprise, Brentwood knew his men's adrenaline was up and racing in a way that that of men, however good, just hauled out of bed could not be.

"*Zdes!*"—"Over here!"—called Aussie in one of the Russian phrases. "*Zdes!*" he repeated to three SPETS making heavy going of it near a wind drift of snow as they cleared the end of the park between the arsenal and the COM, Aussie pumping his forearm in the Russian infantry signal for "hurry up." Hesitating for only a second, they turned toward him. When they were seven yards from the Australian, a flare changed night into day, but it was too late. In two quick bursts, Lewis felled them. Crouching low, running for the COM door and calling out to three members of Laylor's A Group and Choir Williams, like himself from B Group, to cover him, Lewis quickly pushed three balls of Play-Doh plastique from his left pouch against the lock of the big door, the ten-second-delay detonator-firing unit inserted like a small matchbox in putty. The searchlights were nearly all out now, easy targets for SAS men, especially those on the Palace of Congress roof.

"Clear!" called Aussie. Choir Williams and the three men from Laylor's group moved quickly to the protection of alcoves on either side of the door. Now there was a veritable rain of parachute flares fired by the Russians, brilliantly illuminating the yellow sides of the COM building, the trees fifty yards or so in front of them, and beyond, the roof of the arsenal, where a parachute had wrapped itself around a chimney, the SAS trooper crouched behind the chimney, raking the trees below. The dull thump of the plastique was followed by a tremendous crash as one of the doors buckled, its falling weight ripping out its hinges as it slid down the marble stairs into the snow, black, acrid-smelling smoke pouring out of the building, rising quickly, billowing into the snowy air like some abandoned locomotive, the echoing sound of AK-47 fire erupting from inside the building. Another two SAS men, using the explosion as cover, were sprinting through the knee-deep powder now, one of them David Brentwood, who, without so much as breaking his stride, went through the snow-curtained smoke, returning fire, shooting down the two guards, not SPETS, he noticed, who had been blasting away at the door with more panic than accuracy. Probably KGB auxiliaries.

Aussie had started to move into the building with Brentwood, but seeing a rush of six or seven SPETS, and these were not auxiliaries, dashing from the trees, he had stayed to provide covering fire for three men from Laylor's troop who were setting up the 5.56 light machine gun, which quickly cut down two of the SPETS, three more hitting the ground behind them, another two still charging full bore when Aussie brought one of them down in the final burst of his magazine. Choir Williams felled the remaining SPETS, or at least the one still advancing as Aussie, kneeling by the fallen door, quickly slipped another magazine into the MAC's handle housing.

"Hey!" It was Brentwood signaling him and Choir. "No time to play in the snow, Aussie. Let's go!"

"Cheeky bastard!" mumbled Aussie, covering Brentwood's

left flank, Choir Williams on the right, the three of them now in the foyer, the echoing bootsteps behind them those of Thelman and Schwarzenegger. Wordlessly, with no time to be relieved at having found only two men, and these obviously not SPETS, in the foyer, the five SAS men, Brentwood leading, began heading up the red-carpeted stairway as another half dozen or so SAS, some of these Cheek-Dawson's C Group, entered the foyer, quickly pairing off with the other three members in each of their SAS modules, several of them in Brentwood's troop down to three-man modules already, not counting the two he'd lost in the tumble drop. There was a firecracker tempo to the increased firing that was now coming from outside among the trees across from the COM, fire returned by Laylor's light machine-gun crews and other members of Cheek-Dawson's sapper troop, the air outside COM's ground floor zinging with marble chips knocked off by the small-arms fire.

Most of the SAS had now taken off their IR goggles, not so much because they were a dead giveaway for any SPETS who got close enough to see them through the almost zero visibility of the falling snow but rather because, while they indubitably conferred an advantage during the landing and had cost twenty-three SPETS their lives before they got more than ten feet beyond the arsenal entrance, the peripheral vision of the goggles was a hindrance on the ground and indeed could reflect and so draw fire beneath the intensely bright light of the flares.

"Sapper mod!" called out David.

"Here!" came an answer. "But there're only two of us, Lieutenant."

"Never mind," said David. "Do it!"

Within two minutes they had found the COM's main switchboard. Seven seconds later, the entire building was in darkness. David heard the whine of an elevator stopping abruptly. Outside, SPETS fire was increasing. In a way, it was reassuring—the T-90s had not yet entered the complex, the Russian commandos no doubt confident that three SPETS companies could easily deal with the SAS. Besides which, the tanks, whose brutish shapes David had glimpsed before touching down, couldn't do much at the moment—any cannon fire into the east wing as likely to kill Suzlov and his war cabinet as the SAS.

Moving quickly but cautiously up the staircase, David could smell the surprisingly heavy, musty smell of the huge Old World building, and for some inexplicable reason, it gave him a surge of confidence as he, Aussie, Thelman, Schwarzenegger, and Choir Williams moved from the second-floor level toward the third-floor staircase without opposition, the ubiquitous four-globed chandeliers along the hallways lifeless now, the main switchboard had been taken out in the same power cutoff that would prevent the war council from using the elevators. Some chandeliers began to shake, their crystals casting crazy-patterned shadows in the dim, brooding light of the emergency battery packs that had come on at the end of each of the long, narrow, red-carpeted hallways. David's target, which he could see clearly in his mind's eye, was on the third floor of the east wing. There, another hallway leading from the wing's hub would take him to Suzlov's office to the meeting where, as Allied intelligence told them, the decision would be made that could lead to a chemical/nuclear holocaust not only for NATO's forces but for all its noncombatants as well.

Brentwood glimpsed other SAS, a dozen or so, from Cheek-Dawson's C Troop totally ignoring Brentwood's troopers as they quickly went about their business, three men in each SAS module hurrying to place their charges on the Irish "J" beams and other supports, the fourth member of each module providing covering fire. The detonators were set for twenty minutes.

Outside, they could hear the chattering of an M-60 7.62-millimeter machine gun from one of Laylor's A Troop mobile fire parties who were holding off the SPETS while Brentwood's B Troop and Cheek-Dawson's C Troop kept moving up the COM stairwell. David heard a series of steady muffled thumps in the background: two of the SAS's lightweight 60.7-millimeter Esperanza commando mortars, which, as well as laying down several 1.43-kilogram smoke rounds in and about the arsenal, were also firing 1.4-kilogram high-explosive bombs with a fifty-meter damage radius. It was one slight edge that the SAS enjoyed, the SPETS understandably unwilling to lay mortar fire on their bosses in the COM.

Approaching the third floor, Schwarzenegger, Aussie Lewis, Thelman, and Choir Williams behind him, David heard the scream of an SAS man hit somewhere behind them, but not for one second did David look back. Suzlov's office was all he cared about—number six on the right side of the third floor's east wing, the mockup in the Hereford house as vivid to him as the first time they'd run through it. It was a long room, four or five times the size of a Western executive's office, with a highly polished light wooden floor, dark wood desk, and grape-red Persian carpets. To the right of the desk and its neat row of four ivory phones there would be high, scalloped and ruffled white curtains. Behind the desk, a Communist flag and a fifteen-foot-high beige panel between the window and the far door—a door that might connect to the next room. And above the door he would see the burnished brass emblem of the Soviet Union and, though it should be out by now, a large, multifaceted chandelier below which Suzlov and his "merry band," as Cheek-Dawson was wont to call them, would now be clustered behind elements of the elite guard, on station during Politburo/STAVKA meetings.

David heard a bumping, like a heavy ball, somewhere on the stairs above him. "Grenade!" he shouted, dropping to the stairs, firing the MAC into the darkness, the grenade's explosion a crimson flash, its shrapnel taking out a window and zinging against the high walls. In the light of the grenade he saw two figures above him and fired. They both dropped. His group, having paused for only a split second, was virtually untouched by the grenade as it bumped past them, exploding on the second-floor level.

At the top of the stairs David saw one of the four-bulb chandeliers reflecting light from an emergency battery lantern. He gave the lantern a burst and there was no light. He knelt to put in another clip—suddenly a door flew open along the hallway. David flattened, Thelman shot dead, taking the full impact of the SPETS' burst, which now stopped, snuffed out by Aussie's return fire. Schwarzenegger bent down by Thelman.

"Leave him!" shouted Brentwood. "Keep moving." He waved Aussie, Schwarzenegger, Choir, and another man, from B Group, forward. From outside came the approaching rotor slap of a Hind chopper, either bringing in reinforcements or possibly trying for a rooftop evacuation of Suzlov and his crew. The fire from the SPETS told Brentwood he wouldn't have time to play safe and clean out each room, but that they'd have to run a possible gauntlet straight through Suzlov's office. He was also wondering whether Laylor's troop had managed to fight off the determined SPETS attempt to break through the cordon of fire with which Laylor had secured the COM's northern entrance.

There was an enormous explosion, a shattering of glass, and a gust of desert-hot air, the Hind E disintegrating above the COM, sending down a golden liquid rain of gasoline and huge charred segments of what had been the chopper's engines falling down the side of the building, Laylor's M-60 machine guns now in a steady rip, their gunners using the light of the burning chopper to better rake the shapes that tried to make it from the old cannons and trees that flanked the arsenal across from the COM in what was now knee-high snow.

"Watch for more grenades!" Brentwood cautioned as his party split either side of the corridor that led to Suzlov's office about sixty feet away. The cacophony of sound was so deafening outside as Laylor's fire teams kept changing their position and the SPETS counteroffensive grew that Brentwood had to shout to be heard as he prepared them for the rush. Quite suddenly he realized he hadn't had time to be frightened.

Because of the noise, he didn't hear the sound of the opening door, second down on the left, but the light from the chopper lit up the SPETS the moment he'd opened the door to get his line of fire. Schwarzenegger's burst literally punched the Russian back into the room. They heard a high, terrified "Please!" and saw some kind of cloth being waved from the second office, and then, hands high above them, one woman in uniform, the other a civilian in a yellow dress, came scuttling out. David cursed, ordered Aussie and Williams to frisk and "tape" them. It was thirty seconds lost, but for a fraction of a second in that time, Brentwood's action delineated the fundamental difference between the two elite forces joined in battle. It was a microcosm, he realized, of what they were fighting about—about how the trainload of nurses and women like Lili and wounded men would be treated by one country as opposed to another. God knew the SAS were no angels, but David knew from bitter experience that a SPETS team would have simply blown the two women away.

He glanced at his watch. They had been in the COM seven minutes. They'd have to be out in another fifteen minutes, allowing three minutes at least to get well clear of the massive building before C Troop's charges blew. But there was no point in the building coming down until they could confirm that Suzlov and friends had been dealt with.

"Suzlov's office," he reminded the group, "sixth on the right." Suddenly the silence of the building was deafening, and for a moment all he could hear was the ringing in his ears caused by the fierce battle still raging outside, and through one of the shattered west windows he glimpsed small, dark figures of SAS men, four or five of them, who had landed on the Palace of Congress, three still pouring down deadly fire into the arsenal, one crumpled, writhing in the snow. To his right, David could hear the creaking of tanks in Red Square beyond the Kremlin's east wall as more than twenty or so T-90s positioned their 135-millimeter cannons and 12.70 machine guns for the maximum enfillade of fire, all the way from the Historical Museum at the top of the square down past St. Nicholas's Tower Gate to the island that was St. Basil's outside the walls, the variegated hues of the church's onion domes flickering in the light of the SPETS' flares. No doubt the entire Kremlin was surrounded now by armor. The cannons had laser-guided fire control, but aiming, David knew, would hardly be a problem for the Russian gunners. It would all be point-blank. If a 135-millimeter hit you, as Aussie had once told Williams in a cheery aside, there'd be nothing left to identify, the hydraulic punch and superheated shell exploding blood and bone, in effect cremating you on the spot.

As Schwarzenegger quickly finished frisking and taping the two women, the other man from Troop B joined him in covering Brentwood, who was now moving along the right wall of the corridor, quickly ducking across into what had been the office of the two secretaries to make sure it was clear before moving farther down the hall. As he did so, Schwarzenegger pushed the two secretaries back inside the office and moved ahead of Brentwood, taking the left-hand side of the hallway, followed by the new man from Troop B, with Choir Williams behind.

Williams, taking up the rear, could hear a squeaky sound, like unoiled carts. It was the sound of more tanks wheeling into position in the vast square. Choir realized that refusing to take up Aussie's bet about how many SAS would get out after the mission had probably been one of the better decisions of his life. Not that he'd get to spend what he'd saved.

David glanced back, seeing that Schwarzenegger, the new man from B Troop, and Williams were right behind him.

"Fritz," he whispered, motioning to the new man and Williams behind, "you three go forward. Aussie and I'll take rooms three and four, with you covering from halfway down." He indicated the two offices on the right, which, unlike the two on the left, still had their doors shut and so were unknown quantities. "Everybody joins for the party at number six. Got it? No grenades until six. Don't waste time on the doors. Automatic fire. Keep 'em or kill them inside. We haven't got time for housecleaning. Aussie and I'll zip open six. You two as backup. Ready?"

"Ja," said Schwarzenegger, he and the new man moving forward, Williams as tail gun Charlie. Making no attempt on three and four until they had covered Schwarzenegger and Co.'s advance along the left side, Brentwood and Aussie

waited till Schwarzenegger was halfway down, away from any direct line of fire from the two closed offices, before they opened up with angle fire, their nine-millimeters chopping through the Party's utilitarian plywood doors that had been used to segment the older, huger rooms of the tsar. Schwarzenegger and Williams were already "renovating" the third office on the left, just to make sure, but no one was in it. Coming out as quickly as they'd gone in, Schwarzenegger, the B trooper, and Williams moved farther down the hallway.

The explosion was like a whoof of gasoline, the hallway engulfed in smoke, Schwarzenegger's legs hitting the roof, falling amid the debris, the blood from his severed thighs spurting from them like hoses, the smell of his burned flesh mixing with the stringent afterfumes of the Astrolite, the liquid mine which, sprayed onto the ground or in this case on the red hall carpet, had been detonated by foot pressure. Schwarzenegger was still alive, barely—a grotesque dwarf slithering in his own blood and intestines that were oozing out of him. The moment the Astrolite—a mine of American invention which the SAS did not know the Russians possessed—had exploded, the door of the office before number six was flung open. Three SPETS, so big they completely blocked the hallway, stepped out and fired. But Aussie, with the long SAS hours of "nondistraction" training, had resisted the natural temptation to immediately look down at his wounded comrades and instead had gone for the target with a full burst—its backwash searing the hairs on his hands—the burst cutting down the three SPETS. The man who had been immediately behind Schwarzenegger, miraculously saved from the blast because of Schwarzenegger's taking the full impact of the mine, was now reeling back, already dead from one of the Russians' shots, the bullet having passed clean through him, clipping Choir Williams on the shoulder.

"Into the rooms!" Brentwood yelled back to Aussie as he fired a long burst to dissuade any more SPETS from coming out of number six as a blur of two or three of Cheek-Dawson's C Troop, having come up from the second level, now joined Lewis and Williams in the last office before number six.

"Bloody carpet was mined," David heard the Australian yelling out at more members of Troop C who were now reaching them from the second floor and about to run down the hallway. "Stay where you are!" Aussie warned. "Fucking carpet's pressure-triggered."

His MAC in his right hand as he backed into the cleaned-out

office now occupied by the Australian, Choir Williams, and the other men from Troop C, David, not putting down the MAC for a second and still watching the hall, reached across with his left hand, pulled out his Browning pistol from its holster, and shot what remained of Schwarzenegger through the heart.

"Let's go for six!" shouted Aussie. "One or two of us'll—"

"Negative!" said Brentwood. In Pyongyang some of Freeman's troops had found connecting doors between several of the offices in Mansudae Hall, and the NKA regulars had used the connecting doors to backtrack through the offices and bushwhack Americans in the hallways from behind. David decided that, given the short time remaining and the further delay any Astrolite explosion would cause, there was only one way—but he had to raise his voice loud enough to be heard over the battery fire alarms that were now screaming all through the hallway, their beams boiling with toxic smoke. Suddenly another fire alarm started screaming above them in the office. "Fish is done!" said Aussie—but no one laughed, all of them knowing they only had at most five minutes to do the job and get out of COM—one man, visibly in shock, shaking violently, unable to look at Schwarzenegger's remains.

"All right!" said David. "We haven't got time for musical chairs. C troopers—plastique! On the far wall—five of diamonds. If we start taking fire through the wall, hit the deck. Got it?"

"Yes, sir."

"Right! Go!" By this time, several more troopers from C Group had entered the room.

"Fucking traffic jam," said Aussie grimly.

"Ten-second delay!" David called out to the sappers, placing the charges in a three-foot square, the fifth lump of plastique in the middle, the detonator wires connecting. The sappers turned, signaling to one of their colleagues, who ran forward with another khaki vest load.

"Feels like brick," the sapper nearest the wall said quietly, quickly packing double the amount of plastique into the square.

"Blow us into the fucking river!" said Aussie, standing next to Brentwood ten feet back from the wall, their MACs at the ready, the newly arrived troopers from Group C making a line of seven SAS ready to charge through to number six the moment the wall blew—if it did.

"How many in all?" asked one of the troopers. "Besides Suzlov, I mean."

"Twenty-nine," said Brentwood. "Don't sweat it. There'll be plenty of targets."

"Plus SPETS," added Aussie. "They're the pricks I want."

"Calm down," Brentwood cautioned him. "Can't help 'em now, Aussie."

The Australian said nothing, knowing that Brentwood meant Schwarzenegger, Thelma, and the others with whom they'd shared the indissoluble bonds of the SAS.

"All set!" announced the corporal who'd directed setting the charges.

"Behind the desk!" ordered Brentwood, but there was no need. The long desk of dark, highly polished hardwood that reflected the flares streaking up from the tank columns outside was over on its side in seconds, the SAS men down behind it, chin straps undone lest the concussion lift their Kevlar helmets.

"On safety!" ordered Brentwood—a precautionary order against accidental discharge from weapons hit by falling debris. "Aussie, you—"

The room blurred, the sound like a cracking iceberg, an avalanche of plaster falling on them, the snap of one man's collarbone distinctly heard, followed by the shattering of the long room's chandelier, its fragments lacerating the portraits of Lenin, the Politburo, and KGB chief Chernko into thousands of pieces.

"Go!" shouted Brentwood, and within seconds after the blast, the line of seven SAS moved into the choking fog of dust, MACs erupting in an enfillade of orange-tongued fire, none of them knowing whether the wall had in fact been penetrated but taking no chances. As they ceased firing, their bodies still tense as compressed springs, they moved forward over the rubble.

Brentwood had prayed that a hole at least the size of the three-foot-wide pattern would allow them an attack point. In fact, almost the entire brick wall had disappeared, a great gaping hole appearing in the eerie light afforded by the burning Soviet flag behind the desk, a pile of rubble looking like the steaming remains of an earthquake. Then David Brentwood saw three shadows, a sparkle of light—the fire from AK-47s—before them. It was a brave attempt, but the three SPETS, with the loss of one of the C troopers, were dissected by the hail of SAS bullets. Then quite suddenly all was deathly quiet, except for the low moans of the SAS trooper whose broken collarbone made it impossible for him to move, two other troopers coming into the room, dragging him out after one of them had given him a shot of morphine in order to get him downstairs and out of the building as soon as possible.

For a reason no one could explain, the room's fire alarm was still screaming, though its light had gone out. Lewis reversed his Ingram, using the butt to silence it.

"Flashlight!" ordered Brentwood. "Two of you by the door—what's left of it."

"Struth!" said Aussie. "The bastards!"

"They're gone!" said one of the troopers, looking around disbelievingly at the rubble. Brentwood, blinking hard, eyes gritty with dust, spotted a shoe by itself over near the desk. Behind the desk, its dark teak split asunder by the explosion, he saw a man whose face and eyebrows were plaster-white, dead, eyes staring heavenward, a neat bullet hole midforehead, only a faint trickle of purplish blood made dark by the dust congealed on the lapel of his suit, where the blood had dripped from his chin. But no more bodies were found in the rubble.

"Who is it?" asked one of the troopers. "Suzlov?"

"Yes," answered David. "It's him."

"We've got three minutes," said the sapper corporal, his voice devoid of panic but insistent. "We'd better move, Lieutenant."

"Where the fuck to?" asked another, glancing out at all the tanks.

"All right," said David. "Red-green flares, Aussie. Out the west window over there. And watch the carpet." The red-green sequence would be the signal for the SAS troops to don the SPETS overlays and withdraw as best they might.

Aussie took his "Popsicle," so called because the red and green self-propelled signal flares were no bigger than two frozen juice sticks. As he clipped a new magazine into the grip housing of his MAC, the flare pack in his left hand, and moved toward one of the COM's west windows, one of the troopers covered him, shining the flashlight low, its beam a few inches above the carpet so they could see any indication of an Astrolite patch.

A few more men from C Troop now passed through the hole that only a minute or so before had been a solid brick wall, one of them Cheek-Dawson, with a tourniqueted bloody left arm in a strap sling, his Kevlar helmet split down the left side, and a hemorrhaging leg wound. "Come on, Lieutenant," he told Brentwood. "Time to go."

Brentwood was bending down, making absolutely sure, for the record, that Suzlov was dead, feeling for the slightest trace of a carotid pulse. "He's cold," he said.

"Let's go!" echoed another trooper nearby, as the Australian, crossing the carpeted hallway in two steps worthy of a danseur, made his way to the west window and fired the flares.

"Everybody out of the building!" ordered David. "Assumption Cathedral. *Now!*"

In less than a minute, even the wounded Cheek-Dawson had reached the ground floor, the order to "clear out" shouted and repeated down the stairwells.

As they hit the cold, dark air, the snow now falling more heavily, they glimpsed dark humps of bodies in the light of the SPETS' flares, some half-buried in the snowdrifts by the trees to their right, as they headed south for the short, desperate run to the cathedral near where several goshawks lay dead, having been caught in the crossfire.

"Where's Laylor?" asked David as the fourteen men—all that remained of his and Cheek-Dawson's forty troopers—headed for the Assumption's golden domes, which, capped with snow, formed a perfect symmetry.

"On his way," said one of the troopers.

As they ran, David suddenly called out to Cheek-Dawson, "Suzlov was cold."

"What the devil are you on about?"

"Stone bloody cold!" shouted David, adopting the Englishman's swear word to drive home the message, his own voice drowning now beneath the rattle of a machine gun opening up from the top floor of the arsenal two hundred yards behind them, red tracer arcing gracefully through the blizzard, kicking up snow about them.

"He wasn't killed by us," David explained. "They murdered him!"

Cheek-Dawson stumbled. David grabbed the Englishman's collar, propelling him forward toward the steps of the holy refuge. Cheek-Dawson was trying to fit it all together, but nothing *would* fit. With his arm hurting so badly, near to the point of him blacking out, only sheer will kept him going, that and Brentwood, who, he thought, must be as addled as he himself was from the unbelievable noise and shock of the short, fierce battle and now the thundering roar of the COM collapsing. All he could think of was that all the other Russian henchmen—General Marchenko, the KGB's Chernko, et cetera—must have gotten out via some tunnel from the COM, or possibly through some other secret exit that Western Intelligence hadn't twigged to.

CHAPTER FIFTY-SIX

STILL TOO HEAVY, unable to rise the two hundred feet to the surface, the USS *Roosevelt* was crawling at a mere four knots, provided by her twin slit-recessed props in her aft ballast tank, moving toward the area directly beneath the four-hundred-yard-diameter hole that her torpedoes had blown in the ice roof. At five knots, it would take her another nineteen minutes even with the assist of the local current before the broken echoes of her active sonar would tell her she was beneath the ice-free hole.

Within another half hour, however, the heat generated by her torpedo's explosion would be completely dissipated and the ice hole would be starting to crust and freeze over again. Meanwhile the enemy sub, adjudged "hostile by sound," was closing, having fired three torpedoes in response to the *Roosevelt*'s firing of one of its Mark-48 torpedoes to break open the ice. In response, Brentwood had launched the four Mark-48s toward the hostile and they were now running. Meanwhile, the men in "Missile Firing Control" remained as perplexed as the rest of the crew by the captain's earlier order, still in force, to "man battle stations missile" and to begin the missile firing procedure sequence. They had received *no* authorization to launch, and no one aboard had received any indication of conditions that would justify Brentwood exercising his IAL—independent authority to launch.

"Our fish closing . . ." reported Sonarman Emerson, watching the blips of one of the four M-48s from the *Roosevelt* moving toward one of the blips that had been fired from the "hostile."

* * *

"Wire disengaged," advised Emerson, informing Control that the *Roosevelt*'s torpedo was now in automatic homing mode. "Three thousand yards . . . two thousand to go . . . fifteen hundred . . . one thousand . . . veering . . . veering . . . enemy fish closing in . . ." The three blips on the sonar screen—two enemy, one from *Roosevelt*—merged, the luminescent dots becoming one, swelling, then gone from the screen. Emerson swung about excitedly to Link. "We got 'em . . we got—"

"Be quiet." It was Capt. Robert Brentwood, disturbingly calm to those in Control, his words more like an older man's dismissal of a younger, emotional wife, its implication—"Behave yourself"—startling to Zeldman, who was not only waiting anxiously for the three remaining 48s now about to go off the wire into automatic, but who was also envisaging him and Brentwood on the opposite sides of a court-martial over Brentwood's order to "man battle stations missile"—the order continuing the preparatory procedures dangerously close to the point of no return.

All Zeldman's instincts were against interfering, but was he, he wondered, permitting his and Brentwood's relationships with Rosemary and Georgina Spence to mislead him, holding him back from a higher responsibility to the crew if Brentwood could no longer—

Suddenly Brentwood, while simultaneously monitoring the verification sequences of Missile Control, Sonar, and the helmsman's report of the sub's painfully slow progress to the area directly beneath the hole, turned to Zeldman. "You heard the order to disarm?"

"Yes, sir," replied Zeldman, his anxiety increasing with Brentwood's apparent clairvoyance. "Problem is, sir, that you didn't order all missiles disarmed. We still have four with seven MARVs apiece. That's twenty-eight warheads, each of three hundred kilotons, sir."

"The new D-5 Tridents we took aboard at Holy Loch," cut in Brentwood, "are a hundred and fourteen thousand pounds each. The C-4 Tridents were sixty-five thousand pounds each."

Zeldman couldn't see it. Nor could anyone else in Control. So what if you fired a deactivated missile? The tube still filled with water. Besides, wasn't Brentwood telling him the D-5s, no higher at forty-four feet than the C-4s, which also rose two feet "proud" above the fairing of the forty-two-foot pressure hull, were almost *double* the C-4s' weight? But then, with Sonarman Emerson's voice telling them the second two Mark-

48s were closing in on the next hostile torpedo coming at them just over seven miles away at a depth of 1,215 feet, Zeldman now realized what Brentwood had over an hour before. Though the D-5s were almost twice as heavy as the C-4s that they had replaced, when the D-5s were released, the volume of water replacing them would be insufficient in weight to make up for their loss. It meant that rather than the sub being required to *increase* its buoyancy, by having to pump out more water, as it would had it been firing the lighter C-4 missile, in the case of the D-5, the volume of water pouring into the tube would weigh *less* than the missile it replaced. This in turn meant the sub would actually become *lighter* after a D-5 firing and would naturally rise, the damaged ballast tanks not needed.

Overhearing the conversation between Brentwood and the executive officer, Sonarman Link still didn't get it, but Emerson did, and it wiped away any umbrage Emerson had taken from Brentwood's curt injunction to be quiet. Old "Bing" Brentwood was clearly a genius. There was no doubt in Emerson's mind that if they survived the war, Robert Brentwood would become vice admiral in no time and probably, like JFK, would become president.

"Enemy torpedo destroyed!" announced Link matter-of-factly. "Hostile vessel still closing."

At the hostile's speed of forty-five miles per hour, it would be in very close range within eleven minutes, and by now its active radar would have confirmation that its target, the *Roosevelt*, was traveling at no more than five knots. The hostile hadn't fired any more torpedoes, suggesting to Brentwood that it was now going to rely on its superior speed to outmaneuver its slow target. The Hunter/Killer would try to stop him reaching the hole, unless *Roosevelt* could increase speed and so buy time. Brentwood unclipped the hand mike.

"Torpedo firing control. Stand by for snapshot two. One."

"Standing by for snapshot, sir."

"Very well. It'll come in a rush," added Brentwood. "Minimum range—one mile."

"Understood, sir. One mile."

"Just keep him away from me," intoned Brentwood.

"You give me the angle, sir," repeated Torpedo Control, "and we'll get 'im."

"Chief engineer?" called Brentwood.

"Sir?"

"Possible to turn our main prop at all?"

"Sir, it's bent to hell and gone—it'd shake the guts out of

her. Too much torque. In half an hour—maybe less—we'd have leaks popping up—"

"What can you give me?" Brentwood cut in. "*Maximum*, Chief?"

"Five and a half," said the chief resignedly but not liking it. "Maybe six with the help of the current, but we'll wake up every son of a bitch from here to the South Pole, Captain."

"We've already done that, Chief. Give it a burl."

"Hold on to your dentures," the chief advised. "It's gonna shake 'em loose."

It was an understatement, and as if that weren't enough, a report came in that not only was the oxygen generator down, but no attempts could be made to bleed oxygen from reserve bottles because of damage sustained to their valve heads and regulators.

"*Also*," the damage report seaman was shouting, above the bone-shuddering noise of the main prop, "oxygen and Freon gas scrubbers—closing down."

"Very well—light candles!" shouted Zeldman as Brentwood hooked back into missile firing control verification procedures.

"I hope," Brentwood yelled out to the weapons officer, "those tube liners can take a bit of vibration?"

"No sweat!" came the weapons officer's report, his voice loud over the intercom, practically blasting the headphones off Brentwood, starting a throbbing, hot, needlelike pain in his left ear. The prop, though bent only a few thousandths of an inch, was turning the pressure hull into what felt like an unbalanced spin dryer out of control, the torque creating mayhem in the kitchen, where hamburgers became airborne, coffee shot from pots in marble-sized globules, the crew hanging on to every hold bar, nook, and cranny they could find, the men in Control buckled up while the OOD gripped the back of the planesmen's chairs. But the chief, as chiefs were wont to do, lived up to his promise and delivered six knots, which together with the four knots of the emergency "bring it home" twin screws in the after ballast tank, were pushing *Roosevelt* at ten knots, chopping her ETA in the area beneath the hole from what was a minute ago twelve minutes to less than six, the burning of the perchoate candles mixing with the stench of sweat that was pouring out of the men. Emerson gave up on sonar echoes, the sub's din overwhelming its hydrophone sensors.

After three more minutes, Brentwood shouted orders to stop all engines in order to take an active sonar pulse. Emerson's screen showed the Hunter/Killer was now at eleven thousand yards.

"Any fish yet?" Brentwood asked Emerson.

"No, sir." Brentwood estimated the *Roosevelt* would have to stop in another three minutes if he was to engage any torpedoes the attacking sub might fire, leaving him only three minutes to retaliate and hopefully blow the HUK's torpedoes out of the water. He called for full speed ahead, and again they were assaulted by a kind of shaking none of them had ever known.

"Sir!" cried Emerson, alarming everyone who heard him. So ingrained were they with the idea of being quiet on the sub that despite the tremendous roaring of the ship itself, shouting in Control was a "noise short" violation, as alien and upsetting to them as any moral dilemma they could possibly imagine. Emerson was cupping his hands about his mouth. ". . . flow . . ."

Robert Brentwood leaned down, straining to hear Emerson's words, but it was no use. Suddenly Emerson leaned forward, tapping swiftly on the computer's keys, the screen reading, "Hole in ice has shifted—now above us."

Brentwood shouted again for "stop engines," someone shouting in the relative silence, "Thank Christ!"

"Where's the hostile, Emerson?" asked Zeldman.

"Bearing zero four one, sir. Speed forty knots." Brentwood gave the helmsman the order to bring about *Roosevelt*'s bow. On the screen they could see the Hunter/Killer had fired one more fish at sixty-nine hundred yards.

"Torpedo firing control. Stand by for snapshot two. One," ordered Brentwood. "Angle on the bow zero seven."

"Angle on the bow zero seven."

"Shoot when ready."

Final bearing and distance were given and Brentwood heard the firing control officer announcing, "Solution ready . . . weapons ready . . . ship ready . . . stand by! Shoot! Fire!"

Brentwood turned to Peter Zeldman. "Unravel the VLF. I want to be ready to receive the moment we surface."

The planesmen were so tense, the OOD told them to take a deep breath, that it'd be okay. They weren't comforted. This was definitely *not* by the book.

Brentwood told everyone to hang on, cautioning the crew that with the damage already sustained, they were unlikely to be able to slow her down much on the rise.

The Mark-98 missile firing control system was all systems

go, except for tube three, whose humidity control had gone haywire during the severe vibration.

Beneath the hum of the missile verification sequence, they could hear the steady roll of the VLF drum unwinding the antenna that would trail for over a thousand feet behind them if the hole in the ice was wide enough.

After the missile verification procedures and sequences were completed, Brentwood inserted his key to complete the circuit. The gas/steam generator ignited the small exhaust rocket at the base of number one tube. The sudden buildup of steam pressure from the rocket pushed the missile out of the tube, the blue protective membrane cap atop the tube shattering concentrically, the missile rising above the fairing of the pressure hull. The solid propellant of the first-stage booster ignited, the missile's needlelike aerospike, which would extend its range if necessary, slid out of the nose, the missile now clearing the surface of the ice-free hole, back-flooding beginning immediately, the weight of the sub decreasing, the sub rising as the first ICBM burst clear of water, its orange tail flattening momentarily on the sea-air interface, its feral roar heard in the sub, and soon seen on radar screens all over the world, including those in SAC and on the Kola Peninsula, rising high over the vast ice cap in as straight a trajectory as could be attained, then falling back, crashing immediately, clearly unarmed, onto the ice pack and disintegrating.

This was followed by the second missile, lightening the *Roosevelt* further and also viewed on the radar screens of both sides as, unarmed like the first, it went up and fell in like fashion, crashing harmlessly into the ice miles from the *Roosevelt*, which was now broaching. Bursting through the ice hole in the Arctic Sea, the sub was hidden in a frenzy of gossamer white, her bow angle at forty-five degrees, water streaming off her into the churning sea, made more turbulent by the fierce bubbling of the torpedoes exploding a half mile away, breaking the spine of a Rubis-class Hunter/Killer, a French nuclear sub that had attacked *Roosevelt* after failing to get either prop or cavitation matchup because of *Roosevelt*'s damaged prop, the French sonar operator, running blind with only sound to guide, having misidentified the American Sea Wolf as a Russian Alfa.

Within five minutes of the *Roosevelt*'s surfacing, her VLF aerial was receiving the message from the E-6A TACAMO aircraft out of Reykjavik, Iceland, informing her that limited chemical and nuclear war had broken out in Korea and that "nuclear engagement" might soon occur on the European front. With this in mind, the president had authorized retaliatory strikes should the Russians . . . The message broke off, then resumed a few seconds later as Murmansk launched three ICBMs on North American trajectories despite the fact that Murmansk HQ, as they had seen clearly on their radar screens and as the TACAMO aircraft had advised them, knew that the *Roosevelt*'s ICBMs had not gone into intercontinental trajectory, had clearly been disarmed, and had been tracked to destruction on the ice cap. The TACAMO aircraft also advised the *Roosevelt* there was reason to suspect the Soviet leadership was in "disarray," which, Zeldman pointed out, meant that no one knew who the hell was in charge of Moscow.

As suddenly as they had picked up the TACAMO message, it ended, the aircraft disappearing from *Roosevelt*'s sail-mounted radar. Instead, what they did pick up were the trajectories of the Russian ICBMs. Brentwood did not hesitate and ordered two of the remaining missiles, the mid pair—three and four—launched. Firing Control, however, could not get number three to launch, the tube's humidity control having gone haywire during the severe vibrations. Number four, however, was fired successfully, its launch flame buckling the fairings about the tube hatches, increasing the temperature inside the sub by ten degrees in less than four seconds.

Soon the second of its three-stage boosters took over, the missile streaking into the stratosphere, its seven 330-kiloton warheads independently targeted on seven of Kola Peninsula's major submarine and military bases. Even given a CEP—circular error probability—of plus or minus two thousand yards, the military targets, including the superhardened sub pens in Murmansk, chosen by Brentwood in retaliation for the Russian launch of the three SS-19 model 3s, were all certain to be destroyed.

Most of the *Roosevelt*'s crew had been evacuated to the ice through "charge-blown" exits through the hull. Their escape was so quick after the long, tension-filled hours behind them that for many, it had not yet sunk in. Yet leaving their submarine, despite the fact they had no choice, was an emotional affair. It was, *had been,* their home. They had made it so in a thousand little ways that, though conforming to regulation, permitted them to mark it with their singular and collective humanity. And now, in the gray darkness of the Arctic night, rugging up as best they could in their winter issue, they wondered if their fate on the ice cap would be any better than if they had gone down with the sub. For many submariners the sudden implosion of water was a better death than a lingering approximation of life.

It was a torpedoman's mate who, assigned as one of the lookouts while the rest of the crew—first those who had been wounded during the Alfa attack—were taken off, first noticed what he thought were "ice piles" jutting up on the endlessly depressing horizon. He was reinforced in this interpretation by the fact that the ice was moving in all about them and locking *Roosevelt* in. But after several minutes he realized that what he had thought were four dots, moving too low for a radar pickup, were heading ominously toward *Roosevelt*. Shivering in the Arctic cold, the bridge knuckled with ice, the torpedoman's mate was struck by the ultimate irony that the most powerful warship ever made now sat as helpless as a beached whale, the black dots no longer four but five.

CHAPTER FIFTY-SEVEN

AS THE RUSSIAN ICBMs, SS-19s, Model 3s—eighteen warheads in all—were being tracked on the big blue screens deep in Cheyenne Mountain, the mountain itself one of their targets, another being SAC HQ below Omaha, President Mayne stepped from the presidential helicopter at Andrews and boarded "Kneecap." The 425-ton, 331-foot-long national emergency airborne command post aircraft, or "Doomsday" plane—piloted by Maj. Frank Shirer—was capable of staying airborne for seventy-two hours with refueling and with a ceiling of forty-five thousand feet.

As the 747 rose above the blue hills of Virginia, mobile microwave relay and booster stations were being aligned, while the phone network into which signals from the plane's five-mile-long, 5/8-inch cable could be fed into the silos and other elements of the triad were being repaired.

From the line of twenty-eight stern-faced computer operators in Kneecap came the information that the targets of the seventeen missiles almost certainly included Cheyenne Mountain in Colorado, Omaha, Nebraska, the Trident SLBM sub bases at Bangor, Washington, Kings Bay, and the Trident tracking facilities at Point Magu in California and Cape Canaveral. The remaining eleven 550-kiloton warheads were expected to zero in on the MX silos in the Midwest.

The situation, bad as it was, became more terrible because of what General Carlisle, SAC's commander, who had already launched Stealth fighter intercepts to fire "spoiler" rockets and B-1 bombers with cruise missiles, told the president in the last phone call he would ever make—that they were faced with the "old north/south problem."

President Mayne and Paul Trainor, sitting before the banks of small TV screens in the presidential command room aboard Kneecap, knew Carlisle wasn't talking about the Civil War. The old north/south problem was the fact, not generally known among either the public at large or the military, that all tests of Soviet ICBMs had, for no other reason than the geography of the country, been carried out on east/west axes and not on north/south axes, which, in any hostile launch, such as the one now on the way, would be the axis used in attacking the United States.

To the man in the street, a missile, like a bullet, presumably operated the same way, no matter in what direction it was fired. But, as the president's aides explained, missiles, due to the necessity of accurately predicting trajectories that would leave the earth's atmosphere and then reenter it, were not only subject to wind and weather in general but were particularly dependent upon the shifts in the earth's magnetic field. It was the reason why, even under the most favorable atmospheric circumstances, a missile still had a circular *error* probability.

This rather esoteric mathematical consideration translated into a monumental decision for the president because of the fact that, unlike the Soviet Union, many U.S. missiles, such as the Tridents deployed in nuclear sub storage areas such as Bangor, near Seattle, were close to, if not part of, American cities. How could the president know, given the vicissitudes of missiles' circular *error* probability, whether the Russians were in fact engaging in "counterforce"—antimilitary—or "countervalue"—anticity—attacks, when so many American bases, unlike many in the Soviet Union, were often part of an American city?

On one level the question seemed purely academic—even, as the president acknowledged, cold-blooded —but it was nevertheless one he had to entertain, for he would not have much time to decide what the Russian strategy was. And if he made the wrong decision—to go countervalue rather than counterforce in any retaliatory strike—it could mean an escalation that could result in utter annihilation for both countries' industries and most of their people. Could he confine retaliatory strikes to military targets like those selected by the *Roosevelt*'s captain when he had fired an SLBM in retaliation for the Russians' multiple ICBM launch?

Then Kneecap received a flash message that one of the SS-19s had exploded in a nonnuclear detonation during reentry, its warheads tumbling down harmlessly before they could explode.

"An intercept?" asked the president.

"No, sir. Mechanical malfunction."

"Pray God the other two will malfunction."

They didn't.

Intercepts took out three of the remaining twelve warheads of the other two rockets during reentry, but that left nine incoming.

The SAC B-1 bombers were disappearing quickly, the screens full of swarms of intercept fighters from both sides. Trainor was shouting, "Mr. President! Goddamn it—we're down to the wire here. If we don't strike back now—"

Mayne raised his hand to steady him. He felt strangely calm. It was now down to a Hobbesian simplicity: "If you use your sword, I must use mine," and the life of man did indeed appear to be "poor, nasty, brutish, and short." Accordingly, he wanted to alert General Carlisle to the possibility of all-out countervalue, city-for-city attack. But Carlisle was already dead, Omaha no more. The last thing Rick Stacy saw was the incoming trajectory, the computers' cold neutrality announcing the incoming missile's CEP was plus or minus three miles.

"Way off," someone in Cheyenne Mountain said. It was, but the air burst of the SS-19's 550 kilotons at four thousand feet above Omaha produced a multilevel but quickly flattening mushroom cloud, its coronas, like enormous smokers' rings, transforming the merely colorful sunset of Nebraska into an explosion of astonishing beauty, the stunningly vibrant orange core of the mushroom turning the vast, undulating snowfields to watermelon pink, the circles now rising about the mushroom's stalk vermilion-tinted, thinning as the red stalk rose through them, the circles now fading to purest white, like a host heaven-bound.

The overpressure of six pounds per square inch produced winds in excess of 130 miles per hour over an MDZ—maximum danger zone—of fourteen square miles, flattening every house in the area, pressures on them in excess of 115 tons, the supercyclonic winds blowing people out of office towers and buildings not already destroyed by the wind.

Three-quarters of the four hundred thousand people of Omaha were killed in a hurtling cyclone of debris as it rose higher and higher, obscuring the lower rings of the air burst, turning the atmosphere a reddish brown. Much of this "shrapnel" swirl consisted of thousands of bodies, superheated, many vaporized—the number of outright fatalities estimated by the superhardened-domed sensors to be 67 percent, the remainder fatally injured.

There were no survivors in a sixteen-square-mile area directly below the air burst's center, and while, beyond the maximum danger zone of fourteen square miles, the survival rate climbed from 10 percent to 90 percent, at two hundred miles from the zone, these "survivors" were the unlucky ones—faces melted, all body hair gone, and for many, no visible injury, but all of them, particularly given the flatness of the terrain, walking receptacles of huge doses of radiation, doomed to agonizing deaths caused by radiation sickness and multiple cancers, those in SAC HQ dying through suffocation, trapped by the millions of tons of rubble over the venting systems and air intakes, the fireballs having raised the temperature so high that emergency oxygen-generating plants either exploded or were too warped to operate.

The first priority of outside rescuers, for whom not nearly enough anticontamination suits were available, was to get to the children of the outlying districts. For many of these, a half hour delay in reaching them meant death.

As the first tremors of the Omaha "strike" registered on the silo cluster known as Romeo, 750 miles away in Montana, Melissa Lange, deep in Romeo 5A on her last shift before her vacation had been due to begin, knew that Rick Stacy was either dead or dying. Immediately she informed both her crew partner, Shirley Cochrane, and Romeo's MLC—master launch control—that she was "in violation of WESSR—weapons systems safety rules."

"Reason?" inquired the duty officer in Romeo's MLC.

"Emotional stress, sir." Her voice was thin, all but inaudible. She paused. "My fiancé is—was—in SAC HQ."

"Hold on." There was a two-second delay, Shirley Cochrane tense in her chair, already buckled up, fully expecting the launch code to come chattering in at any moment, her seat pulled forward on the guide rails, her hands checking the belt for the third time. The Romeo MLC duty officer was back on the line. "Lange, you able to carry on?"

"Yes, sir."

"Very good. Your WESSR violation duly noted and negated by circumstances. Override command issued by Colonel Beaton. You are still on shift. Repeat, you are still on shift. Go to prelaunch status."

"Yes, sir."

Melissa turned back to her console gratefully, for the console was now the real world. She was allowed—had been *ordered*—to shut everything else out. "Hands on keys," she instructed Cochrane. "Keys—" Her voice gave out. She coughed. "Key them on my mark. Three, two, one—mark!"

"Light on," confirmed Cochrane. "Light off."

There was the ten-second delay before Melissa could instruct, "Hands on keys."

"Hands on keys," came Cochrane's confirmation.

"Initiate on my mark. Five, four, three, two, one. Now. I'll watch the clock."

"I've got the light," said Shirley Cochrane. "Light on. Light off."

"Release key," said Melissa.

"Key released."

Even now Shirley Cochrane half expected that the launch code would not come in, that the vote required from another LCC—launch control center—which was required before they could go to "strategic alert" would never come and that instead an ILC—inhibit launch command—would come in its place.

But the launch code did come, as the yellow lights turned to white into the waiting mode for "launch-fire-release"—the alert's arrival announced by a high-pitched electronic ringing and then the voice of the man they had never seen, only heard, delivering the sixteen-word, four-numeral mixed sequence in clear, calm, modulated tones: "Sierra . . . Papa . . . Foxtrot . . . Hotel . . . Tango . . . Lima . . . Acknowledge."

"Copied," said Cochrane, advising Melissa, "I see a valid message."

"I agree," confirmed Melissa. "Go to step one checklist. Launch keys inserted." Both women unbuckled and went to the midpoint red box, each of them taking out her red-tagged brass key and returning to her console, flipping up the clear safety cover and inserting the key, then buckling up again.

"Ready?" said Melissa.

"Ready."

"Function select key," ordered Melissa. "Switch to 'off.' "

"It is."

"MRTCEP to MRT," instructed Melissa.

"MRT."

"Sixty-five select."

"Sixty-five."

"Initiate activator clockwise."

"Activator clockwise," confirmed Cochrane, her delicate hand turning the black knob hard right.

"Take up alarm," instructed Melissa. A deep buzzer sounded. Melissa then reached forward to the progress control panel, turning the knob clockwise to the fourteen-hundred-watts position.

Soon, after the launch code was checked, the keys were moved from "set code used" to "launch."

"One mark!" commanded Melissa.

Both keys were turned.

"Got my print?" asked Melissa. "You armed?"

A bell started ringing, but above the sound was another, like a waterfall growing in crescendo, the concrete-muffled sound of cold-gas-forced launch.

"Mark your process," said Melissa. ". . . Out of inner security . . . outer security . . . missiles gone. All gone."

With that, two MX ICBMs with twenty MARVed warheads, each of 335 kilotons per warhead, were en route to their military targets in the USSR. Three targets, ICBM complexes in Kamchatka Peninsula, were allotted two warheads apiece against superhardened silos. The first of the two warheads allotted each of these three targets was set to explode in high air burst in order to prevent "fratricide"—in which one bomb's electromagnetic pulse, combining with airborne debris, could rise as high as sixty-two thousand feet, interfering with the second warhead's trajectory.

Every one of the MX warheads, unlike those of the Soviets, *had* been tested in the United States on a north/south trajectory in the Pacific, their circular error of probability reduced to only plus or minus three hundred feet. They were ideal for counterforce attacks—against military targets.

CHAPTER FIFTY-EIGHT

IN MOSCOW, GENERAL Marchenko, already in shock over the news that his son's Fulcrum had been shot down over North Korea, and Admiral Smernov sat whey-faced, having just scrambled for safety with the rest of the twenty-six Politburo and STAVKA members through one of the tunnels once used by Rasputin to see the czarina when he was out of favor with the czar. The superhardened concrete bunkers below the Council of Ministers had been ruled out, the VIPs fearing that explosives set by the enemy commando raid in progress would entomb them under rubble.

Inside the Lenin Library, where the secret tunnel exited, Marchenko found himself sitting close to the admiral. He couldn't stand Smernov's breath. Though he had wanted to broach the subject, albeit diplomatically, several times in his career, Marchenko had resisted, and he did so now, for he neither had the courage nor the instincts for political suicide. It was a small thing, he knew, and perhaps with the blood of Suzlov still fresh on their hands, his preoccupation with the admiral's breath was a kind of petty escape, an avoidance of the terrible responsibility in which they were now all involved. But what other choice had they? Even *before* the meeting had begun, it was obvious President Suzlov had been chafing at the bit to order chemical and nuclear artillery weapons used against the NATO front. He had been waving reports from Beijing of American nuclear aggression and announcing with growing hysteria that he was ready to unleash the entire Soviet arsenal against the Americans, that he wouldn't go down in history as the leader of his nation's greatest defeat. Marchenko and Chernko had argued with him, but they could see no way out. He was set on his course and said he would use his power of veto. But above all else, it was the SAS commando raid, still in progress inside the Kremlin, and not Suzlov's ranting that had persuaded Chernko, the natural leader among the rest, that drastic action was called for—the SAS attack a clear sign that if the enemy's conventional forces could reach so far into the Soviet Union, then it was indeed the beginning of the end. Chernko was a man of unfettered ambition, but he was always the realist. He knew that they must quickly come to some "arrangement."

"What arrangement?" Suzlov had screamed, quite deranged by now and having already launched the ICBMs from the Kola Peninsula against America. Reason was beyond him, but the nine-millimeter parabellum bullet from Chernko's Walther P38 wasn't. It settled the matter.

Now, even as their SPETS elite guards were trying to dislodge and annihilate the SAS attackers, they were, under Chernko's leadership, formulating peace proposals to NATO. Marchenko moved away from the admiral toward Chernko, who immediately interpreted this as a political move away from the navy and into his camp. For the wrong reasons, he was correct. Marchenko, who was opposed to Suzlov in the final meeting, now wanted to disassociate himself, despite his military rank, from the three chiefs of the armed forces, for from the moment he had seen Suzlov *temyat' um*—"cracking up"—and heard of the ICBM launch from Kola, he knew the Soviet Union was nearing the abyss. Only with Chernko's power, with the KGB at his disposal, could they hope to convince the others, particularly Admiral Smernov, not to launch from the nuclear fleet and hope to persuade the cocky, relatively untouched Siberian republic to surrender.

But the admiral had been stubborn in the Council of Ministers' meeting, questioning whether the reports of Soviet launches from the Kola could not have been merely enemy propaganda to justify an all-out attack on the Soviet Union. "Have we firsthand reports from Murmansk?" he'd asked defiantly.

At that point, Marchenko had lost patience with Smernov. "Are you mad, Admiral? Madder than Suzlov? What do you think *reports* will tell you? Is it photographs of the mushroom clouds you want to see—or the dust cloud that will obliterate the sun?'' Marchenko had remembered the awesome outpouring of the American volcano Mount Saint Helen's many years ago, its dark cloud darkening entire cities, turning midday into midnight, and the volcano's explosion was only a fraction of the nuclear arsenals both sides had at their disposal. ''Is it the dust of millions of vaporized bodies you wish to see? We have no time to lose, Admiral. If we don't contact the Americans now, they will bury us.'' He paused. ''The trouble is, Admiral, we don't know exactly where most of our warheads will land. Our propaganda has covered our technological deficiencies for years, but you and I—all of us here—know that the circular error of probability of your submarine-launched missiles might be as large as twenty miles. Anyway—''and here Marchenko turned to the KGB chief ''—Comrade Chernko will attest to the fact that we have reports of shoddy workmanship—explosive bolts that don't explode to separate the second and third rocket stages. Let alone the navigation system.''

''Our space program is the showpiece of—'' began the admiral defiantly.

''*Was*—our showpiece!'' cut in Marchenko. ''And we have hidden how many launch failures in that program? Even at best, including the American *Challenger* disaster and the like, we have only matched the Americans seventy percent of the time. That other thirty percent, that inaccuracy, Admiral,'' said Marchenko, leaning forward, risking Smernov's bad breath, ''could mean whole American cities are destroyed instead. Then what do you think the Americans will do?'' He paused and sat back. Smernov's breath was too much. ''At least when Murmansk used the American submarine launch of the deactivated missiles as an excuse to launch, they had the sense, minimal though it was, to go for military targets in the U.S. But if we were to launch from our fleet—the more rockets we fire, the higher the danger—''

''General Marchenko,'' said Chernko, staring at the admiral, his tone the most threatening any of the Politburo or STAVKA had ever known, ''is correct. The American technological edge will do us in in the end. We must tell the American president it is over.'' He looked about at each one of them. ''Let us not compound our error, Comrades.''

''How will we let him know?'' asked the minister of transport. ''What about an EM pulse if his plane is near one of our targets?''

''The president's airborne command post, Comrade, is sheathed against EMP.''

"And what if one of our missiles detonates in air burst too close to the plane? Can you guarantee communication then?"

"No," said Chernko, exasperated. "But we will try, Comrade."

Chernko's assurance was uttered with such deadly and understated charm that the transport minister fell silent. Chernko then turned to the admiral. "We have your word then, Smernov, that your nuclear fleet will not launch?"

"Yes," said the admiral reluctantly, beginning to say something else but catching himself, deciding against it.

Chernko was still looking at him searchingly. "Go on, Admiral. What is it?"

The admiral mumbled something about Suzlov.

"We had to shoot him," said Chernko brusquely. "Are you not prepared to accept your part in our collective responsibility, Comrade?"

"No—no," the admiral hastened. "I mean—no, I'm not discussing that, Comrade Director. Besides, history will not know who shot him. We will blame the Allies."

"Don't be an idiot," said Chernko dismissively, the first time Marchenko had heard the director's tone move from one of icy calm to undisguised contempt. "The Allies will be writing the history books, Admiral. Not us. The irony is, they will correctly say we killed Suzlov, but no one will believe them, given their commando raid. But history will end, Comrade, if you cannot assure us your fleet will not engage the Americans—goading them into a second strike against us. Have we your assurance?"

The admiral dabbed the bridge of his nose with his rolled-up khaki handkerchief where an AK-47 bullet had scraped the skin when he'd tripped in the tunnel and two SPETS had dragged him to his feet. Chernko could tell the admiral was hiding something.

"*Speshi!*" Hurry up!" Chernko shouted. "What have you *done*, Admiral?"

"I—I've *done* nothing. The nuclear fleet has been ordered not to launch, but . . . well, we have several diesel-electric boats. We've lost contact with two diesel boats operating off the American West Coast."

Chernko saw it at once. "*Gospodi! U nikh atomnye rakety!*"—"My God! They are carrying nuclear missiles!"

"Two each," said the admiral.

"Tactical or nuclear?" snapped Chernko.

"Eights," said the admiral quietly, dabbing at his nose again, "out of Vladivostok."

The minister of transport was looking from Chernko to the admiral. "What are 'eights'?"

"You fool!" shouted Chernko, causing several of the members to start with fright. He turned to his comrades. "Eights are submarine-launched *ballistic* missiles. Over seven-thousand-kilometer range."

"Only one warhead each," said the admiral, as if this were some kind of enormous concession.

"Yes!" bellowed Chernko. "One warhead of seven hundred and fifty kilotons. Twice as big as the American missile. And you have *four* of them. What are their targets?"

"It was insurance," the admiral retorted. Far from being cowed by Chernko's outburst, his tone changed from apology to defiance. "Insurance against the Americans hitting *our* cities."

"You—" Chernko began, pausing, fighting for self-control. "You have targeted them on American *cities?* Not military targets? Four *cities*?"

The admiral didn't answer.

"Which cities, Admiral?" pressed Chernko.

The admiral rolled up his khaki handkerchief even more tightly. The bridge of his nose was still bleeding. "San Diego, Seattle . . ." He stopped as if he couldn't quite remember the rest. Everyone was waiting. He shrugged. "Washington."

In the room there was utter silence, and they could all clearly hear the crackle of small-arms fire from inside the Kremlin. The faint ticking of the library's pendulum clock sounded to Marchenko like a time bomb.

"That's only three cities, Admiral," Chernko said, waiting.

"New York," said the admiral.

"New York!" repeated another Politburo member, the minister of supply. *"Gospodi!"—"My God!"* He turned to Chernko. "Can it reach that far?"

Chernko swung on him in displaced fury. "Of course it can, you idiot. And further. Over a seven-thousand-kilometer range. You think he would have targeted New York if he couldn't reach it?" Chernko's rage was now directed at the admiral. "We cannot contact the two subs at all?"

"No, sir."

"We can only hope the Americans find them," said Chernko. "If Washington and New York are hit, we will suffer . . . Do you know where they are now?"

The admiral shook his head. "They are on silent running. Especially now. No further communication is acknowledged once nuclear war is in progress." He looked about at the others. "You must understand the targets were only chosen in consultation with President Suzlov."

"Can we do nothing?" pressed the minister of transport. "Nothing at all?"

"*Molis*"—"Pray"—muttered someone.

"*Molis?*" said Chernko. "Yes—that the Americans find them and sink them."

The admiral's professional pride was ruffled. "The commanders are well trained, Comrade."

Chernko seized on one last chance. "What are their instructions upon detecting nuclear war has broken out? Will they not surface and try to contact us to confirm whether—"

"Oh no," said the admiral. "That's the whole point, you see. That is strictly forbidden. An enemy could be feeding false messages over any number of bands. That's why I said no further communication would be—"

Chernko's voice was calm again. "We should have shot you along with Suzlov, Admiral."

"What are we going to do about the commandos?" the minister of supply wanted to know. "We have them bottled up, but if we have to go in and root them out one by one—it will mean we will have to use tanks. It'll destroy the cathedral—perhaps the whole Kremlin—Lenin's Mausoleum . . ."

"You want us to worry about a few artifacts when we are on the brink of annihilation?" retorted the minister of transport angrily. "For all I care, send in the tanks if necessary. We wipe them out or they surrender. It's as simple as that. Unless—" He paused. "Unless the two diesel submarines are destroyed, pulling us back from the brink. Then we could use those commandos. A good bargaining card. The Americans are especially vulnerable in such things. They worry about losing a few of their own."

"But what," interjected Chernko, "if the two diesels aren't found? Their cities are hit and then ours, then we've had it, Comrades. Completely. Saving the Kremlin won't mean anything."

"But what do you propose meanwhile?" pressed the minister of transport. "Let these SAS gangsters run rampant?"

Chernko shrugged. "Of course not. Move in the tanks."

"What," asked another Politburo member, "will the casualties be like for the Americans if the four missiles are fired from the two diesel submarines?"

"Millions," answered a STAVKA member, "killed outright. More millions will die from the radiation dust—over a thousand rems for everyone, Comrade. No favorites. More, not in the immediate area, will die from the invisible radiation. I don't mean that in the dust cloud, but in the food chain, water table. Bone marrow death, especially . . . Everyone in the whole country, Comrade, will become more susceptible to disease—their immune systems destroyed, you see."

The comrade could not see. He could not imagine such disaster coming back tenfold upon the Soviet Union. But he knew it was true.

CHAPTER FIFTY-NINE

IF EVER THERE was to be a Churchillian moment in Ray Brentwood's life, it came the moment he, so recently of IX-44E, sludge removal, "propelled," was appointed overall commander of the task force set out to find the two diesel-electrics his oil samples had determined must be close in to the American coast. And with his command came even more power once the Soviets had contacted Kneecap, giving the Americans the information that the two diesel-electric Golf-class submarines, though they did not know where they were on the western American seaboard, were carrying four SSN-8s, each of the four warheads carrying 750 kilotons.

Issuing orders so quickly that at times runners with their cellular phones, or at least those with phones that were still functioning, literally bumped into one another, Brentwood quickly assembled his antisubmarine warfare force of frigates, destroyers, MAD—magnetic anomaly detector—aircraft, and sonar-dunking choppers. He knew it was not only the most important race in his life, a race against time at the end of which lay either glory or utter defeat, but the most important race in American history. If the four American cities were hit, in addition to those already struck but explained away, like Omaha, as legitimate targets by the Soviets, the public pressure on the president to unleash countervalue strikes—against all major Soviet cities—would be enormous, and indeed, militarily, would be the only thing the United States could do unless it was to be annihilated.

But for military targets such as the Trident bases at Bangor, Washington State, and Kings Bay, Georgia, SAC HQ in Omaha, and NORAD control in Colorado Springs near Cheyenne Mountain, it was already over, the mushrooms from the impacts depressingly the same. Only over Bangor, Washington, and at Kings Bay in Georgia had the mushroom clouds looked different, their shape essentially the same, but on a bright, clear winter day the mushroom stalks above Bangor and Kings Bay were infused with millions of gallons of superheated water evaporated by the ten-million-degree-Fahrenheit heat at the center of the fireball. The wide V-shaped bottom of the stalk, before it rose and grew thin, had become blindingly white, the sun catching the vibrant iridescence of the countless billions of sea creatures that were sucked up in the whirlwinds of the explosion's core, the radioactive cloud sweeping out to sea.

The sick and dying overflowed out on the lawns beneath makeshift tents as rain, caused by the hot air of the explosion meeting the cold mountain air of the Rockies and the Cascades, poured down, washing much of the radioactivity into the water table faster than it normally would have been absorbed. And as in the case of those who had tried to get to the children first in Omaha, would-be rescuers were thwarted by an almost complete lack of antiradiation, anticontamination suits, the hospital budgets having been slashed in the halcyon days of Gorbachev.

High above the midwestern states, the most dreadful thing that those aboard the ADS—antiradioactive-sheathed—Kneecap experienced was that here they were, safe, at least for the moment, high above the earth, supposedly in command of the situation while all the distant mushroom clouds told them how helpless they were to do anything for those people who were dying by the thousands, the unlucky ones who had not died outright.

Twenty miles off southern California's coast, Ray Brentwood stood in the stiff breeze that had come up since they had left San Diego aboard his command ship, the USS *John T. Munro*, an Oliver Hazard Perry–class frigate, a sister ship to his first, the USS *Blaine*.

On officers' call, he instructed his department heads that they were to keep the mission short and simple when describing it to the men. "Our job is to search for and destroy a force of two Soviet Golf-Class V diesel-electric subs which are carrying two ICBMs apiece. The Golf's surface speed is seventeen knots. And on battery power, gentlemen, they're very quiet. I repeat, *very quiet*. We suspect they have anechoic soundproofing tiles on their hulls and enough battery power to run for seventy-two hours without recharge. Which is the reason why they've been able to sneak past our SOSUS network."

"Torpedoes, sir?" asked the officer in charge of the two Mark-32 triple-tube torpedo launchers on the *John T. Munro*.

"Ten. Twenty-one-inch diameter. Six forward, four aft."

"Radar, sir?"

"Snoop tray and sonars. Medium frequency. Now, my guess is that given they're out of contact with their headquarters and their orders are to remain so—that is, to launch on their own initiative—and given the fact that there is no way they cannot know a nuclear exchange has been under way, I suspect that for the sake of coordinated action, they are likely to stick together in preparation for a short, simultaneous attack, because they know that if they send those four sons of bitches off together, we're going to have twice as much trouble stopping them. It's a pretty good bet that they won't go it alone." He paused. "We've got one thing working for us at the moment, and that is that the electromagnetic pulse from the strikes they've already made is going to scramble communications everywhere for a while."

"You mean they're going to wait a day or so until they can be sure of proper trajectories?"

"That's what I'm hoping," said Brentwood. "But we can't rely on it. We'll have to try to pin 'em down faster than that."

"How we going to do that, Captain?"

"That's my job. What I want *you* guys to remember is that we're going to have sonar pinging out there, magnetic anomaly detectors, and all the other ASW equipment. I don't want anybody getting 'signals mixed up.' Navigators—you make sure where your ship is every second. Day and night. I don't want any incoming noise from one of our own search ships to interfere with our sonar either, so the distance between ships'll have to be watched closely. Should *Munro* be attacked, I expect the officer of the deck to bring her broadside immediately. This'll present a bigger target to any incoming. It'll free our radar masts and Phalanx defense system of upper-deck obstruction. Last thing—from now on, we're Condition Four." This meant that more than two hundred of the ship's 453 complement of men would be on alert at all times, four hours on, eight off.

"That's all," said Brentwood. He took the salute and made his way to the *John T. Munro*'s combat information center, along with his tactical action officer, James Cameron, one of the young officers aboard USS *Blaine* whom he had requested along with several enlisted men who had served with him on the *Blaine*. It was to demonstrate that there was no grudge on his part about what had happened on the *Blaine*. Because he could not truly say how he had ended up in the water after the *Blaine* had been hit, he saw in the *John T. Munro* a chance to redeem himself.

"Can I speak freely, sir?" Lieutenant Cameron asked.

"Shoot," said Brentwood.

"None of the men I know thought you jumped ship. Bosun reckons one of our boys picked you up, pulled the tab to inflate the preserver, and tossed you over. Then he got it."

"Well, Cameron, for what it's worth, I've gone over it a million times. I don't know what the hell happened. All I remember is one minute I'm on the bridge, then bam, the lights go out. The next minute I'm floating. But thanks for the vote of confidence—appreciate it."

"No problem, sir. Ah, Captain—if you think their subs are only going to wait a bit until all this electrical fuzz clears from the upper atmosphere, we're not going to have much time to find them."

"I've got a few ideas."

"Such as?"

"Well, first I think we have at least a day. It isn't just my guesswork that they're sticking together. The oil patches proved that, so I don't think they'll separate."

By this time they were in the combat information center, looking over the charts of the western seaboard, Ray Brentwood using the dividers to measure how far the *Munro* was from the site of the oil spills. "Fair assumption is they're doing no more than ten knots submerged. They won't try to run at full speed—too much noise. Twenty-four hours steaming would give 'em a two-hundred-and-forty-mile radius."

"That's one big area, Captain."

"Yeah, well, it's a damn sight smaller than the whole Pacific, Cameron."

"Yes, sir."

"Besides—we'll have our helos out and our long-range magnetic detector aircraft. Besides—don't forget they're leaking oil. Typical Soviet construction."

"But won't they have fixed that, Captain?"

"Well, if they could have, they would have—wouldn't they? I want somebody on that satellite photo reconnaissance console all the time. We spot an oil patch like that again, we're in business."

"Yes, sir."

It wasn't until he was by himself, poring over the chart, trying to think like a submariner, that Ray Brentwood realized that during the debriefing, no one had taken any notice of his face—they'd all been too busy taking notes to brief their respective departments. Soon, he knew, every sailor in the battle group would understand it would be the most important battle of the war. If they couldn't stop the Russians, prevent the American cities from being hit, then it would be all-out nuclear holocaust—no distinction made between city and military targets—both countries razed, and the living envying the dead.

CHAPTER SIXTY

FOR DAVID BRENTWOOD'S SAS men in the darkness of the Kremlin's Assumption Cathedral, the air thick with the stench of cordite and smoke, it seemed the war was over. The SPETS were closing in, and some of the SAS had seen one of their own—from Cheek-Dawson's Troop C—lying alone about sixty yards beyond the cathedral. Wounded and out of ammunition, he had put up his hands. *"Ne stretyayte!"*—"Don't shoot!"—he'd said. The advancing SPETS beckoned him forward, waited until he was halfway between the Council of Ministers Building and the line of old Napoleonic cannons in front of the arsenal, and shot him down in at least four bursts.

"I thought," said the Williams they called "A," to differentiate him from Choir Williams, "we were supposed to bloody abseil out. Hook onto the wall and over we go in all the confusion?"

"That's still the idea," said David, his voice rising above the tearing sound of the SAS machine gun opening up from the partly opened cathedral doors. "Put on your SPETS overlays," he ordered.

"Sir!" came one of the troopers' voices through the darkness of the cathedral. "Sounds like they're bringing the tanks up."

"Is nothing sacred?" quipped Aussie, zipping up his SPETS overlay. "Bastards are gonna shoot up a flamin' church. Dunno what the world's comin' to, David. Honest to Christ I don't."

"It'll fall in on top of you," answered David, "if you don't get a move on." They heard a scraping noise, then a rattle like stones on the roof—an SAS man who'd taken up sniper position by one of the golden domes had been spotlighted by one of the tanks that were now coming toward the Church of the Twelve Apostles just north of the cathedral after having led its column from Red Square through the Savior's Gate.

"Antitank?" called Brentwood.

"Over here, sir!" It was Choir Williams, he of rousing hymns and football songs sung against the English "barbarians." He was already in his overlay and quickly grabbed the two disposable French Arpac antitank missile launchers, the launchers so small—forty centimeters long, with a bore less than three inches wide, and weighing just over three pounds, with a range of one hundred yards—that the joke among the SAS troopers during training was that if you weren't careful, you'd lose them in your pocket.

"All right, Choir," said David. "Out the side door—and Choir?"

"Yes, sir."

"After, come straight back. We're not going out the way we came in."

"Yes, sir."

Watching the night illuminated every few seconds by flares and the flashes of exploding grenades, Choir, having waited for two seconds of darkness, slipped out of the Assumption Cathedral and within moments was flat against the southern wall of the Patriarchal Palace, easing his way down toward the black hulks of tanks that had come in by the Savior's Gate on the Kremlin's east side, heading toward the SAS at the bottom of the triangle.

Inside the cathedral, Cheek-Dawson was groaning, slumped against one of the ornately frescoed columns nearby, cradling his arm, the morphine wearing off. David glanced down at him, and for a moment Aussie thought Brentwood was going to try to take Cheek-Dawson out with them. But he knew Brentwood knew there was no way they could "lug out" badly wounded. It would hold up any attempt to scale the Kremlin walls—not a formidable exercise at all with the SAS training, but a suicide mission if you were trying to get over with an injured party. "Best thing we can do," said David, "is to give him another shot of morphine before we leave. Maybe they'll take him prisoner."

"Yeah," answered Aussie.

David looked around in the darkness of the huge cathedral, its columns and priceless gold icons momentarily lit by a distant flare. He called out to the men, but his words were immediately drowned by the rattle of SPETS machine-gun fire, its tracer arcing into the marble columns and smashing into the priceless wall of ancient icons that separated the nave from the sanctuary. It was coming from the first tank, now fifty yards away.

There was another long burst of heavy machine-gun tracer smacking and ricocheting in a high, buzzing sound about the cathedral. For a moment Brentwood glanced at the dim outline of the saints, the columns reminding him of the marble pillars of Mansudae Hall and the great statues of the hero workers of North Korea, all of which now seemed so long ago. Not for a minute had Freeman let them think they were beaten, and David could only wish that the general were here now.

"Listen!" he called, his voice echoing in the cathedral. "We've got a chance once we get over the wall. We'll be in SPETS overlay and it's still a few hours till dawn, so we'll be in curfew. No civilians to give you trouble. So just go through the streets as if you own them, as if you're SPETS looking for *us*. Got it? Once you reach—"

There was a clatter that reverberated through the cathedral, an SAS man catching a full burst, the force of the hits slithering him about on the floor. "All right, everyone, go! Now! Aussie leads." David turned to the Australian. "Remember, out and down through the Hall of Facets, Annunciation Cathedral, and into Taynitsky Park. Lots of tree cover in there. They won't know whether it's their own or SAS even if they see you. Then use the old hook, and one, two, you're over the wall and we're out. I'll follow on with Choir. Rear guard. Got it?"

"Got it."

"And Aussie?"

"Yes, sir."

"No gold souvenirs on the way."

"Wouldn't think of it."

"Not half."

"Too bloody heavy anyway."

"See you at the helos."

"Right."

With that, in their SPETS overlays, the remaining sixteen SAS men, all that was left of the three troops, were gone, moving quickly, silently, behind Aussie toward the Hall of Facets.

Choir, invisible by the wall of the Patriarchal Palace, moved up closer in the darkness, then used the side of the Church of the Twelve Apostles for cover. He could hear the lead tank, about a hundred yards away to the left of the Great Bell Tower.

Choir lifted the Arpac, its barrel so short that aiming it made him feel as if he were playing with a toy. The tip of the shaped charge warhead with its point-detonating fuse was barely visible as he leaned against the ancient stone of the Church of the Apostles, waiting for the next glimmer of flare light to illuminate the tanks, their creaky, unoiled sound coming closer.

But there were no flares. There was no light. But Choir, his eyes growing more accustomed to the snow-curtained darkness outside the cathedral, began to make out the hump of the first T-90, then its machine gun opened up again and he could hear its rounds cracking into and about the cathedral's door to his far right. He needed only a second for the tank to fell the peep sight. He inhaled, held his breath, and fired. The sliding barrel recoiled, and the missile's motor, which gave off no flash, blasted from the barrel at over seventy-six meters a second. Less than one second later, the tank was belching flame, the crew screaming, the charge having penetrated the cupola, flame from the tank lighting up the snow so that Choir feared that he'd be spotted in the short sprint back to the cathedral.

But then the tank's 135-millimeter shells began exploding, and as he ran back through the cathedral's side door, the lead T-90 and the two behind it exploded, sending white-hot shrapnel whistling into the infantry behind the tanks and the jumble of smoking concrete that had been the Council of Ministers.

"Good work, Choir!" yelled David. "Fourth of July out there!"

Choir didn't get the reference but he understood it was congratulatory, as Brentwood smacked him on the back, pointing him toward the doorway leading from the Assumption Cathedral to the Hall of Facets.

"You coming, sir?"

"Be along in a second," said David. "Have to give Cheek-Dawson a shot."

"But—" began Choir.

"Well, we can't take him with us, can we?" said David.

"No, sir."

"Go! See you at the choppers."

"Yes, sir."

David knew that Choir knew, but the Welshman didn't linger and did as he was told.

CHAPTER SIXTY-ONE

IN THE ARCTIC grayness around the ice-locked *Roosevelt*, the Sea Harrier, though having left East Spitzbergen, two hundred miles to the north, well before the five Sea King helicopters, was having difficulty finding a suitable spot to land.

The Harrier's forward-looking infrared radar showed such an uneven chaos of jagged ice that even for the versatile vertical-takeoff-and-landing fighter, putting down on the ice would have been a risky venture, so that the pilot couldn't justify risking the multimillion-dollar plane. In any case, his very presence circling the sub, riding shotgun for the approaching helicopters, was message enough, in the radio silence, for Capt. Robert Brentwood and his crew that they were about to be rescued.

As the five choppers neared, two fore and aft of the

Roosevelt, the fifth helicopter starboard midships, all five about fifty feet away from the sub's hull, they began lowering their rope ladders, while Zeldman and the five chief petty officers, their voices battling the steady roar of the rotor slap, began dividing the crew into their various departments and then into groups of twenty, for each of the Sea Kings.

Robert Brentwood went back aboard *Roosevelt* to Control, and set the scuttling charges, double-checking that all code books and deciphering coils were destroyed. After he pushed the timer, he would have five minutes to clear the sail and get on the last chopper.

While the chopper pilots fought to keep hover position in the unpredictable gusts and sudden shears that were caused by the wind blowing over the jagged serrations of the ice pressure ridges, Zeldman and several others struggled to steady a stretcher containing one of the men who was too badly wounded to either climb or be winched up in harness. The chopper, rising suddenly in a gust, shifted only two feet or so, but in doing so, tore the stretcher from the grasp of the ground party, who, as they stood helplessly by, saw the man would have been lost had it not been for the restraining straps. After the chopper steadied enough to allow them to snap on the backup safety ring and began to haul the injured man up, Zeldman walked down the line, his fur-lined parka stiff with ice particles, the rising wind and the sway of the choppers combining to create a wind-chill factor of minus sixty degrees as he shouted above the noise of the rotors, making sure every man understood that if a chopper should suddenly rise in a gust or drop in a wind shear, they must stop climbing immediately and hang on until it steadied itself. Otherwise, as the Royal Air Force corporal who had climbed down to assist told Zeldman, a man who continued to move on the rope ladder could start a swinging motion in concert with the chopper, resulting in a sudden lurch. This could cause a man to either lose his grip or, in the extreme case, as the chopper tried to right itself, create a pendulum effect that could throw him into the rotors. Soon after Zeldman had returned to the head of the line to help the chiefs, whose hands, like his, were frozen despite their gloves, one of the petty officers slipped on a rope rung and lost his grip. Fortunately he fell only a few feet onto the hard ice, his worst injury appearing to be a bruised ego from the severe ribbing he got from the waiting crewmen, who from then on would forever call him "Ice Man."

* * *

In Taipingshao, thirty miles north of the Yalu, the North Korean Army's General Kim's personal interrogator made his way down through the deep subterranean tunnel HQ into the dank interrogation room—or rather, the six-foot-square mud pit with a three-foot boardwalk and bare table.

"Mikuk chapnomtül"—"American bastard!"—he yelled. "You kill our people with gangster weapons." His breath was steaming in the frigid tunnel air, his short, lean frame in the drab olive green of the baggy NKA uniform barely visible in the light of the lantern which he placed on the bare table. "If you do not confess, it will make the general very angry."

The prisoner, who had been kept sitting naked for hours, lashed to a rough bamboo chair, didn't answer. He couldn't sleep, for then they would wake him with a bayonet. He was forbidden to use anything, not even a bucket for a toilet so that he was forced to sit, chained as he was, in his own urine and excrement.

Three of Kim's earlier interrogators had been women, and throughout the questioning and persistent demands for a confession of war crimes, they would make derisive remarks about the prisoner's genitals, warning him that where he was going, he would have no need of his member even if he knew how to use it, which, they taunted, was doubtful. It was this kind of adolescent brutality that was easiest for Freeman to withstand. What was far more deadly was the lack of sleep.

Other things were bearable. Sitting in your own shit wasn't as bad as the gooks thought it was—besides, no one was as repulsed by the smell of his own ordure as were other people. In fact, as a young soldier at Camp Lejeune, he had been told by the drill instructor that people secretly liked it. In any event, this was the kind of humiliation most men could bear—at least for the first few days or so. Lack of sleep was the killer, physically and spiritually. That and their damned stinking "facecloth" torture—during which a large piece of sodden calico was slapped over his face so that every breath he took sucked it tighter against his face. Then they'd jerk the chair back to the point of tipping, and on the already supersaturated cloth they would drip water from a gourd, its rope cradle attached to a hook jammed hard into the semifrozen earth above him. The feeling of panic, of being unable to breathe, the single drops of water creating the sensation—indeed, the reality—of drowning, was almost too much for him, and the hero of Pyongyang wondered how much longer he could last without publicly—on TV for all the world to see—abjectly confessing his part in "the conspiracy of U.S. warmongers to wage chemical warfare on the peaceful, loving peoples of the Democratic People's Republic of Korea."

"I'll confess nothing to you scumbags," he had told his interrogators. "It was your forces who started this business. You can dish it out, but you can't take it—is that it?"

But that had been three days ago, an eternity in the mind of a captive, when stripped, his watch taken, nothing allowed that might assist him in the organization of his thoughts or help prevent disorientation, he had been lashed to the chair and refused all food, offered only his own urine to drink.

"Sign," the drill sergeant had advised the marines. "We all know it's bullshit back home."

Yes, they would know a confession was bullshit. But underneath, in America's heart of hearts, after the news clips were over and the outraged eyes of the American public had watched the humiliation of their fellows, and after they had voiced their disgust with the enemy tormentors, there remained, for all their understanding, a quiet, unspoken shame—that an American had shown he'd broken.

Already his photo with the caption of "War Criminal" had been circulated throughout China to stiffen resistance among the masses to the increasing U.S.–ROK attacks which were now pushing the NKA and the Chinese troops back over the Yalu into Manchuria, using the low-radiation but nevertheless devastating atomic shell artillery fire.

"General Kim is coming to see you!" announced the interrogator. "If you do not confess, you will make him very angry."

Freeman said nothing.

"Do you hear me, *mikuk*?" he shouted again.

"No."

"You—you do not be clever people with the general." The interrogator was shaking his finger like a schoolmaster, cautioning him against disobedience. "You must confess or you will make him very angry."

"I wouldn't want to do that," said Freeman wryly.

"Excellent. You are thinking correctly." With that the interrogator barked several orders and two NKA guards, in full winter uniform, ear flaps down, came in, wearing white cloth face masks against the stench, which, interestingly, the interrogator either didn't seem to mind or took pains to hide his distaste for.

They untied him and took him away to the cold shower

which meant that in half an hour he would have some thin rice soup, bread, and an injection perhaps of vitamins to help get his color up. He would be going on TV again. So far they hadn't got a confession, but Freeman knew the power of the box. With all the will in the world to defy them, once you were shown unshaven and bleary-eyed, despite the new change of olive-drab pajamas that were supposed to pass for fresh clothes, it would be next to impossible to look anything else but defeated, which the NKA and Chinese propagandists well knew. Unless you were one of those who had extraordinary imagination and determination, it was difficult to beat the medium when *it* was the message. He remembered how, years before, the Chinese had so successfully covered the memory of the Beijing massacre among their people with TV confessions and "cooked" footage that in the end, many people believed a massacre had never taken place.

Peter Zeldman was the last man to step off the ice onto chopper number four's ladder port aft of the sub. As he began his ascent, he saw Capt. Robert Brentwood starting to climb the rope ladder dangling from the chopper hovering uneasily amidships off the *Roosevelt*'s starboard side about forty or fifty feet above the ice hummocks, and Zeldman chastised himself for not having gone down to Control to press home to Brentwood the chopper crewman's warning about just how powerful the gusts were a few feet off the ground. As the chopper hauling him up rose, Zeldman turned his head to check that Brentwood was doing okay when suddenly there was a tremendous jerk, the chopper above him buffeted sideways in a heavy gust. Zeldman's right hand, numb with cold, tried to hang on as his left hand flew away from the rope because of the jerking motion. But he couldn't hold and fell thirty feet onto a hummock below. Almost instantly the air force corporal, though busy in the chopper's cabin assigning the men for the best possible distribution of weight, came quickly down the rope, not only from long practice but with the knowledge that the sub would explode in four—now three and a half—minutes. He'd seen Zeldman's dark outline on the white ice rebound from the hummock as it hit, and while he hoped for the best, he feared the worst.

The worst was what he found. Though Peter Zeldman had fallen only thirty feet, his head had struck the wind-carved, concrete-hard ice of a pressure ridge. The corporal felt for a pulse, but there was none, the warm back of the man's neck lolling as if there was no bone there, the neck broken as cleanly as if it had been struck by a steel beam.

"Two minutes—come on!" came the voice of the loud-hailer, barely audible under the frantic slap of the rotors. There was no more the corporal could do as it would take more than two minutes to heave the dead body up. Quickly he reached about Zeldman's neck, took the dog tags, made the sign of the cross, and ran for the ladder.

President Mayne, without taking precious time to confer with Looking Glass, the EC-135 out of Offutt Air Force Base in Nebraska, or his advisers, or the seventeen "options of attack" that were laid out in the ostensibly simple but in fact very complex seventy-five pages of the football's "black book," ordered an MX launch against the massive Soviet oil refineries at Kuibuyshev, Ishimbay, Perm', and Angarii. And, via satellite communication, he told Chernko, in a deadly calm tone, that the Soviet warhead that had penetrated the generally impenetrable ABM screen now thrown up along the NORAD line, and which had burst above Detroit, was the reason for the four-to-one retaliatory attack against the four refineries, and that this would constitute U.S. policy until all Soviet attacks *ceased*.

Chernko understood that Mayne wasn't threatening him—that it was a promise, a promise backed by the undeniable demonstration of American technological superiority, still very potent despite the enormous damage it had already sustained.

"What will happen if you do not find the two submarines?" asked Chernko, trying to sound unflappable but something in his voice betraying tightly reined panic, a panic heightened by the unhesitating willingness of the American president to have had the audacity to actually *name* the retaliatory targets in the Soviet Union.

"What will happen if we don't find your two subs," replied Mayne, "is that if another U.S. city is struck, whether it contains a military target or not, I will take out four of your cities. You may have some difficulty reining in some of your Politburo members, Mr. Chernko, but with four of your cities gone, I think you'll have the best of the argument to cease and desist. Wouldn't you say so?"

"I am doing all I can," snapped Chernko.

"If a U.S. city is hit," repeated President Mayne, "I will take out four Soviet cities."

Trainor stood unusually silent, exhilarated, terrified by the president's cold delivery of America's terms. Mayne was talking unconditional surrender.

Trainor waited several seconds before he spoke, and then, as the president sat calmly watching Kneecap's monitors, his aide, trying to remember exactly where he had put the president's migraine medication, asked "How's the head, sir?"

"Clear."

On Kneecap's monitors they were now receiving the first pictures of Detroit, in real time, relayed by one of the few remaining observation satellites that were still working, the hope for Star Wars rocket-killing beam satellites the biggest single technological flop on both sides of the war, the Star Wars satellites easily taken out by supersonic aircraft firing "pebbles"—clusters of small antisatellite satellites—into orbit.

In Japan, because of more favorable atmospheric conditions over the northwestern Pacific, TV reception throughout the Japanese archipelago was exceptionally good, enhanced by the high-density Japanese screens that were now showing pictures of the one-megaton air burst over Detroit, eighty times more powerful than the bomb dropped on Hiroshima in 1945, the Japanese people horrified.

The Soviet warhead over Detroit was 1.2 megatons, exploding in an air burst at seven thousand feet above the city, fifteen miles in from Lake Saint Clair and approximately six miles north of the Canadian city of Windsor, which, because of a dip in the Great Lakes border, lies south of Detroit. The hydrogen bomb, detonating 1.3 miles over the intersection of Interstate 75 and Interstate 94, about 3.5 kilometers from the Windsor-Detroit tunnel, created a fireball. Different in shape from a ground-burst mushroom, the halos spreading about the shock front and fireball were extraordinarily elongated, forming elegant oval-shaped smoke rings, the fireball passing through their centers. There was no crater, as there would have been with a ground burst, but the air burst, unlike a ground-zero burst, which would have lost much of its energy going into the ground, was much more devastating. First it created an enormous vacuum over the city, then its overpressure collapsed buildings and people alike, as the firestorm-accompanied pressure rings moved from twelve p.s.i. at the center to one p.s.i. across a twenty-six-mile-diameter killing zone. Over a half million died outright from the blast, blast-related injuries, and from the fires and thermal radiation which injured or killed another 760,000 and reduced the automobile factories to ashes.

Not only were Japanese TV viewers horrified—their industrialists were sick with concern. The destruction of America's major auto factories would be a short-term gain for the Japanese auto industry, but the Americans, who could clear and rebuild faster than anyone on earth, would—unless the nuclear exchange became a total holocaust—soon have the newest, most modern and up-to-date auto production facilities in the world, and then Japan would be the country with the outmoded and obsolete equipment.

But they knew, as did Mayne and Chernko, that everything depended on whether or not the Americans found the two Soviet subs. Should Washington and/or New York be struck, the psychological effect throughout the world would be enormous. With the U.S. political and financial capitals in ruins, her loss of prestige, that intangible yet all-important quality in the world of realpolitik, would be disastrous for America, as a ravaged Berlin had been for Germany. America might survive, but her influence in world affairs would never again be the same, and she would forfeit it in favor of Japan.

CHAPTER SIXTY-TWO

RAY BRENTWOOD'S DISCOVERY that the oil patches revealed the presence of the two diesel-electric Russian subs off the American West Coast had propelled him overnight into the national spotlight, but he knew spotlights could shift very quickly. If you failed, they went out altogether—you would be yesterday's man—the man who got the scent but lost the hunt. With this in mind, he was concerned that the very size of his twenty-four-ship "armada," as Vice Admiral Rutgers grumpily called it, while essential to cover the area, could be as much an obstruction to the hunt. If the sound of every one of the twenty-four ships was not read and understood correctly by each ship's sonar operators, it could be mistaken for the enemy. Ray Brentwood also realized something that he hadn't dwelt on during the officers' call—that if any one of the Russian's four big ballistic missiles exploded in the middle of the task force, it would, in the parlance of the military, "neutralize" them in seconds.

CHAPTER SIXTY-THREE

NEITHER SOVIET SKIPPER nor their crews could prove it, but, although the odds of both boats having leaked oil on the same patrol weren't beyond possibility, given the relatively old hulls of the Golf, it was still highly unlikely. It was, they concluded, sabotage. Not of the kind that would have caused "noise shorts" which would have been quickly noticed in the first hour out of Vladivostok and which could have been corrected quickly in port. Something more subtle—a small oil leak, slow, insidious, which wouldn't be noticeable immediately, and by the time it was, could not be so easily located or repaired. There were no dry docks on America's continental shelf. And rather than each going its own way, they'd had to stay hidden and waited together should mutual assistance be necessary. It was the price they were paying for what they believed were *"Yevreyskie sabotazhniki"*—"Jewish saboteurs"—who had been known to pinprick oil feeder lines. Whether it had been done by the likes of the three Jewish brothers the KGB had arrested in Khabarovsk near the railhead for the Eastern TVD, they didn't know, only that if they could get their hands on whoever had done it, they would drown them in oil—very slowly.

* * *

Ray Brentwood sent ships out over the search area radiating from the position of the two oil spills he had collected. As well as those naval vessels assigned to his task force, Brentwood commandeered every available ship he saw—even seconding three coast guard vessels en route to San Diego for liberty. As well as the twenty-seven American ships, there were four Canadian frigates, which, though little better than target drones compared to the equipment aboard the American Oliver Hazard Perry–class frigates, were, typically, crewed by seamen as brave as those on Brentwood's ships and especially adept at making do and squeezing the best out of near obsolete equipment. It was from one of these Canadian frigates that a Sea King helicopter took off, towing its yellow MAD—magnetic anomaly detector—below its tail assembly, covering a search grid 258 miles northwest of San Diego. The Sea King thought it detected a magnetic anomaly, but the Canadian chopper, devoid of ASW torpedoes, could do nothing but radio the Americans.

Within twenty minutes U.S. MH-53E Sea Stallions had closed with everything, as a Canadian observer described it, from dunking sonar, MADs, and MK-37 acoustic homing ASW torpedoes to Chateaubriand. The graph traces of the MADs from two of the five-man-crew Sea Stallions instantly concurred with the Canadians' report that there *was* a magnetic anomaly and that most likely, "by nature of trace," it was a metallic hull that was distorting the earth's magnetic lines of force—in the same way as a magnet drawn beneath a sheet will redistribute the position of magnetic filings on the paper.

But whether the anomaly was caused by a submarine hull, the traces could not tell. Sonars were dunked—so many of the champagne-magnum-size listening mikes being lowered into the sea that Brentwood's executive officer, Cameron, said it looked like a "salmon derby." Still, the passive sonar mikes couldn't add any more to the active traces, unable to determine whether the hull was that of a sub. It could be a wreck—the coastal waters strewn with them. But then again, as Ray Brentwood pointed out to Cameron, the two oil patches had been found *together,* so that one would have expected a bigger anomaly unless it *was* the hull of a sub they'd found, the other hiding beneath it, the two traces merging into one magnetic anomaly.

Brentwood was faced with a classic subhunter's dilemma: If he dropped a torpedo and it wasn't the subs, the torpedo's explosion would immediately alert them, whether or not they were in the immediate area. And they could launch within minutes.

Brentwood ordered sonars dunked to three hundred meters but forbade any active pulses. At three hundred meters the sonars would be very close to the crush depth of an Echo III–class diesel-electric sub. At that depth the bulkheads begin to moan. There was also the possibility that if the anomaly was a sub, it was just that—*one* sub. The other could very well have taken cover in the noise umbrella of the task force. Running on her batteries, the second sub would not easily be detected amid the cavitation noises of the surface vessels. Think! Ray told himself, think like a man who is hunted—like a submariner, a man closed in, as he had been in the darkness of his own trial, when he'd gone under anesthesia time and again, unsure of whether he'd ever surface again. Would *you,* he asked himself, simply lie down there quietly and wait for death? No, he decided. If they had come this far to their American station, they too were brave. They would fight.

He radioed all ships to stop engines so that the deep sonar might hear the slightest sound. He could tell the officers were itching for him to go "active" with the sonar, but he wouldn't be tempted merely to break their tension, to get it over with. If he couldn't wait, lost his nerve, he reminded himself, a million faces—and more—would be melted and disfigured as his had been in the inferno of the *Blaine*. And for these, as for any victims of a nuclear blast, no surgery would save them from the radiation-bred cancers that would eat them away inside.

The officer of the deck checked that all auxiliary machinery and air-conditioning were shut off. "Ship secured, sir."

"Very well. Now we're all quiet, let's hear what's down there."

The sonar operator switched the incoming noise track to the PA. Sometimes, as now, the sound from the depths was so much like the noise of frying fish that some men claimed they could smell it and even taste . . .

"Contact! Bearing two one niner."

"Range?" Ray Brentwood asked.

"Estimate . . . contact gone."

Brentwood was behind the operator and saw the screen himself, the amber arm uninterrupted by any blip. "What was it, Sonar?"

"Noise short from a hull, sir. Definitely."

"Sir?" It was the OOD.

"Yes?"

"Sir, one of the Sea Stallions didn't get the hook quickly enough." It meant that as one of the helos, probably out of fuel, had come down on the white circle of the *Munro*'s flight deck, a "snapper"—the seaman responsible for snapping the hook onto the U-bolt beneath the chopper—wasn't fast enough, and in the pitch and roll, the chopper had lurched forward, thwacking the bulkhead, creating the noise short.

"I want whoever it was," said Brentwood, "on a charge. Immediately."

"Yes, sir."

That was another misconception Ray knew he had to deal with—the idea that because he'd had a tough run of it, ending up with "sludge-removal-propelled," he'd somehow feel sorry for the underdog, the man who made a mistake. He also knew if he screwed up, they wouldn't even give him sludge removal. Lieutenant Cameron as OOD couldn't remember when he'd heard a bridge so quiet—so much so that he now heard noises, the creaking of metal fittings, which he'd never been aware of.

CHAPTER SIXTY-FOUR

THE ICY WIND blowing the Spitzbergen howled about the choppers that were bringing in the crew of the scuttled *Roosevelt*. Because of the radio silence that had to be in effect while they were in the air, it wasn't until they landed that Robert Brentwood and the men in the other four helicopters learned that Lt. Comdr. Peter Zeldman was dead.

The Royal Navy liaison officer assigned to the Norwegian Base expressed his condolences, and while the crew were "mugging up" with cocoa and biscuits, he informed Robert Brentwood, in a decidedly Oxfordian accent, that Brentwood and the remainder of his crew had been ordered back by

SACLANT "posthaste" to Holy Loch. "Balloon's gone up, I'm afraid and—" He stopped. "Of course, you of all people know about that, sir."

Brentwood nodded, but he was still thinking about Zeldman and Georgina.

"Point is, sir, SACLANT's canceled all leave. And, ah . . ." The lieutenant, for all the Firsts he'd earned at Oxford, was suddenly tongue-tied, realizing that, *if* the world survived, the man he was looking at would go down in history as the unflinching American who, upon seeing the Russian ICBMs streaking up from Kola Peninsula toward his country, had immediately launched the West's counterattack.

None of the *Roosevelt*'s crew spoke much as they filed into the Hercules transport that, escorted by six heavily armed Harriers, would take them back to Holy Loch. The next worst thing to having lost your ship was being split up. Half of them, on the orders from SACLANT, were to replace only those crewmen killed aboard another Sea Wolf II which now lay waiting for them in Holy Loch, a titanium patch on her hull where a Soviet ASROC had grazed her hull aft of the sail.

It made sense to split up the *Roosevelt* crew and they knew it, but for men who had lived and worked so closely together, knew one another's joys and failures and shared them, it was still a gut-wrenching business on top of having to send your own ship to her grave. And while they were glad to have survived the ordeal, their first view of Scotland's Cape Wrath was greeted with mixed feelings. There was, too, in the Hercules an unspoken fear as heavy about them as the steady roar of the great Hercules engines: the cold, scientific fact that no matter how they felt now, some of them were going to die within the next few months, others having no more than two, possibly three, years to live—if they weren't killed in action. No one had spoken about it on the way in to Spitzbergen, the dosimeters still on their belts but hidden beneath their Arctic parkas, but it was far from a case of out of sight, out of mind.

The Hercules pilot said something over the PA which no one understood, and Robert Brentwood went forward to find out what it was. Below he could see a wrinkled, gray sea barely visible in the dawn's early light—Cape Wrath. Just as quickly, it was swallowed by cloud.

"Holy Loch!" the pilot told him. "Half an hour. Bet you're pleased to be back?"

"Yes," said Robert. He wondered how much time he would have with Rosemary. It might be better if he had none, he thought, and immediately felt ashamed, disgusted by his own despair. Holding on to the strap webbing for support as the plane hit a patch of turbulence, he made his way carefully back from the cockpit. He told the chiefs of the boat to instruct each man in their department to take off the dosimeter, and when they'd collected them all, to give them to him. Each man's name was on each dosimeter, and he told them they would address the problem of radiation through the base medical officer and the radiation lab in Oxford. Meanwhile he didn't want any family or friends—if any had been alerted that *Roosevelt*'s crew were due back at Holy Loch—to see the dosimeters and start worrying. There'd be enough time for that later when they had the lab's reports. Several of the men—those who, like Brentwood, had sustained more than permissible levels of radiation—felt greatly relieved, and in his concern for them, the bond they felt with old "Bing" was cemented even further.

The SPETS had completely surrounded the Cathedral of the Assumption. Five 135-millimeter rounds had been fired from the third T-90 in the column before the first two battle tanks had been destroyed by the direct hit from Choir Williams on the first tank, which then spewed burning fuel on the SPETS immediately around it. As Williams, following David Brentwood's orders, made his way quickly out of the cathedral into the Hall of Facets, the glorious colors of the priceless fifteenth-century frescoes, lit up by parachute flares, didn't warrant even a glance from him as he hastened to join Aussie and the other SAS men, only fourteen in all, not counting David Brentwood and Cheek-Dawson. Another two men were cut down as the fourteen SAS burst out from Annunciation Cathedral at the Kremlin's southern end, across the snow-covered quad and into the pristine snow of Taynitsky Park. Another man died, beheaded by the sustained burst of heavy machine-gun fire, for despite his SPETS overlay, he was spotted in the floodlit park opposite Annunciation Cathedral because part of his SPETS overlay had been torn. In the next seven seconds, however, three floodlights and the SPETS manning them were shattered into perpetual darkness by at least five bursts of SAS submachine-gun fire as the remaining eleven SAS, including Williams A and Choir Williams, made for the wall. There was more firing, a hundred yards or so west of them, near the high water tower that marked the southernmost tip of the Kremlin's stronghold, where SPETS, mistaking one another for SAS troops, were unintentionally creating a diversionary tactic that the eleven SAS men couldn't have planned better themselves. It was the one flash of luck most of them would remember as, going over the darkened wall, the small band of commandos fell into the soft snow amid the trees that faced the Kremlin Quay, and beyond, in the darkness, the frozen Moscow River. In the air raid blackout of the city, the Kremlin now looked like an island of fire.

"Where's Brentwood?" Aussie whispered to Choir Williams as they headed away from the Kremlin, eagerly seeking the cover afforded by both blizzard and blackout.

In the pitch-black cathedral, its air choked with the smell of cordite, gasoline fumes, and the sweet stench of burning flesh from out by the tanks, Brentwood, taking out his own last shot of morphine, had dragged Cheek-Dawson up by the altar, having had to hold the frozen ampule in his mouth to warm it before injecting it. He loosened the Englishman's tourniquet for a few moments but then tightened it again and clipped the last magazine of nine-millimeter shorts into the MAC's grip housing. Then deftly, considering the unnerving *shooshing* sound of boots in the snow as SPETS closed in toward the cathedral, David snuffed out a tiny candle flame left burning by one of the men who now lay dead beneath it by one of the frescoed columns.

He heard Russian voices coming from somewhere outside by the cathedral's marbeled entrance, and racked by fatigue, he was momentarily back in the vast, marbled hall of Mansudae, where he, Freeman, and another marine had stormed the stairwell leading up to General Kim's office. But the NKA general had fled.

The cathedral was so huge that Brentwood thought he and Cheek-Dawson might luck out—that if they kept quiet enough, the SPETS might pass right by them through the doorway into the sanctuary. It was the fatigue that was doing it, that was making him entertain such fantastic notions of escape—as if, after the SPETS passed through, there would be no one to discover him and Cheek-Dawson in the morning light.

The morphine had given Cheek-Dawson new life, and with it, the clarity that David had often seen in the wounded following a shot. Though unable to walk by himself, the cold stiffening his immobile leg even further, the Englishman was fully cognizant of what was going on. Gently he nudged David and whispered, "Get going—damn fool."

David ignored him.

Suddenly there was a horrific bang, not of munitions but of the huge entrance doors being thrown back at the far end, a sharp order given—the SPETS clearly gathering, readying to charge in force.

"Here we go," whispered Cheek-Dawson. "Think things are going to get a bit sticky, old boy. They're—" Cheek-Dawson winced from pain, despite the morphine, as he tried to sit up into a better firing position. "They're going to light this up like a Christmas tree."

"Well, hell," said David. "At least we'll see what we're doing."

"I'd take that overlay off if I were you, old boy," said Cheek-Dawson, grimacing.

"Why?"

"They capture you in that—you're technically a spy. They don't like spies very much."

"You sound like they're going to ask me to surrender."

"And if they do?"

"You're dreaming, Dawson. Morphine's gone to your fucking head."

"Then if you're going to leave it on, old boy," Cheek-Dawson whispered, tugging the overlay, "I suggest you make a run for it. No point in you staying around and—"

"Shut up," said David. They heard a loud hissing noise, then a bump, the pillars with the saints on them flickering brilliantly, then disappearing, the flare having presumably hit the edge of the main door, bouncing back off into the snow.

"Lousy bowlers," Cheek-Dawson said.

"Pitchers," David corrected him. "They'll get better." They could hear loudspeakers and a lot of shouting.

Cheek-Dawson dragged himself over behind one of the sainted pillars, David now behind the pillar to his right. "Don't know what they're carrying on about," said the Englishman. "They can all have a turn."

CHAPTER SIXTY-FIVE

THE SONARMAN ABOARD Ray Brentwood's guided missile frigate had frozen a pie-slice segment of his screen—restricting the arm's sweep between 200 and 350 degrees—where the noise short from the hard helo landing had been picked up by the *Munro*'s passive sonar. Brentwood, however, quickly had him put it back on continuous sweep from zero to 360 degrees in order to prevent the ship from being surprised by an attack from any other segment—his insurance against the assumption, now held by most of his ships, that the metallic anomaly a mile ahead of them was caused by the two subs they were looking for.

The *Munro* was so quiet as Brentwood and the others listened to the steady stir-fry of incoming passive, they could hear the slopping of water against the ship's starboard flank. Ray Brentwood knew they might be losing valuable time, but the dunking helos were insistent that the anomaly was "within the significant" range—that it *could* be a sub. The trouble, as Brentwood well knew through his careful attention to the minutiae of the charts, was that while they were on the continental shelf, they were very close to where it started to plunge down to form the continental slope. The "significant" anomaly could well be an outcrop of metal-rich rock or even mud slowly shifted by the turbidity currents. The other possibility was that it might be one of the many wrecks that littered the coast, some of them not marked on the charts. Was he being too cautious?—the legacy of any captain who had lost a ship.

"Inform the helos to fire torpedoes," he ordered.

"Yes, sir."

Ten sleek blue Mark-37s dropped from the hard points of the five Sea Stallions, the "wrapped" control wire unraveling behind them like tightly bundled spaghetti.

Almost immediately the cobalt sea boiled with air bubbles—a classic sub antisonar tactic, the effusion of bubbles normally blanking any acoustic homing torpedoes. But as the Mark-37s were being guided toward *magnetic* anomaly, the noise of the bubbles could not deter them.

For a moment it seemed as if the whole sea had swollen into an enormous green carbuncle, then it turned white, bursting in an air-shattering explosion, permanently deafening a sonar operator aboard one of the dunking helos who'd forgotten to turn down his volume control. There was a series of other explosions, the sea's foaming surface littered with the torn and shattered detritus, human and material alike.

"Quiet on the bridge!" shouted Ray Brentwood, determined not to let either ship or helo crews get carried away with the kill, lest the second one had escaped, though he seriously doubted it. OOD Cameron, summoned by one of the lookouts, saw flashes of silver amid the debris, indicating that some of the Sea Stallions' torpedoes might have been chaff-activated—set off by metal balloons full of fine metal foil excreted by a sub in order to detonate the metal-homing warheads prematurely.

Two miles away from the explosion whose noise smothered all target indicators in Ray Brentwood's ships and helos, the sea's surface was broken by what looked like two porpoise-nosed shapes, seeming to leap from the sea, whitish-green water running down their flanks.

"Bearing!" yelled Ray Brentwood. "Zero two two! Fire harpoon! Fire ASROC!"

The OOD immediately relayed the order to all ships while, in less than eighty seconds, the Soviet Golf 5 had launched its two SS-N-8 missiles from its fin tubes.

Two of Brentwood's ships fired Harpoons within two seconds of hearing his order, the American missiles having less than twenty-seven seconds to reach the sea-launched ICBMs after the Soviet missiles had cleared their fin housing, popping through the water like rubber balls suddenly released beneath the surface, their engines already ignited in boost phase.

One was hit, everyone surprised by the lack of flame, its debris smacking loudly into the sea, other pieces of it spinning away in cartwheels, the two halves of its midsection split and dangling like a broken white cigar crashing harmlessly into the sea. But in drawing the fire of the Americans, this missile allowed the other missile from the Golf to escape, passing quickly from subsonic to supersonic trajectory, evading a phalanx of American antiballistic missile defense batteries—their radars confused by the sheer volume of information coming in from the task force's firing—the Russian missile further aided by the usual winter storms above the mountainous coastal ranges in Oregon and Washington State interfering with advanced radar warning stations. Minutes later, it hit Seattle in air burst.

In President Mayne's mind, the Russians had no doubt chosen Seattle as a "technically correct" counterforce, or military, target, as his adviser Schuman had told him, because of the massive Boeing works. It was a lawyer's point, Mayne's advisers aboard both Kneecap and Looking Glass telling him that though Seattle was the most populous northwestern city in the contiguous United States, this could not be used as a "countervalue" argument against the Soviets, who would no doubt, correctly, claim that because of Boeing, Seattle was a bona fide "counterforce" military target. Mayne, though in no mood for lawyers' points, nevertheless had to confront the cold logic of their reasoning in a nuclear world. But cold logic also told him the Russians, who had started the nuclear "exchange," might well be lying through their teeth in claiming they could not contact their subs. Was it Chernko's test of U.S. will? It was only a second in his mind's eye, but in that second, the long memory of what America had forfeited because of Russian lies and subterfuge at the end of World War II lay heavily upon him. And what were the Russians planning? Were they moving their SLBM fleet closer, to attack should America weaken?

He decided that for the sake of everyone, and not just the United States, there must be absolutely no question—no doubt left in the Russians' minds. He would not order the four retaliatory strikes, and as they had not taken out Washington, he would leave Moscow standing, but ordered Leningrad taken out as payment in kind for the millions who he now knew had died in Seattle and would die in the weeks to come.

As the MX warheads came down over Leningrad, the overpressure caused the Neva to burst its banks, flooding Nevsky Prospekt. The rubble that moments before had been a golden glory of imperial architecture housing the general staff headquarters in Palace Square mixed in a sludge with the ashes of what had been the burnished gold of St. Isaac's Cathedral, its vaporized frescoes infusing the sludge with speckles of gold.

The entire Hermitage was razed to the ground, Rembrandt's *Flora* and millions of other exhibits vaporized. The docks, where only minutes before, battle cruisers and missile-carrying destroyers were setting out to sea, were now infernos, the huge dockside cranes tumbling into the Neva, boiling it with their heat. The fires from the air burst cremated over a million—and there would have been many more were it not for the extensive underground shelters in the outlying suburbs.

Now even Chernko knew the war was over—that America could no longer be resisted. In the crude measure of body counts, no doubt America had suffered millions more dead than the Soviet Union because of her lack of nuclear shelters and evacuation schemes, but her technology and, now it was clear, her *will*, were indomitable.

For his part in detecting the presence of the two Russian ballistic missile subs, which, had it not been for his prescience, would have surely increased America's dreadful losses of over six million dead into more than forty and would have turned the radioactive-dead zones of several midwestern states and north Washington State into an entire country of dead zones, poisoned for decades, Ray Brentwood had become an overnight hero—celebrated not only in every state of the union but all over the Allied world.

But even at this moment, when Chernko, "on behalf of the Politburo and STAVKA," delivered Russia—despite the threat of the Siberian Republic to secede—into "unconditional surrender to the United States of America," it would take hours in some places—days in others—before the word was out, and in those places men would continue to die as if there had been no surrender. And despite the euphoria embracing the return of Ray Brentwood's "fleet," he stood alone at the ship's stern, disturbingly hypnotized by the ship's wake. At one moment it was a sea alive, its effervescence catching the morning sun like an ice cream cloud in summer, yet at the same time it seemed to him a massive and ever-moving grave, its vastness taking him into itself, making him feel insignificant and lost.

"What the hell's gotten into him?" asked a jubilant third officer. "Christ, he's won the—"

"Quiet now," said Cameron, who was still officer of the deck. "His wife and children live—lived in Seattle."

As in all modern wars, it was one in which the civilian casualties far outnumbered those of the combatants.

* * *

In Khabarovsk, Alexsandra was hysterical. Her three brothers had come home, released by Nefski, who had apologized, saying that there had been a "grievous error" committed by his second in command, that the three brothers' arrest had been nothing more and nothing less than a case of "mistaken identity." He very much hoped the family would understand, and as a sign of his sincerity, he would be "most honored" if they would be his guests at The Bear Restaurant—*kosher*, of course. What he meant, as they well knew, was that the Allies would go easier on him, given his apology and his subsequent treatment of the family. But Alexsandra didn't hear a word of what he said, still crying hysterically at the sight of Ivan, her oldest brother, whom she had seen shot in the courtyard of the KGB prison. She kept hugging him, pushing him away to see that it was really him, pulling at his beard like a small child, hugging him again and crying and laughing and weeping as she hadn't done in years. Ivan had been told, Alexander explained, to fall in the snow when he heard shots—blanks or, more likely, said Alexander, live ammunition but aimed at the wall, away from Ivan, Nefski not wanting to shoot a source of information before he had to, hoping to terrify the girl enough before he moved to more drastic measures.

They did not accept his invitation to the Bear, for apart from it never having entered their heads that they would do so, it would only confirm the suspicions of others in the Oblast that what Nefski had said about them being turncoats and opportunists was true.

CHAPTER SIXTY-SIX

IN THE PALE light of Moscow's dawn, the sun's rays grew brighter by the second, and despite the air being filled with dust from the rubble of the COM, the colors within Assumption Cathedral grew richer, David hearing the SPETS moving outside, their boots crunching the tightly packed snow, their commanding officer obviously having decided to wait for more light to aid him in rooting out the last of the SAS holdouts. Cheek-Dawson was in great pain again, his left foot so swollen that the boot looked like it was about to split. From his position behind the pillar to the left of the altar and from David's position behind the pillar to the right, they had the entrance well covered, but both knew they could not realistically hold out for any more than a few minutes once the final rush came, both of them having donned their masks for what they were sure would be a tear gas attack.

Then they heard the tolling of the bell tower in St. Nicholas, and the very beauty of the sound, muted by the snow-laden roofs, was hardly over when the attack began, not with tear gas canisters—which would have obliged the attackers to have the encumbrances of gas masks as well—but a cluster of smoke grenades, which rolled into the cathedral, their thick, spuming white smoke churning sunbeams and obscuring the cathedral's chandeliers.

Neither Cheek-Dawson nor Brentwood fell for the trap of firing to give away their positions but instead quickly rolled four "flash-bangs" into the smoke, immediately cupping their ears and pressing their helmets hard up against the pillars. There was a purple flash, a splintering of glass, the sound of someone running, off to David's left. David wheeled about the pillar, saw denser white on white—the SPETS's overlay in the smoke—and fired a quick, three-round burst. The SPETS's feet shot from under him as if he'd slipped on ice, and he was dead the moment he struck the floor. There was a series of shouted orders and now they all came in, Cheek-Dawson throwing two more grenades and David three in quick succession. The cathedral erupted in machine-gun fire, orange tongues darting in the thick smoke, a man screaming somewhere down by the entrance, David knowing he had only four or five good bursts left.

"SAS!" It was a booming Russian voice with barely a trace of accent, coming through the smoke of battle and the mist born of the heat from the COM's rubble blowing across the snow.

"SAS! It is useless to resist further. Surrender now and you will be treated well—as prisoners of war."

Cheek-Dawson, his face grimacing from the pain that even the effort of speaking caused him, added wryly, "At the Ritz, no doubt."

"Intourist," David said, and called out, "What are your terms?"

"Clever lad!" said Cheek-Dawson, but David's attempt to buy more time for the SAS men who had already left didn't work, the Russian recognizing David's ploy for what it was immediately and shouting angrily in return, "Come out now or you will die!"

Cheek-Dawson pulled his last two flash-bangs closer to him, saw David had none, slid one across to him, then, teeth clenched in pain, pushed himself up against the Pillar of the Saints. "Thanks for staying, old boy," he said to David.

"Keep quiet," said David, "and they might take you prisoner."

"I will."

David smiled at the Englishman's transparent lie.

Glass broke somewhere, and within minutes the cathedral was filled with more smoke pouring out of two or three canisters. Suddenly David saw a way of buying a little more time for those of his men already over the wall. "Always the unexpected, son!" had been Freeman's motto. Pulling the pin on one of the grenades, holding down its lever and dashing forward through the heavy smoke toward the cathedral's entrance, David tossed out a grenade hard left, then dashed out to the right through smoky mist. He heard the crash of the first grenade, saw two shapes—one of them a man writhing on the ground, knocked down by the first grenade, the second shape two figures to his left. He fired a full burst. One fell, knees knocked from beneath him as if hit from behind with a club, the second man behind him still coming. David dropped to the snow, firing another burst, the heat wash hot on his face, his Kevlar jacket feeling like ice picks were hitting it. A warm sensation flooded his chest, shadows flitting by him through the smoke into the cathedral.

Garlic, so strong it made his eyes water, was the next thing David was aware of, and a burning pain as if a red-hot poker had been thrust through his abdomen down into his thigh. The SPETS medical officer, a woman, who looked as if she towed tanks to keep fit, was glowering down at him. "You are lucky." Her garlic breath made him turn away.

"Where's my friend?" he asked.

"The English?" she said. "He tried to be brave, too."

David stared at her, but his focus was blurring.

"He is dead," she said matter-of-factly. "Comrade Malek wanted him, too, but—" she shrugged "—his earlier wounds. We could not save him."

"Malek—?"

"Comrade Malek is the new head of SPETS," said the medical officer. "He wishes to know all about SAS."

"I've never worked . . ." said David, gasping from his pain, "for Scandinavian Air—" He was a little deranged from the pain—and thought his answer hilariously funny. Cheek-Dawson would have liked it.

"General Malek is in no mood for jokings."

Neither, as it turned out, was the president of the United States nor the prime minister of Great Britain—nor any of the other Allied leaders. They demanded immediate repatriation of all prisoners and said they were holding Chernko and his Politburo personally responsible for any harm that might befall *any* Allied prisoners in the Soviets' possession—including those "personnel" who "have participated in the raid against the Russian capital."

But it wasn't the tough talk that caused the Russians to repatriate David Brentwood back to London, where he would rejoin the few SAS men, seven in all, who had made it out, but rather the enormous press coverage now being given to the Kremlin raid. Chernko badly needed a highly visible propaganda act of "humanity," and David's hurried repatriation became part of it, due in large measure to the simple fact that only an hour earlier, the Australian, Choir Williams, and Williams A had already been airlifted after being captured in

Moscow. Infrared photos from the Japanese news satellite had embarrassed the Russians by showing the world that the final SPETS attack against the SAS holdouts in Assumption Cathedral was still in progress after President Chernko had agreed to the unconditional surrender of all Soviet forces and their allies to the joint Allied command.

It was often said to David afterward that the satellite pictures had probably saved him from being hauled off and shot as a spy and dumped in some unknown Russian grave. It didn't seem to occur to those who told him this that the satellite pictures hadn't saved Cheek-Dawson and that, as Aussie would have said, his fate had "simply been in the roll of the dice."

David's identity, like that of the other members of the raid, was protected for a time, because of the legendary SAS penchant for anonymity. But for Ray Brentwood, over ten thousand miles away, his ships in sight of San Diego's Point Loma, where the crews could see the fireworks streaming up from Balboa Park and the fighters taking off from Miramar's "top gun" school to form an honor overflight, anonymity was something he could not hope for. Only hours before, the shouts of recognition and streamers of adulation had been all he craved, but now the only thing that seemed in concert with the depression into which he'd been plunged by his fears for his wife and family was the sullen smog that hung above the San Ysidro Mountains, reminding him of the deadly fallout that would even now be blanketing the Pacific Northwest and all of the Great Plains states.

As he returned the salute and descended among the biggest crowd ever seen on the San Diego naval docks, Ray Brentwood suddenly became the most photographed person on earth—the man who, through brains and courage, had saved millions of American lives, and thereby thwarted an all-out nuclear holocaust, the very ugliness of his face quickly beloved by newspaper editors all over the world who saw it as an ironic and inverse measure of his heroism. Among the crowd were beautiful women trying to get close enough to touch him, others from Hollywood to ask if he had an agent—manila envelopes with "option" contracts stuffed inside thrust his way. Ray bore it as best he could—in a silence numbed by thoughts of Beth, Jeannie, and John.

"Admiral! Admiral!" It was a blonde. A military policeman was trying to block her, for SPETS, like Hollywood, had been known to employ beautiful women for their purposes, and who could be sure that some disaffected "sleeper," many of them still at large—

But she wasn't from Hollywood or SPETS, and the young MP, duty notwithstanding, found it decidedly pleasant to feel her pressed hard against him.

"Beth and your children—" she began.

Ray Brentwood pushed frantically toward the MP, the throng so thick, he felt like a man swimming against a riptide, the blonde's voice all but drowned in the hysteria of congratulations about him. The woman, he noticed, was in uniform—a *Wave*, her hat apparently knocked off in the crush. "Sir," she yelled, "your wife and children . . . in Portland. They were on their way down . . . soon as . . . heard your fleet was—"

"They're all right?" Ray yelled.

"Yes, sir. They're fine. They're fine."

He hugged her and flashbulbs popped, something he'd have to explain to Beth when the *National Investigator* and the other tabloids of the Jay La Roche chain printed the photo under the caption "ADMIRAL MAKING WAVES!"

CHAPTER SIXTY-SEVEN

"IT IS TIME for your confession!" announced General Kim's interrogator, a bowl of steaming rice on the bare table beside him as he stood menacingly, a thick bamboo stick tapping his leggings. General Freeman, face hollow, eyes down, blinking nervously, his ravenous gaze fixed on the rice, nodded obediently. All he could think of was the film he had seen of Orwell's *1984* when, in the end, Winston Smith—he of the famous first name and common surname—the embodiment of all mens' strengths and weaknesses—had bowed his head in obedience to *his* interrogator, conceding tearfully and irrevocably that two plus two were five.

"Remember," the interrogator cautioned Freeman, "you

must not try any jokings. You must only say what is printed on the screen."

"I—" began Freeman, "I do not require a—" he had difficulty remembering what it was called "—cue card. I know it."

"Tell me!" insisted the interrogator, the bowl of rice still steaming, holding Freeman captive with its promise.

"I wish," began Freeman, "to apologize for my part in the criminal warmongering activity of the United States against the freedom-loving peoples of the Democratic Republic of North Korea and the freedom-loving peoples of the People's Republic of China. . . ." The confession went on to "acknowledge" various other perfidies against freedom-loving peoples all over the globe. But Freeman was so weak, he could barely proceed. Despite the vitamin shots giving him some color, the effects of malnutrition were evident in his speech. But he knew that before the camera went on, he would be given the rice if he agreed and the promise of a full meal of vegetables and fish, which was a promise, whatever the brutalities the NKA inflicted on their victims, they had never reneged on. He had smelled it after others had confessed—the smell a torture and incitement in itself. No one, Freeman knew, who had not been starved could possibly understand how quickly one's resolve broke down. As they took him up from the tunnel cells, a guard on each side helping him, he thought of Winston Smith again and of Jeremiah Denton, the senator from Alabama who had been so badly tortured by the North Vietnamese.

In the glare of the lights, he looked like an animal out of *its* tunnel, blinking almost continuously.

General Kim, unsmiling, dressed in immaculately pressed NKA fatigues, his flat gold-striped and red-starred shoulder boards showing to maximum effect, waited patiently, smoking contentedly.

Kim cleared his throat and suddenly the bevy of technicians, producers, et cetera, fell silent, and in the surreal glare of the kleig lights, the smoke of his cigarette rising voluminously about him, filling the small studio, he spoke to the interrogator, though Freeman knew that Kim spoke quite fluent English from his days as the NKA's chief negotiator at Panmunjom, where he was in the habit of informing the Americans that "you had better be careful or you will die like the Kennedys—shot like dogs in the street." The interrogator turned to Freeman. "The general says to remind you that this is on videotape and that if you do not say exactly the words, then there will be great punishment. No food. More beatings." The interrogator was shaking his finger at Freeman. "You understand?"

Freeman lifted his head and nodded.

The session began, and Freeman, the glare bothering him, asked that the lights be turned down. They refused. Still blinking like a frightened spaniel, he began, "I wish to apologize for my part in the criminal warmongering activity . . ." astonishing all present by getting the confession word-perfect on the first take, the interrogator pointing out to Kim how Freeman had been celebrated for his attention to detail.

When it was aired on American networks via a South American neutral country, the American public saw the general making his confession on all three networks and the public broadcasting system. So did army intelligence. They wound back the tape and went forward in freeze-frame. Freeman's blinking was a carbon copy of what Jeremiah Denton had done in Hanoi. Well, almost a copy, as Army General Grey explained to the president. Denton had blinked "T-O-R-T-U-R-E" in Morse. Freeman had blinked "B-U-L-L-S-H-I-T."

Freeman got the vegetables and fish hours before Beijing caught on. By then, the surrender of all Communist forces had been made, and within two weeks, Douglas Freeman was recuperating in the Walter Reid Army Hospital, regaling his wife and cat, whom she had illegally smuggled in, about those "stupid sons of bitches in Pyongyang."

CHAPTER SIXTY-EIGHT

IT WAS RAINING in Portland, but Beth didn't care, crying uncontrollably though she knew it was very "un-navy." Both of them explained to the children, albeit gently, that being proud of their dad was okay but not to get any swelled heads.

"Oh, Daddy," said Jeannie, bursting with pride. The sad note in their reunion was Beth's report that the newspapers were listing Melissa Lange—David's old flame, Beth remembered—as one of those killed in the Russian ICBM attacks against SAC in Omaha, and that their officers' quarters house in Seattle was presumably "gone," like so many others. Meanwhile they would have to remain billeted in the Marriot Hotel, which the children thought was "great!" Ray's dad was on the line from New York, though it had taken him over an hour to get through.

"Well, son," he said, voice tight with emotion. "Well done. Well done. Well done."

"Oh, John!" It was Ray's mom on the extension. "Sounds like you're ordering a steak! Let me speak to him. Ray—I'm so proud. I'm just so—"

"Now, Mother," began John, but his wife, Catherine, took no notice, her joy unreined after hearing from the Pentagon that David, though wounded, and Robert had survived the war. The War Office had seen no point in raising the question of Robert's radiation dosage. This was something that the navy thought would best be kept unaer wraps for a while, largely in an effort to dampen public concern over the number of "Chernobyls," or downed subs, which now lay littered about the ocean's floor and which would seriously affect the food chain for some time to come. The navy also justified its position by pointing out, correctly, that the effect of an individual's radiation dosage could vary widely and in any case was something best left for those affected to discuss with their families as they saw fit.

When David arrived at Heathrow in the Red Cross ambulance, his stretcher wheeled into the army waiting hall, where the other seven survivors of the SAS raid were still being debriefed after exhaustive medical examination, he was conscious, but the painkilling shots he'd received on the flight had made him dopey, putting him temporarily at peace as they readied him for transfer for the operation to remove two 7.62-millimeter bullets from his thigh. As his stretcher passed by, it was the first time David had ever seen the Australian genuinely shocked. "Struth!"

"What's up with Aussie?" David asked Choir Williams groggily.

"Oh," explained the Welshman in his basso profundo, "'e's lost a bloody fortune, that fellow has. Bet a packet on you, he did—that you wouldn't make it back. Or that Laylor chappie from Troop A. Very depressed, Aussie is."

"Sorry to disappoint him," said David croakily, his throat parched from the morphine.

"Oh," said Choir philosophically, "I wouldn't worry about 'im, sir. 'E's probably taking bets from some poor sod that the surrender won't hold or t' sun won't come up in the morning."

"Almost didn't," said David.

Choir Williams shook his head as David's stretcher passed on, and looked over at Williams A. "You know, Williams, that Yank's a nice fellow. But terrible morbid sometimes."

"Listen," said Aussie, wandering up to Choir. "Five to one Davey boy comes through the whole operation with flying colors. *Dollars!* U.S.!"

"Go away," said Choir.

"Yes," said Williams A. "Go home, you terrible man."

"All right, all right," said Aussie. "*Yen*. How about *yen?*"

CHAPTER SIXTY-NINE

THE PACT BETWEEN the surviving members of the USS *Roosevelt* was kept and none went public with the knowledge that at least a third of them were probably dying. The secret of their invisible yet deadly illness was not a difficult one to keep in a world where the visible horrors of the war were so widespread. It was a secret Robert Brentwood believed he could keep from the moment he and the others had landed in the wild and beautiful Highland dawn to the time he and Rosemary visited his brother David. They took him down from Middlesex Hospital after the operation to convalesce at the Spences' in Oxshott, where Mrs. Spence spared no effort looking after him, doubtless seeing in David the chance to repay Lana Brentwood for her kindness to young William when he had been wounded in the Atlantic. At times Richard Spence felt his wife's attentiveness to David Brentwood was almost too cloying, but remembering the terrible emptiness that William's death had caused in their lives, he was loath to interfere. In any event, he was as much worried about the effect of Peter Zeldman's death on Georgina. But she, like her mother, had rallied, and while the loss would always be with her, Richard could already see in her a sudden maturing. She was still passionate about her ideas, and at times as argumentative as ever, but much more willing now to listen. Peter Zeldman in a way had tamed her, forced her to look at her innermost self beneath all the varsity-bred and nourished pretensions, so that when she met David, there was none of the petulant, knowing air of superiority she had once held toward "soldiers," but more understanding of what young William and others like him and Zeldman must have been through, a new respect for action as well as for intellect.

"Would you like me to do that?" she asked David one morning as he struggled valiantly but in vain with knife and fork, his right arm particularly painful.

"Yes," he said. It was the way she did that simple thing, smiling as she sat down beside him, a wide open smile, utterly devoid of connivance or any intent to impress, that touched him.

Richard Spence, interrupting his puzzle in the *Telegraph,* watched her and David looking at each other and inwardly groaned for his savings account at the Midland Bank, wondering yet again what unjust and perverse origin lay beneath the pernicious custom that decreed the bride's father always got stuck with the bill. And Georgina's taste in champagne exceeded only that of her Great Uncle Geoffrey, who never helped matters with his exuberance for the Spence family forming as many connections as possible "with our cousins across the water."

It had been only a few days after the surrender when, at about 2:00 A.M., the Spences' high-pitched burglar alarm awoke everyone in the house. Robert was up and out of bed before Rosemary realized it. As he made his way down toward the staircase, Richard Spence was coming up in his robe, apologizing profusely to everyone gathering at the top of the stairs, "Mea culpa . . . mea culpa. Terribly sorry . . . sorry, everyone. Went down for a snack, forgot to switch off the ruddy second beam."

"Oh, Richard!" Anne chastised him, shaking, holding the rail for support, one hand on her chest as if to slow her heart.

"You frightened the dickens out of us! Well, you'd better stay up and answer the police call. It's your own silly fault."

"Yes . . . oh dear. I *am* sorry, everyone."

"No problem," said Robert, who went down to the kitchen with Richard to wait until the police called. Richard said the station at Leatherhead would either call or send a car already in the area.

"It's a knack," Robert said, watching Richard preparing the tea. "You won't believe this, but before I came to England, I thought the only way you made tea was with tea bags." Richard was opening a quarter-pound packet of Bushell's, the small black India leaves measured by hand before he dumped them from his palm into the brown pot into which he'd poured hot, roiling water. At two o'clock in the morning, Robert wasn't in the mood for anything more profound than a conversation about tea.

"Even when we use pots in the States, we just dump in the bags," he said, but Richard didn't seem in the mood for small talk. He gave the impression that his ritual of tea making was more an escape from something he wanted to say—an awkwardness that Robert hadn't sensed before in the Spence household. "They say," Robert continued, "that when Prince Charles went to visit Reagan in the White House, they asked him whether he'd like tea or coffee. He said tea, of course, but they brought him this little bag and he didn't do anything with it. Must have been on old Ronnie's mind, because next day he asked Charles at a formal dinner about it and Charles told him that he simply didn't know what to do with this 'funny little bag.' "

Richard didn't respond, merely pouring the steeped tea, moving the spout up and down, his left hand pressed against the lid—something robotic, if expert, in his movements that indicated his thoughts were elsewhere. He handed Robert a cup of dark, amber Darjeeling. "I didn't trip the alarm," he said quietly. He pushed the small packets of rationed sugar toward Robert. "There *was* someone in here. Two of them. I was on my way down for a snack. I rang the police just as I saw them take off. Couldn't get the car number or anything, but there's a good chance the police might cut them off at the roundabout." He was stirring the tea thoughtfully. "No use frightening the women."

"No," agreed Robert. "Was anything taken?"

"No—that's the thing. You see—"

The phone rang.

"Yes," answered Richard. "Oh—yes, Inspector. I see. Yes—of course. Now?"

Richard returned to the kitchen table. "They caught two people—not at the roundabout. In the cul-de-sac down a bit. They'd like you and me to go down to the station."

"Me?" asked Robert, surprised.

"Yes."

"I didn't see them. I'd have no idea—"

Richard was handing him the Identikit sketches of the "charmers" that Robert had sent him from Holy Loch. "Oh Christ—"

"Look, Robert—they said we could come in the morning if we liked, but I think under the circumstances—might be better if we nipped down there. I'll tell Anne you're coming along to keep me company."

"All right," said Robert.

Robert knew it was them the moment he stepped inside the Leatherhead police station. The desk sergeant was typing out the pink sheet, charging them with "breaking and entering" and "illegal possession of firearms"—.22 high-vels—the very make the superintendent at Mallaig had supposed SPETS abroad had been issued with. High-velocity, quiet, and very accurate at short range. Robert could still see the bullet hole in Price's forehead. The two charmers didn't look too happy—no confetti this time. The identification was simple and straightforward. There were no lineups given for Chernko's people abroad. It would be "in camera" and they'd either be shot or, now the surrender was in place, exchanged for two of the Allies.

It hadn't taken Robert and Richard long, but it had shaken them both to realize that even after the official surrender, the two SPETS had pursued their mission, and they wondered how many around the world were still at large. Both of them agreed to say nothing to anyone else. There was no point. Besides, for Robert, the diagnosis to be given him by the radiation lab at Oxford was a much more immediate and pressing concern.

CHAPTER SEVENTY

ON HIS THIRD visit to what he'd told Rosemary was a "special submarine update" school at Oxford, Robert Brentwood was informed by the specialists at the radiation medicine lab that the initial diagnosis was confirmed—he had indeed received above-acceptable levels of radiation.

"Am I dying?" he asked the doctor simply.

"We're all dying, old chap."

"Come on, Doc."

"Truth is, we never know for sure. In a case like yours, I'd say—" the doctor shrugged "—fifty-fifty. We can speculate, predict, all we want, but there are other factors: will to live, fitness, individual metabolism . . ."

"Even in a case of radioactive poisoning?"

"Oh yes, though it's not generally recognized." He gave a warm, cheeky smile. "Sounds a bit too mystical for most M.D.s, you see. Difficult stuff to measure."

The day of the third visit, as he strolled back from the radiation lab through Oxford's rain-polished streets, the golden spires of the ancient university caught the wintry sun with such brilliance that only nostalgia and hope seemed permissible at that moment. He was shocked to find Rosemary waiting at the station. One look told him she knew where he'd been—her lips aquiver, though she was trying to be brave. She was wearing a scarf, the same one she'd been wearing when they had first met—a light pastel green covered with the wildflowers of an English spring. They held one another before either spoke.

"How long?" she asked finally.

"They don't know. No one does."

She didn't go on at him about why he hadn't told her. She knew his motive, though she might not agree with it, came from all the old-fashioned virtues of a silent service.

"You'd have nothing to worry about anyway," he told her. "You and the *bairn*." As usual, his Scottish accent was atrocious to her ears, but she felt his love all around her like a warm embrace on a wintry day.

"Anyway," he hurried on, "I'll be here to see the boy—"

She was in tears, as they stood hand in hand on the platform.

"Oh—" she said bravely, "what makes you think it's a *boy?*"

"Or a *lassie,*" he said, and he stopped, turning her to him. "Rose. Let's not be sad. I see the glass half-full, not half-empty." She sobbed uncontrollably, told him she loved him and that there'd never be another man for her, and he held her tightly and prayed there would be if he went before his time—whenever that might be.

On the train back, the peaceful winter countryside rocking gently outside, he went to the bar and ordered a double gin and tonic for her, the British Rail attendant astonished, proclaiming, "A *double?* You'd be bloody lucky, mate. Been a war on, you know."

"Ah—yes," said Robert. "Then—I'll just have the single." He left a hefty tip, not really thinking what he was doing.

"Oh, ta very much," said the attendant, suddenly solicitous of the American's well-being. "You're a gentleman and a scholar, sir."

Rosemary refused the single gin and tonic, said she didn't want to do anything that might harm the baby. "Have it yourself," she said.

He did, and looking out at the land flashing by, the smell of frozen earth thawing, he felt so glad to be alive to feel and see and touch the world about him. It was like a longing fulfilled, and he was sure that what he was feeling at this very moment was what it must be like for Rosemary to feel the warmth of a life, his life, theirs, growing inside her.

"It's going to be a boy," he said.

"A girl," she contradicted, snuggling into him.

"You've cheated," he said, looking down at her with mock accusation. "You had a sonogram—"

"Ultrasound," she said.

"Yes."

"No. I don't know, but my pulse is faster and—"

"Ah—" said Robert. "Superstitions. Anyway, I don't care. As long as she, or he, joins the navy."

"Or becomes a teacher," she countered. "No—really, whatever they decide."

"Yes."

"Oh, Robert—"

"Now, now," he said. "No tears. Silent running."

CHAPTER SEVENTY-ONE

OUTSIDE DUTCH HARBOR'S Paradise Motel, it was twenty below. Inside, it was much hotter, Shirer already down to his T-shirt, Lana La Roche, née Brentwood, letting him undress her. Soon he was getting out of control.

"Slowly," she laughed. "You're ripping my uniform."

"I can't wait," he said frantically. "I don't care about your uniform. I'm hornier than a toad."

"Well—*sit,* toad!" she instructed him, laughing. "I'm not ready."

"Not ready?" he challenged. "That isn't what you said in your lettergram. It said, 'Landing field ready'—"

"Yes, I know," she said. "Ready for landing—not attack. And Frank—"

"Yes?"

"Please take that awful eye patch off."

"Why? Thought it would kind of remind you of old times?" He made a Groucho Marx expression, tapping an invisible cigar, rolling his good eye. "If you know what I mean."

"I remember," she said. "But that was before Jay. I want to forget those days. *Please* take it off."

He did, though she didn't know that this time he hadn't meant it as a joke, that this time, while the electromagnetic impulse of the air burst over Detroit had not penetrated Knee-cap's sheathing, the light of the massive explosion, "brighter than a million suns," as the experts were so fond of describing it, had damaged his "steering" eye as well as blinding the navigator. He had to fly the plane alone, reading the instruments with the eye that had been protected by the patch. If it hadn't been for the soft light inside the Paradise Motel, Lana would no doubt have seen the faint, milky whiteness where the microwave radiation had penetrated the aqueous humor of the damaged eye, literally cooking its clear protein, turning it white as easily and quickly as a microwave cooks the clear protein of an egg. But right now, neither the laser operations that might help repair some, though not all, of the damage, the air bursts that had caused it and had injured so many others, nor the long wait he might have for any corrective surgery while America struggled to rebuild herself into something approaching prewar normalcy were on his mind as he turned the light's dimmer switch to low.

"Lordy," he said, "you look better than a carrier deck on a rainy night."

"Oh, how romantic," she said, smiling, her loose hair falling about her shoulders as she demurely slipped between the covers. "Do you always sweet-talk your lady friends like that?"

"I don't have any other lady friends."

"I believe you," she said, her hand rustling the pillow on the other side of the small double bed.

In her arms, the war, Jay, everything was forgotten. Hopefully soon everyone would be at peace, but if it wasn't to be, then for now at least the world was theirs, the promise of love so close, so urgent, they ached for each other. As they joined, the aching gave way, turning pain to pleasure that mounted and grew, enveloping them, pulling them faster and faster, harder, until they were free—over the cascading precipice, falling in timeless cool space where only rapture was certain.

ABOUT THE AUTHOR

Canadian Ian Slater, a veteran of the Australian Joint Intelligence Bureau, has a Ph.D. in political science. He teaches at the University of British Columbia and is managing editor of *Pacific Affairs*. He has written numerous thrillers, most recently *World War III* and *World War III: Rage of Battle*. He lives in Vancouver with his wife and two children.